TRIUMPHAL ENTRY

TRIUMPHAL ENTRY

Thomas Baird

Harcourt, Brace & World, Inc.   New York

Lo! two have gone among the lions, even into the lions' den: but only one has come forth

 PART ONE

My name, unknown reader, is Edward Cranson Bates, commonly shortened to Ned Bates. I went to Williams College, in Massachusetts, but I was not really typical of the nice boys who go there nor, unfortunately, have I subsequently made as much money as they—for niceness is not just its own reward. I am a shifting sort of person, as you will see, living in doubt and despair, and addicted to mockery, but finding it better to be that way than on my knees at some rail to take yesterday's aspirin. I do not believe that History is God in action, and I know no truths which are self-evident. But I do believe in today and tomorrow, and in about as far away as the next block, and in black honesty which bores through to the nothing that is on the far side of everything. Also, I'd rather be kissed than blessed any old time.

So much for my outlook on life. I hope it gives you a feeling for the "I" in this book.

Neal Brewster is the "he" in the book. I won't sum Neal up right now; not because I don't think I could, but because that will happen in the book itself. What is more relevant here is to state how long I have known him and how well. Our relationship has evolved in three stages. With characteristic perversity, I will start with the latest of them, which is the present one, and which is even now developing—even *right* now, as I compose this introduction. It is characterized, let us say, by custom and wariness. The second stage, from whichever end you start, closed about a year ago, and was marked by a considerable dependence, Neal's dependence, and my leadership. I was both his friend, then, and his mentor, and even his creator and savior, even that; and how the second stage ended you will see and should be able to guess. And there was, finally, the earliest stage, which lasted from the time we met to the beginning of stage two, and during which not much happened, except that I got to know something about Neal and his habits. I would not say we were friends during the first stage—too incompatible, really—but we were acquainted, and we were floormates in the same house, and connected with the same big Middle Western university.

I will start my narrative with the delivery of a telegram which was sent at the moment when the primary stage of our relationship began to close. It was, in fact, in the chemistry of our relationship, the precipitant. Most telegrams, except those sent on obvious holidays like Christmas, carry the threat of disaster. That is why there is something ominous in their appearance. That is why they are so interesting. Only a very strange person, a real weirdie, could receive an unexpected wire with indifference—but I am jumping ahead of myself, for the scene must be set.

2.

Let us start like an exploring camera. Imagine traveling over a house, an early-morning house, cold after an early-spring night, bright with early-spring-morning sunshine. The hall, living room, and dining room are still in a chilly disorder of books, magazines, an open telephone directory, some worn playthings. The doors to the kitchen and breakfast room are closed, but from behind them come warm sounds—voices and water taps and dishes. Climb to the second floor. The silence increases; the beds unmade in the bedrooms—our camera pauses at each one—testify to a depopulation in favor of the kitchen. Up in the third-floor hall all is still as death. There are a few pieces of furniture and three closed doors, but no windows. The only light is that which seeps up from the second floor or leaks under the doors. The camera stops. Listen

4

in the darkness and cold. To the right, the floor creaks. There is a thump. Is the house settling, or is somebody there?

Then the doorbell rings. Brrrr. The audience jumps.

The camera, back down in the entrance hall, discovers a pair of pale-blue mules which flop across threadbare rugs, slap on wooden floors, and come to rest at the front door, where white ankles, one of them streaked with an enlarged blood vessel, come clearly into focus. The door is opened, and the first words are spoken.

"Telegram for Neal Brewster. He live here?"

A signature is exchanged for an envelope, and the door closes, but since its latch doesn't work properly, it has to be kicked—a delicate operation in mules. The feet start back across the hall and approach the stairs. They climb.

We jump to the third floor again, to Neal's bedroom, the one on the right, and there he is in the middle of it, brushing his hair. But shut off the camera: this is life!

He had heard the doorbell, heard Mrs. Peters go to answer it, followed her climb up the stairs to the second floor and on up to the third. Normally one is not surprised that a landlady moves freely around in her own house, but the early bell was irregular, and moreover Mrs. Peters was a most distant landlady and never came up to the level of her rented rooms. Such a break with habit and principle disturbed Neal. He stopped, brush up.

She reached our hall and paused a moment, then came onward to his door. Her knock was light, but it was amplified by all those thin partitions. He stood paralyzed, like a man who fears the police. She knocked again. He tiptoed across the room, squeaking floor boards betraying each step, and dithered at the door.

"Mr. Brewster," she called softly.

At this moment I chose to appear. I had got out of bed when she reached our hall, my curiosity needled, crossed to my own door with a spraddle-legged gait which dodged my own squeakers (a trick that had come in handy several times), and was peeping through my keyhole. Now I opened my door.

"Oh, Mr. Bates," she said. "I have a telegram for Mr. Brewster, but he doesn't seem to be in."

"He must be. Try his door. He probably sleeps with those wax things in his ears."

Given time, she might have caught my sly reference to the noise made by her children early in the morning, but she didn't have the time, for Neal, knowing he was caught, rushed out of his room with such a nervous spurt that he nearly collided with her. They came so close that a spark might have jumped between their noses if either had been charged; for he was stooped to avoid the low lintel, and she was quite tall.

I laughed. "You've flushed your rabbit, Mrs. Peters," I murmured.

"Did you want to talk to me about something?" Neal blurted out, backing away.

Mrs. Peters, a professor's wife, gaunt from the double duty of caring for his three children and at the same time living the Life of Ideas, came straight to the point, with typical abruptness. "No, I don't want to talk to you," she said, "but this telegram just came for you." She held it out. Neal retreated even farther, a real surprise, but she handled the situation, in her impersonal way, by putting the wire on the ancient table next to his door. Then she turned and walked briskly to the top of the bare wooden stairs, the blue mules flopping bawdily.

I crossed the hall and leaned over the banister to observe her descent. When she was back in the kitchen with the door closed, I straightened up and turned around, pushing one hand through my checked-flannel bathrobe to scratch. I had a slight case of the itch those months in and about the left armpit, which no dermatologist was able to alleviate, perhaps because I enjoyed it so much. I think it had to do with

6

Pounce, a girl who will appear some pages hence. But I digress. Let me only add, to get tiresome description out of the way, that I was in my earlier thirties, was tall, my blond hair thin, my smile—and I was always smiling—amiable, my general manner a trifle phlegmatic. Unlike Neal, I was not handsome, but I was not ugly either. We were not beauty and the beast on the same floor.

I pursued Neal into his room, whispering. "She didn't know whether you were in or out. She really doesn't watch us at all. If we bribed the cleaning woman we could keep tarts up here, if they didn't eat too much." He had left the wire on the little table where Mrs. Peters had put it, and I picked it up as I went by. "Aren't you going to open it? People are supposed to tear open telegrams, then crumple them up in a fist while their eyes fill with tears." I yawned. "That's the way it always is in the movies. What better guide to action?" I yawned again. "Maybe it's money."

Neal wouldn't touch it. "In a minute," he said. "I have to tie my necktie now."

"So that you can loosen it in your distress? An action which speaks louder than words. Have you finished in the can?" He nodded. I sensed that he wanted me to leave, so naturally I went to his dresser, found his nail file, and began to polish down a little hangnail. "Ready for the daily plunge back into the centuries?" I nagged. "Where does Clio await you today, Brewster? Is it true that Henry the Eighth was such a fearsome farter that Catherine of Aragon complained about it in a letter to her ex-confessor?"

"I don't know," he said.

"Look it up and tell me." I finished my hangnail and started out of the room. "Wait five minutes if you feel like it, and I'll have breakfast with you."

I should explain how we were connected with the university. Neal was a graduate student in history; I, his senior by five or six years, an associate librarian for Special Collections, the sweetest portion of any library. Since we lived on the same floor of the Peters house and shared the bathroom, we inevitably saw quite a little of each other and found it convenient to have breakfast together occasionally or a beer before bedtime. I found Neal rather dull, tending to pedantry; yet, as I think about it, that wasn't quite all. He had promise, even then. I have always been a connoisseur of the hidden underside of the conventional, the kinks and bends that don't show, the secret vice, the slip of the tongue. Neal had as monotonous a façade as any I had ever seen, yet something about him aroused—languidly—my collector's instinct. He was too subdued, too conventional, too sober and industrious, too withdrawn, even too boring. And too secretive. That was really what caught my attention. He never left anything personal where it might be seen by someone else. Letters were burned in an ash tray or torn to tiny pieces and put down the toilet—I caught him at it one time when he forgot to lock the door. Even paper he had used for work was carried out of the house and thrown away in a street trash basket. I had investigated one such discard, and could find no reason to dispose of it so furtively. It was unnatural, and, therefore, to me, interesting.

But to return to the telegram morning. I came from the preparations for the day smelling of bay rum and peppermint, and found that Neal had waited. It was quite possible, and within the rules of our relationship, that he would have gone on. And the telegram? Still unopened. I put it in my pocket to flash on him later. Down we went and out through the child-worn front yard. About six blocks separated us from our breakfast, and we took them briskly, save for one stop about halfway to the small and septic café where we would eat, when we had to pause because a girl hailed us from the porch of another house which took roomers. She was just the kind of a girl I would have expected Neal to know—bloodless and wispy and blond, with reddish eyelids, sexless transparent skin, a bony structure like that of a heron, and goody-goody make-up. For all that, I sensed that this washed-out studentessa might have her uses, connected with the Pounce I have mentioned. She was introduced as June Bliss, another history student, and she had descended to tell Neal (the lip commenced to quiver) that she had been turned down for some kind of fellowship, at least for the fall term, and wouldn't be able to go to France in September, although there was still hope for February. Neal was distant and unsympathetic—perhaps that was what she expected—and I guessed that it was one of those cases where panting nymph pursues reluctant satyr. After we left her behind I asked him about her, but he didn't have much to say. They had gone out together once or twice, but he didn't know much about her. "June Bliss. June Bliss." I said her name over to myself several times. I observed that she was not at all my type, but that I knew people who liked them skinny and bleached. Was that what Neal liked? No reply.

The little restaurant where we went was one of a group of stores opposite an entrance to the university campus. Inside, there were a counter, some dirty wooden tables, and booths along the windows, one of which was free. We sat down and waited for the famous waitress to come up, a slow, good-natured girl with heavy bosoms which figured largely in the fantasies of lonely freshmen each year. I ordered my habitual breakfast, known on the food-stained menu as Number 3, which, to limn a still life, included fruit juice, eggs and bacon, toast and coffee, and cost a dollar. Rather extravagant for my salary. Neal got a large dish of butter-pecan ice cream and a Danish pastry. Imagine!

At this point I produced the telegram. "Here," I said. "Why won't you open this?"

"I don't like telegrams," he answered. "They interrupt."

I received my fruit juice and took a gulp of the tinny stuff. "That's very uncinematic, Brewster. Half of Bette Davis's greatest scenes were built on them." I should note here that it was just about this time that my great interest in movies and movie-making was beginning, but I was still such a novice that I thought Clark Gable as important in the history of the art as Francis X. Bushman.

He opened it, frowned, and stuck it in his pocket. "It's nothing. It's about my family."

"I take it they must have more interest in you than you do in them."

"I don't have a they, only a she."

Breakfast went on. Neal stared out of the window while he ate his ice cream, raising his spoon to his mouth in an idiotic rhythm. While he watched, an old woman was almost erased by a Welcome Wagon, the Chancellor of the university got out of his limousine across the street with the sheeted Prime Minister of the newest African state, and a bitch in heat loped along the sidewalk followed by four eager suitors and some laughing students yelling "Go, Team, Go" at them; but neither comedy, statecraft, nor love aroused Neal's interest in the slightest. He continued to eat until his tongue touched only metal. He looked down. The dish was bare.

"According to the message," he said, "she's supposed to be sick. But she isn't."

"But she isn't?" I repeated. "That's an odd remark. You don't believe the telegram?"

"You'd have to know her. It's a gesture, like a stage gesture, like an actress dying on a stage, then getting up and walking off when the curtain is lowered. It's a kind of trick."

"Would you say it's a dirty trick, or a funny one?"

"Neither. She probably believes there's something wrong with her, and she needs me around to fill out the picture. She dramatizes everything."

"I like that. Make every moment sing. Let me read the wire."

He didn't mind. He handed it over.

YOUR MOTHER ILL STOP RETURN HOME IMMEDIATELY STOP
TELEPHONE ME COLLECT REGARDING ARRIVAL TIME STOP DAVID
WALLACE

"Who's David Wallace?"

"A friend of my mother."

"He wouldn't be gesturing, too, would he?"

"She got him to send it," Neal said sullenly. "I know them."

"Why not at least telephone him, since he says to call collect?"

"I'll lose the whole day if I call him," Neal took the wire back and reread it. "I won't be able to concentrate afterward."

"Why won't you be able to concentrate?"

"I don't know. I just won't."

"But why?"

"I don't know."

I shrugged my shoulders. The whole thing was quite incomprehensible and slightly distasteful. I surmised that it skirted on very private matters, and I really didn't care about knowing Neal that well. I lighted a cigarette, got instantly delightfully dizzy, and was about to change the conversation when Neal involved me further in spite of myself.

"Why don't *you* telephone?" he asked.

"Me? Why in hell should I phone?"

"David Wallace can't beat you down. You can make up some excuse why I can't call right now—say I'm in a class and asked you to do it. See if you can find out how serious they are."

"It's a crazy idea," I said. "No."

"I'll give you a bottle of whisky."

That was different. "All right. Give me a dime to get the operator, and give me the telephone number, if you know it."

I left the table and was back within a few minutes, still smoking the cigarette I mentioned, which will give an idea of how quickly that call went through. I stamped it out back at the booth without resuming my seat.

"Would it make any difference to the Dean of Graduate Studies if your Mr. Wallace called him?" I asked.

Neal nodded. "Yes, it might."

"I thought he sounded like a man a dean might pay attention to. It looks to me like a trip home is in your immediate future."

"He threatened that. I was afraid he'd do something like that. Otherwise I would have torn the wire up."

"And put it down the toilet?" I asked.

"I suppose so."

"He was also very angry you had me call, and he was very curious to know who I was, too. I told him my name was Bates. I have the idea he'll remember it."

"He will," Neal said. "You'll probably get in trouble, too."

I laughed, for I found other people's bogies comical.

He looked at me seriously as he got up. "I mean it."

We paid our bills and started out the door. "You know, you've forgotten to ask me if I found out anything about your mother."

"My mother?"

"Of course, Brewster. Naturally I said you were anxious to have news of her. David Wallace said she has had a heart attack."

"So that's what it's supposed to be." He grunted. "All this trouble and worry and lost time," he added, "and all of it over nothing."

"That wasn't exactly my impression."

"I know them," he replied. And then we separated, for he had to go down the street to a travel bureau to get information, and I was going to cross the campus to the library.

I watched him walk away, shuffling and somehow unintelligent, maybe even boringly mad, yet, with his good looks, made for all kinds of successes he wasn't having. Then I crossed the intersection and pushed on into campus, following, at a suitable distance, a group of coeds in low socks, comparing them in my mind with Pounce. There was, I concluded, no possible comparison, and I turned off to my destination without regret.

3

I have now reached a point where I must describe a scene to which I was not an eyewitness. This raises the question of my method, if not of my honesty. At least it raises the question to me, although I realize that had I chosen to go arrogantly forward pretending to omniscience, almost any reader would follow me without asking any questions at all, which explains, I suppose, why universal literacy will not improve the world. It so happens that I know that the following episode took place, partly because I have been able to interview some of the actors, and partly because David Wallace was careful to keep notes on his affairs. However—*I wasn't there*. And so, it is quite obvious that there will be bits of my own invention, and that the shape of the dialogue is mostly mine. Nevertheless, my work remains far truer than fiction; for —and let this be enough of my method—it is my principle, where I must represent a scene I did not see, to invent at will in order to give the illusion of actuality, but this much I can promise: I will invent only the possible.

David Wallace—a small man. In fact, a little man, his body light and frail, the skin tight over the bones of his face. One could see that he had once been handsome, his body neatly proportioned, and formed, as often happens with small men, with elegance and precision. At the age of seventy-one he was still distinguished, his intelligence bright and cutting, his manner genteel and old-fashioned. At the same time, there was a chilling authority about him, the steel of the Late Victorian tycoon. In a city where parvenu power frequently brayed to the heavens, his quiet voice got heard.

Everyone in town knew who he was, including Ida Gladstone, the pursy practical nurse, who sweated with deference when he stopped by Mrs. Brewster's apartment in the middle of the afternoon. She had been napping in the living room, and after he had hung up his coat in the hall closet, he went in and looked about, noticing the empty coffee cup on the table in front of the couch and the disorderly pile of women's magazines she had been reading before she fell asleep.

"I take it," he said softly, "that everything is all right here, Nurse."

Gladstone felt a giddy slip in her status. Nobody had called her "Nurse" in years. "Yes, indeed, Mr. Wallace," she said, touching with her clean handkerchief at some moisture which formed under her eyelids. "Mrs. Brewster is asleep."

"And you?" His eyes moved up and down her hefty body, remarking, she felt sure, her thick upper arms. She fidgeted with the seat of her uniform to get them partly behind her. "You've found everything you need?" he asked.

"Yes, Mr. Wallace." They looked together at the coffee cup and the spoon, which had slipped off the saucer onto the top of the table. "I was just having a cup of coffee and lying down here. I was up a lot during the night to check on things." Their eyes met, and his gaze was so steady and cool that she felt compelled to say something more. "I hope you don't think I'm making myself too much at home."

"Do you think so?" he asked.

"Well, you know, when you live in on a case . . ."

"Quite. I'm sure Mrs. Brewster would want you to be comfortable, and I certainly agree. Can I look in on her?"

"I don't think it will do any harm," Gladstone replied.

He nodded, then walked briskly but noiselessly across the living room, stepping economically around the delicate chairs and spindly French tables which were scattered about. Mrs. Brewster hated rooms in which furniture was backed up against walls, because, she said, they allowed no social counterpoint. He turned in to the hallway and stopped at Mrs. Brewster's door, daintily rotated the knob until the faintest click indicated that the latch had cleared, then went in. He had not invited her, but Gladstone followed him anyway, on duty, but also curious. She waited in the doorway.

The shades in the bedroom were drawn, darkening the predominant greens of upholstery, rug, and walls. One ray of sun, dissonant in the general twilight, slanted from the edge of a window and glittered amidst the spikes of the cut-glass bottles on the dressing table. Mr. Wallace noticed it and adjusted the blind, then returned to the foot of the bed, his back to Gladstone, and looked at the woman lying there. For several minutes he did not move, his head bowed. Then the sick woman shifted slightly in her bed and began to breathe more heavily. He cocked his head and listened, as if trying to catch behind her breathing some clue to the strength of the beat and flow of her life. He lifted his right hand from his side and stroked the back of one of the gilt-bronze sphinxes which ornamented the posts at either side of the footboard, then, bending forward, he moved it onto the bedspread itself near her feet and let it lie there a moment. Then he turned and walked out of the room without looking at Gladstone, who moved to let him pass. Avidly she glanced sideways at his face and was disappointed to find it quite composed.

She closed the bedroom door and followed him to the living room, where he stationed himself in front of the fireplace with one hand resting on the mantel. He invited Gladstone to sit down, and she took the straightest and most uncomfortable chair immediately available.

"She isn't likely to awaken, is she? I don't want her to overhear what I have to say to you."

Gladstone shook her head. "Not for a while. She's under

sedation." She put her hands on the slim fruitwood arms of the chair and half rose. "I can go and make sure."

"That isn't necessary." He tapped his bone-thin finger. "I did not primarily stop by to see Mrs. Brewster this afternoon," he said. "I stopped by to see you, so that we might discuss a private matter which will concern you because you will be living here for some time, presumably."

"Yes?" Gladstone moistened her lips and her eyes shone.

He noticed it, as he noticed everything, and the faintest ironic smile flitted across his face. "You may or may not know," he continued, "that Mrs. Brewster has a son. He's about twenty-six now. I have been in touch with him, and he will be coming here this evening. He's supposed to land at 10:05, so that he'll certainly be here by eleven, assuming his plane is on time. I think you had better wait up for him. He might forget to bring his own house key."

This sort of thing, if this was all he wanted to say, was familiar to Gladstone, and she permitted herself to relax into the commonplace. "Now isn't that nice. I know she'll be so glad to see him."

Mr. Wallace ignored her and went on quickly and precisely. "I have inquired about you today, and I am told that we are fortunate you were free to come here. I am told that you are experienced, good-natured, strong, and particularly good on a case like this." He let her sun herself a moment in all this warmth, then added: "I have not been told that you are discreet."

He paused while the meaning of this last revelation about her reputation got to Gladstone.

"Nevertheless," he went on, tapping the rhythm of his sentence, "I am going to explain something to you which is a private matter. It is not of grave importance, certainly, but I do not want you ever to discuss it outside."

"I'm very careful. I can't imagine who said I wasn't. A nurse sees plenty, but I know when to keep my mouth shut."

"In that case, let me only emphasize that this is one of those times. So much for that. Neal—that is the son's name—may possibly offer us some difficulties. He is . . . erratic. He has very little spirit, yet he is not easy to manage."

"I'll watch him."

He smiled again. "I'm sure you will. He called my office a short while ago. He wanted to delay his coming for several days, using his work as an excuse. His work! I told him that he was to come at once, and he will, because frankly my will is stronger than his, and he will do what I tell him to do." Gladstone nodded her approval of this crude use of power. "I am telling you this because I may need an ally here in the apartment. Yes, an ally," he repeated with distaste. "Together we can keep him from causing any trouble which might set Mrs. Brewster back."

"I'll be glad to help."

"As I say, he is not very spirited. But it is quite possible that he will attempt to leave. I want you to be sure that he behaves like a normal, dutiful son." He rotated the vase that stood on his end of the mantel a full circle, thinking. "It will be better if his mother doesn't know he is coming tonight. Let her see him in the morning."

He put on his coat in plain view of the living room, where Gladstone remained, standing at attention. From the doorway he fixed her with his sharp old blue eyes. "I am counting on you. All that matters is Mrs. Brewster's recovery." Then he started through the front door, but stopped and stared down at his hat. When he turned around again to look at Gladstone, his face was troubled. "Don't misunderstand me. I have probably exaggerated because I am so anxious to make sure nothing goes wrong. I don't mean to imply that the boy is strange. He is difficult, it's true, but he is not really strange."

He left the apartment, and a few minutes later Gladstone, who had hurried to the front window, saw his driver let him into his car and take him away.

4.

Should we pass the rest of the afternoon and early evening
with Ida Gladstone, waiting for Neal to arrive? I don't think we
will want to spend all that time. Fond as I am of Ida, it would
not be very interesting, for she is undeveloped. She belongs to
the community of prurient minds, of which I, too, am a member, and had we met that day I would have recognized a fellow spirit, a recognition made particularly delicious by the
fact that hers would have peeped forth at me from under layers of Middle Western Protestant respectability, like a kitten
playing in bedclothes. "Now, now, Mr. Bates, none of that
talk," she would say. Yet . . . Yet, she is undeveloped. Poetry
abounds in melancholy regrets over lost opportunity, such as
Indians throwing away pearls, and Miltons who never come
into voice; but one inhibited talent has never been the subject
of such lament, and perhaps it is up to me. Let me then de-
plore . . .

> *Some chaste Priapus, in whose solemn band,*
> *Starched Gladstone steps, a douche bag in her hand.*

Dear Gladstone, had fate been kinder, I can imagine you quite
otherwise, leading us into secluded glades and scented bow-
ers, there to preside right willingly over many a lusty scene,
clapping your hands, those fat upper arms joggling as only
flesh can, the three golf balls of chin and cheeks all ashine
with jollity.

Alas, sweet Ida, nobody has ever asked you to find a feather
to tickle with or to steal a key.

So anyway, my duty done for the literature of lost chances,
let us go on, pass quickly over Gladstone at her duties—magazine reading, face washing, white stocking soaking, medicines,
rubs, and so on; but we might just go with her to the kitchen

18

for a moment, where she tried to pump the maid, Daisy, who came every day in the afternoon and stayed until after dinner. Daisy was at the stove baking cookies, and Gladstone took a fresh one, all hot and aromatic and sagging, to have with her glass of milk. She remarked that a gentleman had stopped by to see Mrs. Brewster.

"Mr. Wallace, I suppose."

"That's right." Gladstone eyed Daisy's back, squinting. "He's here a lot?"

Daisy nodded over her shoulder. "I should say he is. Don't you know about *that*?"

"I've heard something." Gladstone thought it over. She wanted to ask more, but she was mindful of David Wallace's remarks about discretion, so all she said was, "He came to tell me that Neal is flying in tonight to see his mother."

"Huh. That's a surprise."

"Why?"

"He never comes here. Every once in a while she gets in one of her moods and cries about it."

"What's he like?" Gladstone took another cookie.

"He's quiet enough."

"I like to know something about the people I have to deal with on a case, particularly a heart case."

"Well, you don't need to expect much from him. He's real quiet, and he doesn't make any mess. That's about the most I can say for him."

Gladstone was offhand. "Would you say he was nervous?"

"Nervous?" Daisy thought the adjective over. "No. If anything, I'd say he was too quiet. My husband had a cousin who was quiet like him—didn't talk, mooned around. Then one day he up and slit his wife's throat and filled his thermos bottle with her blood, but he forgot his lunch box on the bus, and that's how they caught him. He wasn't only quiet, he was crazy."

"Neal reminds you of him?"

19

Daisy nodded. "A little. I guess I'd better make up his bed for him."

Gladstone took all this with a grain of salt, but it did worry her a little, and after Daisy left that night she went exploring in Neal's bedroom, to see what she could find in there, thinking maybe she could get a clear idea of what he was like from the place he had once slept—typical undeveloped Gladstone, if you stop and think about it. She found nothing surprising about its appearance. Bed, chest of drawers, desk, bookcases, some hunting prints on the walls, rather too elaborately framed—Mrs. Brewster's taste. The room didn't have much personality, gave no feeling of belonging to anybody or of being a particular boy's retreat.

Gladstone then went through the dresser drawers, the closet, and the desk, but found little in any of them. In one drawer were some uniforms carefully folded in a particular way, which she was careful not to disturb in feeling between them for something hidden. She found odds and ends of clothes, but noted the absence of old sneakers, baseball mitts, toy automobiles, pennants, or anything else that spoke of normal youth. As she was leaving she picked up a leather box on top of the dresser to look inside, and was about to put it down when she felt something pasted to the bottom of it. There was a small piece of paper glued to the leather, and on the paper some writing, quite faint. She carried it to better light. It was no price tag, for written there was the standard four-letter word for intercourse, followed by "U.D." It made no sense, but it was hardly a normal thing to find. She went back over the room, this time feeling under things or on top of them. It was like an easter-egg hunt, and at least as rewarding, for she found a dozen additional messages, none of them, because of the use of private symbols and codes, entirely comprehensible, and several using words Gladstone would never have used. Such secrecy! What was she to make of it? Had it not been for an accident, Neal's magical formulas might have remained indefinitely, whether efficacious or not, permanent wee scribblings of hate.

She turned off the light and stumped grimly back to the living room. No physical horror had the power to move her, no grisly wound could make her blink; but mental health—that was a different matter. Would Neal have outgrown whatever was wrong with him, she asked herself? She went back to her own room to get a pill which would calm her nerves, then returned to the living room, where she turned out most of the lights. At least if she could not sleep that evening, she would rest. She sat down on the couch, then stretched out on it on her back, one hand shading her eyes. In spite of her apprehensions, and perhaps because of her pill and because she had been up early, she fell asleep, flat on her back, her mouth ajar. Time passed. Her sleep deepened. The hand over her eyes fell and hung over the side of the couch. There she lay, unprotected, liable to surprise, when the outer door of the apartment opened and a young man tiptoed into the living room.

5.

I will leave Gladstone thus ready for outrage, like a patient prepared for an operation, and stop to discuss some of the circumstances that "condition" (to borrow a term from one of the lesser sciences) the writing of this book. What I meant by the "I" and the "he" in the book must by now be apparent: that this is not just the story of my life; it is also the story of Neal Brewster's. It is a union of those nonidentical literary twins, biography and autobiography. The question arises, why am I writing it? Why write about two relatively obscure people, named Neal Brewster and Ned Bates?

I am doing so out of self-interest. Neal proposed that I should write it. His quirky kind of vanity found the idea appropriate. Naturally, I need a place to write, food, leisure time, et cetera, and he is obligated to provide them. Tit for tat. As long as I write, I eat. The Scheherazade of the dinner table. But I am also writing because I want to. I do not try to deny how great my interest is, natural enough in myself, but also in Neal. For his biography is also my autobiography, and he is my creation, although the creature turned against its inventor with the proverbial sharpness of an ungrateful child. My feelings still smart from that unkindness. Neal the surprising survivor of my creative act. Neal my mutation. Neal my graft. Can I help but write with some rancor about him? Friendship is a tangled web, filled with knots and tears and loose threads and errors—a special kind of fabric, good only for a remainder sale.

I am not, by the way, a writer of prose books. I am not a scholar. Currently I am most interested in aspects of the cinematic arts; that is the work I am going to be able to carry on while kept by Neal as his pet biographer. I have a dozen projects our arrangement will make possible. I toil in obscurity, but that doesn't matter, so long as I can toil. Even this manuscript will never be published, I should guess. Similarly, you will not encounter my films now, because I have been dogged with bad luck. But encounter them you will, and they will eventually be as well known as those of Eisenstein or Cecil B. De Mille; and one day, when age has made them sufficiently respectable, they will be shown at the Museum of Modern Art.

One caution. There are many areas where Neal and I disagree about meanings. Neal's life, my life, this book, all mean one thing to me, another to him; and we are enemies. I ought to restrain my language, but I will let that stand. Our Truths are at war. And you, dear reader, my other enemy, must adjudicate between us, if you ever get the chance.

But I ramble, always a great danger with me when I am not visualizing what is supposed to happen. What I have been touching on will eventually become clear, and all that I need point up here is the complexity of my project. That is the reason I am going to introduce certain primary documents now and then, which, in effect, permit Neal to speak for himself. I really can't insist on having the only say, although I may insist on having the last one. I don't want my own way by omitting the opposition. Let the opposition speak for itself. Give it its moment. I have no fears.

The first bit of original Brewsteriana comes right now. Neal considered, some time before he hooked and landed Yours Truly to be his court historian, writing his own autobiography, and he put down some random thoughts on the subject. I have culled the material that follows from the Manila folder containing these thoughts, and have been conscientious in trying to retain the flavor of Neal's personality and of the operation of his "mind," at least as it was then.

And so, exit Ned Bates for a while. Enter Neal Brewster as hero. Enter our very own tipsy-turvy, trans-Appalachian Hamlet.

Thoughts on an Autobiography

Should I write an autobiography?

There are only two reasons for writing an autobiography. One is for self-instruction. Flay the past, if you can stand the smell. Pluck the flabby blood vessels, the loose muscles, the machinery of heart and bowels, and learn what you can about yourself. The second reason: to instruct others. I revel in today; I rejoice in tomorrow; I do not need to whimper my confessions about yesterday, not for my own use. So I would be addressing myself to others, for their illumination.

Who would ever want to read about my life and learn its lesson? Who, of this feckless and fastidious generation, pliable as chewing gum, could understand it?

Could the ten-toed sloths, waiting each night for the bus, understand it? No!

Could the buyers and sellers understand it? No!

How about the clergy? Heavens no!

The wolves and the eagles are gone; the tigers prowl our encampments no longer. The only menace on the horizon is a scavenger, its shifty yellow eyes looking for strays, its mouth watering at so much rotten flesh. Could he understand my message? No!

Yet a hero is a hero, in spite of it all. And somewhere there is another. Somewhere there is a reader who would understand and close the book with a new stirring in his blood, and a new brightness in his eye. My brother, we will take hands and cross the mountains.

Once I was a slave; now I am a conqueror.

Once I was abased and covered with dust; now I am glorious and a marvel.

But where are the great deeds, the pyramids of skulls, the stone bulls of my victories, the uncharted worlds? There aren't any.

Mine has been a life of becoming, not of doing, of becoming what I am now out of what I once was. And in such an unlikely way, too, through means available free to everyone, for the simple taking.

So you have changed, you have become, says the skeptical sociologist. Who was your analyst?

Mother Nature, I answer, with her loving indifference, has been my psychoanalyst, and Life the lumpy couch upon which I tossed.

Who wants to read about that?

Should we be kind to our former selves? I think not. Change is strength. The coward is always the same. The fool makes up his mind once and for all. The man who looks back embraces death.

I despise the person I once was. I was listless and weak, pulpy and pale, living under the bark of decaying stumps.

How can I remember what I was like, worm back into that soft body, that timid mind? What did I say? How did I think? What, if anything, did I feel? I ask myself, could I present a true account of myself as I was then? Do I even know?

We must hate our former selves. Yesterday's baby is dead, and who cares? Throw it out with yesterday's water and make new.

I kick aside the corpse and leap to the center of the clearing. I pound my chest to the dawn and howl my greeting to the new day. The leaves of the bamboo shiver above me in the cool light, and drip with the mists that trail across the valley; and all around my head an audience of gaudy parrots with green wings and scarlet bodies and eyes like chips of jet scream their admiration while I dance the Dance of Life. Listen. Listen to me stamp out my joy on the great drum of the Universe.

Genesis was written in the third person. Someone was watching. I am the watcher and the watched.

I do not believe in evolution. I do not believe in special creation. But I do believe in miracles, wrought spontaneously out of the inner substance of things.

It is too easy to lay an egg and then sit on it until it hatches. I don't take my hat off to any hen.

I seek a school which has no schoolmaster.

I would believe in God if I were God.

I think of the frog, blinking on the bank, think of the tadpole he once was, and of the magical changes, the shriveling tail, the budding legs, the flow of fresh juices, the new desires, the higher sun and longer days that produced him out of that lumpy creature bound to the slime. I think what happened to me was a metamorphosis, a spontaneous change from one

25

form to another. Yes, to that standard example, the frog, should be added that of Neal Brewster.

Death and Life are at war forever. All around me was the stink of Death. How I longed for it. How I longed to sink back into it and be warm.

Should I begin my autobiography with the great question: Why was I tapped? Why me? Why then? I certainly never expected the metamorphosis to take place, and it was the last thing in the world I wanted. I was contented with my murky existence, smug over its small satisfactions, cozy in its monotony.

I was like a cat that lives in a little store and sits in the window at night. I was a tabby cat, perfectly adapted to life in the library stacks.

I wasn't like other graduate students. I only pretended to be. The others sought Truth, or wanted to make a major contribution, or to mold the minds of youth. I wondered at them, and hid my own aims, the way you might in a crowd try to hide bad breath behind a hand. All I wanted was to teach in the most obscure place possible. I didn't aspire to great scholarship, and I certainly didn't want to be the kind of professor the old students come back to see. I simply wanted not to be bothered, from the time I was hired to the time I dropped dead in front of my last class, my fingernails biting into a piece of chalk.

There was death everywhere, death all around me. My whole life smelled of death.

That is how I want to begin my autobiography, with the smell of death.

6.

There now. The sun is up. The mists have cleared. The Dance of Life is done and the dancer has peeled a banana and swaggered off into the thickets, picking his pelt over for lice. The Drum of the Universe is silenced, and Ned Bates turns off his tape recorder, crawls down out of the crotch of the tree from which he has watched the scene (flicking off the droppings from an occasional parrot), and will now journey back into the hot and unpleasant lowlands of reality, which smell, incidentally, of the usual mixture.

It occurs to me that certain references have been made to Neal's appearance, but that no real description of him has as yet been given. I have described myself, blond and grinning, and I have described other people; but for some reason there hasn't been any occasion to describe Neal. The reader has been introduced to two or more Neals of the mind, but no Neal of the body. There is only one of that, for a body doesn't change in a matter of a few years. The Neal of the body is a few years older, but they don't show much. No metamorphosis.

He took after his mother. Everybody was always saying that, and it is quite true. It is also true that she was a very beautiful woman. Neal was, and is, a very handsome man. He was tall, a little over six feet tall. He tended to be lanky, with a flat stomach and no arse, like a cowboy, but no great width in the shoulders either. His hands and feet were large, and his hands had long fingers, so that if he played the piano, there would be unusual stretch. The most arresting thing about him was his hair, a dark chestnut color, somewhere between brown and black, the color of certain cordovan leathers when there hasn't been purple used in the dyes. It was an unusual color, and he had it directly from his mother.

Ditto the eyebrows, which had an angle in them. The eyes were dark brown and round. Lashes long. Cheekbones high and cheeks flat. Will eventually have lines. Head well formed. Ears small. Nose narrow, not too small. Cleft in the chin. Good smile, with even, rather small white teeth. Big smile, with lips drawn quite far back. It all adds up to a very good-looking man. People took a second look at him, I mean nearly all women, including the wrong kind, and the wrong kind of men.

When I first knew him at the university he had no sense of his body at all, certainly no pride in it. And one thing I will say for Mr. Dance-of-Life, and that is this: He is still not vain of his handsome face and his well-formed body. He takes them for a fact, a pleasant fact, like an inheritance. He is aware of them now, and he uses them when he wants to, but just the way anybody will use any attribute, like a sense of humor or a knowledge of Russian. A handsome man who exploits his looks actively, as Neal does, instead of just passively letting them work for him, is a dynamic force and should be watched—and not just by husbands.

Now I must describe Neal's homecoming, and to do so involves me in a problem, because just what happened that night can never be established. Versions vary, all are grotesque, and none seems to me to tell the whole truth. Truth, as we all know, depends on your point of view. Truth also varies with the level at which you sample life, in the sense that a geologist samples a core of the earth's crust. What *really* happened that night? We could ask Gladstone, and she would tell us one thing now, would have told us another thing then, might tell us a third tomorrow. Neal would certainly tell us as many versions, and none of them would be like any of hers. What, then, is a poor chronicler to do?

Well, I think he must do this. He must arbitrarily choose a window to look through. I therefore invite you to step up to the window with me; but just remember that I make no claims for what you will see. It is make-believe—but then, what isn't? We will be seeing only what I think Neal did, not what he did do, nor what he thinks he did. But if I don't get on, I will have you and me wrapped up like the prey of a spider.

Read on, then, but believe at your own risk.

7

Neal's plane arrived about twenty minutes late, and by the time he had collected his suitcase and got his taxi, it was nearly eleven. The driver, probably a Swede in from one of the country towns, judging from his coloring and his faintly Mongoloid eyes, wore a plaid wool cap with the ear flaps tied up. The windows were all up too, because early April is cold in country that is so far away from the ocean. Neal slumped back in a corner, not seeing anything, not saying anything, not thinking much of anything, his mood over him like a dense black cloth used to cover some object that is best not exposed to the light.

Then they stopped, and he got out, paid the driver, picked up his luggage, and climbed the three or four steps to the door of the apartment house. When he was small, it had been just about the only apartment house in town, the only respectable one, that is. Everybody tried to have a private house, and everybody he knew did have one. That was a great difference, at twelve years of age. The lobby was redecorated now. There were now pictures hung on the walls, prints of North American birds, and Neal stopped to read the titles. One was of a scarlet tanager, which was not a bird native to the region, probably also true of the decorator.

He worried a little because the elevator had been resting on the second floor, that is, on his mother's floor. He wondered if the person using it had just arrived, and had been going to his mother's apartment. If so, who was it? A doctor? Or someone timing his arrival to correspond with Neal's—David Wallace? Within him apprehension strove with apathy for a moment, but lost. He went up in the elevator, then got out and walked down the corridor to his mother's door and listened, trying to hear what was going on on the other side. His arm got tired, and he put his suitcase down. Nothing. No sounds. There was, he knew, a nurse, but possibly she and his mother, too, were asleep. Everybody was asleep, and the elevator had brought somebody to one of the other three apartments on the floor.

Then he had an idea. He schemed a dull little scheme. If everybody was asleep, he could sneak in and not awaken anybody and spend the night without being discovered. He would have to avoid using the plumbing in that case, so he left his suitcase and toilet kit and coat and went back downstairs and outside, where he scrambled behind some spiraea bushes and urinated, a farmyard sound, or a sound of the woods. Then he returned upstairs and tiptoed in. He saw nobody in the living room, only a lamp burning in a near corner, and one of the wall fixtures on. He listened for sounds from the bedrooms, but there were none. He went to a chair near the door and undressed, taking off his suit, shirt, shoes, and socks.

The fireplace faced the door of the living room. In front of it was the only really comfortable piece of furniture in the whole room, a long, deep, high-backed couch, its back to the door, its front to the fireplace. Mrs. Brewster liked to sit almost hidden in that deep, voluptuous sofa when she received guests, because all they could find of her at first was her voice. That was when the maid was there to answer the door. Then she would stand up, and she and the guest would make their way to each other, weaving through the furniture to a dramatic confrontation, so she thought, and she would then lead the way back to the fireplace and arrange herself magnificently on the couch again and talk. She was the only woman in town who wore long gowns in the evenings, and even she not always, because she was never sure whether she was setting a standard or was considered ridiculous. That depended on her mood, too.

Neal turned out the lights and then did a thing that he had liked to do when he was a boy, and wasn't supposed to do because it was so hard on the furniture—namely, mount the sofa from behind. It was not just forbidden, but also fun, like something in a children's park. He tiptoed forward in the darkness, a hand out to make sure he didn't bump into anything, got to the back of the sofa, turned around, hoisted his buttocks up until he was sitting on the middle of the back, brought his legs up, let himself down backward until he was horizontal, lying like a cat along the top of the couch, only on his back, then, with a sigh of satisfaction, rolled onto his right side and fell down onto the deep soft cushions, the trick being to land square on the stomach, stretched out ready for sleep.

That deep sigh of satisfaction—Neal is very insistent upon how he breathed it. It was part of the game, too, since one was supposed not only to land on his stomach, all stretched out, but also land with the breath gone from the lungs, so that the first action was to breathe in deeply.

In this case, Neal gasped. He landed as he was supposed to land, but he landed squarely on top of another person, who was much shorter than he and rather spongy and who choked and struggled. He heaved up, but his arms were stretched out straight at his sides, and the other person, confused, unintentionally held him back. They got hopelessly tangled together, flailing too hard to untie the knot. He barked his shin on the coffee table, and the pain that shot up his leg shocked him into speech.

"Lie still," he whispered, clenching his teeth. "Lie still or you'll get hurt."

"Don't. Don't do it," said the other person. A woman.

"Lie still," he hissed. Their faces met, and his cheek was cut by her glasses. He dug an elbow into her middle, whereupon she grunted and grabbed his flank so hard he had a bruise on it for a week.

She got her breath. "Help!" she cried, much of the sound lost in the cushions.

"Be quiet," he said. "You'll wake up my mother."

She stopped and relaxed as if her neck were broken, and he rolled off the couch and fell between it and the coffee table. That word "mother" had broken the spell holding them together.

"Your *what?* Are you Neal?"

He wormed backward until he was clear of furniture and got up on his feet. Then he turned on a light, and there took place a dramatic confrontation of a sort his mother never even imagined. Most men look unprepossessing in their underwear. If they are embarrassed, being in their underwear makes them look even more embarrassed. In its way it is worse than nudity, if you're going to get caught in it. And so we may be sure that Neal looked very drawn together and elbows-in, and that Gladstone, red in the face, hair pulled apart, glared with horrid venom from the couch, where she was planted in soft down. She adjusted her uniform. Her lips worked. Those three golf balls, cheeks and chin, were aflame with color, like the face of an enraged troll. Knowing what one does about Gladstone, one knows that she took a very good look at the abject man in underwear before her, the searching look that any just nearly raped member of the confraternity of prurient minds would take.

"What were you trying to do?" she said finally. "Is that your idea of a joke? Let me tell you, Neal Brewster, that men get put into jail for jokes like that. A college education won't help when it's a rape charge." She fiddled with her glasses, which had been bent, and finally had to take them off to fix them. That didn't help, because people who wear glasses suspect any damage to them is intentional. She was sitting up by now. "What have you got to say for yourself, you dirty-minded rapist?" She was climbing to new moral heights, was Gladstone. "You vile criminal," she added, glaring at his legs.

"I just wanted to sleep on the couch. I didn't know you were there."

She snorted and got to her feet. "Try that on the police."

She brushed off the front of her uniform, then dusted her hands together. "You ought to be locked up right now." Both of them looked at the telephone, and it may be that Neal was saved by the fact that he was between her and it.

He moved backward toward the chair with his clothes on it and began to dress as fast as he could. "Don't call the police. It wouldn't be good for Mother," he said.

"Why didn't you think of her before?"

"I did. That's why I didn't want to make any noise. If she's really sick, she ought to have quiet, isn't that so?"

"What do you mean, if she's *really* sick?"

"I don't know. All I wanted to say was that I was trying not to make noise."

"You expected me to go through that and be quiet? What kind of a person did you think I was? You must be a maniac, just like everybody says."

Neal stopped dressing a moment, interested. "Do they?"

"Some do. Including me."

He went on, his interest dead. All he wanted to do was get out. "I didn't mean any harm," he said.

"I noticed you didn't let me alone until I called for help."

"But I couldn't get up. You were hanging on."

That made Gladstone furious; let us not question too closely why. "So that's the story you're going to tell, is it? So that's how you plan to keep my mouth shut? Well, it won't work, not with me. My reputation's good and safe." Then, feeling some action was needed, she said: "You get away from that door. I'm leaving here right now, patient or no patient."

"But you don't need to," Neal whispered. "*I'm* leaving." He was dressed by this time and, taking his suitcase, he started for the door.

Gladstone moved fast behind his back, and he became aware that she held his topcoat tail and had her feet dug into the rug. He wasn't going to go anywhere.

"No you don't."

33

"But I don't mind going. It's more important for you to stay here than for me to."

"Just stop trying. You're not going to go. If anybody leaves, I'm going to. But not you. You're going to stay here and do your duty," she said fiercely. "You're not . . ." Tug, tug. "Going to go . . ." Tug, tug. "Anywhere, and I'm here to see to that, and I'll stay that . . ." Tug, tug. "Long. Put down the suitcase, Neal Brewster. You come back in here."

She had lots more resolution than he did. He followed her back to the fireplace, limping. She noticed it.

"Say, are you handicapped?"

"What do you mean?"

"That limp. Nobody told me you were handicapped."

"I'm not. I hit my shin trying to get off the sofa."

"Oh." Gladstone didn't know quite what to do. It is perhaps surprising that she didn't call the police or run out of the house screaming for help, or panic in some other way; but once the lights were on and Neal fully revealed to her, she knew it wasn't necessary. Also, she had her conscience—about Mrs. Brewster, about her duties, even about Mr. Wallace, who would be highly displeased, she knew, if there were a scandal, newspaper pictures, and all the rest. But what to do? She fiddled with her glasses, which now kept slipping down her nose, until she had an idea. "I'll go call Mr. Wallace."

Neal, who had sat down and was staring at the floor, looked up. "No, don't do that," he said.

"Why not? He's got to know about this sooner or later. It's my responsibility to tell him."

"Not tonight."

"But tonight's the night I'm not safe here."

"Yes you are. I didn't know you were there on the couch. I didn't look."

"Your aim was mighty good for somebody who didn't look." Her attention turned from what to do to what had happened. She measured the back of the sofa with her eyes, then walked to the front hallway and looked at it from there. "It's just possible," she admitted. "But your kind always has an explanation for their crimes. No, I don't believe it." She snapped her fingers. "Now I've got it. Sleeping pills." She took his suitcase and disappeared, but was back in a few seconds, holding out three little capsules in the palm of her hand, and carrying a glass of water. "Take these," she commanded.

"I don't want to."

"Then I call Mr. Wallace."

Neal took them.

"Now, then, you get into bed. They'll work in twenty minutes or so, and then you won't be able to. Three of those pills would knock out a bull for eight hours."

She followed him to his bedroom and wouldn't even let him close the bathroom door, for fear he'd stick a finger down his throat. He began to undress, but still she didn't leave, so he did without pajamas and got into bed in his underwear. She opened his window for him, threw a blanket over his feet, and stood in the doorway, waiting for him to show signs that the drug was working. Talking half to herself, she said, "Your color's not good. And when we were so close together there, I noticed a smell I didn't like. Too many French-fried potatoes and things like that. Bad food. You need to get on a healthy diet. Bad food makes everything go all wrong." She looked at her wrist watch, big as a man's. "In five minutes you won't know what's hit you. I guess you can't run very far in five minutes." She turned out the light and closed the door.

But while he still lay awake staring at the bars of light against the far wall, which had shone there ever since he could remember, he heard her prowling the hall outside. She wasn't taking any chances. Then, in just about the five minutes she had prophesied, he got a chemical taste in his mouth. He clicked his tongue dryly against his palate, wondering about it. Then—foof! He blacked out.

*

The following morning Neal awakened about ten o'clock, still doped, neither able to move nor wanting to. He kept absolutely still, partly because he could hear Ida Gladstone snooping outside his door, waiting to hear him as soon as he came to, partly because of the torpor induced by the narcotic, partly because of his sluglike outlook on life. He wished he weren't there. He wished he were back at Mrs. Peters', and that was about all he did feel. Then, he insists, something began to happen to his brain. Someone began to knead it into shapes, like a blob of gray plastic, first into the shape of a loaf of bread, then a flat muffin, then a long, snakelike shape. His room wavered in front of his eyes, and he closed them, but he couldn't get over the feeling of a watery medium invading the four walls, of currents and waving weeds and caverns. It was menacing, but he didn't care.

Then he began to wonder what they would do to him as a result of the night before. He found he couldn't care about that either. He lived through the incident again, feeling Gladstone's plump little belly beneath him, waiting, in his re-experiencing, for the pleasanter moment when he fell onto the floor.

Suddenly—and I have questioned him several times about this, for I find his concept unacceptable—he had the conviction that *something was up*. He says he can't put it any other way. A power was at work he didn't understand; another presence was with him in his room, which was him and yet not him, a counterpart which was connected with an opening of doors, lights going on and off. A double, with different choices. He had the feeling that, could he have overcome his lassitude, he might have leaped out of bed, found the other entity, merged, and been remade on the spot. He didn't. He half sat up, and that was all. Heaviness closed back in. Apathy smothered him. He turned off his mind and retreated from the edge.

It was inevitable, he says. There were things to go through.

When Ida finally broke into his stupor with some remark about a lazybones and said his mother was dying to see him (that was well put, Ida), she found the same old Neal. He had been allowed a glimpse of something else, but still had to earn his right to it.

8.

Getting up in the morning was not the problem for Gladstone that it sometimes is for less organized people. Everything—shoes, pale stockings, sensible underclothing, uniform, and the little cameo pin she allowed herself to wear at work—was left in its place, so that she had no decisions to make, nothing to hunt for. She began with a shower and ended with a touch of witch hazel, and it took her almost exactly twelve minutes from the alarm clock to her final appearance outside her room.

She went through this routine quite as usual the morning after Neal's arrival. Next she had to take care of her patient. Then she fixed her own breakfast and forced herself to eat, although she had little appetite for it, being eager to get on to the excitement of the day. She took precautions—closed doors, lowered voice—so that Mrs. Brewster wouldn't hear her, then looked up David Wallace's number in the directory, flipping the pages in the book with a moistened forefinger. She found it and left an unsanitary little patch of damp on the page by it. Then to the dial, where she hesitated, lost her nerve, approached and retreated from the first letter like a coy adolescent calling her boy friend for the first time. A man answered, whose formality and accent identified him as a butler, Gladstone's first. He wouldn't promise her Mr. Wallace, but he took her name and the fact that her business was urgent away from the phone. While she waited she tried to imagine the fashion in which Mr. Wallace must live. She thought he probably wore smoking jackets and carnations and sipped brandy from huge glasses after dinner. Also, did he ever get sick, she wondered.

Then he was on the line. He wanted to know if Neal had come in all right, and if he had seen his mother yet.

"Yes, he came home. He's asleep. I hope I'm not doing the wrong thing calling you like this, but I thought . . ."

"Of course. Is that all?"

Gladstone realized that there could be no pleasant prolongation to the preliminaries of her story. "No, it isn't all. I can tell you, I've never had anything like what happened last night happen to me in my *whole professional life*. I almost ran out to call the police."

"Come to the point."

"I was waiting for him in the living room, and I fell asleep on the sofa. He came in without waking me up, and then he took off all his clothes and turned off the lights and jumped right on top of me."

"Good God." There was a pause. "I'm very sorry."

"It was the last thing in the world I expected."

"I'm afraid I must ask you what happened next."

"Not what you might think. I thank the Lord for that."

"Did he . . . try?"

"To tell you the truth, I'm not sure." For the first time Gladstone realized that her experience might be considered anticlimactic. "What happened was, I struggled and he fell off and then got up and turned on a light, and he said he hadn't known I was there."

Mr. Wallace spoke in cold fury. "This is outrageous."

Having now brought him to this pitch, Gladstone reversed herself. "He was a perfect gentleman after the lights went on."

"What do you mean?"

"I mean he didn't try anything else. I got him to take sleeping pills and put him to bed."

"That was well done."

"Thank you. Something else. He wanted to go away. That was the first thing he offered to do—just the way you said he might. He put on his clothes, just like he had it in his mind all the time, and he started to get out of the apartment so fast I almost couldn't stop him. I wonder if he didn't do that thing before just so he'd have an excuse to leave. You know, thinking he'd be chased out of the house."

"I find that somewhat far-fetched, Mrs. Gladstone, but I'm not surprised that your imagination is running wild this morning. How do you feel about staying there after he wakes up? Shall I send a man over?"

"I don't think so. I don't feel very comfortable, I can tell you that, but I'm not really afraid of him. I'm a match for him in the daytime."

"You're a brave woman, and you've handled this very well. I need not tell you how glad I am that you did not call in the police. I congratulate you on your nerve."

"Thank you. I try my best." She dared to be personal. "It helps a lot, knowing that I've got somebody backing me up. And he's not so bad. I'll say one thing, he certainly is a handsome fellow. I'd expect a son of Mrs. Brewster to be good-looking, but I wasn't expecting a movie star." The image of Neal in his underwear passed through her mind. Gladstone now made a really daring remark, indicative perhaps of a new power. "What did Mr. Brewster look like? I haven't seen his picture around the house anywhere. Does Neal take after him at all?"

"I hardly knew him," Mr. Wallace answered shortly, "but I believe Neal shows no resemblance to him whatsoever."

"Is that right? Sometimes it happens that way." She let a moment pass. "Should I go ahead and tell her he's home? I don't want her to think I've been hiding it from her."

"By all means. Although you might let him have his sleep out." Mr. Wallace gave her his office number. "They will always know where I can be reached, and don't hesitate to call me again if you think it necessary. I'll be in touch with you later in the morning."

As soon as they were disconnected, Gladstone hurried in to tell Mrs. Brewster the good news; but Mr. Wallace sat by the telephone thinking, while his breakfast got colder. The primary thing was to protect Mrs. Brewster and get her well. But he had other plans, too, involving Neal, and this recent absurdity raised questions concerning them. He looked up a number in the directory, started to dial it, then changed his mind. It was really still too early to telephone a doctor unless it was a great emergency, and he preferred not to give that impression. He would wait and call from downtown.

9.

I take passionate interest in the idea of sickness and the behavior of sick people. In fact, I have thought of making a film on sickness, in which I would try to splice together its characteristic aspects into a kind of sickbed crazy quilt, not a neat little documentary—that couldn't interest me less—but a total presentation, a summary, an epitomizing: the *Gestalt* of illness.

I would want a series of initial moments. The first shiver runs across the shoulder blades of the man who is coming down with flu. A slight frown crosses his face, ruminative rather than ill-tempered, as little minor psychological and physiological adjustments are made in preparation for the uninvited guest who must be entertained, and who will occupy so much time with such bland insistence. Or a shopper, her arms filled with packages, gets up to leave a bus, and the camera lurches with her when the driver swerves, and down she goes, prepared to voice her outrage; but then she doesn't say anything, because she is staring curiously at her ankle, which is wrenched into a nasty pseudo-hoof. Then there are those more subtle cases, an unaccustomed tickle somewhere, a bit of an ache or a tiny pain, a slight obstruction, a spot. Winter turns to summer, but *it* doesn't go away. Finally there is a visit to the doctor; and you know the answer, because you are looking for it within yourself every day.

Very interesting things would, in my film, be done with the progress of disease, too, its erosive effects, the gradual expression of exhaustion or fear or depression, the aimless wiggling, all the usual concomitants to pain and pathology. One could do something quite beautiful, for instance, with the head of a Negro, white sheets and white pillowcases, the metal bedstand white, white cloth screens acting as a shield from other patients, the nurses all in white. Only that one dark head, turning from side to side, back and forth, back and forth, sweating.

One trouble with trying to make such a film is that I'm coming along one hundred years too late. Science has turned sickness into such a banal sort of thing by eliminating so many of the more interesting diseases, restricting others and pulling their teeth, and by regularizing treatment so much. It would be hard nowadays to give the film variety and interest; and my point would most emphatically not be to shock through presenting the atrocity of disease, its outrage. I will leave that kind of cheap moralizing to others. It is the visual beauties of it, the delicate psychological and physiological harmonies as they show to the eye, a strumming of strings which would set an audience to vibrating, that would be my aim, my point.

All these little personal moments, these vignettes of the still living, could be brought into subtle formal relationships with the inanimate adjuncts of disease. What downright moving sequences could be made of microscopic enlargements, if skillfully selected. Or the molecular patterns of instruments—knives with the glare of operating lights glittering along their keen edges, clamps, probes, forceps, all the other fine shiny bits of operating tableware. Or test tubes, rows of drug bottles, and a thousand other laboratory shots. There would really be luxuriant possibilities amidst the paraphernalia of sickness.

I thought of using a character at one time, an ironic little man, like the protagonist in an animated cartoon, who would be known as Mr. Sick. I thought of calling my film, also ironically, "The Adventures of Mr. Sick." He would be a sad, ingratiating, timid, Charlie Chaplin sort of figure, in an overcoat too long, with tremendous circles under his eyes, paper handkerchiefs in each pocket, the perpetual sniffles. And he'd live in a furnished room with nothing much in it except a hypochondriac's patent medicines and health foods, and a lot of little boxes, in each of which would be little slips of paper, with the name of a disease printed on each one. Every day he would gather a lot of these up and put them in a paper bag and go "shopping." Now and then he would sidle up to someone and tuck a slip of paper into that someone's pocket or handbag or market basket, or perhaps just pin it to a coattail. And then that person would become the subject of a subsequent film sequence. The idea of Mr. Sick was an early one; my conception of films has gone beyond devices like him, in spite of the feeling of indifferent malice he might convey; yet Mr. Sick would give coherence to the film. The irony would probably be lost, though, and the sense of fierce comedy I would want. My audience, turning him into a clown, would escape me through the door of its customary sentimentalities.

I suppose all that sounds like digression, but it is not entirely irrelevant to the course of this story, because the dominant influence on these first days I have been describing was, after all, sickness. Putting it another way, little Mr. Sick had come on Mrs. Brewster in the beauty parlor and pinned a slip of paper square on her bosom. Who knows how long she wore that little ticket around, until one morning when she was sitting at her piano, playing one of the *Novelletten* by Schumann, the 7th, just getting ready to move from the first section into the beautiful melody in A major. She played quite well. Listen to the sound of that wonderful, energetic music. She hesitates and goes back over a measure or two, then suddenly she feels Mr. Sick's ticket and dislodges it. It flutters to the floor under the piano, and she staggers to her feet and collapses.

Mrs. Brewster would work rather well for my film, because no greater contrast could be imagined than the way she was before and after. Before, she was a great, heavy-limbed, voluptuous goddess of a woman, slightly out of style in our century, when it is fashionable to be too thin, but of proportions and heft to delight the connoisseur of another. She wasn't fat —there is no emphasizing that too much. Her chin was full, for instance, but not double. Her arms were heavy, but the flesh was firmly attached round the bones. She walked with energy, not in that chirpy way skinny women walk, but with the solemn grace of Aphrodite, Juno in Progress, a sense that something besides a skeleton was under way. She had the extraordinary hair which Neal had inherited, and hers never turned gray, although she was over sixty. Above all, she left a tremendous impression of vitality and interest and life— everybody who knew her agrees about that. She was vain and sometimes foolish, but she was never stale or flat.

But then our weak, sniffling little Mr. Sick, with his sallow face and skimpy mustaches, a man Mrs. Brewster would have brushed aside as any great courtesan would brush aside a scabby beggar, pinned her with his little slip saying *Coronary*. The Life Principle which had always flowed so warmly around her ebbed away, and she was left exposed to a chilly void. She proved to have little stamina, little fight, when that happened, and from the time of her seizure, everybody agrees that Mrs. Brewster never returned to normal.

As soon as Gladstone had told her that Neal was home and asleep in his own bedroom, she began to fret weakly. She wondered if his bed had been properly made up and his room straightened. Gladstone quieted her about that. Was Gladstone sure he wasn't waiting right now in his room, thinking he shouldn't come out so early and disturb his mother? It was then that Ida made her first trip to Neal's door and listened outside. Then Mrs. Brewster worried about her liquor cabinet. Was there any Scotch? Gladstone went to see, found there wasn't much, and said she would order some. Did Mrs. Brewster know what brand Neal drank? She didn't remember, and it was important to get the right brand, because men were particular about that. She didn't, in fact, remember whether or not he drank at all. She fretted about that. It seemed very important to her for as long as she could concentrate on it.

"I'll just order a bottle of any brand. He'll drink it, at his age," Gladstone said, patting pillows. "And if he doesn't drink whisky, there's plenty of milk and ginger ale for him."

"I can't remember if he likes those either."

"Oh, he'll like them. And we'll get him anything else he wants."

"Yes, anything. It's very important. I want him to have everything he wants. If only I could see to it." Gladstone repeated that she'd see to it. "Yes, do see to it, Mrs. Gladstone. I have to depend on you. I want to make him feel really at home." Mrs. Brewster sighed, and her attention slipped away.

She was quiet for a while, but then returned again to the subject of the whisky. "I wish I could remember," she said plaintively. "I ought to remember." Gladstone, used to the ways of invalids, was patient and hardly listened. But Mrs. Brewster got more upset. "I have to remember. I just have to," she complained.

Gladstone got up, patted and smoothed. "Now don't you worry about it. That's the way it always happens. People forget things when they get sick, but they remember them again later on. I have two children, and right at this moment I can remember all kinds of things about them. But when I'm sick I can hardly remember their names."

"Really?"

"I'm telling you the truth."

"I don't think I ever noticed what Neal liked to eat or drink, or details like that."

"My goodness. I think that's all children are—details."

"To me Neal meant love."

Ida moved away from the bed. "I think I loved my children, too, Mrs. Brewster."

Mrs. Brewster noticed and was sorry. "I'm sure you did. People grow apart, even families. I wonder if he's awake yet. Why don't you go and see."

"I will, in a minute. And as soon as I hear a peep out of him I'll get him up and bring him in to see you. Sleep's good, but lying in bed isn't."

When Neal finished shaving he found Gladstone waiting outside the bathroom. She looked at him suspiciously as the thought crossed her mind that he might be constipated from his trip—but later would be time enough to take care of that. She gave him his instructions. He was to be quiet. He was to be very nice and agreeable and not contradict his mother no matter what she said. Finally, he was to leave when Gladstone gave him the signal.

After he got his shirt and tie on, they went into the sickroom, where Gladstone indicated to him with a point of her finger and a pucker of the mouth that he was to go over and kiss his mother. He did so, remarking that she had on no lipstick, that she didn't raise her head to meet his, and that she didn't smell of anything in particular.

"I'm so glad you have come," she whispered, smiling weakly. She rolled her eyes to Gladstone. "Could you open a blind more, so that I can see him better?"

45

He stood, stooping awkwardly, while the room grew brighter. Then he felt the edge of a chair seat pressing the backs of his knees, pushed by Ida. He sat down. Across the room, in the full-length mirror, he could see himself and part of his mother, and, behind, a white Gladstone, fully lighted, her glasses glittering.

"You haven't been home in so long," Mrs. Brewster was whispering. "I've missed you very much."

There followed a long silence. "How are you?" he asked finally, mindful of the white figure behind him.

"Better now."

"She's much better," Gladstone said.

"You won't go away soon, will you, Neal?" When, after a prolonged interval, he didn't answer, Gladstone did, saying of course he wasn't going to go away soon. "You won't, will you, Neal?" Mrs. Brewster repeated, wanting to hear him say it. He felt Gladstone push him in the shoulder, and he shook his head so that his mother could see. She turned her eyes forward and sighed. "Thank God for that," she said.

They sat quietly. Then Mrs. Brewster said, "What are you thinking about, Neal?"

"I wasn't thinking about anything."

"I was. I was thinking about the way you used to follow me around, once upon a time, when I'd let you. But you're grown up now, and moved away."

"Boys grow up," Gladstone murmured, "but they never forget their mothers."

After another interval Mrs. Brewster began to talk, almost as if to herself. "You slept a long time, didn't you? They didn't tell me you were coming in last night. David arranged it, I suppose. I hope you got a good night's sleep. Do you have everything you need? If you forgot anything, or if you need anything, go downtown and get it. I hope you brought enough shirts along. Get more if you need them."

"I'll have enough."

"He's got plenty," Gladstone said.

"If anything should happen to me, don't think you have to keep all the old photographs around the apartment. Just keep a few. But throw the others away. I was so proud of my clothes, and my idea was always to have my photograph taken in everything nice I bought. Throw them away."

"Don't worry about that. Nothing's going to happen to you," said Gladstone.

"When do you think you'll get married?" Mrs. Brewster asked, her voice weaker. "I never cared before, but I would like to have grandchildren now. David calls it something— wanting biological immortality, I think it is. That doesn't sound much like the way I feel. I just think it would be nice."

"Don't you worry about Neal. A good-looking fellow like Neal won't have any trouble finding a wife when he gets ready."

"Yes, Neal is good-looking, Mrs. Gladstone," his mother said. "But I'm not sure it's been a good thing for us. It makes it harder when something happens. I wasn't ever expecting to get sick." She began to cry.

Neal thought he would like to leave and looked to see if the door was open.

Meanwhile, Gladstone got a pill and some water and gave them both to Mrs. Brewster. "Now don't think about it. You'll be all right again in no time."

"Do you think so?" Mrs. Brewster had closed her eyes, tired of talking. The telephone in the living room rang—her bedroom extension had been unplugged—and Gladstone went to answer it. Mrs. Brewster said, "She's very good, but I wish she wouldn't stay so close all the time. I wanted to tell you what I have really been thinking. Lean nearer, Neal."

He bent over, and she whispered. "I have always loved you, Neal, but I haven't ever needed you. Now I need you. I'm afraid, Neal, and I need you near me."

He stood up. "Don't say things like that, Mother," he said.

"Now is the time I must say them."

Gladstone came back at that moment and motioned to him to leave. She herself stayed on a moment with his mother, then came into the living room. She was unsmiling. "You didn't help out much," she said.

"You told me to be quiet."

"I didn't mean that quiet, and you know it. I think she's too sick right now to notice much, though. She knew you were there, and that's what matters. But you're going to have to do better later on. The telephone call was for you, and I took the message. It was Mr. Wallace. He wants to see you downtown this afternoon at two o'clock. He'll send his car. He said for you to be sure to be ready on time."

10.

I have tried to find out what happened to Neal during his first interview with the psychiatrist, but here I have not been successful. Neal refuses to take this whole thing seriously and will never give me a straight answer; and the psychiatrist, Dr. Legg, will not discuss his former patient. I tried him, and he was affable, talked just like somebody's brother who was two years ahead of you at Yale, but cleaved unto his ethical system like a barnacle to a sunken scow. I do know that the Wallace car took Neal downtown, where Mr. Wallace met him, shook hands with him coldly, and led him to Dr. Legg's chambers, which were inevitably furnished in the latest thing in teak from Scandinavia, and had a rubber plant expiring in one corner. Dr. Legg was a youngish man in his later thirties, newly minted at the New York Psychoanalytic Institute, who had come out to this smallish city in the Middle West as something of a sacrifice. "*They* need us too," he must have said to his friends in announcing his move, rather as Saint Columba might have spoken when he set off for hairy old Scotland. Anyway, he was well qualified, and I suspect he had other things in mind for the patient than did David Wallace.

Mr. Wallace, on the other hand, left a careful memorandum of his conversation with Dr. Legg after the interview. What he wanted was to get the doctor to say 1) whether or not Neal had committed a deliberately criminal act the night before, and 2) if so, whether or not he was likely to try it or something like it again. The doctor wouldn't commit himself. All he would say was that Neal was depressed and inaccessible, and ought to be in treatment. This had the old boy wallowing in uncertainty, and may seem unfair; but on the contrary, that's how you get patients, and Legg certainly did think that Neal should come to him.

It was arranged at once, I think because Mr. Wallace figured that if Neal did anything erratic while in therapy there was a certain legal shield. Neal was to go three times a week for as long as he was in town. I know practically nothing about the therapeutic hours either, because, again, nobody involved will talk about them. I have tried, because I feel that some simple clinical material might offer a rather satisfactory figured bass to the romantic stuff that Neal writes about himself. No luck. And so much for Neal and psychiatry. At least I have mentioned it, as must certainly be done by any respectable biographer in our century. Perhaps I will bring it up later in connection with the reverse—or the obverse, should I say?—in any case, the other, the autobiographical aspect of this book. All that need be carried away from these paragraphs is the knowledge that Neal went to a doctor several times a week during the period when he was home. I believe the total treatment came to less than twelve hours.

During these same several weeks Mrs. Brewster was slowly mending, nor did her new attachment to her son grow weaker as she grew stronger. In truth, it thickened and coarsened, like a jungle creeper, and spread out to bind him tight and to explore every aspect of his life.

Neal, darling. Yes, Mother. How much time do you have to spend in classes? About eight or ten hours a week, Mother. Neal, darling. Yes? What is the climate like there? About the same as here, Mother. Neal? Yes, Mother. Where do you take your meals? In restaurants around town. But what restaurants, Neal? I'd like to hear their names. Well, Mother, there's the Varsity Café, and the Wet Hen—that's for sandwiches—and there's Spund's, and then there's a Chinese restaurant which is cheap, but I can't think what it's called. What sort of thing do you eat in those places, Neal, darling? Oh, sandwiches and sometimes steaks and French-fried potatoes, and hash, or maybe pot roast. Neal? Yes, Mother. What sort of a schedule do you keep? The usual schedule. But what is it, Neal? Describe an average day to me, darling. Well, I have breakfast. Then I go to the library and work until lunch, with maybe a break for coffee. Then after lunch I work until dinner, unless I have a seminar, in which case I go to it. Then after dinner I usually work in the library until ten or eleven, and then come home and go to bed. But Neal, how dreary! I don't suppose you realize it, since you're all involved in it, like being a wild savage. You don't know what you're missing in life. I like my life, Mother. I don't think it's dreary. Tell me something, Neal, dear. Yes, Mother? Don't you have any fun or recreation? Parties? Ladies-and-gentlemen sorts of things? Once in a while, Mother. A few a year. Well, at least that is something, dear. I suppose that conversation is very witty and intellectual at them. (Here she lays a hand on a finely bound *Sonnets from the Portuguese* which sits on her bedside table.) Just the sort of thing I miss so much here—good conversation. I don't think the conversation is what you think it is, Mother, at least not at the parties I go to. Neal, darling. Yes, Mother. Tell me this—tell me that—explain to me the other thing. Yes, Mother; yes, Mother; yes, Mother. And so on for three weeks.

One conversation, held at the end of this period, I will report at greater length, since it shows the way the wind was blowing. Mrs. Brewster was out of bed, lying on her chaise longue in some sort of green robe, which flattered her famous hair. She was having tea, and had Neal sipping—and spilling —tea in her room with her. It was late afternoon.

"Here, darling, take my napkin and wipe your saucer. I can see it dripping on your lap when you raise the cup."

"Yes, Mother."

"Neal, tell me something. Are you enjoying yourself here, or are you anxious to get back to the university?"

"I'm anxious to get back to the university."

"I don't think it's nice of you to say so."

"Well, you asked me, Mother."

She looked out of her window. "I know it's your life, of course. But I've liked having you here so much. I can't bear the thought of your going away."

"I'm already way behind."

She faced him again, put her cup down, and folded her hands. She smiled, conscious of her beauty returning. "I want to tell you about a project which involves some people I know. Will you listen?"

"Who are they?"

"Never mind. Perhaps you'll recognize them as I go along. There are only two members of the family. The son is a quiet and studious boy who lives away from home. He lives in a dark old furnished room and doesn't get proper things to eat, and he works too hard. He really doesn't have any *delight* in his life, and since he isn't married yet, there isn't anybody to create it for him."

She smiled at Neal, who was listening with his mouth ajar. "Isn't that too bad? The only other person in the family is his mother. She hasn't been well, but she is much, much better, and she's going to take very good care of herself in the future. But she is sad, because she is a little tired of the worldly life she has been leading, and she longs for a little more stimulation. She misses her son very very much. She doesn't feel right without him around her. But he has to be at his university." She raised a forefinger. "*She* could live *anywhere*, though, for a few years, anywhere she wanted to live. Now what do you think about these people I'm describing?"

"I don't know."

"The mother has a plan which might be very nice for both of them. She would love to keep a nice house for her son, where he could have a study and work and have nice wholesome meals. And he could have other intellectuals come in for evenings or for small dinner parties, when it wouldn't interfere with his work, and his mother, whom most people find a not unattractive person, and some even think charming, could keep all this going for him, and even give it a certain graciousness and tone. She would keep a salon for him, a place where people would try to get themselves invited. The mother and the son would do it together. Don't you think that's a nice idea?"

"I . . . I . . ."

"Don't say yet. I think you ought to think about it and tell me what you decide. I think it a wonderful idea."

Neal stood up. "I don't want any more tea, Mother. I think I'll take a walk."

"If you must walk, then walk," she said a trifle sharply. "But think over what I said."

"I will, Mother."

Nobody will ever know quite what his mother thought about the way he looked or his quick departure from her room, but, being the kind of person she was, she probably found an explanation for it that wasn't too harsh on herself. As far as that goes, one might wonder why Neal didn't take to her idea. She could have made him much more comfortable. His biographer can only state that he didn't want to be more comfortable through her arrangements; he wanted neither to move back into her house nor to have her move into his. He just wanted to be by himself and to be the way he was, poor Neal.

Where he went on his walk would be a matter of indifference if, as was usually the case with the Neal of those days, he had plodded along looking neither dextrally nor sinistrally, occupied with no thoughts at all. But during the course of it he had what he considers an important psychic experience, about whose nature and import I again find myself skeptical; but I cannot reasonably leave it out.

He had no particular place in mind to walk to, so he let old controls work on him and took the route that he had always taken to school as a little boy. He passed in front of the large white house with columned veranda across the street from his mother's apartment—now made into apartments itself—then down an alley where a cat skulked around a concrete incinerator the way a cat was always skulking around a concrete incinerator years before, thence into the neighborhood that lay below. He turned into a side street where the houses were smaller, then crossed an intersection and walked about two thirds of a block to the school building. It was a red brick building, with one large entrance in the middle, and two wings on either side; and compared to the schools they build now, with all their colored panels and glass and open courts, it looked rather like a reformatory. Lying to either side of it were the playgrounds, and Neal walked around one of these, stopping at a basketball post for a moment. Behind the field was a low hill which commanded a view of school and fields, and he climbed to the top of it and sat down on a stump.

There his despair closed in on him. Why wouldn't everybody let him alone? Why did they make him go to a doctor and stay when he wanted to go away? And why did they want to change his diet and the way he lived and what he was doing? Why wouldn't they let him alone? Why wouldn't they? Why?

A little blond boy about ten years old came up behind him. "What are you looking at?" he asked.

"Nothing. I was thinking."

"What about?"

"I don't know."

"You must know. What about?"

"I don't remember."

"I won't go away till you tell me."

"Everybody wants to make me do things I don't want to do. That's what I was thinking about."

"Why do they?"

"I don't know."

"You must know. Why?"

"They don't want me to be the way I am."

"What are you going to do?"

"I don't know."

"Why don't you kill them?"

"I don't know how."

Disgusted by such incompetence, the little boy went away. And then, when he was alone once more, Neal had the second of his *petites épiphanies*, the first having taken place the morning after his arrival home. This one brought him to his feet, his heart pounding. It was not a thought, he says, but a feeling about himself and the world. Put into words, the feeling would go something like this:

Brewster is Brewster! Yes! Brewster is Brewster!

Then it subsided. He sat down again, and despair sat down beside him. He passed a quarter of an hour staring out over school and fields before he got up to go back home.

*

One last incident needs to be told of that day. When Neal got back, he found Mr. Wallace's car waiting outside, so he sneaked up the service stairs and through the kitchen, thus avoiding both Mr. Wallace and Ida the Watchdog, on duty in the living room. Mr. Wallace was in Mrs. Brewster's bedroom, and he was in a rage. Neal stopped in his own doorway to listen and find out what it was about.

The first word he understood was "impossible." Mr. Wallace said something was impossible. But why shouldn't I, was Mrs. Brewster's question. Because of me, among other things, was Mr. Wallace's reply. Of course, I was expecting that you'd spend much of your time with us there, said Mrs. Brewster. How preposterous, said Mr. Wallace. How could I do that? Moreover, there's every reason to think he won't be going back in the fall anyway. I get reports on him all the time, and I am told his work does not show very much promise, and they have far more applications than they can admit students; therefore they may not let him return. I have not discouraged that decision—I mean, I have not attempted to bring any influence to bear—although I have not approved it either, since I would prefer that he decide to return here of his own free will. He'll be crushed, my poor darling, Mrs. Brewster said. Even that might be good for him, Mr. Wallace answered. The boy is slack and weak and undirected, and I think he is a prig, too. He isn't like you, Harriet, and he isn't like . . . Well, it's difficult for me to understand it. He is very gentle, said Mrs. Brewster. No, he isn't; he is indifferent. He is also a bore, and where in the world could he have got that from? From Mr. Brewster, she said with a laugh. Stop it, Mr. Wallace rejoined. This is no time to make tasteless jokes. Who are you to say it was tasteless, and don't be so sure it was a joke, said Mrs. Brewster. And in any case, I am not joking when I say that I need Neal around me now, and if he isn't here, I am going to go there. I know you think I am being silly and emotional, but . . .

"Neal Brewster! I didn't see you come in. How did you get here?" cried Gladstone, who was also eavesdropping from her end of the hall and had come closer during the latter part of the conversation just repeated in order to hear more clearly, and had thereby surprised Neal. She called out her warning to the two in his mother's bedroom.

Immediately Mr. Wallace came forth, small and terrible. He stared at Neal and judged him for a sneak. "So you've been here. And did you hear what we were saying?" Neal nodded. "Very well. So be it. You had better come and have a talk with me in the living room."

"Now, David, please . . ." Mrs. Brewster said.

"Mrs. Gladstone, go in to Mrs. Brewster and please close the door behind you. Follow me, Neal."

When they were seated, he asked Neal a series of questions, the same kind his mother had been asking him, about his life at the university and how he felt about it. When he had let Neal have his say, he summarized his reactions. "In short, you are leading a life more or less apart from normal obligations, normal worldly functioning, I mean." Neal said he hadn't ever thought of it that way. "And I suppose it is a great temptation to somebody like yourself, Neal, since you are withdrawn to begin with, and there is nobody to direct you there into more active channels. Frankly, I don't understand your lack of ambition."

He stood up and walked around the room. "It is awkward to have to talk to you with so little preparation," he said. "But it is high time. In the first place, I want you to understand one thing. I am devoted to your mother, and I am . . . I love you, Neal, very much, and want your own good. Understand that.

"Now, that out of the way, let me be frank with you. I have hopes and plans for you. I need not tell you about my own position in this town. You must have some idea, and further explanation can wait for another time. But I hope to convince you that you should return here of your own free will, where you will have an unparalleled opportunity to influence affairs, if you take hold. Nothing could stand in your way. I will live a while longer, and I will see to that. I will train you, *really* educate you in the way things *really* get done. You may become, as I am, the most powerful man in the city. You may even become the richest one. That is a career worth trying. It is better than being a teacher, however good a one, or a scholar either, as far as that goes, and you know now that nobody thinks you will be very good at either. Not that that should discourage you about yourself. It may just be that you were cut out for other things—the power, the money I have just spoken about. You can sit on the boards that rule—rule colleges and museums and civic affairs."

He sat down again opposite Neal, and spoke more quietly, in great earnest. "I want you to come back here. I want you to come back home and settle down. You have no time to waste."

Most young men would have been bug-eyed at the prospect of slipping so certainly and so painlessly into the ranks of the mighty, but not Neal. "I don't care whether I'm a good teacher," he said.

"It's unworthy of you, I repeat. It's unworthy of your heritage not to care, to be willing to be mediocre."

"I can't help it. I don't care. And I don't want to come back here to live."

David Wallace didn't raise his voice or turn purple in the face—that wasn't his style. Opposition calmed him and made him much more dangerous. He stretched out his hand to indicate that the conversation was over. "I will talk to you again. I said I hoped you would do this voluntarily; I did not say that only if voluntary would you do it. If you won't come back of your own will, you will still come." He passed sentence, a hanging judge. "You will come back here and you will become what I have described. Whether you want them or not, you are going to have them—power, wealth, even Wahnfried." Wahnfried was the name of the Wallace mansion, which sat in the middle of a large estate out on the river, and commanded the town like a feudal fortress. "You will take your place here, if only because I say you will." And he left the apartment, feeling he had been caught out at something and forced to reveal his hand too soon, and feeling it was unfair that he should have to feel so.

And Mrs. Brewster called for Neal to come to her, patted his hand, and told him not to worry about anything.

That night, after the house was asleep, he lay in bed thinking. He had a pad of paper on his lap and drew on it endlessly. Strange images, polyps, ectoplasmic manifestations, the internal organs of impossible animals, and, on the last page, hundreds of tiny dead birds lying with their feet in the air. About eleven o'clock, he put the paper aside, got out of bed, and got dressed, put a few things into his suitcase, and tiptoed out of the apartment. His flight was not discovered until the next morning, when Gladstone went to call him for his breakfast. She found the papers with his drawings on them and saved them to show to Mr. Wallace, who, in his turn, showed them to Neal's psychiatrist, to whom they were a cause of some concern.

II.

Neal came into my room to see me the afternoon he got back, which was a Saturday. I had all my lights out and the blinds drawn, and hadn't gone to speak to him when I heard him arrive. He knew I was at home, though, because I was playing my recorder, and he could hear my melancholy, lovesick piping. He knocked, came in, and crept over to stand beside me while I went on playing, the somber melody falling slowly to the place where the orchestra comes in. I looked up.

"Hail, Kurvenal," I said dreamily. "Have you come to tell me that you see a ship?"

"What do you mean? What were you playing?"

"The shepherd's tune from *Tristan*," I replied. "I am sick with love and in love with Death right at the moment."

"That's odd," he replied. "Uncle David has a room in his house decorated with pictures from *Parsifal*. His ballroom."

"There is no such thing as coincidence. Look for the meaning. Well, I don't want the Grail Parsifal wanted, and we'd better not go into the matter of the spear." I played a few more bars of that infinitely pathetic tune. Almost overcome by the music's poignancy and my own hard lot, I groaned. "Don't ever fall in love with a witch princess," I advised him.

"Who are you in love with?"

"With the Princess Pounce. I am sick with my love for her, because she won't telephone me, and she promised she would."

"Why don't you telephone her?"

"She told me not to. She said she wanted to think things over." I piped on, wishing he would go away, but he stayed beside me, a person who didn't know how to get himself out of the room. "I feel lousy and depressed," I said as a hint.

"So do I," he replied, and sat down on my bed. He put his head in his hands.

"How was your mother?" I asked, giving up.

"She's all right. It isn't that."

"Are you in love?" I asked. "You, too, wounded?"

"No." Then, after I asked him what the matter was, if it wasn't love or his mother, he told me all about the conspiracy to change his life. "So I left home," he concluded.

"And do you think they'll come after you?" I asked, intrigued by such an old-world situation.

"Oh, yes. Uncle David will do just what he said. I won't have a chance. I don't know what to do about it."

"Let's go get a cup of coffee," I said, "and think it over. Maybe I can help." Just as on that other morning, we set off down the street. And again, just as on that morning— and is there such a thing as a meaningless coincidence?—we encountered a pale-lashed, weepy June Bliss, she of the skin like skimmed milk. This time she was going toward her rooming house, so we met her head on. Her brief talk with Neal gave me an opportunity to size her up again, and I decided, with the ruthlessness of the lovesick, that she would be my sacrifice to Eros. "I will call my lady," I said later to Neal, "and arrange to take her out to dinner tonight, if you will ask that girl and come along with us. It will take your mind off your problems. And in return for the favor, I will do my best to solve them for you." He had nobody else to turn to, so he agreed. When we reached our café, I telephoned Pounce, who was furious at first to be called from her darkroom, but I told her that something was afoot for the night, explained what it was —a double date with my regressed floormate and a wispy, red-eyed blond—and she agreed to come along. Neal did his part, too, and seven o'clock found us all drinking together in Pounce's studio.

I will sketch in the evening on a few pages only, although if this were purely my autobiography, it would deserve a whole gathering. For on this night I finally enjoyed bliss in May; but let me add, in case there is already worry for her, that nobody enjoyed June Bliss. Brief though I will be, I must take the time to describe Pounce. Her real name was Nancy Dakin, and she had black hair, dark eyes, heavy brows, and a low forehead, and a set, determined chin. She was slender, with a rather boyish style, and looked elegant and, to me, very desirable, whether in blue jeans or formal dress. She was very imperturbable, cool, as they now say, disinclined to show any emotion: a lift of the corner of her delicate mouth signified laughter, the raising of an eyebrow indicated anger, scorn, or intended murder. To keep herself busy—she had some money of her own—she ran a photographic studio, where she did a few commercial portraits of sorority presidents and kindred subjects who happened to interest her, and also did a lot of special kinds of subjects—nature studies, light effects, nudes. She was a superb and imaginative photographer, and, at the time I am writing about, was beginning to experiment with movies.

All this was in great contrast to shrinking little June in her baby-blue cardigan sweater and colorless nail polish.

The studio consisted of one very large room, about forty-five feet long and twenty-five wide, with an efficiency kitchen off in a corner, a bathroom, and a darkroom. Part of the studio was furnished with day beds, Japanese pillows on the floor, bookcases, and a few stools and homemade tables. The rest was work area, inhabited by the great insects of the photographer's trade. Pounce turned the lights off and the radio on, and we sat and drank far too many Martinis by its red glow. She liked that. I think she would have entertained in her darkroom if there had been enough ventilation.

The immediate results can be quickly catalogued. I got tight and jolly. Pounce didn't change—alcohol has no effect on steel. Brewster got stupefied. Blissikins got absolutely plastered. She wasn't used to Martinis, I imagine, and Pounce took on the job of servicing her with drink, and did it with gruesome dedication. Every time I looked in that direction there was a full glass in June's hand. June was complaining in a tedious way about something—I think it was the obtuseness of the history faculty and the fact that they didn't recognize the merit of the best students, and how international fellowships were awarded on arbitrary geographical bases instead of to people who *really* had *important* projects. Etc., etc. Pounce was sympathetic, supplied her with Kleenex when Bliss got the weepies, showed her where the bathroom was, patted her consolingly, and insisted on riding in the back seat with her when we left for dinner, so that she could take care of her if she didn't feel well, which June had already announced to be the case.

June didn't eat any of her dinner, but at least she didn't throw up. That Pounce of mine—she was a crack shot.

After dinner it seemed in order to go for a ride with the sun roof of my Volkswagon open, to clear everybody's head. This makes for quite a rush of air, particularly when you go fast, and the girls in the back seat—they were there together again —huddled against the chill. I watched them in the mirror, feeling a bit wry what with my after-dinner-after-Martinis slump and the all-too-obvious acceptability of my sacrifice. Neal went to sleep, his head dropping onto his chest like a spastic's. I heard June say something that I couldn't understand, followed by a remark from Pounce. Then, more clearly, June said, "No. Leave us alone. I want to get out and walk." We were at the edge of town, and nobody paid any attention until June reached forward and shook Neal's shoulder. "Let's get out and walk," she said plaintively to him.

"Let's all go back to my studio," Pounce said.

"No," June answered. "You go back. Neal and I will walk."

"Suit yourself," Pounce replied coldly.

I stopped the car and let them out. They had about a mile to go to get home, part of it along an artificial lake which formed the boundary of the campus in that area. They sat down on a bench to watch the waterfowl float on the dark water, and June edged rather close to Neal. "They're very strange people," she said.

"Who are?" he asked.

"Those friends of yours. Ned and that Pounce."

"I guess so," Neal answered, somewhat disloyally, I think. "Ned's in love with her."

"Really? That's even stranger. I don't understand at all."

"Don't understand what?"

"Well, she said she preferred sitting in back with me because men are so harsh and domineering. I thought I understood something about her I won't say. But maybe I'm wrong. Are they having an affair?" Wistful, innocent June Bliss. She put a slim and icy hand as close to Neal's own as she decently could, but he didn't take it. "I'm glad that we're away from them," she said.

"How did your paper on the regency of Blanche of Castille go?" Neal asked.

She sighed. "All right," she said.

Neal took her home, and I meanwhile had taken Pounce home. I asked if I could come up, and got no reply, which I took to mean yes. We dumped the ash trays and carried away the jetsam left behind by the Martini hour. I made two highballs and lay back invitingly on a day bed while Pounce, to my dismay, sat down on a campstool and began to read a book by the light of her radio dial. I mentioned that she was going to hurt her eyes and got the raised eyebrow for my pains. Normally that cowed me, but this night I was desperate. I stood up, walked over to her, took the book and hurled it twenty-five feet off into the studio, and, while she watched me impassively, stormed at her for ten minutes about how lovesick I was. I gave full details on my symptoms and my desires. Toward the end I punctuated my speech by throwing coat, trousers, shirt, and shoes after the book. "And tonight," I concluded, aquiver with emotion, "I went as far as a man could go. I produced just your type for a double date. Your files are full of negatives of June Blisses, and I found you a brand-new one. Well, the pimp wants his pence—it's not my fault if you flubbed." I collapsed on her couch and pulled a plaid throw over my trembling body.

"You can leave if you want to," I said, exhausted, "but I'm going to stay right here until morning."

"Leave . . . ? Oh, hell!" she replied. And then, joy unending. The corner of her mouth twitched. "Who's going to go to so much trouble?"

And that is how the great love affair of *my* life began.

12.

I was miserable and self-pitying during the next week, for
Pounce, having once yielded to my persistent, if odd, courtship, did not suddenly become a sweet and gentle creature,
broken to the bit. She got up the next morning, and while I
lay in her bed, my eyes closed, daydreaming in a foolish haze,
she performed a cursory toilet, slipped into work clothes, and
made breakfast in a tense, silent way which should have
tipped me off that scene two was not going to be quite as
idyllic as scene one. The breakfast was good, but the conversation during it thin, for Pounce read the sports section of
the Sunday newspaper which she fetched from her downstairs
entryway, and left me to talk into the air, which I went ahead
and did.

I asked for more coffee, which she brought without speaking. She had tossed a kind of smock to me to wear, and I tee-
tered on the back legs of my chair and sipped my coffee, my
golden-haired shanks exposed to the knees. "This is really living," I said, unwilling to recognize that all was not perfect.

She lowered her newspaper by about one and a half inches,
until her glowering eyes showed. "Good God, but you're an
ass," she exclaimed coldly. "Why don't you get dressed and go
home?"

"What's the matter?" I asked, clattering forward, spilling
my coffee, and clutching close my smock, which had divided
at the sudden movement.

"Just go home," she growled. "I'm not letting myself in for
this." And she raised her sports page again.

I should have said "To hell with you" and got dressed and
left, or perhaps I should have knocked her out, or I should
have done just about anything but what I did, which was to
argue. I did worse than that. While seeming to argue, I

wheedled. Naturally she saw through the false positioning to the shivering and cowardly voluptuary underneath, begging for her continued favors. She was merciless to that creature, and quite rightly. The actual words that the painful dialogue took are not very important, and I will not ask the reader to go over them, since they would add no insight to either Pounce's character or my own. Let us simply settle for the concluding vignette, in which I, hastily dressed, necktie askew, am at the door, smiling ingratiatingly at Pounce's back. She had finished the paper and was sitting staring out of her window, chain smoking.

"I'll call you, Pounce," I said timidly.

"Drop dead," she replied.

"Is that all you have to say?"

"No. Go to hell afterward."

I plodded down her stairs and out into the bright spring world, now a dead world for me. I remember thinking as I returned to Mrs. Peters' to shower and change that I would very probably kill Pounce if she kept this up.

But I didn't really think she would hold out on me. I thought she was probably suffering from that not unusual morning-after revulsion, quite to be expected after the first time of making love, which would lessen by noon, and by cocktail time would have turned to appetite. I and a Martini would become simultaneously desirable again. I quite underestimated the complexities of my Pounce's character. The Martini may have come back to favor that afternoon, but I did not. Nor the next, nor the next, nor the next. Then, on Thursday afternoon, she did agree to see me for a drink, but it was only to explain to me, with all the tenderheartedness of a vivisectionist, that, while she liked me, she was very contented with her life as it was, that she was a damned good photographer and I didn't amount to anything, that I had an archaic conception of a woman's place in the world, and that she was sick of having men around.

"I don't see how all these things get involved in our shacking up," I said indifferently, trying my new tack.

"They're all there, though," she replied, with a lift of an angry black brow. "They're all implicit, even in the very God-damned hierarchy of the act."

Her words brought back the night we had spent together as vividly as my dreams had been able to do. I almost choked on my own heart, but I stifled the emotion and kept it out of my voice and off my face. I shrugged, and began to set my watch by her electric clock, which was always accurate. "We can change that," I said. "I'm not doctrinaire."

"I don't accept charity, in or out of bed," she answered. "I care for nobody, no not I—and that's the way I like it."

Then, keeping the light touch, I told her that I had thought about killing her. "I suppose I'll do it, too. I'll carve you into pieces and store you in the canisters in your own darkroom."

The idea amused her, and her lip curled.

"Besides," I added calmly, "I really love you."

"That again," she said gruffly. "It's time for you to go away."

"Fine," I said, and got up. My new tack was not to beg anything from her or demand anything, but just to insist on the facts of the case when they came up. I had come to the conclusion that if I was going to win her, it would have to be man to man.

I had the feeling that I had made some progress, and I was hopeful, but I was also abstracted and preoccupied, once again playing my recorder, when Neal knocked on my door that night. I had not seen him since our double date, and I was rather shocked by how ill he looked, as if he had neither eaten nor slept. His eyes had enormous circles under them, and his cheeks, dark with the beard of two or three days, were drawn in. I stopped piping. "You really look like hell," I said.

"I know. I feel terrible, too."

"Have you tried the infirmary?" I asked. "Maybe it's just

something that's going the rounds." I blew a phrase of "Three Blind Mice."

"It's not anything they could help," he said. "It's worrying. I can't stop worrying."

"Worrying about what?"

"About what will happen to me. It's started, you see. It started a couple of days ago when Uncle David called me and I said I wouldn't come back home. Then this. It's a summons to appear before the Dean tomorrow. That'll be it."

"Don't work yourself into a false crisis," I advised him. "It may be just something routine."

He turned back to the door. "Maybe you're right," he said, clearly not meaning it. "Good night."

"Good night, Brewster." I piped "Taps" as he walked across the hall. I should have been ashamed of myself to dismiss his troubles that way; but I really wanted to be by myself and moon over Pounce.

Neal was right. David Wallace had wasted no time. He later alleged, and I have no reason to doubt that he meant it, or, rather, that he thought what he was saying was true, that the steps he took were for Neal's own good. He was alarmed by Neal's erratic behavior and got in touch with Dr. Legg, Neal's psychiatrist, as soon as he found out on Saturday morning that Neal had left town. Did some new pattern now show that the doctor could perceive and that warranted drastic action? Dr. Legg was worried too, and suggested that perhaps Neal might have to be put in an institution for a while. He would certainly have to stay in treatment. Was it more probable than before that Neal might be led into some irrevocable action? The possibility was certainly finite, opined Dr. Legg. Armed with this weapon, and with Neal's own refusal ascertained, Mr. Wallace then got in touch with the university authorities by telephone, and, after hinting at that finite possibility, which to the university meant possible scandal, blood on the snow, he raised the question: Was it wise for Neal to continue his studies at the present time? Wouldn't he be better off in treatment at home? The Dean got in touch with the university psychiatrist, who talked to Dr. Legg, and then said he naturally wouldn't want to go against the opinion of a qualified colleague, particularly one who was in a position to know about the background of the case. Doubtless the point was passed between the two doctors that home might not be the best possible place for Neal; but doctors must be resigned in these matters. Anyway, carefully fuzzed up though the issue was by all concerned, and with merely a hint, a nudge, an inflection or two to go on, the action that the Dean felt he must take was clear, and he so notified Mr. Wallace. With that, the latter began to travel.

When Neal appeared in the Dean's office the next day, he was confronted not just by that high official, but also by Mr. Wallace and the university psychiatrist. They had spent the preceding half hour together to their mutual profit. The psychiatrist had new funds for research he was conducting, the Dean a substantial addition to his scholarship monies, and Mr. Wallace, of course, had, or thought he had, Neal. Not that any of them was aware that a transaction had taken place. They had discussed Neal's case, then had some time to wait, and their talk had naturally turned to the university, the infirmary, the Office of Graduate Studies; Mr. Wallace was a millionaire, and his family was known to be interested in education—they had founded a college which bore their name, back in Neal's home town. The system worked automatically. In the higher administrative levels of our educational institutions, bribery is given an exclusively personal definition.

The decision of what to do with Neal having once been made, everything was done to keep it from being executed with too great an appearance of haste or harshness. The Dean was a kind man, after all. So was the university psychiatrist. So was Dr. Legg. So, in his own way, was Mr. Wallace. And I ought to emphasize here that none was a villain, none even a wicked or cruel man. However compound their motives may have been, primarily they all thought that Neal was mad, or going mad, that this was a bad thing, and that something could and should be done about it—to say nothing of Neal's worldly prospects, about which Mr. Wallace hinted enough, revealed enough of provisions he had already irrevocably made—trust funds and the like—to make even a Dean's eyebrows rise. So he was handled gently in that interview. He was told that everyone concerned thought it might be better if he had a little rest and more therapy, maybe even a spell in a "rest home" somewhere. It was his decision, and there was no hurry—Mr. Wallace fidgeted here, but the Dean quieted him with a look—as far as the university was concerned. But (a significant downward glance at some papers lying on the blotter) he hadn't been doing well in his studies, and it might be wiser to leave the semester's work as incomplete, in case he wanted to return. At this the psychiatrist, lighting his pipe, said there was no point in giving oneself too many problems to solve all at once. No, the Dean agreed. And he would be glad to take care of the record. All that would appear would be a notation that pressing personal reasons had caused the student to leave before the end of the term. But it was Neal's decision, of course. Nobody was forcing him to do anything. Well, Mr. Brewster?

Mr. Brewster looked at the Dean, and he looked at the psychiatrist, and he looked at Mr. Wallace. "I'll leave now," he said.

"I think that's wise, Brewster," the Dean agreed.

"It's a heck of a lot easier to study, Brewster," the doctor said, getting up, "when you feel inside your skin."

"I'll take you to your room to pack, Neal," Mr. Wallace said.

There was handshaking all round, and Neal followed Mr. Wallace away as passively as a puppy dog. When the door was shut behind them, the Dean said to his psychiatrist that he was glad the man was leaving, that he didn't much like the looks of the case. The psychiatrist agreed. Too quiet, hardly registering, possibly not even understanding what was said to him. Precisely the type that might blow up unexpectedly. "At least I don't see how he can harbor any ill will against *us*," the Dean said, thinking of the future.

Mr. Wallace had rented a taxi for the day he was to be in town, and it was in it that he took Neal away. He had traveled much of the night before and was tired, so he suggested that he get off at his hotel, where he had taken a room in case he wanted to rest, and that Neal could take the cab on and use the driver for errands if he needed him. He asked Neal to come with him to the doorway, where, out of hearing of the taxi driver, he prudently extracted a promise. He asked Neal to promise on his word of honor that he would not try to go away again. Mr. Wallace waited until the formula had been said, while the hotel's marquee, striped in the university's colors, flapped above their heads and people went in and out, swinging the doors. Mr. Wallace had also considered alerting the driver, but he disliked allowing a man like that even a glimpse into private areas. No one had told him not to leave Neal alone, and he thought he was doing more than the necessary in getting his promise. But of course no one had figured Ned Bates in the picture. I was the unforeseeable factor that ruined everybody's plans.

"I promise," Neal mumbled.

"On your word of honor."

"I promise on my word of honor."

"Good. You won't break that." Mr. Wallace, it seems, thought word of honor equally binding to sane and mad. "It wouldn't do any good to run away anyhow," he observed, "since we could easily find you. You get packed and come back here before dinner." He looked at Neal closely. "What are you thinking about? Did you hear me?"

Neal had been looking at the ground, his brows drawn together in thought, with that intense worry over a small prob-

lem which people will sometimes have when the foundations and walls of their lives are crumbling away. "There's
something I don't understand, Uncle David. That's what I was
thinking about."

"And what is that?"

"Why everybody cares so much whether or not I stay here
or what I do. Why do *you* care?"

The old man's temper, worn thin, flared up. "If you don't
know the answer to that, Neal, you are more of a fool than I
thought you were," he snapped.

13.

Such questions were still on Neal's mind when, after an hour
of ineffectual packing, he brought some magazines I had lent
him to my room—French pictorial weeklies, they were, filled
with the grimacing faces of movie stars at Saint-Tropez and
knobby-kneed bicycle racers pumping along the desolate
roads of the Massif Central. I happened to be at home when he
came in, for I was coming down with a cold that Friday. He
thanked me for the magazines and idly looked through them
after he had put them down.

"God, what's wrong with you, Brewster?" I asked, sounding
like a man with asthma closing in. I had a fit of five sneezes.
"You look the most unutterably miserable wretch I ever saw."

"I am miserable."

"What did the Dean do to you?" Neal recounted the events
of the morning, and, after allowing a dramatic pause, I said:
"The answer is simple. Your Uncle David knew it, and he even
told it to you. You run away."

"But I promised I wouldn't."

"What's in a promise? No promise extracted under torture
means anything."

"I suppose you're right."

71

"Good. It's agreed, then. You're going to run away. Put on your track shoes and go, man." I leaned back on my pillows.

Some time passed while he thought about it. Then he sighed. "I can't run away. Where would I go? And how? I wouldn't know what to do."

"Let's go back over it again," I said irritably. "In the first place, they've all ganged up on you. Right?"

"I guess it looks that way."

"Right! Now they've done it by implying you're crazy. Are you crazy or aren't you?" I have to confess that at this point I was listening more to myself than to him.

"I don't know. I don't think I know what being crazy really is, so how can I say?"

"That's easy. Do you feel crazy?" I grinned, delighted at the whimsy of my test.

He considered the question for several minutes, while I watched his answer gradually cast its shadow across his face. "I feel loaded down and heavy. That isn't the same thing as feeling crazy. No. I don't feel crazy. But I wish somebody would do something about how loaded down I feel. I wish somebody would just turn everything off and close all the doors. That's how I feel."

"Nobody will, and don't you do it either," I said, for the first time really aware that perhaps I was meddling where I had no business to meddle. "Mind you, I don't want to interfere," I said uncertainly.

"Please. You've got to help me, Ned."

"Well, let's go on, in any case. Now then, if they're ganging up on you, the thing to do is to serve them right. Get the best revenge you can. Slip through their fingers. Disappear."

"I don't want to take revenge on anybody."

"Begin to want to. Begin to feel a lot of things you've never felt before, Brewster. Come alive." Certain that no matter how obvious my device was it would not put him off, I got up and started a highly affirmative piece of middle-period Beethoven on the phonograph—I think it was the Seventh Symphony. I let it play a few minutes, then said, "There. Feel like that."

Neal seemed to find the music's message a real puzzle. "I don't think I can," he said finally, putting a hand over his eyes. "Ned, I want to ask you a question. What's wrong with me the way I am, or the way I was yesterday, or maybe two months ago? Why does everybody want to change me in some way?"

"Everybody wants to change everybody, Neal. I want to change you, too. I have an image of you, and I want to change you to fit it."

"What is your image of me?"

"It's all there in the music. Here you are, still young, remarkably handsome. I want you to get out and overeat and pick fights and make love and do all sorts of great, affirmative things. What do you do now? You sit in a box where you read and take notes. What do all those other people want you to do? They want you to sit in a different box. I don't want you to sit in a box. I want you to do things which I'm sure you can do if you try—murder, torture, rape, seduce, steal, rescue the drowning, kill dragons, build a pyramid of skulls when you sack a city, discover America. I want you to dig truffles, learn the tea ceremony, become king of the pygmies—who gives a damn what it is, just so you don't go back to them and don't stay here."

He was really disturbed. "You think I can do things like that? Whatever makes you think so?"

The whole idea was ludicrous, but since I'd started it, I decided to carry it through. "I know you can," I shouted, over a tremendous climax in the music. "You can if you choose to, with my help." I turned the record on even higher. "You must," I yelled.

"Why don't you do all this yourself?" he shouted.

"Ha! A good question. Because if you do it, then I won't have to." I turned the record off suddenly. "You'll do it for me."

"You'll help me?" Neal asked.

"Certainly. We'll correspond."

"But you know, Ned, I don't know what to do out in the world. I don't know how people act. I don't know how to act myself. I don't know why people do what they do. I don't even know what they feel."

"That's easy. You'll learn. Think of yourself as an actor learning a role. Better still, follow the Rule of Imitation. Without it America would totter, the Soviet Union fall. The Rule of Imitation means quite simply this: You watch what other people do, listen to what they say, how they think, what they appear to believe. It's not only data, it's also your desideratum. Imitate it, or them, whatever my object now is. Assimilate your lessons until acting, thinking, believing like other people is reduced to reflex, like playing exercises on the piano."

"How do I know what to imitate? Where do I see it?"

"Watch television. Go to the movies. Read comics. Do anything that is essentially popular. It won't take you long."

Here he tripped me up on a point of logic, which was the last thing I ever expected. "But what does this Rule of Imitation have to do with rape and all the other things you mentioned at the beginning? It seems more like what the others have in mind for me."

"An astute point," I said. "Yes, an astute point. A telling point," I repeated, stalling while I thought. "But in my system it's only a beginning, or, I should say, it's only for the part of you that shows. The part that doesn't, that's the part where you can develop in any bizarre way you want. You need some protective coloring, but consider it a façade. It doesn't have anything to do with what you *really* do or what you *really* are. But it's the essential beginning." I looked at my watch. "See here, I think if you're going to run away, you'd better get started." I pushed him out of my door. "Pack two suit-cases," I said. "One should be the stuff you'll need the next few months, the other winter things I can send on to you. I'll hide it in my closet."

He was obedient. I had only to command; and he to obey. He started for his own room. "I'll do it, but you're going to have to write to me. I'm going to need your help," he said.

"You can count on it," I assured him.

While he packed, I invented a plan of escape. It was very simple, hence quite workable. He gave me his two suitcases, his briefcase, and his toilet kit, then he took an armful of library books downstairs and had the taxi driver put them into the trunk. Then the driver took him first to the bank, where he closed out his savings account, withdrawing almost $9,000, then to the library. Meanwhile, I put the summer suitcase into my car, along with his raincoat and the few other things he would need right away, and drove to a side entrance of the library. I also bought him a money belt as a going-away pres-ent. He came out, jumped in my car, and we sped off about thirty miles to a good-sized town where he could get a bus that would take him in two hours into a large city, where he could change buses again and disappear without being no-ticed. Just to give the whole enterprise a nice gothic touch, I gave him a map of the United States, too, with a scattering of cities numbered on it. I had its duplicate for myself. That was how we were going to be able to correspond without giving away his plans, should the mails be watched. I dropped him at the entrance to the bus depot, but we thought it was better if I didn't wait around. The last I saw of Neal for some time was his timid hand wave in my mirror as I pulled away from the curb.

14.

On my way back into town I dropped by Pounce's studio to tell her what I had done, and to complain about the cold I had developed since seeing her the day before. The furnished end of her living room was all she had for waiting clients on those rare times when she had overlapping appointments, so her door was kept open. I went in, sat down, and picked up a copy of *Crampons*, a hiking and mountaineering magazine Pounce subscribed to. I had a fit of the sneezes, which would have brought her wrath down on my head without delay if she hadn't been doing live work and had to control her temper in front of a stranger. She had a remarkably plain girl posing for her, one with drawn-back hair and a right-angle bend in her upper back, who was wearing a shapeless knit dress twenty years too old for her, and was introduced to me as Miss Ferney, President of the Women's Science Club, and as an up-and-coming astrophysicist. Pounce, so stunning and smart herself, had an astounding knack for doing wonders for that type of girl. Somehow she took photographs of their minds and rendered the fleshly envelope transparent and transfigured. When Miss Ferney had drawn on her mantle and departed, Pounce slipped the lock on her door and stood, her arms folded, glaring at me.

"What did you come here for? It's really too much when you also interrupt me at my work."

"I'm sick. I've got a cold. I want sympathy."

"I never have colds and I don't intend to catch one from you. One more reason I'm glad I've thrown you out of my life."

"I've also been doing something interesting." I told her about Neal. "And, lest I forget, I should warn you that you are going to be used for a contact," I concluded. "Neal will write me, put the letter in an envelope and seal it—that was his idea, not mine—I don't care if you read his letters—then put that envelope in a larger one and mail it to you. You will then give it to me. We thought it might get too risky sending letters directly back and forth. He'll use the name Christopher Dakin, your cousin Christopher, on the envelope when he needs to, or on a wire or a postcard where he has to give a name."

She sat down on the opposite end of the day bed from where I was sitting. "Swell," she said, lighting a cigarette with a kitchen match which she ignited with her thumbnail. "Just swell. I suppose you know that you may get into real trouble over this. I don't know what the charge would be, but I'm sure it's illegal to help a lunatic run away from his family."

"He's of age, and no legal steps had been taken," I replied.

"You had no right to interfere," she said.

"I only wanted to give him a chance," I argued. "Hell, how much chance would he have had if they got him?"

"And what makes you think he has any this way?" she asked. "What in hell is the poor guy going to do, floating off into the continent somewhere, with no place to go, no friends, and no sense?"

"He has money, at least." I pulled an enormous wad of bills out of my pocket. "This five thousand is his, too. I'm to keep it and send it to him as he needs it. We didn't think traveler's checks were safe—too easy to trace. I want you to put it in your safe."

"Folly," she said. "Real folly." But she took the money, put a rubber band around it with a piece of paper carrying my name and address, and put it away. "I think you're damned presumptuous, to say nothing of cruel and frivolous," she said when she came back from the safe in her darkroom. "And you've involved me in it, too. Thanks a lot."

"Why do you care so much what happens to Neal? You care for nobody, no not you."

She stared me up and down, clicking her front, that is, her biting and tearing, teeth together. "I care what happens to any

77

helpless creature," she said. "I don't care what happens to you, because you're not helpless." Feigning indifference—I saw through it—she added, "Did he have a chance to say good-by to June?"

"Hell, no. He barely got away at all. No time to kiss his moll."

"Poor thing," she said.

"Which?" I sneezed, groaned, and blew my nose, while she looked disgusted at my question and the frailty of my body. "Now listen to me," I said when I was finished. "I'm not being frivolous or cruel. Neal's problems have their comic side, but that doesn't mean we can't take them seriously, too. I seriously think what has happened is for the best. I think he'll come out of it all right, and I stand by what I did." I stopped to think over what I had just said, and found it easy to be courageous through others' adversities. "Yes, by God, I'll stand by it." I sneezed again.

She went into her bathroom and came back with a bottle of pills. Pounce was the kind of person who had all necessary first-aid supplies and knew how to use them, as well as how to administer artificial respiration and apply a tourniquet. "Here," she said bitterly. "Take a couple of these, and I'll give you more to take home with you."

"I thought you never had colds," I taunted her.

"These are for hay fever." She put a hand on my forehead. "You idiot. A fever, I think." She brought a thermometer, took my temperature, found I didn't, and told me to go home.

"I'll go if you'll come around with some cold supper for me tonight and stay and eat it," I said, slowly getting up.

"I'll bring you something, but I won't eat with you," she replied.

"I'll accept the compromise. You know, I imagine they'll be coming around to see what's happened to Neal. They must be discovering just about now that he's missing. All hell will be breaking loose. I've been over to see you, remember, in case

I need an alibi. I don't think I will, though. They'd have no reason to connect me with his getaway."

"Christ," Pounce said angrily, pulling off the heavy silver bandeau she wore to hold back her hair, then replacing it—a sure sign of fury. "You're a fool, Bates. If anything happens to Neal, the very least it will do is cost you your job."

"So what?" I called from the stairs.

They didn't get wind of Neal's escape until very late in the afternoon, because the dumb taxi driver sat outside the library for several hours on the supposition that Neal was working inside. When he finally realized something funny was going on, he drove over and reported to Mr. Wallace, and then the wires began to hum. A telephone call came to the Peters house. Mrs. Peters and I together went into Neal's bedroom and discovered the evidence of his hasty departure—she had been out the earlier part of the day. She reported that he seemed to have packed and left. A little later I had visitors. All my visitors, in fact, arrived at once—Mr. Wallace, the taxi driver, the Dean's representative, the psychiatrist, and my sweet Pounce. But since I later wrote Neal what happened, I think I'll stop right here and introduce our first exchange of letters. His escape, incidentally, took place on the eighth of May.

 PART TWO

PART TWO

May 14

Dear Ned,

Well, here I am at Destination #5, but I don't expect to remain here more than a couple of days. When you write me, send the letter to General Delivery at Destination #8, which I intend to make my next long stop—in about three days. I'll probably stay there about a week. Let's say I'll be there May 22nd for certain, if you can get a letter to me by then.

I don't know whether or not this code is going to work, because of the postmarks on the envelopes. If he really watches the mail, he'll undoubtedly discover a letter like this, even though it goes through Pounce. He'll have her mail watched, too. That's why I won't be here any longer by the time you get this. We'll have to test the system out before I'll trust it. Keep your map hidden.

I think I got away safely. I *think* so. I have gone back over all the movements we made, over and over them, and I don't see where my trail can be picked up, unless an accident happened. I got off at X, as you suggested, and went to the bus depot. I felt really bad there, and scared at what I was doing, and I checked my suitcase in a locker and went and hid in the men's room in a pay toilet for almost an hour until the cleaner discovered me and I had to leave. Then I took the first bus, stayed on it all night, got off, and have made my way here by zigzag steps. I hope his detectives haven't picked up my trail, but I can't be sure. I think I see them everywhere, particularly in hotel lobbies. There was a man in the lobby here this morning when I went downstairs for a plate of ice cream who followed me into the cafeteria and sat about three stools down from me. I thought for sure he was after me. The trouble is, I don't have any idea how a detective would look or what he would do, so I had no way of proving to myself that this man was really working for Uncle David. Do you have any advice about this? If I knew for sure what a detective looked like I could get away secretly as soon as I saw one. All I know is that they're around somewhere, maybe near, maybe not so near, but looking for me. I don't like the feeling.

I've been taking your advice—going to movies, watching television in my hotel room, and reading paperback novels. They all seem to deal with plots I wouldn't think of as normal, but I'm learning something about the way people are supposed to act and think. I don't have much confidence about trying it out yet. I'm still scared to go up to a hotel clerk and ask for a room.

I want to say in this first letter how much it means to me to be able to write to you, Ned. Not only to ask your advice, although that is certainly a big help, but just to be in touch with somebody I know from my old life, just to have a friend. I wish they hadn't forced me out the way they did. Maybe what I was going to do was unambitious, but at least it made some sense to me. Now everything is senseless, but I do have you to write to.

That's all for now. I'll finish this tomorrow and walk down to the central post office and mail it where I'm less likely to be noticed.

Well, it's really happened. Last night I woke up about 3 a.m. with the feeling that someone was outside my door. More than one person, maybe as many as three. I heard footsteps in the corridor, too, and another person joined the ones already there. I came wide awake and listened. I could catch the sound of their breathing. Then they moved away from my door a little distance and whispered together. I caught a word or two—my own name, something about Mother. I got up and went to the door, but didn't dare open it for half an hour. Then, when I was pretty sure they were gone, I opened it and looked into the hall. There wasn't anybody in the direction of the elevator, but when I looked toward the fire stairs I saw a man disappearing. I'm not sure, but I think it was the man who got coffee near me yesterday morning. So I've packed up and I'm going down to pay my bill—it's only 6 a.m., and I'm hoping to get away before they get up, since they were up so late last night. I wish I knew how many of them there were. How many do you suppose they would put on a case like mine? Write me at Destination #8, as I said at the beginning of this. And wish me luck.

Your friend,
Neal

P.S. How do you suppose they found me?

I was feeling pretty low before this happened, but now it's worse. I was shaking last night when they were outside my door, and I almost yelled for them to come on in and get me and to stop playing with me. Maybe I ought to give myself up.

May 17

Dear Neal,

Good God, what a timid runaway you've turned out. What a failure, I should say, since the point in running away is to be free, whereas you are far less free than if they had locked you up in their mental hospital. That attitude isn't going to get you anywhere, man.

Look at the whole thing rationally. If you were a detective assigned to tail somebody, the last thing you'd want would be to make the fact known to that person.

You don't have to worry about the detectives you recognize. It's the one you never see who will catch you.

I can't tell you what a detective would look like. Probably they look like lots of other people. I don't think there is any generic identification, like a turned-around collar or cowboy boots, or no girdle. I'm sure your Uncle David wouldn't have

85

gone to the regular police yet, but would be using private detectives, and I imagine he's got plenty. Of course they're out looking for you. Looking for you everywhere, but there are lots of places to look. I visualize a central headquarters where they hang the Map, pins with green heads on them stuck in it, each one representing a Neal-chaser, an aspirant Neal-catcher. And one pin with a sparkling diamond head, held in reserve for the big moment. If you haven't been apprehended yet, if you ever get this letter, then you can be sure that your voices in the hall were talking about something else, or were just the wind blowing sadly down the corridor, or some old frump going on her hygienic hegira to the can. If you've been picked up, it's a different matter. I'm wrong and you're right. Remember . . . *if you get this letter, then you're safe.*

I must catch you up on the news from around here. I was in my room when they discovered you were gone. It was a great scene, really a great scene. You remember I had a cold—there's nothing left of it now but some postnasal seepage—and I asked my favorite nurse, Pounce, to come up with some supper for me. That was after I got back from delivering you to the bus. She came around 5:30, and we were having a drink together, I on my bed under a blanket, she sitting beside me, permitting me to flex her sinewy fingers with my free hand. There was a commotion in the hall downstairs and the sound of many feet and many voices. They climbed to our nesting level while Pounce and I listened, went into your room, gabbled and clucked there, then came over to see me and find out what I knew. The party was made up of David Wallace, the taxi driver, and representatives from various concerned branches of the university, with Mrs. Peters pouring. I received them with a limp raise of my hand, which I immediately let drop upon Pounce's knee not far from the point where impropriety begins. There wasn't anything she could do about it with everybody around, since it would have looked worse if she'd moved it.

The fellow from the Dean's office spoke first, wanting to know what had happened to Brewster-Across-the-Hall. I looked at them suspiciously, and exchanged a look with Pounce calculated to raise their curiosity.

"What do you mean, what's happened?" I asked.

"He's disappeared. And most of his clothes are gone."

"So?" I rubbed the knee of my mistress absent-mindedly.

"It's time to take your temperature again," she said, rising and getting the thermometer from the table across the room. She planted it in my mouth.

The natural reaction was one of general exasperation. Several of the assembled dignitaries said my temperature could wait, but Pounce said it couldn't. Then your uncle spoke up and said he thought that it might be well to explain to me that you were not quite yourself, and it was intended to take you home where you could receive some treatment. I gurgled in surprise and rolled my eyes and hit my hands upon my blanket, as if I had had something important to say. Your uncle, who had noted the time the thermometer went in, called the ready notice, and out it came.

"What's that again?" I asked excitedly.

Mr. Wallace repeated himself, watching me closely, so that I wondered if he didn't know everything. "I might add that Neal is potentially dangerous, not to other people, but to himself. Do you have any idea what has become of him?" he asked.

"Why, yes," I replied. "I took him to the train myself. He had me pick him up at the side entrance of the library." I looked from one face to another. "I am profoundly shocked by what has happened," I said. "I feel that there has been real negligence in exposing me in this way to somebody who might be dangerous. He ought to have been watched."

Mr. Wallace made a quick flutter of impatience. His gestures are very avian—have you ever noticed? "Quite. Quite. You're quite right. But nobody realized how erratic he had become. Would you please explain exactly what happened."

I explained that you had wanted a ride to the station and that I was going out for medicine and agreed to take you there, picking you up at the library. So far as I knew, I said, you had caught the next train home; how was I to know that anything was wrong?

"There are no trains in that direction in the afternoon," the Dean's creature said.

Here Pounce, who had taken away the thermometer, interrupted to say that my temperature seemed to be up a little. The psychiatrist came to look at it, then asked me a question or two about my symptoms. All this contributed to the funk of your uncle. And then the grilling began. How well did I know you? So-so, I said. About the way one would be expected to know somebody who peed in the same pot. Did I know if you had taken money with you? I said I didn't know. It was then that the taxi driver recalled, for the first time, that you had stopped at the bank. I played it very cool, like early Dietrich. I blew lots of cigarette smoke. More questions, which I answered honestly whenever I could. Everybody was satisfied, everybody but your Uncle David. When the room had fallen silent, he said quietly, "Weren't you the young man who telephoned me not long ago?"

"Yes," I answered. "I wondered when you'd remember my name."

Silkily Wallace asked if you weren't accustomed to take me into your confidence, considering that I had made such a personal call for you. Then Wallace turned away from me to the others in the room. He wondered, he said, if Neal could have conceived all this for himself, without some kind of help.

"Really," I said angrily. "That is insulting. Would I help a known psychopath to run away?"

"But you didn't know he was 'upset,'" Mr. Wallace said quickly. "At least that was my understanding. . . ."

"If Neal had told me he was trying to escape, he would have had to tell me why, wouldn't he? So if I'm guilty of hatching his plot, then I would have to know about his looniness."

He probed me with his pale-blue eyes, but I held my ground and stared back. "Be that as it may, I advise you to let us know should he by any chance let you know where he has gone. It would be most unwise to conceal the information."

Mrs. Peters came to bat for her elder roomer. She is a Liberal, you know, and had taken a dislike to gold-plated Mr. W. She said she was sure I had acted in good faith, and she thought they ought to leave me alone to nurse my cold.

Everybody left, but that old boy had smelled something rotten. He lagged behind a moment and gave me his card, first writing his address and phone number on it. I took it without a word and pushed it under my moist Old-fashioned glass.

"I suppose, since you acted out of kindness for Neal, that I must thank you for taking him to the train station," he said. "Such a pity you didn't recognize the signs of his mental condition. I find unobservance usually the quality of an inferior mind—and I wouldn't have thought yours was inferior, Mr. Bates."

It was frontal assault, and I rejoined in kind. "But after all, it was you who let him get away," I replied.

Pounce thought it was time to intervene, because otherwise, she said later, I might have allowed myself to be baited into some indiscretion. She came to my bedside, which broke Mr. Wallace's spell, if he had one cast. He recognized the fact and moved away to the door, for he doesn't waste his time.

"Ah, well," he murmured into the air as he went out, "in any case we will find him."

Pounce was furious with me, and told me I was a fool for admitting that I had had anything to do with your escape. She wouldn't stay with me, although I asked her to, sneezing piteously as I did so. She doubted that she would see me

89

again, she said, because she hated show-offs. Is her bad temper a good sign?

I'll mail this now, and try to write some more advice tomorrow. The library is being given a great collection of erotica, and the donor is lecturing tonight, so I must go. I suspect it will be right up my alley.

Yours,
Ned

May 18

Dear Brewster,

What I didn't have time to tell you in my other letter is this: It's time you began to make a few practical applications of what you've learned. You need experience *in* life, not just more knowledge *about* it. Get out on the street!

I've never been in Destination #8 (Thank God!), but I imagine there must be bars there, just the way there are bars everywhere else. You can begin the kinetic phase of your education by breaking yourself into the bar routine, because there's nothing quite so stereotyped as bars and barflies, and the buzzing that the ones do in the others.

Select a bar. Take a post somewhere near the end of the counter and order whatever seems to have the hegemony along the length of it. If you do that, you can't be wrong, even though it makes you sick at your stomach, because the patrons of a bar where beer and blends are drunk would rather have you drink them and throw up than order a Pink Lady and hold her down. Watch people and listen to what they say. Note down the remarks you hear most often. Keep them in a notebook and memorize them. I can't predict what they'll be, but, believe me, they will be repeated often enough for you to get them word for word. Analyze the attitudes they reflect. Then ACT. Use one or two of them, and be sure when you do that you don't make a mistake and get the wrong saying for the kind of bar you're in and the kind of barfly you're talking to.

Don't let anybody know how well educated you are.

Don't offer to buy anybody a drink or accept one from anybody until you really know your way.

Be careful of talking to women who are already with men.

Conversation with a bartender is a really refined art, which you had better not try. He is slow to love and quick to despise, and would betray you for a paltry bribe to your uncle's agents.

Don't talk to them either.

Other things occur to me that you might do to ease yourself into the active life. . . .

Make a study of women below forty. Classify them in your mind according to their availability and what you think they might like to do in bed, car, weed patch, or wherever. You'd be surprised how much time the average idle man of your age spends—should I say "wool gathering"?—in this way. I do it myself while waiting for trains, second showings of movies, in museums, department stores, on escalators and elevators, and pulling taffy. Classify, classify, classify. When you find yourself with nothing else on your mind excepting your troubles, or in one of those moods you get into when you don't even have troubles on your mind, catch yourself up. Pull yourself together and do something useful. Think about girls.

Remember, the movies and television give you the dream, but they won't provide the practical end of the stick. When you go out you talk about how you want to make love to Marilyn Monroe, but you go on that night to lay a beast in bangles and an orthopedic truss.

Study people's walks. Walks fall into a set of categories which express a psychological mood or a biographical fact. For instance: the sexy slouch, which is organized around the crotch; the tough; the intellectual, subtended by the head;

the businessmen's special; the I've-never-been-in-this-frigging-place-before. Etc.

In short, the world is your subject. Go warily out in it. Learn to do.

Get yourself in a situation. Get yourself in a dozen of them.

Yours, as ever,
Ned

2.

In the next two letters I got from Neal, dated May 23 and May 24, he rambled on about things like the weather and its effects on people's behavior, whether or not they could nail him under the lunacy laws, had he by any chance seen me go by in a taxi one morning [!], and so on and on. In the first one, he did report the following:

About all that advice you wrote . . . I've tried some of it. I've spent every night drinking in bars, and I've learned a lot about life in them, I think. Finally last night I got in a conversation, although I didn't intend to. A man sitting next to me asked me why I looked so "down at the mouth," and I had to answer him. Here's what was said, as well as I can remember it. See what you think.

Me: I'm not looking down at the mouth.

Man: Well, I'm looking down at the mouth, even if you aren't. I just had a blowout, because I hit a big hole in the street. These God-damned streets. They never fix them.

Me: Why not?

Man: It's politics.

Me: All politicians are a bunch of crooks. (A phrase I had overheard.)

Man: You mean to tell me you think John Mahoney is a crook?

Me: Who is John Mahoney?

Man: He's a politician.

Me: Well, if all politicians are crooks, and John Mahoney is a politician, then I suppose John Mahoney is a crook.

Man: Yeah? *Yeah?* (He got very angry, and for a moment I think he wanted to start a fight, but then he quieted down.) You're right. He is a crook. How else could he afford a swimming pool?

Ned, I'm sure three weeks ago I wouldn't have been able to talk to him that long at all.

I'll write again soon. You can write me next to Des. #37, where I expect to spend Memorial Day.

Your friend,
Neal

P.S. I wonder how my mother is getting along. I'm sure she's all right, but I am curious.

He concluded the second with a testimonial to me, and a question. I quote:

I don't have anything much to say, but I like the feeling that I'm in touch with you. I had been feeling better, but today I feel very bad. I don't know what I'd do if I couldn't write to you and know that you'd write back.

I wonder if I'll ever be happy, Ned. As far as that goes, what does it mean? You didn't tell me to see how people look when they're happy, but I've been doing it anyway. Whatever being happy is like, I'm sure I'm not.

How is Pounce? Are you happy with her?

May 26

Dear Brewster,

Happy! Ha ha ha! I laugh till the tears run. Being in love with her is the most tormenting experience of my life. It is the

93

only thing I live for, but it is like being torn to pieces by hot pincers.

At least she's seeing me now. We are developing a mutual interest in some of the problems of film making, she those of a technical nature, I those of aesthetics and style. It may well be just this that will cement us finally together. She disapproved of some of the advice I gave you, by the way, particularly that about women.

The first students are receding from town, leaving behind them a noxious litter of examination booklets and notes all over the library floor. I have been busy doing special cataloguing of the new collection of erotica I wrote you about. It has been sheer delight, a serene haven in the midst of a tempest of mad Pounce passion. I'll tell you about it later. The collection, added to what we had, makes our locked cages the erotica hub of America, the Rome to which all impure pilgrims must some day journey. I have amused myself surveying the one or two shy souls who have so far dared request the *droit d'entrée*. I hover about, my lips pursed, as they pursue their naughty studies, grunting, frowning, glancing sideways, squinting, and clearing my throat. If they hesitate a millisecond too long over some choice illustration, I suck in my breath in a scandalized hiss. Sooner or later we will have visitors who will revel openly in their wickedness, and it is they whom I hope to make my friends. As a matter of fact, I suspect that one such is due in a day or two, a man whose name nicely combines Gallic light with oriental mystery— Ahmed Bidault. Ahmed wants to see our early recipe books for aphrodisiacal stews, broths to restore fading virility, and other like concoctions. I wrote to ask him the purpose of his study (a form letter we always send) and he replied, "privates reasons," which I do hope was not merely a French pluralization.

I enclose a letter from your mother to me. Perhaps it will answer your questions about her, although it doesn't answer them to me. I have replied to her with tact and kindness. This is all costing me lots of time and money for postage, and you must be in one of my movies for nothing to repay me. That is my fee, and I'll collect it. Don't forget.

Nothing further from David Wallace. It is perfectly possible, you know, that he has decided to forget the whole thing. After all, he made you a pretty interesting offer, and you turned it down. Perhaps he has lost interest. Perhaps at this very instant he is interviewing another candidate for your place. Perhaps, Brewster, he doesn't give a damn.

Later . . .

I've got a comment on the conversation you reported.

For the *quality* of the situation, the sense of action, suspense, subterranean meanings, sounds and sights and smells, everything that might conceivably interest me, you substitute a kind of court-clerk dialogue. I am not an archivist, I am your correspondent. I suppose you didn't notice any of that.

Why in hell are you so proud of yourself? Kindergarten stuff.

Get busy, I say. You haven't got much time.

Yours,
Ned

You may be interested to know that when I showed this letter to Pounce, which I did over coffee this evening, the clouds gathered, the dark brows knit together, and she got furious with me. She accused me of being a bastard and a false friend, not trying to help you out, but only trying to play like God. You see, Brewster, I don't withhold the facts from you. You can take your choice. Believe her and go your own way, or continue to follow my advice.

Pounce wanted to send you a note, so that is enclosed, too. That makes two enclosures—the letter from your mother, and the one from Polemical Pounce.

Finally, you can worry about happiness when you've earned a little of it.

Ned

Sunday, May 24

Dear Mr. Bates,

I have just learned the full truth about my son Neal's disappearance. David Wallace and the doctor had been withholding it from me for fear that it might affect my recovery, for I have been very ill. But all the time, in my heart, I knew something was wrong.

You can imagine how it has pained me. Pained! What a feeble word to describe what I feel, knowing that my only son has run away like a crazed animal—and why? I can see no reason.

One thing I am sure of—he would never have done it, no matter how disturbed he was, if he had known the true state of my silly health. I am sure he thought that because I was "coming along," as they say, so well, I was out of danger. He would never have left me if he had known the truth. I will not burden you with that truth, Mr. Bates; but I need my son beside me.

David Wallace suspects—I have no idea why—that you may have some inkling where Neal has gone—and are withholding it out of loyalty to him. If that is so, I can only beg you not to act in blindness. I beg of you—and I will ask few things of anyone any more—that you tell him how great my need of him is.

If you do not know how to find him, then all hope is gone.

Sincerely yours,

Harriet L. Brewster

Tuesday—

Neal—

CHIN UP!

Pounce

June 1

Dear Ned,

I got all the letters you sent me. Thank you very much. I'm sorry this is causing you so much trouble.

I don't think you have ever known what it is to have everything go wrong in your life. I won't hope it happens to you, but if it ever does, you'll understand how hard it is to keep going at all.

Your friend,
Neal

I'm quite reassured about my mother.

June 15

Dear Ned,

At last I am having an adventure, just the way you said I ought to be. It doesn't make much sense, but the important thing is that I'm in it, whether it makes sense or not.

It all began in a bar about ten days ago. I was in a small town where I'd gone after Memorial Day, which is a whole story in itself I'll tell you about sometime—all those flowers everywhere. Anyway, I was studying the way people behaved in this small town I mentioned. The tavern I was in was the nicest place in town, and had open space where there was dancing, in addition to tables and the very long bar with its shiny brass rail and no stools or women allowed. Three Negroes in cowboy clothes were playing for dancing. The music wasn't much good, but it was fast and bouncy.

A little fellow stood beside me looking sharply at everybody who came in, and at everybody who was already there. I remember one time watching a hawk through a pair of binoculars. I think I must have been spending the day on one of

Uncle David's farms. The bird was in the top of a tree, and he kept looking around him, his head low and thrust forward, very piercingly. That was the way this little man was looking at the door, like a tiny little hawk, ready to drop on its prey.

I hope you find that that gets the feeling of the person and the place. I worked on it.

Finally he turned on me and stared fiercely at me for a moment, turned away quickly to glance at the door, then returned to me. "What are you doing here?" he asked without smiling. "I'm just having a couple of brews," I replied, trying to sound easy and colloquial. "You're doing more than that," the little man said. "You're looking around at the people. I've been noticing you. I suppose you're hunting for some poor girl." He spat out his last sentence with real fury. You could tell how ready he was to hate.

None of my studies had really prepared me for this, because usually barroom conversation takes a very different moral tone from his. I didn't know what to do, and I had a moment of panic which I filled by emptying my beer glass. I thought I'd better get out of that bar. But then I thought to myself that he was, after all, someone different, not only in size (about 5'4" tall) but in his attitudes. Maybe he would lead me to adventure.

"Not me," I said.

"You're not in here after quiff?"

"Not me."

"Well, you're the only one who isn't." The quick, dark little head turned toward the dance floor. He stared intently at a couple wiggling there. "It's got so a man's sister isn't safe in this country," he remarked gloomily.

"It's a crime," I said. "It really is."

"I'm glad to hear you say so," he said. "There aren't many men who think that way any more. My name's Georgie. What's yours?"

"Neal," I replied, shaking his hand. It was small and dirty, but strong, like the talons of my hawk.

"That's a funny name. What does it come from—Daniel?"

"No," I said. "It doesn't come from anything. It's just Neal, so far as I know. Look at that," I said, indicating the couple who were shimmying out on the dance floor, more incompetent than lustful, I'd say. "It's shocking."

"I'm glad to hear you say so, Danny. That's what your name's from; I know it. Daniel. Daniel in the lions' den." A thoughtful look crossed his face. "It's a Biblical name. So's mine—George, or Giorgio. I'm Italian by descent."

"St. George was later than the Bible," I observed, forgetting for a minute what you said about not exposing my education.

He was skeptical. "Maybe," he said. He jabbed a thumb toward the dancers—the man in the red plaid shirt and the girl in blue (white fuzz around the collar of her sweater)— and added, "Who I feel sorry for is her family. Her father, and her brothers, if she has any."

"Me too." I beckoned for another beer.

Our conversation went on for about two hours. I got tired of it, but I didn't know how to leave without offending Georgie. Every time I tried to, he started talking faster. His outlook on life was very pessimistic. He predicted a depression, and that atom-bomb testing would make a desert out of the Mississippi Valley. He thought organized vice was bigger than government. Our schools were places where children learned to do "immoral acts," as he put it. Our movies were filthy. He was born a Roman Catholic, but he said 90% of the priests were only out after their parishioners' women, and when I said I thought maybe his statistics were a little high, he flew into a rage, clenched his fists, and almost hit me. He offered to give me a ride the next morning when I told him I was seeing the country. He was staying on the edge of town at a motel, and I was in the town's only hotel, a door or two away

99

from the bar. He said he'd come by for me and to be ready early. Then, finally, he let me go. He did come, and I got a ride with him for about three hundred miles—not such a long distance around here. He has a closed-in truck with lots of stuff piled up in back covered with a tarpaulin.

He turns out to be a very entertaining little man, and not so surly when he's sober. He's been everywhere in the U.S., but he's mysterious about how he happens to have traveled so much. However, he doesn't ask personal questions of other people, so it suits me. One thing I'm sure of is that he isn't working for Uncle David.

But I'd better finish the story up to date. When we got to where we were going—this was all yesterday—he stopped on the side of the highway to let me out so I could hitch a ride. There he looked at me a long time, frowning. I met his look. Then he asked me if I'd meant what I'd said about the dancers the night before, and if I wasn't just out catting around the country. I assured him I wasn't. I said I practiced chastity, like a saint.

"Them," he said scornfully.

But after thinking a while longer, his engine idling, my hand on the door, he offered to give me a bed on his place, providing I'd do some work for him. It would be work for my body, he said, and it would be good, clean work. I took his offer.

We drove past this little town to a place a couple of miles outside. I'm not going to describe it too accurately, because that might give its exact location away. I'll only say that it's not exactly a farm, and not exactly a ranch. There are tall cottonwoods growing around the house and the outbuildings, though, and their leaves rustle in the night and sound like rain. He had me wait in the truck while he went inside the house—we parked quite a distance from it, behind a barn. After a while he came out with bedding and a couple of towels and took me off to one of the small buildings where there was running water and a little stove. It must have belonged to the hired hands at one time. He tossed the bedding onto a bedstead with open springs and a thin mattress, then changed his mind and helped me make it up.

"You'll be comfortable here," he said. "Come to the kitchen door for your supper tonight."

He gave me heavy gloves and some work to do—sawing wood. He showed me how, since I'd never done it before, and watched until I began to get the knack. By evening I was worn out. I washed up and waited, not sure about the time I was supposed to go to the kitchen door. At six o'clock he came to get me and took me right into the kitchen, saying he'd changed his mind. It was a nice large one, and a good dinner was all set out, with fresh rolls, beefsteak, vegetables, and a fancy cake for dessert.

All the time, all through dinner, he kept listening. Listening, and watching me. I kept my eyes on my plate and *ate*.

I feel very safe from Uncle David here, which is the main reason I took Georgie up on his offer. But I'll continue to be careful.

Your friend,
Neal

I forgot to tell you that I'll be able to get letters from time to time at Des. #78, which is only 50 or 60 miles from here.

June 20

Dear Daneal,

A most satisfactory beginning to an adventure. Suddenly you are making progress. What has happened to my mousy little protégé, dusty from the library stacks?

Out of my vaster experience with life I am able to perceive already a pattern which you, blind worm, do not. I put several things together and come up with an obvious answer: women! Somewhere in your adventure there lurks a luscious vixen, lolling voluptuously in the pine needles, waiting for you to trot up and nip her. I don't know why, but I am certain of it.

Do keep me informed. I pant with eagerness to hear the latest developments.

Now for my life . . .

The only possible news about me must also be about my core, my fulcrum, my axis, my heart, brain, and nerves, my epicenter, my omphalos, my love. I mean Pounce.

Here I can report progress, progress of my own. It is really surprising how much mere persistence can accomplish. Enough of it can seem like strength of will, like dangerous insanity, like irresistible virile force, like inevitability, and even like sex appeal. So it has worked out for me. Plus the fact that Pounce and I are compatible. I draw a veil across the details of our affair, and only say that we begin to love each other. In me it takes the I-would-have-thought-impossible form of an intensification of the madness I felt for her before, in her a competent control of her ambivalence. It is really quite amusing.

She is interesting me more and more in the cinema, and we go and see everything we can. Summer is not a good time here to catch up on all the old reels one has consistently missed across the years through the most perverse blindness to one's own deepest needs, and I long to tread upon the popcorn of some grubby stick of second-run houses, such as must exist in most major cities of the world. I would even live in Chicago if I were assured that I could see Tom Mix there, and John Bunny. Pounce and I talk and think and look and argue, diagram and analyze, in between our tender sarabands. She is a great photographer, you know, and I have quite a flair for imagining new approaches.

She fills all my life except for the hours I must continue to spend at work, and which I resent more and more. What a terrible waste of time it is. One might as well be a grocer arranging citrus fruit in a window. I thought for a while that dealing with the new collection of erotica would change my ennui to enthusiasm, but it hasn't. What it has done is to cause an outbreak of real animus between me and my boss. He has the strictly vaudeville name of Peebles to go with his burlesque personality. Peebles and I have been at swords' points ever since the visit of Ahmed Bidault. He turned out to be a sloe-eyed, melancholy Levantine type who is in the U.S. for some months on business, and who is really a learned man on the subject of what one might call "provocative medicine." I admired him and he me, and therefrom came my great tussle with Peebles, who noticed us smacking our lips over the courses of a dinner described in an Arabic manuscript which Ahmed translated to me. What a feast! Each dish—at least a dozen of them—designed to send the gourmet coursing after the nearest Circassian slave girl. From that, Ahmed and I went on to other lascivious documents, and all the while Peebles was watching us as I had watched those others. Finally he called me on the carpet (broadloom, alas) and said he thought it was unseemly for me to snigger (his word) over our erotica with visitors, and he was putting me onto the circulation desk until further notice. And that was that. Excepting that Ahmed and I have seen a lot of each other after school hours, and he has asked me to visit him in Paris. Perhaps I will. I'm not going to be able to stand it here much longer. It depends on Pounce.

Lest you feel you have escaped entirely, allow me to twitch the string twixt thee and me, twixt this faded old world you used to inhabit so cozily and the bright new one where you now saw logs 'neath the shade of the rustling cottonwoods. I got a letter from your Uncle David the other day. A reminder that should I ever hear from you, he wanted to know about it. Efforts to trace you so far had failed, he admitted, but there were promising clues. It was only a matter of time.

Ta ta,
Ned

The cancellation on your last was plainly legible, so Des. #78 is out of the bag as far as I am concerned. Don't step on any snakes. And be careful to send letters care of Pounce, since Wallace is still on my trail, and he'd have a posse scouring the country around Des. #78 in no time if he knew its name.

4.

Dear Ned,

Howdy!

I have been working hard, mending fences, felling dead timber, all kinds of things outdoors and in the farm buildings. Everything was very run-down and hadn't been taken care of for some time. I haven't ever had physical exercise like this before, and it's making me feel very good. Yesterday Georgie came out in the fields to have lunch with me, and watched me working for a while with my shirt off; and then he said he thought it was a good thing I was sworn to chastity, because otherwise now that I was getting in shape I'd be quite a temptation for the girls.

I still haven't been past the kitchen of the house. The meals continue to be big and good. The baking gets more and more elaborate. Cream puffs today, filled with whipped cream, drenched with chocolate. When does Georgie do it all? Or does he?

I have noticed that every now and then when I cross the farmyard the curtains in the upper windows twitch. And once when I was out working with Georgie I looked back at the house and I'm sure I saw someone hanging up laundry.

One effect this life is having on me is that for the first time since I can remember I am becoming aware of myself as an animal. I mean, I am becoming conscious of my body and its appetites. I am aware of the fact that I am tired in the evening, filled with the need to sleep, my arms lying out on the arms of my chair like sandbags and my blood thick. I am also conscious of hunger, great hungers which it takes potatoes and potatoes and potatoes to satisfy. Not just now and then, but three times a day. That isn't the end of it. I am growing conscious of my body for itself, if that makes any sense to you. I am conscious of it when I walk or jump or run or lift something, or even sit. I have looked at it in a mirror to see if it is changing, and, if so, how. It seems to me like a friend I have ignored for years and am now getting to know better.

I am committed to chastity. I don't know about my friend.

I really wonder who does the baking and twitches the curtains and washes out my underwear.

Georgie just came to get me and tell me he was ready to leave for Des. #78. He saw I was writing a letter and got very suspicious and flew into a rage. He stalks around with his little legs stiff at the knees, rubbing his hands through his black hair until it stands on end, and he grinds his jaws together until you'd think he'd break his molar points. He is a good-looking little fellow, with a well-shaped head, like most Italians, but I think his brain is addled.

I had to give him an explanation, so I told him I was writing to my Spiritual Instructor. I told him that I had left the world behind and was trying to achieve elevation of soul through physical labor, loneliness, and meditation, and that the only person who knew where I was was my Teacher, who from time to time sent me advice on how to achieve Perfection. He liked that idea. I also added that if anybody came to inquire about me, or asked him in town who I was, or in any way showed interest in me, he was to say I was a friend of his from Florida (which was where he was driving from when he picked me up), and if possible not to say anything at all, because I didn't want all my former worldly contacts to know my whereabouts until I had reached Peace.

After all that he stood in my little room picking at my table with his penknife and finally said that he believed me and trusted me. I was the only man he knew he did trust, he said, and fate must have made us meet the night in the bar, because he and I had a special job to do together which we'd have to get to soon. What do you suppose that meant?

I've now protected myself against being surprised by Uncle David's agents. And Georgie is such a fiery friend that I think he'd help me escape from them even if they did catch up with me, and might even shoot a couple. He keeps plenty of guns around, of every size and type, because I see him cleaning them out in the yard. He's started to teach me pistol shooting, and I'm not bad. Together we could make it pretty hot for Uncle David and his goons.

Your friend,
Neal

July 4th

Dear Brewster,

Panting Pounce is nagging at me to leave for the local *feu d'artifice* sponsored by the town fathers on the occasion of this, our hottest national holiday, so I have only a moment.

I am delighted to be your guru. I haven't time to go into the series of exercises I want you to take up, but they could all be contained in the following: Keep a sharp eye on those fluttering curtains.

I think you ought to keep a fairly sharp eye on Georgie, too. I'm not so sure about Georgie. And be sure to touch any scratches you get from the barbed-wire fences with mercurochrome.

Yours, faithfully,
Ned

P.S. Pesky Pounce insists that I send you her love and asks if the girls out there wear blue jeans.

N.

Dear Ned,

I have your letter of June 20. Uncle David's letter to you doesn't need much comment, does it? He's desperate.

I know more about what goes on now. Also about what's on Georgie's mind, though I don't know everything yet. It has to do with somebody who has been hanging around his place but whose name he isn't sure of. I don't know exactly what the trouble is—maybe some thefts? Or maybe some peeping?

Have I described the ranch? Georgie doesn't work it. Most of the land is let out to neighbors who use it partly for cattle and partly for irrigated potatoes and hay and things like that. We also have some timber up against the foothills. It was run for years by his father, who was an American success story, an Italian immigrant who made good by going west; but Georgie went away and the old man died, and now it's better to rent most of the land. Georgie has told me all this.

There's a pretty stream running through the place, which has lots of trout in it. Georgie caught some the other morning at dawn, while I watched him. Then he cleaned them at an outside trough and took them to the farmhouse, and came back outside to wash up. I noticed something about him. He has very strange and terrible scars around his neck and shoulders.

He really likes me, Ned. I mean, quite apart from all I've told him about my spirituality, I think he likes me just for myself. That's something new. I like him, too, strange as he is. For one thing, he's very clever with his hands, and quick on his feet, like a cat. He can jump up on a stump using only one foot, and he can do good carpentry work. Perhaps things like that aren't so very important, as things go, but here they have a place, and I admire them. He's also a patient teacher. There's only one thing wrong with him, aside from his melancholia, and that's the fact that he goes on crazy drunks. I hear him yelling and talking to himself in the kitchen—his favorite place to sit—when he's in the middle of one.

He seems to have very strange feelings about the little town nearby. I don't mean Des. #78, I mean the town four miles from here. What the hell—I'll call it by its name, Oreville. He's suspicious of the people in it, and doesn't like to trade there any more than he has to, which is why we do so much shopping in Des. #78. Oreville is typical of the region, with the new hospital and the new school which seem to be everywhere in small-town America, plus a few places to eat and drink, a bank, a barbershop, a motel or two, and some stores. The old buildings and houses have some flavor—like hitching posts still preserved here and there—the new ones none. That's typical, too. Day before yesterday he made his first real visit to Oreville, although everybody knew he was back.

"Hello, Georgie," they'd drawl when we walked in anywhere. "You back home?" Friendly, but cool. I sensed they may have a few strange feelings about Georgie, too, and don't want to get mixed up with him. He introduced me to everybody as Daniel or Danny, a friend of his from Florida. They took me as a matter of course and only said the most obvious things about Florida, like how the weather must be nice, nothing that I had to reply to. That is, until we met the sheriff. We were in the bank, and this tall, good-looking man with blue eyes and a day's growth of beard was ahead of us in line. He had a certain swagger which, from watching television, I guessed must belong to the Law, even before I saw his star. His name was Cory. (I think that's his last name, but I'm never sure around here.) When he turned and saw Georgie, he said, "Well, if it isn't the mighty Medici back in town," in a very patronizing way. Georgie turned red and ran his hand through his hair and gritted his teeth. But Cory was the sheriff, so Georgie just said, "That's right, Cory," without offering to shake hands. "I've got a little business here in Oreville to take care of. That's why I've come back," and he walked on up to the teller's window. But then he remembered me and introduced me. "From Florida, are you? I guess they have a big floater problem down that way," was Cory's dig for me. "It's changed a lot for the worse since the days of my great-grandparents," I replied. "It's full of retired policemen now." I never would have said *that* two months ago.

All over town Georgie was asking questions—about hired men, about strangers, about what had been happening while he was gone—without ever seeming to come out and ask what he really wanted to know. People were guarded with him, and he wasn't getting anywhere. Then in the hardware store, where he went to get some ammunition, he got some results. It belongs to a middle-aged widow named Mrs. Baskin, who has a sharp eye for what's going on, and whose house is way outside of town and has a view, so Georgie told me, of his own. She was nicer to Georgie than the other people in town and asked him about his sisters—that was the first time I had heard any sisters mentioned.

"Never mind about them, Mrs. Baskin," Georgie said, glancing in my direction, "just tell me who's been hanging around my place."

She checked to see that her store was empty, and even went to see who might be just outside. She spoke softly. "If I were you, I'd ask the sheriff about that, Georgie Leone."

I forgot to say that Georgie's last name isn't Medici, it's Leone. I don't know why the sheriff called him Medici. Probably a crack.

Georgie was upset all the rest of the day, and drank a lot, starting about four in the afternoon—at least a full pint, which is a lot for such a tiny guy. That night, when we were sitting in the kitchen having supper, he was very drunk, and crazier sounding than I had ever heard him before. Finally I couldn't control my curiosity and I asked him about his sisters.

He scowled at the swinging door into the rest of the house.

"I was waiting for you to ask that. Well, you're as dependable a friend as I'm likely to find, so you might as well meet them. Come on out, girls."

With a shrill squeak the door swung open, and into the kitchen filed three women, ranging in age from about forty down to about twenty-five. They were all big girls, too. I've commented on how little Georgie is. Well, his sisters are just the opposite. They were all at least 5'10" tall and looked even taller because they clustered around him. They must have been waiting just on the other side of that door, and from the way they were fixed up, and came in so fast, I think he'd prepared them for an appearance that evening. I stood up, and they were introduced to me as Opal, Pearl, and Ruby. Opal was the eldest.

She was plain, but the others were nice looking, and very, very developed in the bust and elsewhere. They were all dark, and all of them had Georgie's black eyes; but where he is quick and nervous, they were slow and on the sweet side, excepting, again, possibly Opal, who was a little jittery. They were shy and wouldn't say much, and Georgie didn't let them stay long, either. After introducing them he glared at them for a few minutes while I tried to talk to them, then he growled, "Now you can get out of my sight," and hiccuped. Whereupon they all sniffled and dabbed at their eyes with handkerchiefs and withdrew in single file, Opal at the head of the troupe.

When we were alone again, Georgie left the table and his hot dinner and began to pace up and down in the kitchen, banging at the old wood stove, the table, and the floor cabinets as he went past them, rumpling his hair wildly, and muttering. "I shouldn't have stayed away. I should have known what would happen." He shook a fist at the door they were now vanished behind. "God damn it. Oh, God damn it," he said, over and over.

"What's the matter, Georgie?" I asked.

"What? What?" He turned, baring his fine white teeth almost like a wild animal. "Are you making fun of me?" I shook my head, and suddenly he relaxed. "No, of course you aren't. You're just innocent, that's all. You really don't know, do you? I've got no right to pull you into this." He turned green and swallowed hard—the tail end of that pint was on its way up. "Finish your supper. Finish your supper, Danny," he said, and ran from the kitchen.

That's where things now stand. Is this an adventure, would you say, Ned? I think it is.

Yours,
Neal

Georgie got drunk again yesterday afternoon, and when I came into the kitchen for supper I found all his firearms sitting out there and on the back porch. He played with them all through the meal, until one of them went off accidentally and tore a big hole in a window screen. I think he's already at it again today, although it's early in the morning, and I'm worried.

July 11

Dear Ned,

Tell Pounce that lots of the girls around here wear blue jeans, but not the Leone sisters. The two younger girls, I've discovered—and this is my big news—are going to have babies.

Georgie told me, finally. That's what's been on his mind. They're pregnant. He talks openly about their "shame," and about how he has to revenge it. The great problem is that he doesn't know who the men are, and the girls won't tell him, not even Opal, who wrote him the bad news in the first place. I guess they're afraid of what we might do.

I say *we*, because I'll help him if he needs it. I'm getting pretty good with a gun now. Also, Georgie has taught

111

me some judo. You can kill a man easily with judo. Did you know that? Just a tap on the back of the neck, and click! It's all over.

He's drunk all the time now and his fits of anger are getting more and more violent. So is his melancholia. It's not as pleasant here as it was before he started his investigation, and frankly I wish the whole thing would die down. I have the feeling it's not going to, though. He's still asking questions in town. Yesterday Mrs. Baskin warned him that he was being watched, whatever that meant.

I wish you were here to advise me about what comes next. I hope it won't be something fatal.

> Your friend,
> Neal

July 14

Dear Brewster,

I have your letters of the 8th and the 11th, both of which I have read with some uneasiness. I think you're in over your head. It's all more than I bargained for when I helped you clear out of here.

The thought even crosses my mind that you should consider returning home. You've had your outing. Isn't it time to call a halt?

I wish Pounce were here to consult, since she'd have some good common-sense answers to my questions. Alas! she is temporarily absent, visiting her Uncle Bobby, who seems to be perishing of athlete's foot, and from whom she hopes to inherit a boxful of worthless securities.

By all the laws of the horse opera, that helpful Mrs. Baskin is marked for destruction. Caught in cross fire, she will receive a 45-caliber dumdum bullet in the left rear cheek and die on her feet.

But we don't want that to happen. So please stop thinking,

talking, and writing about guns and judo and killing people. It's that which worries me. Move on. I want to hear from you again right away, from somewhere leagues beyond Oreville. The Guru has spoken.

Yours,
Ned

I know that when Pounce returns she will be furious if I haven't ascertained just how short your three Norns cut their hair.

HAPPY BASTILLE DAY!

5.

July 17

Dear Ned,

After all this waiting, the situation has finally come to a head. It is a terrible mess, and I feel very bad about it.

Georgie knows something definite now. We were in that damn Baskin Hardware Store this morning, and Georgie asked her if she couldn't tell him anything more. "I told you to ask the sheriff," Mrs. Baskin replied. "And what I meant was not to get information, but that he was the only man I saw around your place, and he was there plenty."

Georgie was rocked. "Not him. Not *him*," he kept saying on the way home. "I've hated him ever since school, when he called me names and made fun of my size." Then he did what you'd have expected. He got very drunk in the course of the afternoon, and when he was full of whisky, he called in the girls and asked them point-blank about the sheriff. There was consternation. "So he was one of them, was he?" Georgie shrieked. "Who was the other? Who was the other, and who did it with which? Was it his deputy? Who was it?" The girls wouldn't tell, and actually didn't even admit the part about the sheriff. "All right," Georgie said. "There are other ways to find out. Follow me, Danny. We're going to pay a little call on Cory."

The rest really was a television show or a Western movie. Georgie rushed into the sheriff's office like an angry black terrier. It's at the back of the jail. He pulled out his gun when he saw the sheriff (who was reading the *New Yorker*). "So you're the son of a bitch who got my sister in trouble," he cried.

"In trouble?" the sheriff asked, his mouth falling open.

Georgie pranced with rage. "With child. With child, you fornicator," he yelled.

"My God," the sheriff said, glancing at the open window.

"Everybody in town's told me it was you."

"Which one?" the sheriff asked.

"You tell me which one," Georgie answered.

"Good God," the sheriff said again, going white. But he had begun to collect himself. He was watching Georgie carefully, especially his gun.

"I'm going to kill you for it," Georgie yapped. "But not until you tell me who the other man was." He raised his hand.

Moving very fast, the sheriff reached out, turned the gun aside, and removed it from Georgie's hand. "Now, now, mighty Medici," he said, "everybody knows you've lost your nerve ever since you almost got your head taken off." With as much *sang-froid* as if he had been doing it in front of a million video watchers, he emptied the chambers and tossed the cartridges into his desk drawer.

It was too much for Georgie. Moaning, he jumped up on the sheriff's desk and kicked everything on it down to the floor, then he leapt down and scattered all the papers in every direction, dumped the wastebasket, and started in on the drawers. Inside sixty seconds he had that office in a terrible mess. Cory circled him, then grabbed him like a baby, held his hands together, and dragged him to a cell nearby. Georgie yelled to me as he was being pulled out of the room. "Help me, Danny."

But the sheriff said, "You just keep out of this, Danny Boy, unless you want to go back to Florida in handcuffs." A self-locking door closed behind him before I could do anything anyway. I heard some howling, and a terrific splashing of water, and then the sheriff came back into his office, dabbing at his face and clothes with a towel.

"You can go on home," he said, lighting a ready-made cigarette. "I'll bring him out tonight after he's had a chance to cool off. I don't want him shouting any accusations when folks are up to hear them, because then everybody in town really would be talking. You tell his sisters I'll be there." He took me to the door and gave me Georgie's keys so I could drive the truck. "He'll never believe it, but I'm really sorry about this. I really am. It's just one of those things a man falls into. See you tonight." He didn't go back inside until he was sure I had the truck started and was on my way.

What a panic there was in that hen coop when I arrived and told the girls the news. At first they rushed around the kitchen weeping and crying out, but finally they settled on chairs, where they wept and worried. Pearl and Ruby ate some apricots, while Opal smoldered and gnawed her fingernails. Then I asked them to tell me the truth, so that I could help, if help was possible. It was the sheriff, I said, and who else?

"It was only the sheriff," Opal said. "Only him."

"Both of them? You mean, he's the father of both of them?"

Opal gave the girls a terrible look, passing from the head of each down to the swelling belly. It was the look of an old maid who has spent many a night wracked by who knows what frustrations. "Both of them," she whispered. "He came out to court me, but they waylaid him on the road or on the porch or in the barn—I don't know where—and look where it got them." Then she used a little language which wasn't nice.

"Whatever he came for, it wasn't to court anybody," Pearl said, sniffling.

"No," Ruby agreed, taking another apricot. "He's already got a wife and children."

"He would have divorced her," Opal said fiercely.

"You couldn't have married him anyway, even if he was divorced," Ruby replied, "being a Catholic. And besides, you don't have to be so mean. We didn't do anything you didn't want to do."

A look of anguish passed across Opal's plain face. "I know. I know that," she said. She began to cry.

This set them all off again, and I decided it was time for me to leave. But when I said I was going over to my house to wait for night and the sheriff, they jumped up and gathered around me and offered me coffee and cinnamon toast and said I didn't need to go, and why didn't I stay with them. I got the funniest feeling that— Well, I won't say it. It would be disloyal to Georgie.

Next day . . .

The sheriff came about eleven o'clock last night with Georgie handcuffed to a metal bar welded onto his back seat. He let him out, but locked him right up again to the stove in the kitchen. Georgie looked terrible. He had a black eye and was limping, but I don't think the sheriff had roughed him up intentionally; they just happened while he was getting him into the cell. He was also still wet, and I guess the water treatment had continued after I was gone, because things dry out awfully fast here. Georgie wouldn't look at any of us. I'm afraid his heart is broken. More than that, I'm afraid that for the time being at least his reason is pretty well gone, too.

The girls were all dressed, and Opal had a rose in her hair, but nobody paid them any attention. I was the person the sheriff talked to. He gave me the key to the cuffs and said I was to unlock them only when I thought Georgie was under control, that we were all responsible for keeping him quiet, that he wouldn't have him running around with a gun, and that if he got loose and came into town that way again, there might be some pretty nasty consequences. Cory would see he went to jail for a while.

He looked at Georgie, slumped over on a straight wooden chair, his hands locked to the iron leg of the huge, antique range. "Or the State Hospital," he added grimly.

"You'd better get him back to Florida as fast as you can," he said to me, as he was leaving.

None of those threats is very dangerous, of course, because the sheriff certainly doesn't want Georgie to come up for any kind of trial, or even hearing, where he could tell people why he behaved the way he did. On the other hand, we don't want Georgie to get into any trouble, and don't want anything to happen that would expose Pearl's and Ruby's shame to the whole town. I don't trust the sheriff, either. He might shoot Georgie to keep him quiet, and lay it all to self-defense. Those poor unborn children—their uncle murdered by their father. Their relationship to each other is going to be difficult enough in any case.

That's the way things stand right now. Georgie hasn't eaten or slept since he was delivered last night. He won't talk to any of us. He is perfectly docile, stands up when he's told to, goes to the bathroom, sits down, etc. I've had him out in the woods today and over at my place for a while, but I haven't taken off the handcuffs yet. I'll keep you posted, when something happens.

Your friend,
Neal

Uncle David and all that certainly seem pretty far away from me right now.

July 22

Dear Ned,

I'm writing this from Reno. We can't continue with our secret destinations, because I left my key behind when I had to leave the ranch in a hurry. I'm not staying here long enough to get a letter, but will let you know where I finally settle down.

When last I wrote Georgie was still handcuffed and very depressed. He continued quiet. The humiliating incident with the sheriff seemed to have drawn his stinger, and I was afraid that he'd pine away. He went along like that for several days, until both Opal and I thought it was safe to let him loose. We kept the keys to his truck hidden from him just in case, although we both felt that he wouldn't make another attack on the sheriff. What was the use, unless it was violent, and Opal told me that the sheriff's remark was true, that Georgie had lost his nerve. Whatever remnants he had left were all used up the afternoon he roared into town. I took the cuffs back to their owner the afternoon we finally removed them. He tried to talk to me about the Leone family, about how strange they had always been in the neighborhood, never mixing, like suspicious European peasants dropped into the heart of the friendly West, so that the sisters never even met eligible boys. He had been summoned originally to the house by Opal, because she thought there was a prowler. Only he didn't think she really had seen one, and anyway, well, things just got started. He suggested that I should be sure to see the younger girls got proper medical attention. They might not, otherwise. He thought it would be better to go to Des. #78 for it. He was nice enough, at heart, but his position was awkward, to say the least, and he was worried about his job, his family, his reputation. If he'd been a millionaire I think he would have provided handsomely for his bastards, although that doesn't prove much, does it, because for a millionaire to provide for his bastards is the easiest thing in the world. I heard the sheriff out, but, loyal to Georgie, I didn't talk the situation over with him the way he wanted me to. As I was leaving, he asked to see some identification because, he said, he was going to have to write up a report for his confidential file, leaving out certain allegations, of course. I showed my old library card to him, which might be dangerous, but I doubt it, because after all, he's on the spot and won't do much talking around.

When I got back, Opal came running into the yard to tell me that Georgie had started drinking and I'd better drive right back in to get the handcuffs again. I refused to do it, saying we couldn't keep Georgie shackled like a vicious dog, and that if he was going to get dangerous every time he drank, which I doubted, we ought to know about it, and if all he did was to yell and curse, then it might do him some good, like lancing a boil. I also told her to hide all weapons.

How those three sisters did move, while Georgie drank himself wild in the kitchen. The place was filled with the clink of metal, and when I peeked through the door I saw gray forms flitting through the twilight of the late afternoon carrying implements of every kind to secret hiding places. Several hours later, when Georgie was really drunk, that farmhouse was as innocent of possible weapons of death as the wards of a mental hospital. It may be that greater tragedy was avoided thereby; but it is strange that it never occurred to them to hide the one thing Georgie best knew how to use.

Meanwhile he brooded, now and then rubbing his black hair till it stood on end. By this time he had enormous madman's circles under his eyes from not sleeping. He muttered about his parents, about his responsibilities, about sin and fornication, and the condition of his two sisters. Once, when I asked him if he wouldn't like some food, he muttered: "Give me stones to eat. Opal, Pearl, and Ruby—my three precious stones." Yes, he was raving mad, but putting everything he said, then and before, together, I realized that Georgie sniffed sin everywhere; and while he blamed his sisters for succumbing to temptation, he saw the desire to seduce as a wicked impulse shared by all male creatures, as if the source of all evil were the universal presence of the rutting drive. That

119

evening he suddenly grabbed my arm as I went by and told me he included animals as well as men. The tomcat on the prowl, the bull mounting the heifer, dogs running loll-tongued after a bitch—he mentioned them all.

"You don't know about all that, though. You're pure, Danny," he said.

"Not really," I told him. "I'm ready to go out into the world now."

"You mean you're going to be a fornicator, like the others?"

I should have been warned off, but I thought a little truth might help clear the air. "My purely spiritual phase is over, and now I have to take the next higher step," I said. "Those are my teacher's orders. I must become like other people, only greater and more splendid. Don't take such a black view of mankind, Georgie. Men may not amount to much, but they could be worse. Now and then they think, now and then they try. You're obsessed," I told him. "You see fornication behind every bush." Then I launched into a eulogy of the body as the partner to the mind, and the foundation for the soul. I lifted my wings; I soared. "Through it we may express our deepest longings," I concluded. "Not only is it a unique instrument of joy, but also it is the only instrument we can play on which sounds through the universe."

I think you'd have liked my speech, Ned. It sounded like you.

He stared blackly at me, then jumped to his feet and ran around the kitchen table spilling whisky from his glass. "So you're like all the rest," he shrieked. "Like all the rest, are you? Why did you lie to me, Daniel? As if I didn't know." And he stared at the doorway.

"I didn't lie to you then, and I won't lie to you now," I replied.

"That doesn't make any sense," he answered furiously.

"Neither did my life at the time we met," I said.

He crashed his glass down on the table. "Get out," he

shouted, beside himself. "Go away. Go away from here. You're just like all the others."

"I'll go tomorrow, Georgie," I said sadly. "I told you this because I wanted to be honest with you. It was done out of respect."

Opal, from behind the kitchen door, fluttered into the room. "You can't leave us, Danny," she cried. "You can't."

Georgie stared from her to me to her to me again. He rubbed his hair, hid his eyes with his hands a moment, then, shouting "Fornicators, fornicators," he ran out of the house.

Perhaps five hours later, about midnight, I was awakened by some sound. I got up, very sleepy, and looked out of my window. It was dark outside, that starry darkness of the open country which hides so quickly in the memory after a few weeks in town. The lights in the house were all out. Then I heard my name called, not from there, but from the old barn. I waited, thinking I was mistaken, but I knew something funny was up, because patches of light showed through chinks in the barn walls and from its upper windows, and that barn is unused. Then my name was called again. I pulled on a pair of trousers, slipped on some shoes, and bounded across the open space like a fugitive.

It was Georgie who had called me. He was leaning out of a ventilating window at the upper level of the barn; and when he saw me, or, rather, heard my "What is it?"—he couldn't see me in that black farmyard—he told me to come on up, that he had a treat for me, a going-away present. I slipped through the door, which hung ajar, and headed for the ladder to the storage room above.

Upstairs there was one big light bulb burning, which dangled by a ten-foot cord suspended from a rafter. Giant shadows cast by the beams and supporting posts haunted the outer edges of the vast room and came to life whenever the draft—there was always a wind at night—swung the light to and fro. Then I saw the posters tacked onto the walls. They were circus posters, and all featured an entertainer, the Mighty Medici, a tiny man in a big cage confronting a mass of toothy carnivores with only a long whip for protection. In one of them he was lashing at an enormous tiger which was springing upon him, its great paws spread-eagled in mid-air. In another a whole pyramid of snarling felinity was backed into the corner of a cage, while the Mighty Medici, whip snapping, gestured imperiously toward a flaming hoop. In still another, the little man was allowing his head to be taken into the mouth of a great male lion.

Standing in the midst of all this was Georgie, raving drunk, dressed in a kind of spaceman's costume made half of silver, half of gold cloth, with blue sequins glittering around his neck and on his slippers. Georgie, the Mighty Medici! And he carried his great whip, just like his picture in the posters, but unlike them, he carried his bottle in his free hand. As soon as he saw me, he cracked the whip and began to mutter. I stood paralyzed, particularly when I saw the rest of the treat he had invited me up for. Sitting on three pedestals of varying height were his sisters, dressed the way they were the day the sheriff brought Georgie home, Opal with another red rose in her hair. Most ominous was the fact that a fourth perch, a brightly painted barrel, highest of all, was unoccupied, awaiting its big cat.

Crack went the whip. Crack, crack, crack. Georgie strutted around, playing up to an imaginary audience seated back along the dark walls. Then he pretended to see me for the first time. He made a magnificent gesture, ordering me up onto that red, white, and blue barrel. "This is too much. You're mad, Georgie," I cried, but a crack of the whip, within inches of my head, made me realize that, mad or not, he wasn't joking. I decided I'd better go ahead and do what he wanted and up I jumped. I might have made it back down the stairs, but on the other hand, I might not, might have felt the burn of that vicious whip; and anyway, what would I have done about the three sisters? I couldn't decently leave them to play alone in that act with their poor demented brother.

There followed the strangest, most pathetic scene I ever expect to see. One after the other he made them come off their stools and do tricks. Pearl he had twirl in front of us all, but particularly right in front of me, round and round four, five, six, a dozen times, then reverse. Ruby had to zigzag between the pedestals and circle my barrel. Then Opal, the one who wasn't pregnant, he made lie down on the floor and roll over, then pick up her flower in her teeth. They all went through their tricks, Ned, with a kind of seriousness, even a sort of enthusiasm born of desperation, like galley slaves straining to win a race. Finally, all three together had to play a game of musical chairs and change places at his command.

When that part of the show was over, he cracked his whip wildly over their heads and ordered them to roar. A chorus of screeches and sobs greeted this command. The girls were all incoherent from fright and shock, naturally, all nearly as wild as their brother, but when he told them to roar, they roared. They seemed to know what he wanted right away, and I wondered as I watched if this were by any chance the sequel to a game they had all played innocently together as children, those four little Italian children, so set off from the rest of the community. It sounded like a madhouse, and he kept the whole thing going for several minutes with his whip, shouting for ever louder choruses.

Suddenly, after making several cracks in quick succession, he yelled, "Quiet!" When they were still, he swaggered up and down. He came to a stop in front of my barrel, where I was squatting.

"All right, Danny," he said. "Now make your choice. You've seen what they can do."

"My choice of what?"

"Your choice of what you followed me home for, of what you've been sneaking around here after all these weeks."

"What are you talking about?"

"Your choice of mates," he answered.

"But I don't want a mate," I replied.

"I'm telling you to choose." He lashed out with his murderous whip again, this time close over my head, and hopped madly around the floor in front of me, beside himself with fury.

"Georgie, come to your senses. Help me, girls," I cried.

He lashed his whip again; they screamed; he lashed, and this last time he let me feel it on my bare shoulder, just a little. "Ow!" I yowled. "That's it, that's it," he shouted when he heard me, and he capered up and down in ferocious glee.

Only one way to escape occurred to me, based on the principle that if you can't lick them, join them. I began to roar in earnest, as much like a lion as I could. I roared and roared, which sent poor Georgie into a further frenzy. I really tried. In fact, I found I rather liked doing it. I stood on my barrel and bellowed, baring my teeth, tossing my mane. "Good, good, good," he shouted. "Louder. More." His sisters began to scream sympathetically. And then, showing his courage before his imaginary audience, he turned his back on us and bowed. It was just what I had hoped for. I leaped off my barrel with a particularly horrible snarl. One of the sisters called a warning to him (imagine that!), but before he could turn and drive me off, I was on him. I carried him down with my weight, grabbed him around the neck, and pretended to sink my teeth into his shoulder. He struggled just a second or two, and actually I bit him.

Do you know what he did, Ned? He fainted. We were saved.

A lot of thanks I got for it. The girls ran forward. "Oh, oh, oh, you've hurt Georgie." "What have you done to Georgie?" "How dare you do that to Georgie?" Opal fanned him. Pearl ran for smelling salts. Ruby tried to pour some of his whisky down his throat, as if he hadn't already had quite enough. I tell you, that entire family was crazy, not just Georgie. When they got his eyes to flutter, they had me lower him down the ladder to them, then I came down myself and carried him over my shoulder back to the house and put him in his bed. He was alive, all right, but either he couldn't or he wouldn't talk to us, and the last I saw of him he was lying in his bed staring at the ceiling.

That ought to be the end of the story, but it isn't—not quite. I decided, you see, that I'd get what sleep I could before dawn, and then go out on the highway and hitch a ride west. I didn't fall asleep for a couple of hours, worrying about Georgie and thinking about everything that had happened to me; but then, maybe an hour before dawn, I did doze off. I don't think I slept more than a couple of minutes—you know how you have that sense of the duration of time occasionally— when I awakened with a conviction, an absolute knowledge, that there was a prowler in my room. I lay still, wondering if it was Georgie, and if he had got hold of a knife or something like that and was going to kill me. Or was he just checking on me? I pretended to snore, hoping he would go away. Something touched one of my feet—a hand!—then prodded at my ankle and calf, getting bearings, identifying. Involuntarily I shuddered, just once, but I lay still. The hand was withdrawn. Would the next thing I felt be cold steel in my heart?

Far from it. The next thing I felt was a moist hand on my chest, then a body lay beside mine. We tussled until—well, until I changed my mind.

Somewhat later I said, "I've got to get up now. I've got to pack my things and be out on the highway at daybreak."

"No," said my companion. "Don't go away. Stay here with me."

"It would kill Georgie," I said.

"I'll hide you from Georgie."

"And your sisters?"

"I'll hide you from my sisters, too, somehow."

I thought about it. "No," I said finally. "One time is an accident, but more than once would be betraying Georgie. I must leave."

She slipped out of bed and glided to the door. "Wait," I whispered.

"Farewell. Farewell," she said, and disappeared. When I dared put on the light, I found a rose on the pillow, and I packed it along with my shirts.

So now here I am in Reno, and I'm having a mighty good time here, too. I feel lucky, you know. I've been playing a little roulette and blackjack and watching the girls waggle their bottoms, and I'm planning more of the same for tonight. Maybe I'll break the bank, and if I do, then won't those bottoms waggle—and for me. I've learned one thing for sure, and that is this: That the second time you do anything is a lot easier than the first.

All the best to you and Pounce,

Neal

August 5

Dear Ned,

I've finally come to a stop. What a town! San Francisco: the Golden Gate, two knees and a sling of pudic drapery; rolling Pacific, no mother of mine; dappled gray receiver of suicides, the great north-south Bay; sounds of horns and bells and ships' whistles; up-and-down buildings on up-and-down streets; domesticated exotics, japs and chinks, queans and beatniks, niggers and wops, glorious! Wind, wind, wind, blow, blow, blow; fog and sunshine, damp and dry. Me in the middle of it, wondering how I spent so many years avoiding redwood trees and 2 a.m., both of which are local specialities.

A great city, and I feel great in it.

I've fallen in love, too. I saw her in a coffeehouse the other night after the bars had closed, serene face, but wistful face, hair drawn back in a knot, like a governess. It was 2 a.m. With not a redwood tree, but only a stick—regimental stripe, prematurely gray hair clipped that morning, more blood than necessary. We ogled each other, I from stool, she from wrought-iron chair. Electricity. The likelihood of something absolutely cosmic taking place, like the explosion of a nova. Stick noticed. Stick displeased. Glare 'twixt me and stick. Stick took her away, but she returned for her gloves while Stick watched, and I watched, and she watched, we watched, and they (boys behind coffee counter) watched.

That was three days ago. I've been back in the same place at the same time every night since. She'll be there tonight or tomorrow or next week, and this time it will be by herself.

I walk all day, sometimes six or seven hours. I sit in the park and feel the cold damp wind, and every morning I watch the fogs roll in and disintegrate themselves toward noon on the bay-side hills and I think of the waiting sun, like a principle whose complement is everything that changes and transmutes and explodes and is volatile and unstable and—jazzy.

I contain a part of the sun's constancy. Playing all around and in and out and above and below it is change—jazz!

I talked to an old woman today in front of the jaguars at the Fleishacker Zoo. Feeding time. Lots of noise from behind the bars. She always visited zoos, she said. Particularly the big cats, which had a fascination for her ever since she saw a lion tamer maimed during a show a couple of years earlier. What? What? Named Medici. Got shaken like a rat by a terrier. She wondered why they didn't put cat repellent all over themselves, like what she used in her garden.

Georgie . . . Good-by, Georgie.

It's late. Almost time for my coffee. No cream or sugar with it, just a twist of rewarded vigil, please. I'll mail this on the way. I'm at the Hotel Montmorency, Constable Street, and hope to hear from you there. It's been weeks and weeks.

What present can I send you, Ned? Without you I'd never have come this far. I don't think I need to say anything more than that, knowing how understanding you are about motivations and feelings.

As ever,
Neal

6.

This is Ned Bates again, once more head cook, boiling up an auto- and biographical bouillabaisse. I would willingly let the Bates-Brewster *Briefwechsel* continue indefinitely, since it involves so little work for me, but I am committed to follow Life, and our lives ceased to contain any exchange of letters. There was, in fact, only one more, a final note from me to him. If only I had had better luck. If only I had either written immediately or not written at all. As it was, I fell between two stools, and, in a way, it hurt.

What I said was innocent—that I was fascinated by his adventure, that I was glad the lion had lain down with the lamb, and that San Francisco seemed like a good place for him to stay a while. I was in a hurry when I wrote; also, I wanted some time to think over what he had written me. He never got my letter.

The next evening I was at Pounce's. It was a hot night, dog days, the fourteenth of August. We had celebrated the Ides of that month the night before, or at least I had, with a spot too many gins, and I was without energy or much thought, certainly disinclined to enthusiasm over anything. I was lying on her day bed enjoying her air-conditioning after the hot library. The telephone rang. Pounce answered. It was for me, long distance, which was a surprise, for who would call me there?

I went on the wire in time to hear the hysterical clink of silver coinage tumbling into the coffers of the Bell System.

Then, after so many weeks, came a familiar voice, only not low and depressed now, but full of thump.

"Ned? Is it really Ned?"

I replied that I was Ned, if there was such a person. "Which I sometimes doubt," I added.

"This is Neal. I guessed you'd be at the studio. Listen, Ned, I've been discovered. They've found me."

"And put you right on the phone to me?"

"No, no. They've located me, but they haven't netted me, or whatever they plan to do. I'm still at large. The elevator girl, night shift, waited outside the Montmorency to warn me, and somehow got some of my clothes out of the room. It was very nice of her, I must say, but then—well, anyway, I can't go back."

"How about your money? How about your identification?"

"I always carry them with me."

"That was fortunate," I said dryly. "Do you have any notion how they found you?"

"It must have been Sheriff Cory. Once they got me that far, tracing me the rest of the way would have been easy. I cut quite a figure in Reno." There was a pause, and I heard noises in the background. "I'm off now. I just wanted to let you know that I was on the move again. This time I'll give them a good run for their money."

"How do you plan to do that?"

"Oh, plant false clues and keep moving. They'll never get me, you know. Think of them right now, waiting in the hotel lobby." He laughed gaily. "Isn't this the greatest thing that ever happened, Ned?"

"Why don't you stand pat and defy them, now that you're so much in command of things?"

"Too unpredictable. I'd rather not meet Uncle David face to face just yet. Besides, it's more fun this way."

"And you've got plenty of money since Reno? Pounce still holds a lot for you, you know."

"Sure, plenty of it. Although I discovered that waggles aren't free. There goes my call—I'm over at the Oakland airport. Say hello to Pounce. I'll be in touch. Say, Ned, would you like to go to Europe?"

"Love to. Been thinking about it."

"Let's plan on it. Maybe in a couple of months. So long."

"Bye-bye." We both hung up.

I summed up his side of the conversation to Pounce. "It's just a little boring," I said, lying down in the draft again. "It has the great limitation of all crude incident—it doesn't hold one's interest."

"It holds mine," Pounce said.

"I'm glad of that, little Pouncelet," I said wearily. "Now what about dinner?"

But my cool, black-browed Pounce was crisp from spending the day in air conditioning. "Didn't you write to him yesterday?" she persisted. "Well, then, maybe if they have found him they'll get his incoming mail, and then just maybe they'll find out that you have known all along where he was. And maybe that'll have a few tiny repercussions."

"Maybe," I said. "And then again, maybe not."

Pounce had a certain trait, caused by the fact that her mind worked slowly over a subject, turning it around to be viewed from all sides, testing it, before coming to conclusions about it. Her trait was to break off a conversation, if she met opposition, in order to have her chance to counter it after having her chance to think. She assumed that her opponent was worrying the subject in the same way, so she would suddenly take the conversation up where it had been dropped hours earlier, without any reference. That is what she did that night, after serving me a delectable and refreshing *salade niçoise* followed by an adequate cheese and an excellent *crème renversée*, after the dishes, and after a half hour of television, a documentary about a national park in Africa. I was getting lions from all sides that summer.

"Anyway, we'll soon know, won't we, which one of us is right," she said, turning off the Eye and settling down on her campstool, a glass of iced coffee held in both hands. Her heavy silver rings glinted barbarically in the dim light of the darkened studio, her brows made a straight line above her shadowy and hostile eyes. How beautiful she was!

I knew from her look and her voice that she had shifted ground, that she was now attacking me. "How will we know?" I said warily.

"By consequences, as I already pointed out."

"Yes, that may be true." I leaned forward and touched her right hand. "But I don't care. Let's forget about it."

"How can you just forget it? Or the way you treated Neal and how you're treating him now. You weren't nice over the phone, you know. You could have been talking to an insurance salesman."

"He was too excited to notice." I sighed. From would-I-get-caught to how-I-treated-Neal. The conversation was taking off in that illogical way one sometimes will, in which unrelated things are brought into a false relationship of sequence. "Look, a little cold water was in order. I talked to him, you didn't. Pride—he's suffering from pride, now. He thinks he's invulnerable, just because he's survived a few bizarre experiences. Also, he wants attention."

"Attention?"

"Sure. He was getting it before, in the form of advice. Now he wants to get it by playing up his danger. It's just a little boring, as I said. Like phony suicide attempts."

"You don't want to admit one other possibility, do you, Mr. Svengali?"

"And that, lambie pie?"

"The possibility that Neal isn't quite the same. That he's managed to get himself on his feet again. I've been thinking about his last letter. That's how it rings to me."

"Bull," I snapped. "People don't get on their feet again. I don't believe in Hollywood endings."

She thought a minute. "Why are you so angry at him?"

"I'm not. But you tell me why you think I am."

She shook her head. "No, I won't guess about that. I'm more interested right now in why you can't concede that he might change—get better."

This time I was careful with my answer, because she was striking tangentially at my affair with her. I answered as honestly as I dared. "Because I think it's illogical, in the first place. In the second, I suppose I don't want him to change like that and get better. It's my mean streak, which is gratified by the knowledge that he's not well off, my envious mean streak that feels that if he's not well off, then I'm better off. I've never denied my mean streak. It's not really a big one. Keep 'em down, not too much, just a little."

"No. You are mean, but that's not it. You're angry because he sounds so independent. You want him to continue to depend on you. You want a slave."

"You're wrong," I insisted. "It *is* my mean streak." I moved forward and knelt down and put my head in her lap, like a love-hungry child, and pulled one of her hands loose from her glass so that she could stroke my hair with it. "Are we going to argue?" I asked. "I will if you want to, but I still have a hangover. I'd rather not."

"No. We won't argue tonight." Although I couldn't see her, the shake of her head was transmitted to me through her body. "Tomorrow, maybe, but not tonight."

7.

Pounce and I did argue quite a lot. I suppose it was the price we had to pay, each of us, for the alternate mode of tenderness. There was much of that, too, but I can't pretend that ours was a thornless affair. It was very prickly, nearer cactus than rose.

But we were greatly in love, I think, as love goes in our location and our generation. Perhaps it was not the love of Anna Karenina or even of Swann, but it was the love Pounce and I could feel, hence, from our points of view, it approached the classic emotion.

I know that people wondered what she saw in me. Who knows? Who can ever explain that? There were some obvious areas of harmony—photography, gin, bitterness, a willingness to fight, good sex. But beyond that, why would she, so beautiful and independent, choose me—broke, not handsome, hard to get along with, demanding, already showing real characterological quirks? (I admit them.) Maybe the way I sat on a chair, one long leg crossed awkwardly, recalled a first crush and was enough to open the doors to her deepest feelings. I know that I loved her because she was elusive and delicate, yet uncrushable. You never just glided over her; you could always get foothold in Pounce. I also liked her because she was black-haired and heavy-browed (my type), and—well, obviously there must have been an X factor with me, too.

Now I wanted to live with her. She didn't want to get married, so I was willing to settle for far less, less even than the same apartment, if she would agree to be my mistress, give me her key and certain official rights. I wanted to know that she was mine every afternoon at five o'clock if I wanted her to be, just the thing I wasn't sure of when I first fell in love with her. Is it any wonder that we had so many fights?

But they don't matter, as I look back. In between, we loved each other. And in between, I dazzled her, too, with my imagination and insolence. Oh, there were reasons both ways for our love.

She had promised to go away with me for the two weeks

ending on Labor Day, and we left on the Saturday morning following my long-distance telephone conversation with Neal. Nothing had happened by then—no consequences—and I had hardly thought about it, I was so sure nothing would, until the next pitch Neal made for concern and attention. Pounce and I were going up to the big woods, where there was a resort on a lake someone had told us about, and where we planned to do some experimenting with a new camera Pounce had just bought. And, incidentally, some experimenting with life in common—same quarters, same schedules, same Pounce, same Ned. The place was called Sacagawea Lodge, although that benevolent redskin had surely never come within a thousand miles of it. I can't really say it was a find, a little bit of heaven in the murmuring pines and the hemlocks. It consisted of a central building of one story and no style, furnished with a few odds and ends of Bunyaniana. The food was right out of the freezer, via the stove, of course, for the length of time suggested by a certain ubiquitous cookbook which I dare not mention by name, but which when given as a wedding gift surely plants the seed of later divorce. Grouped dismally about this mother house were a number of ramshackle *dé-pendances*, each with its screened-in porch commanding some sort of view of the lake. Ours was one of the better ones, being on the perimeter of the bacterial cluster, sheltered from prying. It was what we expected, and it was what I could pay for—the vacation was on me—although it was not precisely what we might have wanted. It was there, at Sacagawea Lodge, that Pounce and I spent what was, after all, our only honeymoon.

Our main project for those two weeks was to work on a short film, to run about ten minutes. We called it *Obstacles*. It was a good idea and, I think, a good title. *Obstacles*. Very evocative. Filled with associations, without suggesting any kind of a narrative or didactic program. That was just what I wanted to avoid, for we had no message, no story, no educational or informative purpose at all. What we wanted—I may as well say what *I* wanted, for I was supplying the creative idea—was to represent the state of being frustrated, baffled, the confrontation of a desire and an opposing factor. I wanted to represent through moving, changing visual images, put into a careful succession, the feelings and meanings of an abstract noun. Let me describe a sampling of motifs.

The background to the title and credits was done in Pounce's studio, since it was the kind of thing one wouldn't want anyone accidentally to see, lest it be reported to the S.P.C.A. We bought a little bird, some kind of finch, and I tied its legs with a glittering silver thread, then frightened it. That was all that was on the screen for forty-five seconds, just that image of terror snared. A shorter sequence would have shocked, probably aroused pity, but after half a minute these reactions couldn't be sustained, and the image became oddly obsessive, total, abstract—if I were trying for an analogy, I would liken it to experiencing the nightmare of someone you didn't know. The frenzied bird was constant, but we varied the lighting, so that now there were shadows, now full light, now a dark profile, now clear. Only once did I allow it to settle, exhausted, for a moment, then off it had to go again, trying, trying, trying to escape the threatening mop. (That was what I used to frighten it, although of course the mop never appeared on film.) Then the printing appeared with the bird as background, and the spell was broken. It was extremely effective. Even Pounce admitted that, although the "cruelty" of it angered her, and she gave the finch away immediately, saying she couldn't bear to have it around.

Natural obstacles alternated with artificial ones, dumb creatures with humans. There were scenes of my hands trying to open cans, work loose screws, raise a stuck window. (The best of this sort of thing was where I tried to work a damaged zipper on my trousers.) Then there was the hooked sunfish, struggling at the surface of the lake, never pulled out, never allowed to sound, and later a larger fish—I think it was a bass —thrown onto the dock, flopping in the blazing sun; but each time it would approach the edge, from which it might fall back into the cool water, a foot (mine) would come forward and push it back onto center stage. We stayed away from all inherently repellent or dangerous creatures, like snakes, spiders, or wasps, because it was not fear that we wanted to arouse, but an empathy with frustration, a feeling of not being able, of meeting arbitrary, unexpected, and exasperating opposition. *Obstacles.*

I marvel, as I think back, on how good Pounce was at what we were doing, and at her concentration. The closing shots were extraordinary. They showed ants trying to move through a jungle of grass, black ants, the kind which always hurry. I added obstacles—a twig, a leaf, a stone or two. Unseen, I goaded them with straws and with a lighted cigarette. First, one came on the screen, then more, and more and more, until finally, for the climax to the film, we managed to have about thirty of them at once, all scrambling frantically in every direction. Then, to close it, I took a bucket of water and washed clean the camera's field. First, obstacles, then oblivion. If there was any content, that was it, and I was never quite sure that I hadn't done artistic violence to my film by ending it that way. Well, no point in regrets now.

We shot the ants out in the woods, and when we had finished I put an arm around Pounce's shoulders. I hugged her, triumphantly. I was well satisfied. "Perfect," I said. "Just perfect. Will it come out?"

She loosened my arm and began to pack her equipment. "I think so."

"Lively and lovely," I said.

"Why did you want to flood them like that?"

I felt thorns, but I was too set up to care. That was the way it was with us—just when I was feeling most set up, we would have trouble. Whistling, I picked up the bucket and my sweater—a birthday present from Pounce—which I had thrown to one side, and brushed some relations of our recent cast from it. It didn't matter what Pounce was feeling. I said: "Let's go back to the cabin and celebrate with Martinis before lunch. We've already done a good day's work."

She led the way along the path we had taken out, her eyes on the ground, while I kept on chattering about how well we worked together, etc. I put on the finishing touch while stirring up the drinks. "I wish I knew where we could get some money so that we could stop everything and work together like this all the time. I'd supply the ideas, and you could do the photography. I tell you, we'd be a really great team then." I clapped her shoulder. "We already are, Pounce."

She sat down on a plastic hassock on the porch, pulled off the visor cap she wore out in the sun and tossed it into a corner. "No we aren't," she said. "We aren't a team at all. I don't know what we're doing half the time. I just take orders. We aren't a team, we're a military outfit."

"Somebody on every team has to make decisions," I said. "But carrying them out is just as important, sometimes even harder." I raised my glass. "Here's to us."

She refused to look at me or return my toast. She shook her dark head stubbornly and stared out through the screens at the calm lake and the low, undistinguished opposite shore line with its sprinkling of private cottages. "We aren't a team," she repeated, "if I don't understand what we're doing."

"What don't you understand about *Obstacles*?" I didn't like this turn of things. Personal antagonisms were manageable, but professional difficulties might jeopardize all my plans.

She slowly raised and lowered her shoulders. "My mind is too conventional. I don't understand what is so wonderful about it. I can't feel the layers of beauty in it you talk about."

"I think I said 'beautiful juxtapositions,'" I corrected, "Not layers."

137

"Oh, and I don't understand the cruelty, for instance. Now it seems to me that the whole thing is that way."

"Not really," I argued. "Not *really*. And what if it were? Think of the bullfight. Sometimes art has to be cruel."

"That may be. You may be right. You're the artist, and I'm only the artisan. I'm the one who takes orders. I can see the cruelty, but I can't believe in its justification. I can only take orders."

"I thought you were enjoying this. You've been happy. Haven't we had a good time?" I asked.

"I've liked it, but I haven't. I've been fascinated, pulled along into it, like being dragged into deep water by someone you want to be with. You'll never understand." She held out her glass for some watery Martini from the pitcher. More subdued, she said, "I guess I like being ordered around by you, but at the same time I don't. It's that simple."

Suddenly I got angry. "Shut up," I said harshly. I turn red when I'm angry, and my mouth waters, so that I have to swallow frequently. "I don't want to hear any more. If I'm giving orders, and you're taking them, I'm giving you one right now. We're happy, and we're a good team, and we're going to stay that way and work together that way, and you can damn well curb your instinct to destroy. And that is that."

She stared at me a long time, more a process of memorization than of examination. Then she looked away and nodded. "All right. Only we really have to take the afternoon off."

It was our last weekend, and we had plenty of footage; so we napped, we read, we ate, we slept. Then the next day it rained, and we had to go into the neighboring town for some antacid pills—that awful food!—and I had her bring along her camera, because it occurred to me that we might get some amusing shots of the functioning of that most redoubtable obstacle in any summer resort—bad weather. She didn't want to, she was fed up with obstacles, but she did as I told her. And we got some pictures of people standing out of the rain, boats for rent in the rain, everything dreary in the rain; but they didn't go with the film, and we didn't use them.

As we drove into the parking place by our cottage, Pounce said, "You won't ever understand that I'm neither like you nor just a photographer. I can't help but continue to work with you now. I'm charmed. I'll follow you for a while. But don't forget that I like to be independent and do what I can understand and what I can invent, too. And that's why one day when you tell me to do something, I'll walk off and never see you again." Suddenly she smiled, in her barely amused way. "I'm keeping that privilege in reserve, you see."

I was content. The possibility lay far, far away. It was finite, I knew, but it was distant. And, for the time, I had Pounce more firmly than ever before, for what she had just said was, for her, something of a surrender.

8.

As it turned out, they did intercept my letter to Neal, and they also found others in his hotel room. David Wallace went at once to the university authorities, and, as Pounce had prophesied, there were repercussions.

I had several sessions with my employers, which I will not describe, since they are peripheral to my purpose, although they might go well in some other book, revealing, as they did, rather a lot about administrative operations. The upshot of the interviews was that I was fired, but since I had a contract to run through the academic year, and since I was able to convince them that I would make as much nasty publicity as I could if they tried to break it, they agreed to pay me out my salary, providing I would stop working at once. Need I say that their chief concern was to be able to tell a certain person that I was no longer on the staff? It was the best I could do, and I accepted, but I took my time clearing out my desk in order to bedevil my former overseer, Mr. Peebles, who had been included as a gloating if powerless bystander in the sessions I have mentioned. The official charge against me, amusingly enough, was insubordination. To whom? The Treasurer?

The next problem was to decide what I should do. Another library job was pretty well out of the question. I might have been able to blackmail a token letter of recommendation out of Peebles, but no power on earth could prevent the operation of the grapevine. No, there would not be another library job for me in some time; perhaps there never would be, in fact. With a tepid letter from my only employer it would be difficult to get any job whatsoever. I looked into government service, the possibility of additional graduate work to equip me for some new profession, innumerable other things, but there was always something wrong with them. Basically I guess I didn't want another job. I wanted my freedom for a while, and there was Pounce to stay near to, too. She and I spilled a lot of gin over my problem, until I got the post-card of the Ingres Odalisque in the Louvre from good old Ahmed Bidault, my friend from those days in Erotica, once more repeating his invitation to visit him, and, in a later mail, a note from him. He had my letter by then, telling him the news of my fall; and since I was uncommitted now, I *must* come to Paris, he wrote. That night I asked Pounce if she would go there with me, and she said she would. So in ten seconds we had solved my puzzle.

It was then near the end of October.

On the first day of November—how well I remember it— word reached me through my old boss, Peebles, the despicable Anti-Salacian, that David Wallace was coming through town and wanted to see me. I agreed. Why, one might ask, did I want to see him, since it could only be humiliating? Because I figured that he would not have asked to see me if he still thought he would find Neal. Neal was well away, so he had to turn to me. My humiliation would be greased by David Wallace's disappointment.

Six months of frustration and worry had nibbled away some of his assurance, to say nothing of his health. He looked older than the first time I had met him, more stooped, less quick in thought and action. I told him when we met—neither of us offered to shake hands—that he wasn't looking at all well, and before he thought to defend himself against my malice, the nagging preoccupations of the ill betrayed him into a reply. He hadn't been well, he said. He had had one or two little strokes.

"Yours would seem a bad city for heart cases," I purred.

He looked surprised, then recovered himself and turned to stone. He led me to a quiet corner of the lounge of the local hotel, where he sat, small, in a great overstuffed chair, one hand resting on an arm, the other hidden—I think it might have been a little affected by one of those strokes and he didn't want me to notice.

"You are a callous and inaccessible man, Mr. Bates," he said. "I don't know whether I should threaten you or plead with you."

"About what?" My guess, then, was right.

"We haven't found Neal. I will admit now that I don't think we ever will, necessarily. And it is possible that there isn't much time. His mother has not recovered as we had hoped she would. And I am quite unwell, as I have already said." His thin fingers gathered into a claw. "You did a heartless thing in helping him to escape, then encouraging him to stay away. You had no right."

"Nonsense. I had every right. I obeyed the demands of friendship, and I might say that I have paid for that generosity."

He smiled. "Generosity—an odd word. Friendship—even odder. How could you call it friendship? You forget. I have read some of your letters to him. They are full of contempt, amusement at his expense, condescension—but friendship? I hardly think so."

"Friendship now takes forms never dreamed of by Walter Scott or Rudyard Kipling," I said. "And anyway, I didn't, as you know, try to keep him away," I reminded him. "I suggested once that he come home. I forwarded his mother's letter to him. I didn't force him to stay in hiding, after all; I merely refused to betray him."

"Without you, he wouldn't have gone. His running away was his first real act of overt insanity. He was safe when I let him go back to that rooming house—I know him—but then he met you there, and it was you who helped him cross the boundary. It was you who made him run off. What has happened is your doing." Mr. Wallace grew very shrill as he spoke.

I shrugged my shoulders modestly. Even I had never thought of it in quite such terms. "You overstate," I said.

He shook his head. "No. If I had kept Neal with me, I would have had my way. You got to him, and you have had yours, and so he is probably mad. If I had been able to find him, I still would have succeeded. I mean in San Francisco. That I can't blame on you, not finding him, but I blame you that I had to look at all."

"What could you have done if you'd found him?" I taunted. "He was terrified you would, so terrified that at one point he locked himself in a pay toilet and wept—that's how much he loved *you*, Mr. Wallace. But could you have made him come home? Did you really have any legal leg? Could you have had your way?"

"Of course."

"How?"

"How? You are such a . . . such a third-rate Mephistopheles, Mr. Bates, to have been such a troublesome one."

I flushed. "And you are such a weak old devil, Mr. Wallace, for all your power."

"Do you have his letters to you?"

Instinctively I lied. "No. I destroyed them."

"Where is he now, Mr. Bates?"

"I don't know."

"I don't believe you."

"But it's true."

"You will have trouble getting another job, as you surely know. I can see to it that you do. On the other hand, if you care to co-operate, almost anything would be possible."

"Bribery, Mr. Wallace?" I asked, smiling.

"Why not? I should have offered you money before."

"Yes, you should have. Because if you had, then, at least, you wouldn't be gnawed at by that word *if*. *If* you had offered to bribe me, would you have Neal back now? You would know the answer, whether it was yes or no. That would be worth something, Mr. Wallace, would it not?"

His visible hand closed, then relaxed. He noticed my watching it, and withdrew it into his lap. "That is in the past. I am offering to bribe you now."

"And now it is too late. Perhaps, if I knew where he was now, I might accept your bribe. Perhaps not. But I don't know."

"That is final?"

"That is final."

He stared at the knot in my necktie. "Leave me, Mr. Bates," he said softly. "Leave me now." Only, in the end, he didn't dare maintain his hauteur. He called me back. "Wait. Just remember, should you change your mind, I have made an offer."

I bowed, then turned and left him sitting in his chair, for all the world as if he could never leave it. I couldn't resist one additional bit of cheek. I met the waiter at the door—they served drinks in the lounge where we had been sitting—and sent Mr. Wallace a whisky and soda with my compliments. I was well sacked, no doubt about that, but I had had my modest revenge.

Pounce and I went on with our plans for Europe. She couldn't leave, for family reasons, until after the first of the year. She took me to her uncle's place for Christmas, which was spent listening to how all his investments on the stock market, "with a very few exceptions," were going badly, which meant, she said, that he was richer than ever. Afterward I went to spend a few days with my only living relative, a sister named Isabelle who lived with her husband in Cincinnati. Then Pounce returned to close her studio, which she was keeping while she was abroad in spite of the extravagance, and I went on to await her in New York. It was while we were separated that we finally heard again from Neal.

The night before she was to leave to come to New York, Neal telephoned. We were to fly on the twenty-eighth of January, so this must have been about the twenty-second or twenty-third. He was in New Jersey, for some reason, but he refused to call me in New York after Pounce told him of the interception of my letters and of my being fired, perhaps because he felt I was too dangerous. He found out all about our plans before he hung up, then called her back to say that he thought he'd come with us. She asked about a passport. He had one. What about a ticket, space? He didn't think there would be any trouble. He wouldn't try to be on our flight, but would see us on the other side. Pounce gave him our future address.

The day finally came when Pounce and I were to board our transatlantic plane. The very afternoon we were to leave I made an interesting discovery. I had passed the newsstand in Times Square where every imaginable out-of-town newspaper is sold, and, as a joke, had picked up three or four back copies of Neal's home-town paper—it was called the *Journal* and belonged to guess who—which I was going to give to him as a little present. I took them with me to Pounce's hotel room, where I went to pick her up to take her to the terminal. June Bliss was there helping her pack—trust Pounce. June, who had spent the fall at the university, where we had seen her a couple of times for dinner, had been awarded her fellowship for the spring term, and was leaving for France herself in a couple of days, but she had to go by ship. I sat down to watch, and Pounce handed me an envelope with a short message inside, addressed to her.

"Going on a day ahead. See you there. N."

"Well," I said. "We're going to have quite a party."

"Isn't it wonderful news?" June Bliss speaking, stars in those virginal eyes.

"Uh huh." I leafed through my journals while I waited. Suddenly my eye caught an article on one of the obituary pages. I asked for scissors.

Pounce was irritated. "They're already put in," she said. Pounce packed as one might solder together a high-fidelity amplifier—everything in its place. "What do you need them for?" She came over near me, to have a look at what I was going to clip.

But I didn't let her see it. "Never mind. A secret. But clip it I must." She gave in and got me her scissors, and I removed the article and put it in my billfold, for it was certainly one that would have made my little newspaper joke in the worst of taste. I tossed that issue away, and the others I took with me to the Old World. And what happened to them? In the excitement of landing at Le Bourget, I completely forgot them and left them on the plane; but the clipping, unfortunately, I kept with me.

 PART THREE

I

Paris! How can anybody write anything more about Americans in Paris? Yet there we were, and the Paris period of Bates and Brewster must be next on the agenda.

It was the first time I had been there, or anywhere outside North America, and I was fair overturned, I was (*bouleversé, mes chers concitoyens*), by initial impressions, by such things as the allure of the vermouth ads, the universal preoccupation with the most refined comfort, by my first glorious two-toned menu posted outside a significant restaurant, positively the thematic index to a gastronomic symphony, by all the sparkle and chic I saw everywhere around me.

Except for a bad quarter of an hour when we first arrived in the city, everything went wonderfully well. Ahmed Bidault had written that he would meet us at the *aérogare* in town rather than way out at the airport, but when we got there, we found no Ahmed. I posted Pounce as the gorgeous guardian of our luggage and went to search the nooks and crannies of the place, almost certain, so strange I felt just then, that there had been a mix-up of days or of weeks or of the year, or that Ahmed had had a change of heart and was going to disappear from under us—some catastrophe, large or small. I might have guessed what had happened, and the instant I saw him everything explained itself. He was following a woman.

Ahmed was rather short but quite muscular and trim, and in fact was short only because his legs were short in comparison with his torso—an oriental kind of proportioning, I always suspected. His skin was pale and milky, his eyes and hair jet black. It was the eyes that most betrayed the halfcaste, aside from his name. They were gazelle-like, the eyes of some beauty in a Mogul miniature, liquid, expressive, mel-

149

ancholy, and, above all, profoundly sensual. When I saw him he was pretending to a great interest in a display of perfumes in a case set up to catch the tourist, but he didn't fool me. I stopped and watched the sideways looks, the rubbing of the chin, and all the rest of the courtship dance he was going through for the thin, pretty little girl, rather tan (pancake or Nice?), with pale-blond hair. He became more bold. His head tilted, a smile, sad and tender, came upon his face, his great eyes melted. It was, in American terms, a little absurd, for he was about forty-five, and she a good twenty-five years younger; but this was Europe. Even as I watched, he dared to speak. She answered. He said something more. She replied, smiling, preening in the glass of the showcase. More talk. Engrossed, I moved nearer. Then apparently he discovered something he didn't like—a husband, a mother, a departing flight somewhere?—for he shrugged, and she moved away. And then, only then, that fickle Ahmed looked at his watch, an expression of dismay came on his face, and he started off to where the buses disembark their passengers.

I called to him. "Well," I said. "What a rascal you are. So young."

"But so blond."

"Will you meet again?"

"Never. Alas, when it is a question of a girl so much the color, the style, the everything which one likes, it so rarely works out."

"Sometimes it does," I said smugly.

We went to get Pounce, whom Ahmed, of course, knew. Then he took us to his apartment and set us up in our room. We were invited to stay with him, luckily, for my funds were slim. As soon as we had unpacked, he took us out to a sublime lunch at a place on the river, down across from the Ile de la Cité, then drove us about for a little sight-seeing. It was winter, so the city was at its most characteristic—gray, romantic, beautiful, and we didn't go back to his apartment until the lights had come on, Paris at night, for night settles in early there in January. We rested, and then his own servants prepared us a magnificent dinner. I knew that I had found my spiritual home when I tasted that *soufflé au gingembre duraquoise.*

We spent the next several days the same way—eating, looking around, getting reacquainted. The third night we were there, Ahmed and I had a chance for a good talk after Pounce went to bed. I told him that I hoped to be out of library work forever, even erotica, and that I planned to try to do some films, that Pounce and I had done one good one already. I described *Obstacles* to him.

"Of course, it's a question of money," I said. "But as long as ours holds out, in any case, I'll keep at it. It's a big help having you let us stay here, you know, Ahmed." The remark was just a tiny bit unfair, I know, in that it was tantamount to putting my own lock on his door—in addition to all the ones already there (one of the peculiarities about his apartment I'll describe later)—but I had to take precautions.

"What you should do, Ned, is a film on love," he said.

I smiled and replied that I didn't have the idea for one, and that pornographic films were aimed toward a different goal than the work I hoped to do with Pounce was.

He argued. "And your snared bird? Your trapped insects? These were not pornographic?"

"Perhaps, in the most general sense, there is an elusive element of that in *Obstacles.* But true pornography has to be crassly literary, after all—start with a situation and see it through. Or at least illustrative. It is reportorial, descriptive, not formally beautiful."

"That is the challenge—to make pornography also beautiful, not merely stimulating. To excite all the senses at once. That might be worth trying."

"Well, yes, I admit that it might." I didn't want to be too intransigent with Ahmed my third night under his roof.

"Mere copulation—what animals do—is not necessarily beautiful, that I admit, Ned. But when it is transfigured by imagination . . . Once, in North Africa, I saw an exhibition of love-making between a hideous Negro and a crippled Algerian girl, very expensive. They had a specialty: slow motion. It was all slow motion, like a film in slow motion. Imagine it. Everything, everything from the first kiss onward. Perhaps that was why it cost so much—it took twice as long. It was something to see, Ned, very, very beautiful. It was one of the most romantic days of my life, that." His delicate hands waved in the air like palm fronds. "You must make a movie on love, Ned. And in it you will put many pale blond women with little teeth, to please me."

"*Tenez*," I said. "*Alors.*"

"Like that first day."

"I remember."

Then our conversation veered away from films and pornography. He discussed himself a little, but left so much out that at the end he was still a man of almost complete mystery, and I knew nothing, really, about his origins, his life, or his business, except that they would not bear daylight. Before we separated I brought up the subject of the film again, for in the interval I had had a chance to think.

"A film. A pornographic film, but not all the usual fifteen-positions stuff. A beautiful one. That might indeed be a challenge, Ahmed," I said.

Something in my voice made him careful. "I should think," he said.

I puffed cigarette smoke out in clouds, the very picture of the artist at work on ideas. "Of course, one would need models, special places to work, safeguards against police interference. It would be very expensive. One of the problems would be to find backing, financial backing, for such a film," I hinted.

"I dare say."

I let a little time pass. "A scene in slow motion—one might work that in," I mused.

More time passed. "Have you heard from your friend yet?" Ahmed asked.

"What friend?" I said, close to being cross.

"The one who came a day ahead of you?"

"Oh, him. No, not yet. Now I was just going to say, about that film . . ."

Ahmed yawned and put down his glass, now emptied of orange juice, which was about all he ever drank after dinner. "Could he have been in an airplane accident?"

"Of course not. We would have read about it. I can visualize, right off the cuff, some pretty interesting . . ."

He interrupted. "I am tired now. Some other time, Ned, we will talk about it and exchange ideas."

"Fine. Fine, Ahmed." It wasn't ideas I wanted from him, as he well knew. He hadn't taken the bait, but neither had he turned his back on it. I didn't give up hope.

2.

After a week had gone by and we still hadn't heard from Neal, I did begin to worry. I wondered if I should do something—go to the police or to the American Embassy. Could it be an accident, after all, I wondered, or amnesia, or was he lying dead, his wrists slashed, the gas on, a pill bottle under the bed? I watched for him while we were sight-seeing, hoping for a chance encounter, but none occurred. After almost another week had gone by, I did check discreetly with the Embassy, and I visited some of the more obvious hotels and described him, saying that I had met him on a ship and had lost his name and wanted to repay a small loan. I thought the mention of money would arouse sufficient interest in those French concierges for them to remember my inquiry if they ever saw him. Then, finally, just as I was really ready for the police, there was a note for me in the last mail one afternoon. I was to come to the Hôtel de Carthage et Edimbourg the next afternoon. The hiding was over; *homo transfiguratus Brewster* was about to appear.

Yes, Brewster Resurrectus, that flamboyant species, must now be displayed to a host of devoted believers. The magnificent Brewster, transformed from the slimy creature of so many pages ago into a talking frog, from a tufted caterpillar on a leaf into the Lepidopteral Hero. Omnicompetent, great in love, mighty in the arts of war and peace, unparalleled peacock of soul and body, insufficiently laced up in common sense, perhaps, but otherwise immaculate. How inadequate must one feel for his unavoidable biographical duty. I draw back from my task.

What irony! I created him (David Wallace said so), but I recoil from the creature. Yet another proof of what should be, whether it is or not, an old adage, namely, that it is easier to do something than to understand what you have done.

The Carthage et Edimbourg was a small hotel on one of the side streets not far from the Deux Magots and the Flore, and specialized in semipermanent residents, mostly fairly young, who were spending part of a wanderyear in Paris. One felt that much frolic went on there, and that many an amorous foot had trod those ill-ventilated stairs; later, when I checked the impression, I found it was accurate. The patroness of the place told me, with a sparkle in her eye, that Neal was on the fourth floor, French style, *"Ce beau Monsieur Brewster,"* she added appreciatively, and I wondered if she, upon occasion, indulged in frolic herself. I paused, prepared to hazard an indiscretion—my French was improving fast—but thought better of it.

I was, of course, aquiver with curiosity to see Neal again and find out what in the world had delayed his getting in touch. I had had fantasies of how this meeting would go, and had decided that a certain hauteur on my part would not be inappropriate, for after all, no matter what had been going on, he could at least have sent me a *pneu*. But all control of the scene was taken out of my hands the moment the door opened.

There he was, after all this time and all these events, the man who had cost me my job. And how had he prepared for our momentous meeting? Was he in sackcloth, ready to bathe my feet in gratitude? Did he kneel to kiss my ring (Williams, Class of '45)? Not at all. He was in circus costume. He was dressed up in tights and a bright-blue jacket. He had on twirling false mustaches and a false Vandyke, and he carried a large whip. Nor was that all. Perched on his night table, hanging on the headboard of the bed, sitting on his desk blotter and on the icy radiator, were four stuffed lions. The reference was unmistakable.

"Welcome, Monsieur Bates," he said, with a flourish of the whip, bowing low. "Welcome, welcome. Come in and let's get drunk." There was a bottle of cognac on his dresser.

"Good God," I said, then I burst out laughing. It was all too preposterous, a bad joke, but one that a person had to laugh at. I looked at him closely. "You're all right, Neal?" I asked.

"I'm perfect. Perfectly perfect."

"Well, where have you been? What's been going on?" I asked, my irritation unfolding, a nettly flower of the mind.

"Life is mysterious," he replied, currying a mustache until it fell off. He reached down, retrieved the missing whisker, and replaced it.

"Where have you been?" I repeated.

"You ought to know the answer to that," he said, apparently puzzled by my tone of voice. "I've been making the acquaintance of a new place."

"Why didn't you get in touch sooner?"

"I wasn't ready."

"We've been worried to death." I was getting quite angry now. "We almost went to the police."

"Worried? Why?"

"How was I supposed to know? I imagined all sorts of things."

He poured some cognac into two tumblers and held one out to me. "It is possible that something unpleasant might have befallen the old Brewster person, but the new one is invulnerable. Here."

"I don't want it."

"Oh, come on, Ned," he said. "I didn't mean to worry you. It never occurred to me, I suppose because I was doing such interesting things. And you were seeing Paris for the first time with Pounce. Why would I bother you sooner?"

"What things?" I asked, taking the glass of brandy, prepared, having made my point, to be brought around. "Fill me in."

He shook his head. "No," he said, "I don't think I ought to do that. Let us just take life up again right now. As if we were just meeting."

"But we aren't just meeting."

He smiled and walked briskly up and down the small vacant space in the middle of his room, swinging his arms. He stopped and hit one palm smartly with the other fist. "Yes, we are. Yes, yes indeed, we are, Ned," he said.

I couldn't get any more out of him just then, but Pounce did when, a little later in the afternoon, I took him to meet her for tea, where we were joined by dear little J. Bliss. (Neal changed clothes before we went out—a lion in the streets of Paris might go unnoticed, but not a lion tamer.) We were meeting at one of the famous tea spots of Paris, but June was so thrilled by the appearance of her hero that she hardly touched the heavenly *religieuse* she had chosen from the pastry counter. Of course, I finished it off, rather than let it go to waste.

I said to Pounce: "He won't tell me where he's been all this time. He's not only irresponsible and inconsiderate, he's also secretive." I turned to Neal. "Tell us. Tell all of us all, right now."

He grinned and shook his head.

"Why should he?" Pounce growled. Neal-Ned . . . That combination seemed so often to set my sullen sweetheart asimmer.

I myself was having a pedestrian *baba*, and I poniarded a morsel of the airy stuff on my fork and held it in the air. "I assume when someone won't tell me something that he has something he had better hide. Now let us follow that through logically. If someone has something better off hidden, then that is precisely the something to interest someone like myself, student that I am of *la faiblesse humaine*." I popped the *baba* into my mouth, where I was pleased to discover it contained a piece of perfumed citron I hadn't known about.

June had to go off early to a reception given by the Cultural Attaché, and I had to go off to the w.c. at the same time. When I came back to the tiny wheel of gray marble that had served as our table, I found Pounce and Neal in deepest conversation.

"What were you talking about?" I asked suspiciously.

"Why do you ask every question as if an answer to it were your right?" Pounce demanded in return.

"You've been planning my murder."

"No. Neal was telling me what he wouldn't tell you. That was all."

"Well?" I looked from one to the other, resenting their intimacy ever so slightly. "Well?"

"He can read the journals, too, if he wants to," Neal said.

"What journals?"

"The ones I've kept since I got here. I'm giving them to Pounce to read. You can, too."

A half hour later, after stopping by Neal's hotel, we returned to Ahmed's carrying a sheaf of papers of various sizes and weights, from scraps to foolscap, all of them covered, erratically, with Neal's rambling writing. Ahmed was out for dinner that night—I do not know where, I cannot even imagine—and Pounce and I dined alone in his apartment, then went to bed rather early, where I read my Baudelaire and Pounce read the Brewster journals.

One of Pounce's friendliest traits, one of the ways in which she permitted herself conversationally to cuddle most cozily close to a companion, was this, that she loved to read snatches aloud from whatever she was reading, things that struck her, whether or not they would, thus excised, make much sense.

"That's interesting," she muttered, after we had both been in bed, each at his task, a few minutes. "I think I know what he means."

"Means about what?" I said absent-mindedly, forgetting how hard she was to stop once she had started.

"Listen to this." She began to read, and, after she had gone about halfway through a paragraph, I gave up trying to concentrate through it, sighed, and put my finger in my place.

". . . Finally I am the Outsider, not by habit, not by fear, not by any barrier built out of the self, but by Law. And by choice. And with wonder. I stare at the streets and people. I am outside. I am free to wonder. I am free to love. This is the first time for that. . . ."

Pounce turned to see how I reacted. My shrug was noncommittal. "I prefer Baudelaire," I said, and began to read.

" 'Mère des jeux latins et des voluptés grecques . . .' " I let silence fall between us, and read on to myself.

A little later Pounce interrupted again.

" 'Now I understand what the phrase *on the prowl* means. I am on the prowl.

" 'I prowl through rainy nights past deep doorways, into which I look for adventure. I prowl across squares—is that adventure over there? I prowl the mysterious streets, looking for adventure. Last night I prowled around the horse of Henry of Navarre, and I found adventure.

158

" 'Everywhere I prowl I look for adventure. There is adventure everywhere I look.' "

"Yes, but what kind of adventure? What does it all mean?" I said. "Give me particulars, vivid description, something I can get my teeth into. For instance . . .

"Lesbos, où les baisers sont comme les cascades
Qui se jettent sans peur dans les gouffres sans fonds . . ."

Squelched, for the moment, Pounce read on in silence. Then, "Huh," she said.

"Mmmm?" Why didn't I learn not to make a sound?

" 'I have thought for a long time that it might be true. I think it is. I have a counterpart, a double. Somewhere in the world there is another me. Everyone is a bimorph. One of each of us is in an Accustomed Place, grinding corn or weaving cloth or adding figures. The other is Elsewhere, doing Otherwise. One is having children or involved in representative government or reading books with happy endings. The other has bright eyes, like the eyes of a panther in the night.

" 'Do they work toward each other, through terrible ordeals?

" 'What happens if they achieve simultaneity. Boom? The whole world up in smoke? The end of all time?' "

"What bull," I said. "All fantasy. Pure literature. Adolescent twaddle. Corn. Neal isn't even like all that. When you come right down to it, he's pretty ordinary. Just a few quirks left."

"A hell of a lot you know about it."

"First you want him sane, now you want him crazy. Let me read."

A little later. "Do you want to hear Neal on women?"

"Not particularly, cabbage."

She read anyway. " 'The four most beautiful female images are the Saint Ann-Mona Lisa: Leonardo really had it. The

Winged Victory of Samothrace: because she has no head. Venus from Melos: look at the way the left leg comes forward. S.F. girl: I thought of her today as I left the museum. Who knows? Maybe my Doubleman saw her drinking in a coffeehouse or walking in Golden Gate Park. In my mind, she had her head turned to one side and there was sunlight behind her. She seemed very close to me."

"How gauche of him to have left out the greatest."

"Which is?"

"Stern dark brows, somber eyes, and a terrible habit of interrupting people when they're trying to concentrate. But I won't overlook her—" Then I read:

> "Car Lesbos entre tous m'a choisi sur la terre
> Pour chanter le secret de ses vierges en fleurs . . ."

"Go to hell," Pounce said. Then, unable to control herself, she began to read a long entry which had to do with the preservation of wonder. More of that sort of gushy stuff. It ended: "'No more programs. Exercises are for other people, who need them, not for me. The next time I see "The Embarkation for Cythera" it will be by accident. It will be because, passing it by, I notice it.'"

I waited until she had finished, then reached over and, gently, but oh how firmly, took Neal's journals out of her hand. In it I put the *Fleurs du Mal*. "Here, my precious. You are going to read this; I am going to read Brewster." Pounce stared at me a moment with those intimidating dark eyes of hers, but in those days I could face even my Puissant Pounce down, and I did so. She grunted, tossed the poetry off onto the floor, and squirmed down into the bedclothes to go to sleep. I joined her.

It fell to me to return the journals a day or two later, while Pounce was having a fitting for a new dress she was getting— and paying for herself. I went to Neal's hotel.

"Did you read them?" he asked.

"Of course. They didn't answer my questions about what you were doing."

"The questions they answer are more interesting. Now what about you, Ned?"

"What do you mean?"

"What that is really interesting has happened to you?"

"Should I really tell you? Are you free the rest of the day? Will you take notes to put in my biography when I'm famous?"

He nodded.

"By God, maybe I will." There was something about Neal during those days when we were in Paris together that made it possible to talk to him. *Sympathetic*, that doesn't say it. *Sympathique, simpático, seelenverwandt.* And I guess I must have had a lot corked up. I needed a chance to talk to somebody. I certainly did that day, talk, I mean, to Neal. I said everything, sitting in his dark and chilly little room, with its one French window covered by a dirty net curtain, its threadbare red rug, its battered furniture, Neal's dirty clothes in a corner, all those stuffed animals. I ran through my past, and I sketched in some of my plans for the future.

Neal said: "This is the point of absolute balance in your life, Ned. Everything behind you is closed; in front of you everything lies open. That's wonderful. It really is."

I could almost see it, the endless and beautiful Pacific Ocean of my future, as I stood on the top of a mountain, exhilarated. I talked on and on, and before I was through had said things I hadn't even known were in my mind. I told of obscure hopes, of how I thought I could do something really important if I had the time and the chance, and that a year or two in Paris might do it. That was only the beginning, crashing into the field of the avant-garde movie. There were the larger fields of experimental television—who had ever really understood what could be done there?—of the theater, new conceptions of the dance, even literature. My talk became pure loose ambition and longing. I projected for us a shadowy image of myself as the many-sided creator, I made us feel my potentialities that afternoon. It was a day when anything was permitted, when, if you will, Ned Bates had the courage to dream. Strange, isn't it, that I, usually so cautious, should have offered what I had never offered anyone before, not even Pounce?

Had Neal replied to me lengthily, talked too much, asked the wrong question, agreed too easily, I would have regretted my confidences, but he didn't. He found instead a rather perfect thing to say, once I had worn my mood out.

"It will be very hard, Ned."

And that about summed it up.

3.

I wanted to get going. I hadn't done anything since leaving the university, and I was restless. It's no wonder I got so irritable. There's nothing like frustration to bring out the beast in each of us. I investigated the cost of renting space, of equipment, models, props, of film and processing, and soon was convinced that the idea that things were cheaper in France was a total fallacy, and that if I were to have to do films on my own resources I would be restricted to an occasional dull travelogue, with Pounce the only pretty girl therein. A plan began to form in my mind, or, rather, not exactly a plan, but an association of ideas, the base for a plan, a gathering together of parts which I thought I could somehow build into a structure that would bear weight.

One possible difficulty lay with Neal. Although he didn't know it, I did, and I decided I had better bring him into my party, make him a member of the in-group, in an effort to neutralize his power. So one afternoon when I was talking to him, I gently introduced my subject.

"You know the man Pounce and I are staying with," I said. (Ahmed and Neal had not yet met.) "He's about middle age, but he has a taste for younger women, especially pale blonds."

Neal said they didn't suit him at all. We were in his hotel room again; I had formed the habit of dropping by there whenever I was in his neighborhood, for he was almost always at home in the late afternoon, always had a bottle of cognac, and I found it a relief to get away from the static life on the other bank. He was combing the false beard and mustaches he had on that first day—he had managed to get some tangles in them, I don't know how.

"Girls like June Bliss," I explained. "I've thought I might try to match them up."

"Good idea," he said, putting some spit on his thumb and forefinger and twirling the tip of one half of the mustaches. "Just what she needs. But isn't she too—undifferentiated?"

"You mean too much the schoolgirl?"

"Something like that."

I thought of Ahmed's panting performance at the *aérogare* that first day. "I don't think so," I said. "But the trouble is, June has a crush on you, Neal."

"Me?" He stopped to look at me. "I'd wear her out. My pace is too swift." He groomed the other side and held the whiskers up to look at them. "Do you ever have days when you walk around in an aura?"

"Not that I remember. What's that got to do with it?"

"With what?"

"June Bliss. We were talking about June Bliss."

"Not me. Not any more. I've got an aura today. I'm surprised you haven't noticed it. Squint and see."

"I can't. But is that why you didn't shave?"

He put his hand up and rubbed it over his face. "No. I forgot to. Nothing bothers me today. We could go outside and you could throw stones at me, and they wouldn't hurt."

"Mmm. Well, to return to June and Ahmed . . . Will you help me get them together? All you really have to do is to see that she doesn't get too fixed on you first."

"She'd be afraid of my aura." He picked up the beard. "Say, Ned, would you like to wear these for a while?"

I giggled. I dare to use that odious word for what I did. Remember, he always served me from the cognac bottle. "Should I? Should I?" I stood in front of his mirror and attached the mustaches and beard. "Now give me the whip," I said. I was converted from my usual amiable-looking self—however misleading it was, I did *look* amiable—into a completely different person, a hulking blond villain, an Anglo-Saxon Iago. I postured. I was quite pleased. Then, remembering my dignity, I removed the disguise. "That's enough of that," I said, as if Neal had been making fun of me. I finished what was left of my cognac and went away.

Ahmed overheard me telling Pounce about Brewster's aura and said he would like to meet a man who believed he was invulnerable. He remarked, in his gentle way, his large eyes, it seemed to me, suddenly rather sad, that he certainly could use such an aureole, and wished they were for sale at the Bon Marché.

"I suspect, Ahmed," I replied, "that they are sold in a different kind of institution entirely."

As if merely to please him, I arranged to take him and Neal to lunch, but I also arranged, without saying anything, to meet Pounce and June afterward, the reason for not having all to lunch together being that it was my party, and I saw no reason to be so extravagant when a later rendezvous with the girls would serve my purposes just as well. Ahmed and Neal got along, for Ahmed fell right in with Neal's fantasies. Not only did they discuss Neal's aura, but also his Doubleman, for that bit of mythology had now been incorporated into the Brewsterian daily life, and whenever he had a memory image, particularly one related to life back home, he claimed that his Doubleman had been out and around that day.

"Mine, I think, is probably dying somewhere," Ahmed said, quite seriously. "He dies somewhere every day. Have you thought what that might mean—a fatal accident to your Doubleman, leaving you partial?"

"I don't think that can happen. He disappears sometimes. You know, goes underground, or visits the dead, I don't know what all; but that's his business. I dare say there are days when he doesn't get much out of me, either."

"Are there days when you visit the dead?"

"Yes, there are still days like that."

There was a long pause while Ahmed lit his pipe. I called for the check, and noted that the really rather disappointing red had added a round $4.50 to it. "Why don't you come on with us, Ahmed?" I said. "We're meeting Pounce and another girl from home."

He said he had things to do.

"Just as you will." I turned to Neal. "I hope June's cold is better. She's had a bad cold ever since she got to Paris," I explained to Ahmed.

He clucked. "Too bad, too bad."

"But you know how it is with girls who are thin and delicate. And who have that very fair, Nordic coloring, translucent, like certain porcelains. . . ."

Ahmed was opening the door and stopped so that we could not pass through. "Fair? Translucent? Is that what you said, Ned?"

"Yes. Pity you're busy."

"I will take a moment. Yes, I will take the time to come with you, Ned."

Alas for the best-laid plans. June's cold not only wasn't better, but she was running a temperature and had had to stay home in bed that day; so only the robust Pounce was waiting for us. I don't know who was the more disappointed, Ahmed or I.

That infuriating June went and got a touch of pneumonia, and everything was held up while she recuperated. It wasn't serious, but she had to be careful. I kept her image shimmering before Ahmed by mentioning how large and bruise-blue the circles were under her eyes, how oddly tiny and pointed her little incisors looked when she took her pills, how her hair was just the color of the icing on some *petits fours* he had sent her from his table, anonymously. He began to get the idea, for whenever I would devote a bit of time to describing June to him, he, in return, would mention politely my own work, never committing himself to anything definite, but seeming to show that our two interests were somehow linked. That was the most I could do, and it was progress of one kind. Meanwhile, swallowing my choler, I watched progress of another.

It commonly happens that a love affair is weighted on one side, so much so that the goddess of love should be represented with a shoulder dragging in recognition of her frequent arrangements of imbalance. It may even seem, rarely, that there is absolutely no response from the beloved, that he or she is oblivious to the sighs and ocular caresses of the lover, that all efforts to please fail and efforts to call attention pass unnoticed. Look a little longer, Casual Observer. Go a little closer. There is something just ever so slightly up, is there not? Do we, in fact, ever find a true indifference, such as the indifference of the trellis for the morning-glory, or of the earth to the sea? Can mythology offer us such purity of rejection? Echo and Narcissus, Apollo and Daphne, Galatea and Polyphemus? I think not. Naturally, such affairs, chilled as they are by the draft of lopsidedness, do not come to a magnificent fruition, as did Pounce's and mine. They struggle in the darker corners in love's vast and sprawling compound, yet they may be very pretty in their minor way.

The watchful eye and keen ear of Ned Bates were unable to detect the means whereby Neal encouraged June Bliss in her hopeless love for him, yet I am convinced that somehow he did so. It was, perhaps, unconscious on his part; should we therefore absolve him from guilt? Indubitably not! He pretended to be true to what I considered his gentleman's agreement with me. He seemed neither pleased by her admiration and passion, nor watered by her tears, nor inflated by her sighs. He was nice to her, as if she had been the female of another species entirely, one completely without odor, beyond reciprocity—it was as if June had offered to drop him half a million eggs among the pebbles of a river bottom. Yet she loved; therefore he did *something*. Also, were I forced to speculate clinically, I would say that little Junelet had a wee neurosis. And she was sick and in Paris all alone, and I suppose her daddy had a cleft in his chin much like Neal's, and so on. June was a born dependent. Somebody will always have been taking her off his income tax one way or another, for that's the kind she was. And if the perceptive reader, antennae waving, has noticed that my sympathy for her has failed me at this particular point, he has noted aright.

June made Pounce her confidante, and told her all the little steps she took from the middle of nowhere toward its exit. She got over her pneumonia, but in its place she got the weepies, she couldn't sleep, she ate only to keep alive to yearn after Neal. I saw her pining myself—who could avoid it? According to Pounce, her tearful reflections always wound up on the note of Neal's indifference and the hopelessness of it all, that especially. It would seem that hopelessness was the whole point. Moreover, she wasn't getting any work done (this was the sub-theme). She was betraying her trust, scuttling her fellowship, gyping her foundation, because indifferent Neal appealed to her so much more than the Archives.

Unfortunately, the fact that she knew her love to be hopeless didn't really help me much, until something should happen, some withering—for please remember that I had my own plot to thicken. How could I introduce her to Ahmed while she still loved Neal? What was I to do? Time was passing. Bates grew older. Spring was on its way. As the days grew longer, my temper grew short.

One evening Neal, Pounce, and I were descending into the subway stop nearest June's lodgings after dropping her off— she lived in a furnished room in the apartment of the widow of a civil servant. I was trailing down the stairs when Neal happened to move in front of me, and we collided. I swore, and remarked that he was in my way all the time.

Pounce turned on me. She and Neal had become such good friends that I was very nearly jealous, and I'm still not sure they didn't . . . But why speculate, since I suppose I'll never know. Anyway, at the foot of the stairs Pounce slowed us all, her hands thrust belligerently into the pockets of her mackintosh, her black hair glistening with the mist it had collected outside. She looked like an angry movie star—what more can I say?

(Shall I answer that question? I can say this much more. I don't really believe what I just hinted at. I was never cuckolded by Neal and Pounce, and I know it; for Pounce still loved me then, and I put that in because when one becomes filled with doubt, there seems no reason to stop anywhere. But it isn't true, and one need not provide against every possible betrayal.)

She glared at me, afraid I might have hurt Neal's feelings, and said, "What brought that on?"

"He's interfering with my plans," I replied. "I haven't told you." That was true, for I didn't quite trust Pounce in this matter. "Now move on."

"What plans?" Pounce asked, sidling into the runway that led to the crone who would punch our tickets.

"Nothing important. It's just that June's the type Ahmed likes, and I want to get them together, and how can I when she's mooning and moaning over Brewster?"

"What a fantastic idea," Pounce said. "Why do that? And how? You still seem to think you can move people around the way you want to. What are you going to do, give them a love potion?"

"Do you believe in love potions, Pounce?" Neal asked. He stopped us in our tracks again, holding up several infuriated Parisians. "I've wondered about them. I wonder if they work in coffee, because I was drinking coffee when I fell in love with a girl in San Francisco."

The corner of Pounce's mouth twitched with amusement. "Why not? Ned finds one in every bottle of brandy, don't you, Ned?" Mostly at that time I made love to her only after quite a lot to drink, and she objected.

Because of their dawdling, we just missed a train and were barred by the automatic gate from running for it, so we had a long wait on the platform. Pounce returned to the attack.

"Do you really believe that all you have to do is bring them together?" she asked scornfully.

"When I choose to introduce them," I replied arrogantly, "they will fall in love. *Because I want them to*," I concluded, raising my voice to a shout, suddenly furious with her.

Pounce was never one to shy from a fight, not even when a circle of curious Parisians was around to see and hear. "And so you're going to arrange things, just so you can have the pleasure of watching what you want to happen, happen. It will amuse you. Ned Bates, puppeteer."

I ignored the usual warning voice. "I've got better reasons than that," I said darkly.

"But why blame me?" Neal asked.

169

"Look here," I said, "we've had this out already. But now I think it's time you stopped seeing her. That's the only way I can see to get her over this folly—and to prove your good faith."

"Wouldn't that be likely to hurt her?" he asked. "After all, there's June to think about, Ned, not just you."

I put the steel in. "Now listen," I said, turning, I am sure, red in the face with rage, gulping saliva, as is my exasperating habit, which interferes with effective speech at moments of crisis. "You don't want her. Well, you've got her anyway, and I want you to shake her off. Don't you feel that you may owe me that much?"

He was surprised. "*Owe* you?"

I looked at a poster on the wall behind him, an ad for mineral water from earth's purest spring. "It seems to me that without me you would not be here. You would probably be in a strait jacket somewhere. And I might point out that helping you cost me my job, and that your 'uncle' has told me I won't get another wherever he has any influence. I don't face an easy time. I can't give up and go back and knuckle down and become someone's protégé and be a millionaire. I don't have anything or anybody to fall back on. I've been ruined for your sake."

There was a long silence after that speech. Pounce flushed with embarrassment and turned away from us. Neal reflected. Finally he said, "That doesn't sound like you, Ned."

"You might just as well get used to it, both of you, because I'm going to sound more and more like that. Something really important is involved. All my plans. All my hopes. Let's be clean and sharp about it. Ahmed is the only person with a lot of money I know in all Europe—all the world. I'll spell it out: the way to his pocketbook is through his—well, let's say it's through his heart."

"And you really think that he'll give you money if you can get him June? I don't see why."

170

"Gratitude. Gratitude has its cash value, Brewster."

Pounce had listened to everything. She said to Neal: "It's not very pretty, is it?"

"How easy to be moral," I said, "if you have nothing to lose."

"I'll do what I can," Neal promised, thereby promising nothing.

"Thanks a lot."

"It's all wrong. Damn you both," Pounce said. And she got in a different car from the one we got in.

4.

This unrequited love, though it may seem to have got nowhere, certainly did not leave the psychology of my tale unchanged. If I may be sententious—and I sometimes think it is a failing of mine—I would say that often those events which seem to have the least results in the arena of official actions, such as assassination, the birth of an heir, or the fall of empire, may in fact have finally the greatest consequences. Ostensibly June's love for Neal and my opposition to it and Pounce's resentment seem to have been a mere aside; yet, as I look back, I feel that those weeks made a turning point in our story. None of us emerged quite the same. Let me be more explicit:

Neal: the least affected, I think, of any of us, partly because his own life suddenly took such a dramatic turn. Only, I had been drawn, at the subway station, into clarifying too much. He would never again be quite so innocent.

June: a catharsis was being prepared. And when it took place, Junelet was left with quite a bit of loose rancor toward all of us, especially, for some reason, me, which was to work its way through to the surface.

Pounce: she didn't seem so much changed. She was tired of staying with Ahmed and being obligated to him, and that feeling got stronger. She was even more skeptical about my ethics than before, and she seemed to develop a feeling which I find hard to define, a kind of feeling that what we did, she and I, didn't matter, because in her mind, now, she could see a limit to it. I profited from that feeling at first, for she would never have made some of the pictures I asked her to make had she not had it.

Ned: I sincerely believed that I was acting according to perfectly legitimate self-interest. I really couldn't see the reason for the change in the way Neal and Pounce treated me, as if they detected a certain slight mold on the charisma. My plan did both June and Ahmed a good turn—and even if it hadn't, what did June really matter to any of us?

One of Neal's remarks bothered me those days, I recall. It had the power to move me—I think everyone has experienced that. All sorts of remarks can pass right over one's head, twigs falling on an elephant, but some chance phrase, no more pointed or important than any other, will dig in and fester. That was the way I reacted to Neal's statement that I didn't sound like myself. What did it mean?

I traveled in my mind back to the old days on Mrs. Peters' third floor, and to myself then in comparison with myself now. What basis did he have to say such a thing, after all? He hadn't known me all that well. I knew him much better than he knew me. It seemed to me that we had had a kind of false friendship, as, in language schools, they speak of "false beginners." What did he know about how I ought to sound, he whom the outside world so seldom reached in those days?

Yet I had to admit that I sensed a difference between the two Neds I placed before my mind's eye for comparison. The second one, standing slightly to the right, a little older, with a bright pocket handkerchief that went well in Paris but wouldn't have gone under Mr. Peebles, was somewhat tenser, had taken to biting the cuticle of his fingers, was jumpier, less detached, more given to sudden angers than to irony, yes, downright irascible. Was all this such a bad thing, I had next to ask myself. No! was my answer. I had been feeling pressure lately, pushed and pulled by forces I could not quite make out. My life offered difficulties, both subjective and objective ones, and it was important to me to get my own way; for that was the only possible antidote. I did not feel surrounded with benign influences. Rather, there were reports from the frontiers of ill omens—a black albino, ravens gibbering in the streets, Siamese twins born to a Persian cat. But I was willing to fight, and the only way to get the things I wanted was for me to arrange for them to happen, to come true, to be realized. I intended to put up with no interference. I had Pounce and I would keep her. I had my liberty and intended to use it. I wanted money and time, and would get them. Woe to anyone who interfered. And yet, and yet, and yet . . . The one Ned regarded the other. Irony confronted irascibility. Too bad.

I stopped turning all this over in my mind. I had to carry on as I could, after all. I had to settle for as far as I could see. That was all I could do. I could not be expected to understand, only to hold my course, come safely past the nearest shoals.

Finally there was some action. Kinesis, mortal foe to introspection. A coincidence.

We, the four Americans, were once more together, sitting at a table in the inevitable Parisian café. We had had a good dinner, but I had heartburn from too much wine and rich food, and too much uneasiness. I had excused myself and gone into a drugstore to buy pills—I was increasingly dependent on them, the Lethe which allowed me to forget my most recent rich sauce—and was sucking them at fifteen-minute intervals. I must have looked sour, because Pounce was baiting me. She got me out of my black moods by making them worse first.

"I've been reading about the history of Paris," she said. "All

173

the great boulevards were cut through during the Second Empire, did you know that? It's the most lasting thing they did. Which proves, I suppose, that cutting right through, real power, gets you farther than intrigue and corruption." The remark was too unrelated to everything, too nonsensical, really, not to be directed at me. As least so I supposed. I was just preparing to ask her how she thought Baron Haussmann had got approval for his plans, when I felt Neal, sitting beside me, suddenly stiffen. His foot, which had been resting on one of the stretchers of the table, fell to the ground, barking my shin on its way.

"Ow," I exclaimed, instead of making my point about town planning.

Then, without saying a word, like a man under hypnosis, he got up, took his raincoat, and followed a woman out of the café.

We, three survivors of the crash, looked at each other. I searched back in my memory for a phrase from one of Neal's letters. " '. . . wistful face, hair drawn back in a knot, like a governess,' " I quoted. "That must be who it was."

"If you have the answer to this, I'll buy your coffee," Pounce offered.

"You remember the girl he mentioned once, the one he said he fell in love with in San Francisco. Well, that's who it was."

"Oh." A piteous little cry from Blissikins.

"That's just a guess," Pounce said.

"Of course it's just a guess, but it's an educated one," I replied.

"I never saw him look like that before," June said.

I got up to go. "He's very flighty. He'll never settle down. You need somebody with more substance, June, somebody you can count on. Everybody is supposed to have a love affair in Paris, and where would life be if we didn't live out its clichés? But Neal isn't a suitable partner for you." I saw

174

light ahead. Recklessly, I exposed my hand. "I'm going to introduce you to our host, Ahmed Bidault."

Three days later Ahmed gave a dinner party in his apartment for us. I waited that long to see what Neal would do, to make sure all was clear. It couldn't have been better; he disappeared. I dropped by his hotel twice, but he hadn't been back since that night. He had vanished, but since his room was paid for by the week, and he still had a couple of days to run, his landlady wasn't worried. The point of being a tourist was to travel, she implied. All girls didn't live in Paris, she said. If the handsome M. Brewster didn't reappear within a few days after the rent was due again, then she might take concern. I reported all this to June and Pounce without comment.

The most striking thing about Ahmed's apartment, to me, was its luxury. It was in the fashionable part of town near the Bois de Boulogne, and consisted of the entire second floor of the building—two drawing rooms, a dining room, four bedrooms, a balcony, bathrooms, halls, and so forth. The rooms, all large and bright, were crammed with furniture, works of art, and curiosities which Ahmed had gathered during his travels. Half of it had the quality of an expensive bazaar, but the dining room, one drawing room, and the main hall were furnished in purest Louis XVI, authentic, I believe, and if so, surely worth a fortune. He kept those rooms so—at least this is what he told me—because it was in them that he entertained Frenchmen, and it was during the war in Algeria. The other rooms had the exotic flavor of Islam. The apartment was a true mirror of its owner, when you stop to think about it.

Ahmed's dinner was magnificent—*consommé double, sole Normande, tournedos* with *sauce Béarnaise, pommes soufflées, salade aux endives,* a perfect *Pont l'évêque,* and *crêpes* rolled around preserved raspberries and served with flaming *fram-*

boise. Filling, but magnificent. He left the menu up to me, and I was supposed to choose things June would like—a stipulation I ignored, since her culinary level, at that time, was contemptible, way beneath the great classics of French cuisine which I selected. The center of the table was sewn with iris and tiny white jonquils, each stem in an invisible plastic tube, which Ahmed had chosen to complement June's coloring, and he had produced favors for the females—earrings made of massive garnets for Pounce, who was quite embarrassed by the splendor of the gift, and for June a chaste little pin of pearl and enamel lilies of the valley, which happened to have been made by Fabergé. June simply didn't know what to make of it all, but the pin was obviously becoming, just her style. She put it on, blushing. Ahmed applauded, then rushed out of the dining room to get a hand mirror. She looked at herself, and a smile of pleasure lit up her sad, pinched little face. She suddenly revealed possibilities of life, of coming into bloom, which one had not suspected before. I had seen her worse side, after all—the red and running nose, the timidity, the whining. Ahmed was charming to her, smiling and friendly and easy and inquisitive about her background, her aims in life, her view of things. June bored me to death with her modest ambitions to teach in a girls' college, her wish to write a book on the medieval French bureaucracy in Touraine, her derivative liberalism—everything so predictable. But no matter what she said, it delighted Ahmed. He found her ideas stimulating, it appeared, her ambitions sweet.

And he took her home—alone. *O là là!*

I was triumphant. I poured myself a big drink and got Pounce to stay up with me for a bit. "Not bad for a catered dinner," I observed. Ahmed had not used his regular cook that night, but had got one in from a famous restaurant.

"There was too much," Pounce said. I had been dimly aware all evening of how the party was grating against her fur.

I blew a beautiful smoke ring. "But after all, one had to introduce Blissikins to her new life," I murmured.

Pounce was a square shooter. "You called that," was her dainty way of admitting how right I had been about June and Ahmed. "I was surprised at the way she took to it."

"He tickled her fancy," I said, smirking.

Pounce removed her earrings and examined them. "These are really too much, Ned. I wish he hadn't," she said.

"Keep them. Keep them, and don't worry. In a way, they're a present from me."

She went off to our bedroom, but I waited for Ahmed, who, when he came in, seemed to me transformed. All the melancholia which so often oppressed him was gone. He was whistling *The Afternoon of a Faun* and kept touching a place on his jaw to the right of his mouth, which was the place where June must have pecked him her demure good night. I asked him what he thought of her.

"Perfect," he replied. "She is perfect. Ned, I could grow to love that little girl. Yes, love her." His great eyes shone. "Such pallor," he said ecstatically.

I went around with him while he checked the windows and doors of his apartment. Have I mentioned one peculiarity of Ahmed's living arrangements, that his apartment was a fortress? All the windows had iron shutters on them which Ahmed insisted should be closed and locked for the night, and the doors were armed with enormous bolts. Even the ventilating fan in the kitchen had a special metal shield of steel plate which closed and bolted when the fan was not in use, and the servants had to be let in by someone on the inside when they came in the morning. I helped him that night and skinned a knuckle on one of the shutters.

I swore and sucked on it. "You and your thief phobia."

"No, not thieves." He took my hand and examined the wound. "It's nothing. But we live in violent days, you know."

177

"She was more lively than I've ever seen her before," I said, returning to the subject of June. "Pounce noticed it, too."

"So?" He put a hand on my arm. "Those wrists," he said dreamily. "Have you noticed her wrists and hands? They are the anatomy of a different race from us. So slim and brittle, as if made to pick flowers growing deep within a barrier of thorns."

"Or a single grape from the midst of a cluster," I suggested.

We were on the point of separating. "By the way, Ahmed," I said, "I do want to talk to you seriously sometime about my ideas for this film. Time is passing."

"Yes, yes, by all means," he said, strolling off toward his bed-room.

"I have an entirely new kind of pornographic film in mind," I called after him. "Quite original, but I'm afraid it will be expensive to make."

He turned. "Soon, Ned, very soon," he said. "I am getting in a mood to hear about your projects."

5.

As I write I have Neal's journals in front of me, and I have to marvel at the situation in which he landed after his impetuous disappearance from the café that night. If one goes loping off into the darkness "in search of adventure"—and adventure is certainly, by one definition, what Neal found—he usually either knows after whom he lopes, or else knows that he will never ask. We aren't dogs exactly. But Neal neither knew nor did not know the girl whom he trailed; mustn't one admit, though, that they had some sort of relationship, which existed, if anywhere, in the area of E.S.P? Now before such a coincidence as that which took place in our café—I mean Neal and the girl happening on each other for a *second time*, with half the world to keep them apart—I believe I would have hesitated, fearing in it the devil's handiwork (there is reason to think it was), made inquiries, consulted my horoscope. Neal simply acted, but Neal had his various intuitions, instincts, sixth and seventh senses, doubles, guardian spirits, fate and destiny, One might even say that Neal *had* to act, and then ask whether, given his new temperament, he was really more free than the obedient devotee of some Negro magus in a pointed hat. But that gets really too philosophical, and philosophy we must eschew, for she ends by dividing our minds in useless little pieces.

The journal of the love affair is kept in a separate notebook. Not that it is fancier than the other bindings, but it has a zipper all around so that it will hold photographs, and it is kept locked. It is the only binder, among all Neal's papers, like that. It begins with the sentence: "We are finally back together again, for she has come to Paris after me—I have not slept much since—the air across from her hotel, in the gardens, smells of chestnut trees." And it ends: "Who is to blame? What is wrong? Is it mortality?" Between these two passages is contained our present subject matter.

Well, it *was* the girl from San Francisco, although I could write quite a few pages conditioning that simple declarative. Trust old Ned—I mean, trust me to have guessed correctly. Neal notes that some American laughed at him because he bumped into the wall of a *pissoir* when he first started to follow her, so blinded was he by the goddess. He heard "*Cherchez la femme*" in a bad accent behind him. Then across the street, down another, a few turns, over the Seine, and through the great courtyard of the Louvre. As she walked by the Arc de Triomphe du Carrousel she slowed to admire the splendid vista up through the Tuileries and the Champs-Elysées to the Etoile, all floodlighted.

Neal writes: "She must have felt me there behind her, and that was why she stopped." If so, she didn't do anything about it. He goes on to complain that there were too many tourists around. It interfered with their "communication." Psychic cross talk.

He stayed close to her as she strolled slowly toward the arch, then, as she started to pass around it, he bifurcated and went the other way. He hoped to meet her square in the center, a real setting for a dramatic first encounter, for a seismic hello. But she turned away, and, after waiting a moment, he noticed her walking over toward the Rue de Rivoli and followed. As they came to the street, he got a clear view of her.

". . . withdrawn and pensive," he says. "I wondered, out of the blue, if we would ever speak. Would we always circle each other silently like this? Would we ever touch?"

She went into a hotel, an expensive one. Although he was sure she wouldn't be out again that night, he didn't leave and go home. He stood across the street and watched for a light to go on in one of the rooms upstairs, calculating about how much time it would take her to speak to the night clerk, get in the elevator, walk the corridor—he had no doubt but that she would have a front room. Lights did go on in a fourth-story room at about the right moment, but he had no sure sense that it was she, since people were entering the hotel so frequently. He paced the sidewalk, back and forth, from one boundary of her hotel to the other, as projected across the street, squared the distance to get an idea of the entire building, multiplied by the number of floors, guessed at how many feet of perimeter the average room would command, just to figure what the chances were that that room might be hers. His calculations, like so many others, got him nowhere; but it probably was not, he decided, for if it had been, he would have had no doubts.

He tried outright telepathy. He concentrated on a message: "I am outside. I am outside. I am outside." Time passed, he thinks about three hours.

A policeman was watching him. Neal moved on, for he didn't want to get picked up for questioning, and the police of Paris are not always easy to deal with. He took walks from his post, off onto different streets, coming back, then going away again. He walked like that from after midnight until dawn, never bored, never tired, never feeling he might like to go back to his hotel to sleep. The next morning when he went into the Tuileries Gardens and took off his shoes to empty them of some gravel, he saw that he had walked the soles off his socks.

He sent her another message. "Good morning. I'm still here waiting," and he thinks he got a garbled message back, one transmitted by a person unaccustomed to the medium of pure mind. It was about sleepiness, sleeping on, sleeping until later, fatigue. But I remind the reader that he didn't start keeping the journal in the zipper binding until he finally got back to his hotel and that is quite time enough for the mind to erase truth and correct memory.

He bought a copy of *Le Figaro* so that he would appear to have something to do while he stood across the street. He waited. He watched. An hour or two later she came out, and he started toward her, heedless of traffic. She jumped into a taxi, and he heard her order it to go to the Gare du Nord. He followed, and several hours later both of them got off a train at Amiens.

Here the journals leave us gasping with travel anxieties and curiosity on the platform of the capital of old Picardy and digress for pages about Neal, the girl, chance encounters, above all, love, love, love. Very uninteresting generally. What could be more boring than *mere* love? It will do for the fourteen lines of a sonnet, but I point out that it is not the subject of *Paradise Lost*. Let us jump on; let us skip those pages till we once more read the name Amiens.

I have never been to Amiens, and, frankly, the journals are not much of a guide. They mention neither the regional specialties nor the leading restaurants. They do contain some snippets of architectural description. There is, it seems, a famous Gothic cathedral there—doesn't that come as a surprise?—the town was badly damaged during the late war. Repairs are going on. And thereby results a near tragedy in our story—the devil testing, testing, one-two-three, one-two-three.

Neal followed the girl as she walked from the railroad station toward the cathedral. She walked around the outside first—I gather one bothers only with the entrance to the right transept and the front portals. There is sculpture, it seems—a *Vierge dorée,* who smiles famously, labors of the months on the splayings of the west doors, a noble *Beau Dieu* on the *trumeau.* Then we go inside, and we find the most refined of all Gothic interiors, for the girl said so later. It is white and airy, with a beautiful foliate string course just under the triforium gallery, huge rose windows, vast space. And then we go out again, this time to have another look at the sculpture of the west entrance. Then, the girl leading, Neal skulking behind—it is understood that they have not yet met—they start around the building, coming close to the overhanging roof. A workman, high up in the air, cries out. Neal looks up, but she ignores the sound. He sees the danger—a gargoyle, being hoisted up to replace one worn out by the rainfall of centuries, is slipping in its tackle and may be about to fall. "Look out above you," he shouts. The girl looks up, runs to one side, and the heavy stone monster falls. Was it right where she was standing? Who knows? It makes a better story. And her left leg had a cut on it from a chip of flying rock. She looks around to see and thank whoever had warned her, but Neal has darted back around the corner and inside to think.

I *know* the incident took place, because I read of it in the Paris newspapers. There was a local investigation, to see whose carelessness it was *let* fall a heavy limestone demon. What folly, My Lord Bishop. And demons your métier, too!

Six o'clock saw both our prospective lovers back in the city once more, she again in her hotel, Neal at his vigil across the street. The good weather held, so he was able to pass the second night there, and I feel that is remarkable. Any gentleman raised in the Romantic tradition would have spent one night outside his love's window, but not so many would have spent two, particularly not when terribly bedeviled, under such minstrel circumstances, by that frequent complaint of aspirant lovers, diarrhea—the choice of detail is not mine; it is mentioned several times in the journals. But Neal transcended it—*ad astra per aspera*—and stayed on to spy upon his beloved the next morning, and eventually to meet her.

It happened in an amusing way, everything considered. There he was, waiting around hour after hour, trying to catch her attention through telepathy, following her when he could, yearning from afar. Always, that day, some accident like a too-rapid hailing of a taxi, confusion in the subway stop, or some diffidence such as that he felt at the Carrousel, kept him from speaking to her. Finally, worn out, he fell asleep in the late afternoon in the Tuileries Gardens, and his lover's work was done for him. I need not by now say just how "miraculous" Neal thinks that was. What I should mention, before we become beguiled into a Brewsterian belief in uncanny links and extrasensory bonds, is that Neal inquired about his lady from her hotel clerk, trying to find out her name while she was gone; and, because he was by then the most disreputable-looking American ever to have entered that hotel, the clerk would tell him nothing, not even for money, and in fact reported his inquiry to his superior. The superior asked the Mademoiselle if she knew a Monsieur with reddish-brown hair, an artist perhaps, who would have been asking for her. She said she did not, and the whole matter was handled with such rarefied tact that she took no fright. But can't one assume that the description penetrated her mind and fermented there? And that that is how one might explain her choice of chairs in the Tuileries Gardens? For she sat on a chair right next to the bench where Neal fell asleep, and he was awakened when the ancient who collected the few sous which such a chair costs the weary came around and collected. He was dead tired. He blinked. He looked dumbly about him. Then he sat upright and smiled.

"At last," he said. "I was getting pretty worn out. I don't know how much longer I could have waited."

Neal did not make people suspicious. The girl was amused, and smiled back at him, raising her eyes from her book—it was Balzac. "Did you have a pleasant nap?" she said.

"How did you know I was here—on this bench?"

"That's rather obvious. You're not invisible."

"Did you know I've been waiting for you ever since I followed you home night before last?"

She froze. "No."

"You didn't? I wonder. My only worry has been that you might move out of your hotel before this meeting."

"Oh?" A well-bred chill enveloped them.

"You didn't recognize me by the arch over there?"

"When? Oh—on my way home?" She thought a moment how to handle Neal, and smoothed her hair, drawing the palm of her hand from her forehead back toward the knot in back.

"There. That's your beautiful gesture," Neal said. Anyone who has ever been in love knows how certain gestures often repeated will finally almost define the beloved—a part standing for the whole.

"I didn't notice," she said.

"Yes, yes. You felt the electricity. I'm sure of it."

She shook her head. "Sorry. No electricity."

"My name is Neal Brewster."

She pretended to read.

"Tell me, though. You do remember the coffeehouse in San Francisco?"

For the first time her mingled disapproval and detached amusement at the conversation and situation broke. She was puzzled. "Oh," she said. "That's different. What did you say your name was again?"

"Neal Brewster."

"Brewster," she repeated. She shook her head doubtfully.

"You wouldn't remember my name, because you never heard it."

She asked him to describe the coffeehouse and whatever had happened in it. But no words? she questioned him. He said there had been none, but he emphasized that there had been no doubt about the feeling that had passed between them. There had been an enormous pull. And he remarked that after all, it was pretty clear she hadn't much liked the man she had been with.

"You think not?" she asked, considering the possible truth in what he said. Then: "Just exactly what did I have on? What sort of clothes was I wearing?"

Neal didn't remember that too precisely. "Something dark."

She smiled. "Something dark. That doesn't help much," she said, suddenly laughing (contralto voice). "That really doesn't help me decide whether or not I was really there."

"Of course you were. Don't you recognize the description of the place? Don't you recognize the man? Weren't you in San Francisco last August?"

"The answer to all the questions is yes."

"Well then . . ." Neal jumped up and paced in front of her. "That's settled."

"I'm glad you think so."

"You know, I don't know your name. Here we've been talking to each other all this time, and I don't know your name." He noticed that the toes of his shoes were dusty, and he rubbed them off on the calves of his legs.

"I don't think it will be necessary for you to know it," she said, still the lady.

"On the other hand, if I'd have known it yesterday, I could have warned you better."

"Warned me?"

"When that stone fell."

185

"So it was you."

"Uh huh. I didn't want to say anything to you just then. I hid."

"But I might never have known. I might never have had a chance to thank you. Of course I'll tell you my name. It's Eloise Lincoln. And I do live in San Francisco. And I have a sister named Patricia who lives there, too. We look quite a lot alike."

"Is she older or younger?"

"A little older, but we're quite close together in age. And she likes to drink coffee late at night, too." She looked at her watch, then closed her book and got up.

Neal was shocked. "Where are you going?" he cried out.

"Cocktails. Dinner. With friends."

"Cancel it and stay with me."

"It's a little late. I'm sorry." Then she remembered that after all she perhaps owed her life to him. "But I'll be coming home about eleven o'clock, Mr. Brewster, and I'll be going for a walk in the gardens tomorrow morning. Will I see you over here either time?"

"Both," Neal said. And that is how he happened to spend a third night away from his hotel. It was, incidentally, the night of Ahmed's dinner party.

6.

Eloise Lincoln was by any standards a nice, well-brought-up American girl, and by the standards of Greenwich Village or Hollywood a conventional one, no more offbeat than any other woman with a profession—for she was a licensed architect. She was smarter and a good deal more perceptive than your average suburban bourgeoise, but her *curriculum vitae* since graduation would have aroused no reserve among the principled old New England maiden ladies from earlier classes

186

at Mount Holyoke, her alma mater. In a way, though, they would have erred, for dangerously special about Eloise was her flexibility—no New England specialty—which takes genuine intelligence, and is rare in either sex. She could imagine more than one way of being or doing without going into a sweat. She was, in short, open minded. But she was "nice" enough and conventional enough to have misgivings about Neal and the way she had met him, and she had some *arrière-pensées* about the two dates she had tossed him as she left him in those stunning gardens, standing forlornly amidst French children rolling their hoops. Nevertheless, she turned up. Apropos of which she later wrote Neal, in a letter whose point of perspective belongs—like my own—to the future, but which—as I must—dealt with the past:

"I couldn't decide which of two things I wanted, even then. I wanted to see you again, yet I didn't want to. I almost didn't come back to the Tuileries to see you."

So . . . She *almost* didn't show that night or the next morning. What a word, that *almost*. Satan and I laugh whenever we hear that word, until I must swallow mouthfuls of spit, and his obscene little belly shakes. She *almost* vanished, as Neal once vanished—it's not such a bad trick, actually—but she relented. And once she relented, she was lost. They were lost together, and I use the adjective with full awareness of what it means to be lost. I was clarifying my definition at about that time, as a matter of fact. You are lost if a *person* grows to mean more to you than *things* do. But let's hear from Eloise again:

"I wonder what would have happened if I had disappeared. Believe me, I thought of it. I knew our danger when I heard myself calmly telling a stranger that I would see him not once but twice. You will understand in just a minute or two why it was the last thing I wanted, just then—to get tied to another human being. Believe me, Neal dearest, I didn't want to fall in love.

"As I write this letter, I can't help wondering what would have happened if I had given you a false name or changed hotels or gone on to Rome. Would you have found me again?

"Anyway, I told myself that the situation was harmless. I told myself it was just curiosity and gratitude that brought me back that night and again the next morning. You were such a shaggy, eccentric sort of man to turn up on a bench, saying we had seen each other months before and were meant for each other. Curiosity killed the cat. It also snared the self-confident Miss Lincoln."

My narrative is told for me. Miss Lincoln didn't run off. She came back that night and joined Neal and talked to him until long after midnight, then the next morning they walked together in the gardens till the sun rode high in his heavens. That afternoon Neal went home and slept for about eighteen hours, but . . .

"It was my turn to stay awake. In spite of all the tricks I had learned to put me to sleep, in spite of pills and capsules, I didn't sleep at all that night. It was my second chance. I knew by then that it was serious. I could still have run off, but I didn't. That is what you must forgive. Don't think I am writing you this instead of telling you because I was afraid to tell you. I knew that if I wrote it, I would say everything I wanted and had to say.

"I've put it off long enough. Here goes . . ."

CUT! ! !

Ned Bates, the great director of comedies, isn't going to reveal his plot, not at this point. We'll return to Eloise's secret and her letter in a while.

I met her at the Louvre, and I must say I was rather taken by her myself. She would never have done for me, but I did like her, and that wasn't always the way with me where a woman who belonged to somebody else was concerned. Pounce and I were early for the appointment, for we both yearned to see Eloise. We knew all about her, because Neal had been in touch and had told us. It was arranged that we would all four meet in front of that old favorite of Neal's "The Embarkation for Cythera" of Watteau, where I wanted to get some discussion going which we might expand before other, rather more lascivious and energetic essays in the amorous mode. Like the languorous couples in the Watteau, Pounce and I dawdled as we passed through the Grande Galerie, looking out the windows, observing the crush of tourists—for it was getting along into May. I remarked to Pounce that I felt that the genius of all Western visual experience was snapping at my throat whenever I walked into that museum. How had French art survived the Louvre so well? How had it been so respectful, yet so revolutionary? How was it that it hadn't been suffocated, like the Italian school? She interrupted the course of my pleasant thoughts.

"They're coming," she said. "Lord, don't they make a photogenic couple—I'll do some studies of Eloise," she added.

"I'll bet," I said. I gazed where she gazed, our four eyes converging.

"This is Eloise, Pounce," Neal called from such a distance that fifteen or twenty surfeited Scandinavian heads, members of a tour, swiveled away from their cicerone toward our coalescing quartet. I dare say it was a relief for those Swedes, although they were being told about a marvelous Caravaggio, because Scandinavians like handsome people more than art, and Neal and Eloise were a handsome couple, Pounce just as good in her barbarian-princess way, and I, being tall and blond, at least provided for identification. "And this is Ned, Eloise."

I know I must put in a quick description of Eloise, and it's such a bore. I wish I could simply introduce one of the several portraits Pounce did do of her. There was one in particular, which for some reason isn't in that zipper-bound notebook, which showed Eloise standing in the narthex of the church at Vézelay, near Ahmed's country place, where we all spent a weekend together in the early summer. The architecture was massive, great dependable solids, with some of the nave showing out of focus behind, and, as living counterpoint, there stood that elegant girl with her severe hair and her stylishness, leaning slightly on her umbrella, the way models so often do in fashion mags. It was really a quite fantastical juxtaposition (Pounce! that instinctual genius) of the suppleness of our century against Romanesque ponderosity. Eloise was not pretty, God knows not fluffy and sweet. She had too high a forehead, too severe and removed a manner and expression for that. If she had any flaws worth mentioning, they would be: a slight immobility of expression, and a slight heaviness of arms and legs—rather a relief after the Blissbird. Also, Eloise had blue eyes, nice teeth, and wore no nail polish. Had we orchestrated our girls, Eloise would have played the piano, June the harp, and Pounce the kettledrums.

I hate the dither which so often follows the introduction of friends to friends, so I leapt into the pause.

"Since I'm here to work, let's go look at the Correggio. I want to get some fresh impressions. And I want to sharpen some knives I've got tucked in my pocket on you people."

I sensed that Eloise liked the harshness of my figure of speech, as did Pounce. They shared a directness, which in Pounce resulted from her view of Life as War, her constant fear of being overrun by the enemy, anti-Utopia, but in Eloise came from a kind of poised curiosity. Spartanism versus the Socratic, if you will. We circumambulated the Scandinavians and headed back toward the incomparable "Jupiter and Antiope," that flawless vision of lust. When we arrived in front of it, I said:

"I probably ought to explain to your friend, Neal, that I'm trying to shape up some ideas in my mind for a film on the general subject of love. Now obviously such a large subject must in some way be subdivided. But how? Here, I think you'll agree, Eloise, we have one recurrent theme, one possible subdivision, which I might be able to build into my realization. The 'mode' of this picture is certainly one of the constant ones in art and literature, and has been wherever love has been dealt with at all. Greece, Rome, the Renaissance —they are the best sources for this mode, and the eighteenth century, too. I think of it as a formula, which is varied in every generation, and in each individualization gets tucked into an envelope of specifics, but which remains all the same a constant—like the fact that we all look different, yet all obey the law of bilateral symmetry."

"What's that, what's that, Ned?" Neal yelped. He had quite a wild look in his eyes that day anyway—no sleep and too much excitement, I suppose, over a ten-day period.

"Well, if it's what I think it is, it means that a line dropped from the middle of your head to the ground would divide you into two equal, or nearly equal, halves, except for your inner organs—like the two halves of an ink blot when you fold the paper on it. You have two sides which are identical visually, if not biologically."

"That's true, that's true," he said excitedly.

"Umm. To go on," I continued dryly, "in mythology this formula can be represented repurified of those specific details which tend to make it obscene. That is one of the functions of mythology—to allow the representation of formulae which contemporized would strike us as smutty—or tedious. And yet . . ." I thought a moment, for this was one of the problems that were puzzling me. "And yet, we shouldn't forget that it contains the formula. The satyr, the animal-man, the Man as animal, leers down upon the sleeping nude woman. It's all perfectly simple, really, as an idea. Man, the lustfuler sex, insatiable, eager, his tongue lolling out, scrambling through the bushes to get at the desired object. And she sleeps —but not without coquetry. After all, if you go to sleep naked, your plump limbs disposed in a frozen wiggle, and there are goatmen about, you can expect the unexpected, can you not? That's the rather profound and more modern insight which Correggio has added here, I think. The Renaissance yearned for the particular at least as much as it yearned for the universal. Lots of artists have shown nymphs being surprised by satyrs, but only Correggio has added a vivid psychological complexity: the half-conscious invitation to ravishment. In every sex crime there are two participants—that idea. Rape, violence, he says, are so inevitably preceded by seduction. Well?" I was slightly uneasy as I asked for their reactions, for I knew all the pitfalls of vulgarity which lay about me.

Eloise had a clean kind of mind, clear and logical. She gazed for quite a while at the painting, whose point of view was so different from her aristocratic poise. Then she looked for a perceptible time at Pounce, a similar stretch at me, then back to the picture. Was she wondering just what went on between these friends of Neal, just what the secret of our relationship was?

"So the general idea here, the constant, would be the shy female contrasted with the lascivious male?"

"Precisely. My mind has been running to musical analogies —you realize that when you are planning to work in a non-verbal medium, it's well not to get too entangled in verbalizations—so one could say that this is a constant *theme* of love, or, perhaps even better, it is a kind of tempo marking, which controls the expression of a bewildering variety of individual themes, each a specific embodiment of the tempo. Abstract mythological versions of the tempo, like this one, approach pure rhythm, beats without melody."

"What has this got to do with your film? I mean, we have been dealing with words, after all, which you say you mistrust. But anyway, we have been talking about content. What about form?"

Eloise was not an architect for nothing. Content and form, the eternal dualism of art; all artists are perforce ditheists.

I went up very close to the picture, actually in order to have a minute to gather my thoughts, but with the pretence to see how lovingly the Parmesan master had painted the flesh of his voluptuous Theban princess. Just for some splash before my audience, I ran my hand over her knee, barely touching the paint surface.

Out of nowhere a guard appeared—where do they hide? Gobble, gobble, gobble, gobble—so fast and in such a common accent I couldn't understand him. I stood, my finger tips still pressed against that herb-scented flesh. Gobble, gobble, gobble—much louder this time. I was infuriated, since it must have been obvious that I objected not so much to his meaning, which was clear enough, but to his tone of voice. Then he dared to pull my hand away from Antiope's limb.

"*Allez, allez,*" I snapped. I flipped my hand in his face.

"Ned, what's the matter with you? He's a guard. He's trying to tell you not to touch the picture," Pounce said.

"Really?" The word was drenched in sarcasm. "What a bunch of old maids they get for that job," I said. Then, ignoring both the guard, who continued to rail at me, and a little group of bystanders who watched, I continued to Eloise:

"My tentative idea is to explore the various tempi of love in my film. In other words, I do not intend to recount anecdotes, or to represent complete actions of any kind. I want to go at my subject from a completely different point of view. I have said that I have been thinking of musical analogies. Well, just suppose we had a film organized like a symphony. Each movement pertains to a different amorous tempo, to be consistent. Within that there would be themes, variations, pauses, development, codas, and so on. Bound together, however, not by narrative, but by the more subtle relationship of thematic rapport, and a common marking."

"What are your other tempos, or modes?" Eloise asked, she, too, ignoring the uncouth babble.

"Well, we have just been talking about hot desire and its

193

object or stimulus, of lust and temptation. There"—and I pointed toward the Giorgione "Concert Champêtre"—"is something quite different, an entirely new tempo. The diversions and relaxations of love, the *canzonetta d'amore*, the tender little lyric. Love with its stinger drawn. Love spent. The sweet shepherd, piping, as here, his tune. The bouncy nymph and leering satyr banished to the bushes, where they belong."

"The elegiac and mournful, too, and the fleeting," Eloise said.

I drew my little notebook from my pocket. "Here are some others I have jotted down. Love in motion, that is, everything from the movements of actual copulation to country dances. The violence of love, blood and guts, masochism and sadism, whips and chains, cockfights and spider webs. The orgy and the *bacchanale*—that could come under love in motion, but maybe that is too broad a category and would have to be subdivided. Then there could be the forbidden love, love for the same sex, in men, women, and animals. Ah, yes, and secret places, where Cupid goes on tiptoes—voyeurism, exhibitionism, fetishism, bestiality, all that sort of thing. And I have something down here about deflected appetites, and love sublimated—good manners, art, etcetera. Those are some of the possibilities I've thought of. I suppose I'll think of a dozen others before I'm through."

I became aware of a new voice nagging at me, this time in English, although the language was rendered adenoidal by a heavy French accent. What was I doing, it asked; why had I refused to obey the guard? Would I please move away from that painting? I turned upon this object, some form of being coeval with, but socioeconomically superior to the flunky who had been shouting at me before—a middle-aged hairdresser, one would have guessed.

"Go away," I said. "Shoo."

"Ned, they'll lock you up." Prudent Neal speaking. Where was his alleged heroicity then, may I ask?

"Piffle. I haven't done anything. And I won't be badgered."

The voice asked whether or not I had touched the painting. I stared at the worm. He turned to the bystanders. Had I? These included now most of those Swedes I mentioned, who had stopped on their way back to the entrance. One of them demonstrated what I was supposed to have done, which he had heard from someone else.

"Lies," I said. "He wasn't here. A practical joke. A mere North Caper."

"Fie!" said another Swede. Book-learned English.

After some additional haggling, I was told to leave. We were all told to leave. In fact, we were taken to the door by guards, an international affront.

Out on the sidewalk that stretches along the river, I pretended to feel no smart, although I was nearly blind with fury at those beastly little functionaries. They'll be the death of France, mark my words. However, I didn't let on how I felt, and tried to recapture the attention of my now grim audience of three and get the conversation going again. I had the feeling that they were handling me, for the moment, like somebody else's pet snake.

"Now we can talk in peace," I said. "What about my ideas?"

Eloise was able to pull herself together and answer. "I think you run the danger of falling into formal busyness, being too complicated, too multiple, too much, therefore merely miscellaneous," she said.

"Photography can be used to hold things together, you know," Pounce said, coming to my rescue in spite of her feelings about the recent scene. Eloise going to conceptual flaws, Pounce, the craftsman, with her sense of the possibilities in execution.

Neal said: "What I wonder is, will there be enough sex in it?"

"Little else," I replied tartly.

Suddenly I didn't want to talk about it any more. We had, unexpectedly, reached that point where other people's comments are merely irritating, not helpful. "I can tell that you're all going to begin to invent your own movies instead of criticizing mine," I said. "Not another word right now."

They looked at me curiously, put off by the violence of my voice. But I broke that conversation up, which was what I wanted. The one thing that was really on my mind never got stated at all, either by me or by anyone else: could I really do a pornographic film without demeaning my genius?

7.

Another dinner party *chez* Ahmed, this time for six: the host and June, me and Pounce, Neal and Eloise.

Let us tune in on a hiss from Bliss, the viperette.

"You always talk a lot, Ned," she said. "So many big ideas that it's hard to keep up with them. But I don't see that you carry out very many." This was days later, and we were back once more on the subject of films and love and love films. June poked with satisfaction at a rather frightening French version of fruit-jello salad, which was following the well-done leg of lamb with mint jelly; for Ahmed had probed June's tastes to their bottom, and was granting her anything. "I mean, the proof of the pudding is in the eating," she said, led to that saw, I assume, by horrid circumstance.

Pounce came lumbering to my defense, simian anger showing in her black eyes. June had been baiting me quite a lot those last few days, and that was Pounce's prerogative. It was not open season on me to dear little June H_2O Bliss. "It's like doing a thesis," Pounce said. "A film takes time, often a lot of it." She beetled at June, who flushed and looked down, and I think I heard Ahmed cluck with concern. It was Pounce's turn to jab at that salad, whose recipe, by the way, Ahmed got by calling the American Embassy, which perhaps explains why we are losing the diplomatic war. "Ned has only started, but he may go a long way. How many of us here can say that about anything we will ever do?" This time she looked around the table at each of us, leaping quickly by me, for her protective impulses vis-à-vis me embarrassed her. As I have said, she could not regard truce as quite normal.

Bliss sniffed peevishly, but didn't dare to speak.

Junesie had been rather out of sorts for many days now. She and Ahmed were courting furiously, but it had produced a curious reaction in her. As she moved nearer and nearer toward becoming his mistress—so I would explain it—her niggling native prudery, not strong enough to hold her on the straight and narrow, fixed itself on my carnal relations with Pounce. She disapproved of us. She reproached us, particularly me, since she did feel some gratitude toward Pounce for having looked after her when she was sick. It was hardly what I had hoped for when I brought her and Ahmed together. I had to be careful with her because of Ahmed, but I did use Neal and Eloise to make her uncomfortable, reported everything I knew about them, and promoted a meeting, which she put off as long as she could. That night she was watching Neal and Eloise to see if they, too, were having extramarital relations, so that she could rid herself of them by including them in the package with my Pounce and me—a prude is never more dangerous than when she can condemn where she is herself most tempted.

Bliss's dig at me, with which I began, had come after I had been expounding my views about my new film—much the same stuff I have already reported from that day at the Louvre. Eloise now came in, her low voice, like much of what she said, so medial, so temperate after those two extremes, Tweeter Bliss and Woofer Pounce. One felt at once the hand of Mind upon the reins of conversation. She was sitting next to Ahmed, for Blissbore, the First Wife, already held the opposite chair from him as a matter of household ordinance.

197

"What you want to try is very interesting, Ned. I've thought about it. I believe it may suffer from one great flaw. I wonder if you'll ever forgive me for using this word—but I think it's too grandiose. Or, even worse, I wonder if it isn't pretentious."

"That does it," I said hoarsely, wishing I felt sufficient lack of objectivity in her to take this as personal, not critical.

This time Ahmed defended me, but more as host than as real partisan. "I think that is a conservative, and, if you will pardon me, a womanly criticism, Miss Lincoln. Ideas must be grandiose. We must plan to do the infinite, in order to accomplish just a little."

Eloise shook her head. "No. You have always to deal with what can be accomplished. Otherwise conception and accomplishment will never be brought into any relationship. People are wrong who think that art is a cloudland world. Art is realistic and hardheaded, or it wouldn't exist at all."

Ahmed thought about her point. "I think that in this case you make a mistake. Ned loves his subject. That is very important. That is why his mind ranges out into all its possibilities. He does not set himself a limited exercise, he sets out to create a masterpiece. That requires range."

I was about to ask, screwing my face into simulated jocularity, whether he had enough faith in me to sink some money into such a film—my worries about my finances had reached a point where I was prepared to be pretty crass—but Pounce came back into the conversation.

"I'm not at all sure Ned loves his subject, Ahmed," she said in her slow way. "I love my work. I'm never happier than when I'm working. But I've worked with Ned, and it isn't true about him. He is fascinated by what he does, but still, I get a different feeling from him. I get the feeling . . ." Gradually she worked her idea clear. "I get the feeling that there is a lot of dislike for what he does. No, not dislike, but really a kind of hatred. Do you know that often when he is thinking the hardest about something that interests him, he grits his teeth?"

I was, to say the least, nonplused by the perception as well as the talkiness of the usually rather taciturn Pounce. I realized immediately that she had been thinking long and hard about me lately, and about what we had done together and might yet do. I made up my mind then and there that I would learn a little photography myself, in case I ever needed it.

"Can't we get off these subjects and talk about something *nice* for a change?" Guess who whined that.

Obedient Ahmed turned to Eloise, with that sort of perfumed courtliness he sometimes assumed, in which Frank was wedded to Saracen, and drew her out about herself—how she was a lady architect, sight-seeing in Europe, and was going to meet her sister and brother-in-law later to spend much of the summer in Italy—nothing I hadn't already told him.

"Neal will join us there," she said, with a quick look at her lover lad, just a tiny bit uneasy.

It was the first I had heard of this plan, and I felt a tickle of anxiety, detected a whiff of desertion: was I to be the poor little sibling left to scratch in the cinders while the more glamorous children went off to the ball?

"Why are you asking all those questions, Ahmed?" I said crossly. "I've already told you about Eloise."

He didn't bother to turn to me when he replied. "I don't entirely trust you, my dear Ned."

We had a bottle of champagne later, with which Neal, who had been quite gloomy all evening, proposed a toast—to all lovers everywhere. "I hope we can all drink to that," Neal said. Another little exchange of looks flashed between him and Eloise.

"Yes, of course we can," Ahmed said dryly, holding his glass out toward June. For he was not ignorant of what June had felt for Neal a month before. Yet, so far as I know, he was never at all jealous of Neal. Ahmed, perhaps because he was a metic, had taken up the myth of the Gallic philanderer and lived it very, very hard. Love came, love went. When one was in love, one was engrossed in the beloved; but change was possible, and one might not love tomorrow. And so he was not jealous; he assumed people loved in a series.

Toward the end Eloise began to look very tired, and finally asked if she might go, although it was early. She had been ill recently, she said, and needed lots of rest, had very little sticking power. Ahmed asked her, then, to come down and stay with him in the country. June cleared her throat significantly, but he refused to notice. Eloise was pale, and took Neal's arm when they left the apartment; and I suddenly thought that it was this which perhaps partly accounted for the strange feeling of detachment and poise that one got from Eloise, that she had just been ill, was just recovered, had, so to speak, seen the other side, and was less concerned with what went on over on this one.

This little dinner party was not inherently so very interesting, and certainly made far less difference in our lives than what happened afterward. For it was on the same night that June finally capitulated, and it may be that seeing us all together affected her, rendered her receptive. She hadn't so very much resistance, after all. Her naïve chastity surrendered to Ahmed's learned sensuality, just as her piddling liberalism collapsed before all the luxury he offered her. She not only took Ahmed as her lover that night, but also, during the conversations that followed before daybreak, she consented to move into his apartment, in preference to his having her established in one of her own. She consented, that is, with one proviso.

Pounce and I were still Ahmed's guests, and, as far as I was concerned, we would have continued so indefinitely, although Pounce didn't like it. My checks from the university would soon stop, and I was too worried about how long I was going to be able to live to be proud. I am forced to admit that in bringing Ahmed and June together I cooked, or at any rate parboiled, my own goose; for the proviso she stipulated was that Pounce and I move out. She came back with him that night after they left, presumably to get her home, but she wouldn't stay in the morning because of us. It was embarrassing, so she said, to live intimately with a man when there were people around watching. I heard all the bolts crash and clatter about six A.M., and when I saw Ahmed, quite used up, over breakfast coffee, I remarked, probing, that he had been up damned early considering how late he must have gone to bed.

And then he broke it to me.

I was flabbergasted. Apart from the irony that I had arranged the whole thing, which wasn't easy to take, I suddenly saw my money problem become really acute. What would I do now?

"I am afraid I must not only ask you to leave my apartment, but I must ask you to leave very soon," Ahmed said, deftly mixing hot milk and coffee from twin silver pots. "I know you will understand, although I am very sorry about it."

"Of course," I answered mechanically, adding up some dollar totals in my head, and multiplying by the exchange.

There was a pause while we both drank coffee. My cup clattered, and he no doubt noticed, for he suddenly reached over to put a hand on my arm. "Ned, I wonder if it would offend you if I asked you to continue to be my guest, only to be my guest in a hotel."

"Well, no . . ."

"I have an idea, which occurred to me as I was lying in bed watching the dawn break. I was very happy. Now you have talked of this film, this great film on love. Suppose I commission you to make it. Suppose I pay you a salary and give you some expense money while you work on it."

"It won't ever make any money. You'll lose your investment."

"What does that matter?" Then he mentioned a sum of money which was enough for my needs, although it certainly wouldn't keep me in the style I had lived in in his apartment. "Think that over," he concluded, "and, when it is convenient, I will have the servants help you pack. June wants a separate room, and I will have yours repainted for her. In some light color, I should think, a powdery gray-blue, maybe. Blue goes well with her, don't you think so?"

I made no reply

By the time I discussed the matter with Pounce an hour later my spirits had risen. Wasn't the new arrangement in some ways an actual improvement? "I'm getting what I wanted," I said, "even if it's coming in a backhanded way. Ahmed will pay for us to continue to work. That's the important thing."

"Should you take the money from him, though?" she asked.

I had come to my decision and had no doubts left about it. "Yes, I should. I don't know why not. I don't have an archaic conscience. We won't be sponging off him, and even if we were, the history of the fine arts is filled with artists who have had to do that. We'll take his offer."

"If you've decided . . ." she said, dissociating herself from our new patronage. My fastidious Pounce, I think we both knew that we had taken another little step apart.

We moved the next day. Ahmed's servants did most of the work, but we did private papers and the like ourselves, with one consequence which I should relate. Pounce was going through a briefcase, throwing out old bills, and came across the clipping I had cut from the obituary page of Neal's hometown newspaper. She read it.

"What is this, Ned?" she asked slowly, considering possible meanings, possible consequences.

"That?" I took it away from her. "Just something I clipped

202

from a newspaper the day we left the States. I'd forgotten all about it."

She sat down on the bed and looked squarely at me. "Why haven't you shown it to him?" she asked, with full Pouncian solemnity.

"I will—sometime. But I don't see any reason to ruin his European adventures. There is nothing he could do about it and never was. The news was already stale by the time I saw him. It was already too late."

Absently Pounce pushed a hand back into the briefcase and pulled out more disposable material. "When are you going to tell him?"

"When the time is ripe. Let's go."

A half hour later, as we were riding to our new room, she returned to the subject. "I think he should know about it. You haven't the right not to tell him."

"It's my clipping and I'll tell him when I choose," I replied sharply. "And not before."

We joggled along the Boulevard Saint-Germain, for we were changing quarter entirely. We, too, were going to live at the Carthage et Edimbourg.

"You scare me a little, Ned," Pounce said.

"Of course," I replied gaily. "But isn't that half the fun?"

"Not for me." A hesitation, then, "Poor Neal."

"Why poor Neal?" I prepared to alight. "This is a comedown, but it'll have to do." I paid the driver and directed the handling of the luggage. "Neal is in love," I said.

The lady owner, who so admired his looks, came out to the sidewalk. "*Alors, Madame, nous voilà!*" I cried, lifting my new French-style Homburg.

8.

We knocked on Neal's door to see if he wanted to go out to lunch with us. He called in French to come in—I suppose he thought we were the chambermaid. It was a nice day, and Neal had a front room, so that with the windows open it was hard to hear because of the noise of traffic buzzing through the narrow street below. We were a floor above him, and our rooms—a few francs cheaper—gave on the court and were much quieter, although the air didn't always smell like *muguets*. Neal was still in his gloomy spell, really in a funk. One pays even at the time for the Eloises of this world, I guess. He was lying fully dressed with his face to the wall on a bed that looked as though a really gross orgy had taken place on it—in any case, comparisons of that sort jumped into my mind in those days, what with my film and all. More factually, his bed was rumpled, the covers all askew, and Neal's head was sandwiched between the two pillows so that only the clot of dark-brown hair showed.

"You can come out now," I said, poking his hind end with my walking stick—another addition of the last week or two, and perfect for just such impudences. "It's practically summer. You don't want to be the last chuck to the clover patch."

He didn't look around. "What are you doing here?"

"Graciously put," I replied. "We live here. We just moved in."

I expected, I suppose, surprise. I got none. "Oh," he said dully. "What's your room number?"

"Seventeen. Aren't you going to ask why?"

"Why?"

"It was June. She had Ahmed ask us to leave, or else she refused to cohabit with him. I hope she contracts the French disease and looses her yellow card."

Pounce reached around and put her hand roughly onto Neal's forehead. She had some maternal impulses, although I wouldn't really have trusted her not to show the puppy-eating habit. "Are you sick, Neal?" she asked.

"No."

"What's the matter?"

"Eloise." He turned his head, finally. "I want to marry her. I proposed in the elevator going to the top of the Eiffel Tower. She turned me down."

"Well, congratulations," I said. "You were lucky that time." One of the most necessary things to learn in life is never to appear to want what you can't have; and when I had recently hinted to Pounce that she and I should marry, just for the conveniences (more mine than hers, admittedly), she had refused outright. I aimed my cane at a stuffed lion. "Bang, bang." I shot him, and flicked him on the floor. "Why in the world do you want to marry her?"

"What's the point in not being married?" he said.

"You must be afraid that she's going to get away from you, no?" That just slipped out—I didn't mean to say it.

He thought about it, but before he answered, I quickly said: "Are you two sleeping together?"

"That's not your business."

"You're getting so conventional, Brewster."

"I can imagine being with her when I am sixty," he said. "If you are sharing common human experience, why not go in for the common human formalities. Take what you can get out of them. The rest can't hurt you."

"This is too much," I cried, striking the armed tip of my stick on the floor smartly. "What has happened to the Brewster of yesterday? Where is the Lion of Oreville?"

"But I *feel* like marrying her," he said.

Another knock on the door. Enter Eloise, very smart in a blue silk suit—she never dressed like a tourist. She looked at us all, looked at Neal, surmised what we were talking about, for she must have known Neal well enough to know that he would not have been reserved about her refusal. My impression was that she wasn't very pleased—was Eloise, then, a potential foe, like Bliss, I wondered? There came a crash from the street at almost the same time, and then some excited voices—another of the numerous small accidents that happen in Paris. Pounce dashed for her camera and leaned way out of the window.

Neal sat up and took one of Eloise's hands, but he continued to talk to me. "The funny thing is, what I really want to do is to marry her and take her back to America and introduce her to my mother. And Uncle David, too, I suppose. Just so they'd know there was such a person as Eloise, and so she'd know them."

"What weakness. What a coward," I said to him. "Why did you run away in the first place?"

"Because I felt like it then."

"What was bad hasn't got better," I said. "Only the contrary ever happens on this accursed planet." I flicked a second lion to the floor.

"Mother's not so bad, Ned. You've never met her. And you've seen Uncle David at his worst."

"It's true I've never met your mother, and I don't imagine I ever will," I could not resist saying, since Pounce, who still dangled out of the window, could not hear me.

She drew back inside. "Nothing serious. It broke right up, but I got a picture." She addressed Eloise in her concentrative way. "I won't marry Ned because I can't think of us at forty, much less at sixty. If I could imagine us at sixty, then I might."

"You see," Neal said, down again, looking at the ceiling.

Eloise said, "But darling, what we *feel* isn't at stake at all, only what we should *do* about it."

And that was the only thing she would say, that day, in front of Pounce and me. In fact, she conveyed to us the idea that we might go on and leave them alone, so we went off to lunch.

My mood by then had gone a full cycle. I had started the morning in despair at our eviction, then cheered up a lot after considering Ahmed's offer, but now darkness settled down again. It turned into one of the days when my sense of doom, of unfavorable omens, was its strongest. I slept most of the afternoon and went to bed again right after dinner, although I had planned to go to the movies.

My psychic barometer steadied, of course, as I worked further into my ideas. All the talk we had had was actually something of a help. The necessity to limit what I wanted to do had been brought home to me—I quivered still from that "grandiose," that "pretentious." I narrowed my thematic range, and forewent any ambition to be the Dante of Sex. Following through on my musical analogy, I decided to divide the film into four movements. The first, *allegro,* a kind of universal awakening of and progress of desire, the basic drives and objectives of love, as seen in animals and humans —I planned to use the Correggio in it, and I did some early sequences using Neal's stuffed animals, which would have been a sensation in any toy-shop window. Then came, as I worked it out, the second movement, following all that display of energy: *lento,* love's languors, love spent, the sadness of fulfilled desire, the slaked thirst. Then, movement three, the *Marche funèbre*—violence and cruelty, the Ceremony of Blood. Finally what would have been, I think, my favorite part, the finale, *scherzo.* Here Dionysus was to reign triumphant over his whirling dancers—orgy, frenzy, divine madness. Just as in *Obstacles,* of which this new film was, in its way, the development, I used no narrative connectives, saw no single act through to the end, but, rather, linked a series of visual motifs into temporal and formal relationships with each other—or would have, if I had been able to finish the work. State a subject, then another, vary and intertwine them, relate them temporarily and by optical harmonics. Such was my ambitious formal design.

At the same time I worked out another scheme. I had begun to realize that for practical reasons what I wanted to do was two films, two films that would complement each other, one saying what the other could not. One of them I wanted to go only so far, in terms of your middle-class propriety. It was to remain sufficiently "clean" that it would pass at least a few censorship boards. In it only innuendo would strain the leniency of the law. The other—and I envisioned both as using a lot of the same footage—would dig into the subject on quite another level. The first would go for the high-brow film societies; the second would remain illegal to the end of time. Half my monument would show, half would lie buried.

I found a big room with good light, which I could rent for not too much money on weekends, and I got equipment for evenings, too. No questions asked, needless to say. There Pounce and I started to work, and I got her to teach me, too. She was quite willing, and we both knew why: it drew back another lock.

During these days we didn't see so very much of Neal and Eloise, but I have his journal in front of me, as usual, to fill in their activities. I really see no reason to inflict it on anyone. It is filled with all the goo one would expect from a lover who was inclined to be, shall we say, quite gushy anyway. Perhaps just a sample will serve to fill in this period:

"We walked around the Place des Vosges, Hôtel Carnavalet, etc., today, and some of the streets of that neighborhood where there are old houses. We go somewhere every day. Eloise very conscientious about that. She carries her *Blue Guide* and marks it with a pencil. Also keeps notes in notebook, including lots of sketches. I love to watch her concentrating when she looks at something. She is her most beautiful then. I try to think myself into her mind and see the way she does. Can't. I told her today that we wouldn't ever be matched where seeing things is concerned and asked her if she cared. She said no, that she had almost married another architect once, and one of the reasons she hadn't was monotony. If you bring sight to me, what do I bring to you, I asked her. Energy, she answered. And gusto."

Pounce and I went with them on a sight-seeing expedition one warm Sunday afternoon. We drove out to Fontainebleau in a car Eloise rented, toured the Château from top to bottom, stem to stern (how I should have liked a couple of those Primaticcio nymphs to undulate for my lens), then dallied for a while in the gardens. Afterward we drove slowly back toward Paris through the ancient royal forest where once the lords of France did love to hunt the stag, and where now smelly plebes promenaded and smooched. Those French . . . Tsk, tsk! We stopped the car by the road and walked ourselves, then sat down under some fine old trees, and I got out the camera and shot the strolling couples. It was like photographing animals from a blind, quite surprising what variety of behavior one could get, from a stationary position, in the course of an hour, if one faded cunningly into the background. I got tired and stopped. None of us said much; it was a sleepy time. I had a sudden spurt of photographic interest when two couples came by together, very close to us, about nineteen years old. The boys were identical twins, with the shock of up-ended hair so typical of French university students, and were dressed in tight cotton trousers (the American influence) and coarse sweaters of a different color for each, knit, I expect, by a devoted grandmother so they could be kept separate. I called out to them.

"Hey, we're doing a film on Sunday in France. It's a special project. How about posing for us?"

They looked at each other and at their girls. "Why us?" one of the boys asked, grinning.

209

"I could find lots of sweethearts, but not many twins," I replied. "Evidently."

The other shrugged. "Well, why not?" he said. "Where will we be able to see ourselves?"

"It depends on how the project turns out." I got up and had Pounce check my camera settings, for it was later in the afternoon—less light. "If it gets shown in Paris, I'll send you a note and some tickets, if you'll give me your names." He got a card out of his billfold and scribbled his Paris address on it, for the one printed there was in Besançon. He lived up behind the Sorbonne, on the Rue des Fossés-Saint-Jacques, not far from a little cinema club I'd been to. I told him so and said maybe he'd be shown in his own quarter. I told them to do what they pleased—walk around, sit down, talk, anything. I winked.

They were very good, very natural, particularly the boys, I suppose because, as twins, being on exhibition was normal to them. I stopped shooting when one of them had pretended to go to sleep with his head on his girl's lap, aping Neal and Eloise, while the other tickled his girl with a blade of grass. I didn't quite see them in either my first or second movement; but there was nothing to be done about it. I couldn't very well tell them to step up the voltage toward lewdness, young as they were, and posing for nothing.

"Perfect," I exclaimed. "Thanks a thousand."

They got up and passed in front of us to get back on their path again. "I have a question," I said, holding out Pounce's package of cigarettes. "Don't you ever get mixed up?"

All four of them smoked. "How?"

"I mean, don't you ever find yourselves kissing the other's girl?"

Gallic shrugs. "It's all the same."

I addressed one of the girls. "What about that?"

No shy maiden she. "I could tell which one it was."

"How? Tell me."

She answered me in English. "Charles is very serious. Armand is very gay. I could tell."

"Come on, come on. In French," one of the boys commanded.

Neal's own French was good enough to have followed the conversation, but he had some difficulty in posing a question he wanted to ask them, so that when he had finished I rephrased it for him.

"He wants to know if you can sense each other's thoughts," I explained. I guessed at a French word. "*Télépathie.* Is that correct?"

"That does happen, but only on Sundays," one of the brothers said—let us accept that it was probably Armand. He pretended to concentrate on reception. "I got a message just now that my brother wants to go on. Good-by, Yankees."

We all said good-by.

When they were out of earshot I began to expound on the subject, what a terrible thing it would be to be one of a pair of identical twins. "I mean, there would be all the obvious problems, like being mistaken for each other all the time, having strangers come up and talk to you, assuming they knew you, always having to explain. And then I should think the psychological strain would be terrific. Supposing I had a twin and the twin got on an airplane to go somewhere. I'd suffer agonies until he landed safely."

"He—or she," Eloise said.

"And the terrible feeling that one was sharing essence, genes and chromosomes, was only half of an egg, at bottom, the gnawing frustration of being forever divided, with nothing you could do about it. Forever deprived, forced to share." Back to crises. "Or when the twin was sick—think how you'd feel. I suppose it would be the greatest possible companionship, in a way, but also the greatest possible loss if anything happened, the greatest possible catastrophe. I mean, suppose my twin was on the point of death, imagine my feelings." As

211

I was talking I brought out my notebook and made a note to put such a scene in my film on Mr. Sick, if I ever made it. Little Mr. Sick with a slip of paper in each hand, but only one of them marked with an X. Mr. Sick conducts a lottery. "I'd never sleep at night. I'd shiver when the phone rang. I'd . . ."

Eloise interrupted me so sharply that my jaw remained ajar, ready for the next word, and Neal sat up to see what was the matter. "Stop. Stop, Ned. I mustn't let you go any farther. It will be too embarrassing. I should have stopped you before, but I was wondering where you'd go. You see, I am an identical twin. The sister who's arriving in a few weeks is my twin sister."

"Oh, for God's sake," I said. "Why didn't *you* stop me, Neal?"

"I didn't know," he said, very excited, jumping to his feet. "I didn't know either. Why didn't I know?" he shouted at Eloise, very angry.

They ignored Pounce and me; they slugged it out.

"I was going to tell you," she said, flushing—Eloise, too, had her temper. "But I was waiting until I felt like it. That's a principle you'll understand. You see, I'm bored with being a twin. I was liking not being one for the time."

"It isn't a question of liking it or not," Neal said. "A fact like that is so important that you can't put off telling it."

"Well, I did. Why do you really care so much?"

"Why? Why because it may be the most important thing about you that there is to know."

"Not quite," she answered, turning away from him.

"Then what is?" I interjected. I was ignored, as before.

"I should have been told about it." He walked around her in a circle, all but having to lean inward, he went so fast. "Damn it, Eloise, you've left me out."

Soothingly, now. "You're right, of course. I should have told you. Now that you know, I'll tell you something else. A man I once almost married has married my sister. What's more, when you were in San Francisco, and went into that coffeehouse, everything was up in the air and he was seeing both of us and was taking both of us out. So you see, Neal, it's not quite clear which of us you fell in love with—Patricia or me."

"But what a truly comic situation," I cried, delighted. "Which one are you, really, Patricia or Eloise—and please show proof."

This struck Neal as funny. "What's the difference?" he said, "if they are identical."

"There must be some. No two things in nature are ever alike. Consider the snowflake."

Eloise answered. "Eloise is always serious, and Patricia is always gay. Only that's not true. Eloise does what she feels like doing, and Patricia does what other people tell her is her duty. Now do you know which I am?"

"I think it is one's duty to do what one feels like doing," I said. "So I don't."

"Lord. Oh, lord," Neal said. "I wish I could sing something. This is wild. This changes everything."

Eloise, too, had risen to her feet, and she kissed Neal. "Patricia would never do a thing like that," she said.

"Not even if I told her she should?" I asked. "And besides, wasn't that your duty after deceiving Neal?"

"What a complicating factor," Neal exclaimed. "Twins. And both in that coffeehouse. Now what in the world does it mean?" He put his hands on her shoulders and turned her to face him. "If only you will marry me, you can have a new monogram. You could even have a tattoo. That way you'll always know which you are."

Pounce and I got up, too, for it was time we started back to Paris. "If you decide to do that, promise me one thing," I said.

"What?"

"Promise first."

They agreed.

"Let me choose where the monogram will go."

Everyone found the joke slightly schoolboyish, but, unsuppressed, I went on. "Also, I want to decide on its design, and I think that it should combine all three initials superimposed. That way, ELB would look exactly like PLB, which would solve the problem."

My tortoise-minded Pounce said: "Solve the problem? How?"

Playfully, I struck her bicep with my fist. "Solve it *my* way, sweetie pie," I replied.

9.

One of the modern practices most worthy of scorn is, in my opinion, that of going away for weekends. Mind, I say going away for weekends, not for weeks or months or forever, all of which are quite different and perfectly acceptable. But the brief weekend is a horrible affair, filled with activities, and the more one is promised rest and nothing to do, the more sleep one loses, the more weeds one pulls, the more people one meets whom one will never meet again.

Our weekend at Ahmed's country place, when he honored his invitation to Eloise, fits my description in a good many ways. For one thing, we spent quite a long time coming and going, which necessitated leaving Paris early, and that was sleep lost right there. For another, there was too much to do —not people to meet, for Ahmed never provided people, but places to be visited. His house, which was eighteenth-century, a done-over manor house, never very grand but now at least very comfortable, was built on the edge of a valley, commanding a view of a long backbone of hills on one of which was built the town of Vézelay. That meant that we had to visit the church of the Magdalene there, not once, but often—often!—

including Sunday morning, so that Eloise could satisfy a conceit she had to see those mossy stones in use. And there were other places all around. It seems to me that as I look back we were always crowding, all six of us, into Ahmed's car and spinning off someplace. The important things that happened were all slipped in between the organized sports.

"We" consisted of June Bliss, as well as of Pounce and Neal and Eloise. June consented to come on the weekend; perhaps she didn't really mind very much, I don't know. I have no idea whether they argued, she and Ahmed, over it or not. My guess is that she regarded it as less improper to entertain fornicators in the country than in the city. I am sure she didn't acquiesce through a prophetic knowledge that it would be the last time we would all be together.

Let us see what happened, according to my mental appointment book:

Friday, June 14.

11:52 A.M. We arrive from Paris. We all exclaim about how pretty the countryside is. The yard behind the house is terraced, and there is a very fine view. June has already been here several weekends and is offensively "at home" and familiar when we are being shown around the place. Example: she tells the manservant to bring some chairs *as usual,* as soon as he has put away the luggage.

12:03. We retire to our respective rooms in order to wash before meeting before lunch. Pounce and I have a large room with a low ceiling and a fireplace in it, in a wing of the house where no sense of classic proportions ever reached. Older than rest of house?

12:45. We gather in the garden. Pounce has changed to those tight, below-the-knee-length trousers and a striped shirt, and looks like a girl masquerading as a French sailor in a musical comedy. June demure in seersucker. Eloise, the lady, in more formal summer dress, some kind of brilliant printed stuff. She comes out last, and I see her approach from the house, smoothing her hair back toward the knot with the outer edge of her flattened hand. Does her twin do that, too, I wonder? Neal gets up to meet her as if she were Garbo. Boy, has he ever got it bad, I think. We have vermouth, etc., until 1:30, then go to eat. Lunch delicious.

3:00. Lunch over. Naps all around. Three couples, how much amour? I wonder. Neal and Eloise in separate rooms, but a door between. Ahmed telephoned me night before to inquire about that arrangement before he called people in country. I said adjoining rooms with access. Keep Junesie guessing.

4:30. Walk. We stroll down into the valley and along a stream there. Little traffic. We round a bend in the road and have to cross a small stone bridge, where there has been recent work going on—odd stones lying around, etc. We stop on top of the bridge to look across valley toward Vézelay. Suddenly a very queer thing happens. Just as if the hidden underside of bridge contained a fissure leading into Inferno, a troup of demons comes scrambling out as we stand there, dumfounded. They hurry up the steep banks of the stream and pour out onto the road, dark faces, shredded clothes, clucking to each other in their diabolic lingo. We are surrounded—will we be dragged back? They stop, however, and stare at us—more talk—then, after a few evil leers at the girls, take up tools, etc., lying around. Construction crew, taking a smoke where they wouldn't be noticed. Algerians, like most such laborers in France at that time. All this took only a few seconds.

Ahmed suddenly says, "Come on. Come on, we must get away from here." We turn and stare at him. "Hurry up, hurry up, you fools." He is dead white, and I think terrified, probably more for June than for himself or us. He hurries her away drawing her along by an arm, and he won't let us slow down until we are back in his house. I tease him, and he jumps down my throat, telling me I don't know what I'm talking about, and, in a word, to be quiet. I sulk. He cautions servant to keep close watch and lock everything carefully. We retire to wash some more.

6:45. Drinks before dinner. Americans all have Martinis, Ahmed has vermouth. Still very upset, I can see. Dinner delicious.

10:00. Ahmed suggests we all go over to Vézelay and have a look at the church by moonlight. We all pile in. I sit in front with June and Ahmed. She shrinks from contact. Screw her. Eloise says façade of church nineteenth century. Ahmed says one of the Crusades was first preached here. Violation of Islam by France. I ask him if he has forgotten Roland and all that. Neal and Eloise wander off together, billing and etc. On way home I speculate about a movie in which layers of history would be shown simultaneously. Pounce says she thinks it might be too much like De Mille, and I get furious at her. I mean really furious—I'm not using the word in the watered-down modern sense. Stop tearing down my idea, Pounce. Neal puts his hand on my shoulder, shakes me slightly (slightly, not gently) and tells me to take it easy. Pounce withdraws from further conversation. Everybody else embarrassed. Why?

Saturday, June 15.

9:00. Breakfast in our room. Pounce lights into me for night before. I am contrite and explain that I am worried. We gossip about Ahmed and those Algerians.

10:00. We all pile into Ahmed's car for a day's touring of the neighborhood. Return about five, many churches later. Indefatigable Eloise now looks really tired. A drink helps her a little.

8:00. Dinner. Don't remember menu, but would guess it must have been duck. Ahmed's country cook too ignorant to re-educate to June's standards—*Grâce à Dieu!* Eloise goes to bed right after dinner. Neal looks worried. I tell him he's acting more like a mother than a friend. I stay up after others

have gone to bed and think about the future and about
Pounce and about lots of things, including even David Wallace and his bribe, gradually letting my thoughts fog up with
Ahmed's brandy. I certainly don't feel like a tomcat around
Pounce any more, yet I still have need of her. If she weren't
there, I can't imagine what would happen to me. I wonder
what it all means. I hear a sound and jump. Ahmed. He has
come out to check the shutters and doors. He tells me not to
go out into the garden at night. I sit on. Finally I go to bed
and put my arms around Pounce, who wakes up. I say that
she is going to have to fight off the Devil when he comes to
get me. She promises she will if she is there at the time. I fall
asleep with Pounce in my arms.

Sunday, June 16.

9:00. Breakfast. I ask Pounce what she meant by saying she
would if she were there at the time, and she replies, putting
strawberry jam on a *croissant,* that the Devil probably would
have enough sense to choose a time when I was alone.

10:00. We all pile in to go to Vézelay to see the church in
action. Beautiful day. Striped interior of church surprises me.
Service going on. Several parishioners turn to look at me. I
cross myself with holy water on my way out. Always the
trouper.

1:30. Lunch. Delicious. Strawberries sublime. June describes
old-fashioned shortcake to Ahmed.

3:00. Naps all around. I get up early and so does Pounce. She
goes off to read under some trees. I wander around, bored.
I encounter Ahmed. He puts his finger to his lips and takes
me to a brick wall. Behind it is an enclosed garden where he
has said we could sun-bathe if we wanted to, because it is
sheltered. He takes me to a place in the wall where there is a
peephole, and on the other side I see Neal and Eloise. They are
lying on their backs, but now and then they turn to kiss and
caress. I tiptoe away and get a camera and return. The wall,
the breeze, the distance keep them from knowing or hearing

218

me. They become more heated in their love-making. I take more film. And so on and on, until we pass from Film One to Film Two. Ahmed is disturbed that I am doing this, but I tell him that I will give it to Neal when it is developed. They stop, I stop. Neal leans over her and she takes her finger and touches the cleft in his chin. They talk. Then she raises the hand and he strokes it, running his fingers down each of her own. He takes a ring from one of his and places it on her left hand, fourth finger. I look at Ahmed. Ahmed looks at me. We tiptoe away.

6:00. *Apéritifs.* We all pile in later and drive to Avallon to have dinner there at one of the great restaurants of France. I have the *galantine* followed by *Jambon à la crème,* etc., etc. Groaning, we pile back into the car and return to Ahmed's house. It is the last night, and everyone feels that it should be commemorated in some way—everyone except June. Ahmed gets out champagne (the servants are off) and we drink some. It is then that Neal tells us that he and Eloise are engaged and will be married when her sister and brother-in-law get to Europe. He is very happy. Persistence has overcome resistance. She is happy, too, but maintains her characteristic mood, restrained, a little somber. Ahmed is nostalgic, light, perhaps a teensy bit melancholy. Junelet pouts. Pounce is frankly depressed. I don't give a damn. There's nothing like a little good news to get a party going.

Monday, June 17.

We all pile into Ahmed's car and return to Paris via Vézelay, because Eloise wants a last look at it. The note of sadness again. I remain in the car, out of sorts, with a hangover.

10.

May I confess something? That I feel myself a weary traveler at last, tired by the sometimes rough and confusing, although fairly sunny, terrain through which I have been trudging with you, unknown reader, as my companion, and, to tell the truth, rather depressed by the unfriendly and dark glen I see ahead, through which we must yet go. This moment, standing at the end of one road and at the beginning of another, is worth perhaps a slight hesitation, a stock-taking. Until now, I would say that the crises in our little tale have been . . . civilized. All the characters have behaved as decent and respectable characters should; and the Devil, when he has appeared, has shown himself clownish, grinning. His cynicism and irony haven't really hurt, not *really*. But that old Nick can be quite otherwise. He mocks and giggles, and one giggles right along. Then he turns, and seeing that he amuses you so much, he does something really hilarious—smashes in your face and scuttles off picking fragments of your teeth out of his leathery fist. That's not so funny, friend. You don't smile if your face is ruined.

Whatever grinning devil was guardian over our lives decided at just about this point that he would display another side. With the genial invention of his species, he began his new campaign to the accompaniment of lutes and love songs, and set it in the soft warm nights of the Midi; but the hand which directed that Provençal serenade was doubling up.

I rather think I have put across the message that Neal, under the influence of Cupid, Tamer of Men, had been revealing some tendencies to turn into what is known, in certain repellent strata of American society, as a Square. I have sometimes thought that if he and Eloise had been less star-crossed they might have ended a quite conventional couple, almost, because once that tiresome impulse to be an integrated part of one's kind gets going it has a tendency to take everything over in the end. Today's Socialist, as has been remarked, is tomorrow's Tory.

Neal, in any case, was saved from quite that, as much by

the Devil as by anyone else. Eloise's brother-in-law, ex-beau, whose name was Robert Waters, may have helped, too. Rather well known he is now, for doing modern houses, whose chief distinction is that they always hang over hillsides. It seems to me a small melody to play, but fashion is a great amplifier. Waters was the most propriety-minded of men, and I think that he helped Neal to define himself, clear up some points, decide how much out of his various inherited packages was worth keeping, how much to show, how much to hide, how much to throw away.

They didn't meet in Paris, because Rob and Patricia Waters arrived one evening and flew the next day to Nice. They had taken a villa at Sainte-Maxime for six weeks or so. The fiction was that Rob Waters was dead tired from overwork and wanted a complete rest, but of course he began to do business within hours after arriving on the Côte d'Azur with the renters and owners of neighboring villas, making contacts, all that sort of thing. Eloise told them on their way through Paris that she wanted to stay over a week or so and would join them later. She spent the week with Neal, then went on south, told them then she wanted to have a guest down, and Neal was invited for the tenth of July, to stay as long as he wanted. Until they moved to Florence, that is, where they had still another villa for August and early September, the home there of the Rector of the American Church in Florence, who was a classmate of Rob's (Yale) and was going to be away those weeks.

Now let's have another go at Neal's journals.

I saw the two sisters together today. Finally today I saw them together. The Lincoln twins. I was frozen as the moment came. I don't know what I expected to happen, but I had the feeling that something might, like an earthquake. Patricia was upstairs getting dressed to go out when we came in from the airport. I saw her later. Eloise said that all they do is go out, that and sit in the sun to get over the wine of the night before. Robert Waters, who was much the way I remembered him, crew cut and all, was ready downstairs. I felt suspicion from him, although there shouldn't be any. Like the feeling I felt from him in San Francisco, as if everything about the two Lincoln sisters was his and he wanted nobody to have any of it, including any part of their twinship.

Twinship! What a thing to happen.

The place they live in is called the Villa Chaminade. It has a garden behind it full of geraniums, and from the house a view down onto the bay. There is a great cape across the bay, where there is a town called Saint-Tropez. I gather from the way people were talking later that Saint-Tropez is a place everyone is supposed to have heard of. I'm keeping my mouth shut around here, feeling my way. Eloise did say in the car to watch out a little for Rob, that he had his rough side.

Twinship. What does it mean? I mean, what does it mean to someone like *me,* to love a twin? I keep wondering just how much of Eloise belongs forever to Patricia, hence how much of her belongs to Rob. I wonder if that was what he was thinking? I don't think I resent the possibility, because what is there to do about it? But someone else might.

Question for Eloise: Do she and Patricia have identical dreams?

What does she feel when she and Patricia come together after such a long time away from each other? Like streams of water?

If she and Patricia complete each other, yet each now has a man who also complements and completes her, then what are the mathematical, geometric relations of the four of us? Are we four equal divisions of a large square? Or are Rob and I each attached to one side of a single unit which is divided down the middle by a line? There are other possibilities. I had better jot them down, just to get them clear in my mind. . . .

222

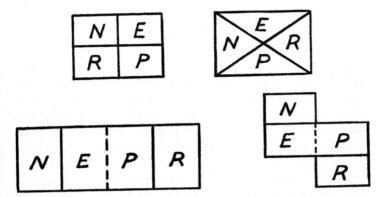

And that's only the beginning. What if we got into circles?

How alike they do look. Eloise was watching me when I met Patricia. So was Rob. Everybody watches everybody else at the Villa Chaminade, and I watch just as hard as the other three. I think they make an effort not to dress alike to save other people embarrassment. I mean E. and P. I'd know the difference anyway. Worlds of difference, I'm concluding. They have a different feel when you touch them. They also smell different.

They are very close. They hardly needed to talk in order to communicate. I tried standing between them—no appreciable interference. I think Rob is better at jamming. They seem to draw back from each other when he is in the room.

Patricia has been very nice to me, but I have caught her looking at me curiously several times, as if she didn't understand something. I need a twin to set her straight. They don't ask personal questions, these people, so nobody has asked me anything about myself yet.

There was an accident out in the bay this afternoon. We saw it from where we were lying on the beach, but couldn't tell exactly what was happening. Word spread fast. Also ambulances and police cars and the like. A boy was swimming off his sailboat, and someone in a motorboat ran over him. Both his hands were severed, so perhaps he was trying to shield his head.

Everybody at the house we went to tonight before dinner was talking about nothing except whether laws and regulations couldn't be passed, only since most of them owned or used both power boats and sailboats, they didn't know who was supposed to be protected from what. They just knew that the death was an outrage during a lovely summer, particularly because the boy was the son of some Hungarian nobility, and the power boat belonged to a Philadelphian who raced thoroughbreds, and there ought to have been some kind of a regulation that would have prevented it. Eloise said it was because they are all rich that they all think there is so much to be gained by passing rules. Rich people probably break more rules than most people, and that is why they have so much faith in them.

After we got back I talked to Rob for the first time, although I've been here now five days. The first time alone is what I mean. The people we had dinner with, who had had us and others for cocktails, are going to build a house designed by Waters, it turns out. Or they probably will. They live in a much bigger place, higher on the hill, which is called the Villa Vertige, and come from Seattle, where they own an island in Puget Sound. They are called Mr. and Mrs. Gould, also Fid and Prissy, Fid being a short form of Fiddler, itself a nickname, Prissy short for Priscilla. Everybody in their circle seems to have a nickname. There was an argument about the house they're going to build. Eloise said on the way home that she could imagine the kind of a house Fid and Prissy would want, a house just like the Villa Vertige, only made of glass and heart of cypress, and fog-resistant, and Rob flared up and said that they could at least pay for it, and the only architecture he knew of that got built was architecture that could get paid for, and that only architecture that got built could be considered architecture. Wham!

When we got back to the Villa Chaminade, the girls went upstairs (only bathroom is on second floor) and Rob and I had a drink together downstairs while they were gone. He took me into the small room where he has been working. I asked about some sketches I saw lying around, but he pushed them into a pile so I couldn't see them.

"Later," he said. "They're ideas for the Gould house, and some others." The drinks he poured were big. Then he sat down and for the first time seemed to realize that he and I were alone together, and he was going to have to do something about it. I had already figured that out.

He gave me a funny look, not very cordial. "So you're the guy who kept Eloise in Paris," he said.

I was surprised. That seemed the least of it to me, but these people depend heavily on what they call "arrangements." "I guess I am," I said.

"How the hell did you ever get to know her?"

I thought carefully before I answered him. Should I tell him the real truth or not, all of it or part of it or none of it? I decided the truth was best. "I saw her one time with you in San Francisco," I said. "I never forgot her. I recognized her in Paris and introduced myself."

"Saw her with me? You mean, just from a distance."

"There are distances and distances."

"That was all?"

"That was all."

"Christ," he said. Patricia came into the room, and he told her what I'd told him. "That's all she knows about him. Imagine that—that's all she knows about him," he said. "She doesn't know who or what he is at all." Eloise joined us. "He could be a bum or anything else, including dead broke and aware that your father owned half of Palo Alto."

"I don't think that would mean much to Neal," Eloise said. "That would mean a lot to you, Rob, but not to him."

He turned red in the face. "Of course it would," he said slowly. "I can't understand anybody that wouldn't mean a lot to."

"Just concede that it could happen," she said.

"I can't."

I felt it was time I said something. "Palo Alto does mean something to me," I put in. "That's where Stanford is."

"You see. I said so," Eloise said to Patricia. And suddenly they had closed in and both Rob and I were left out of their understanding.

Eloise and I drove into the back country today for a picnic, to get away from crowds of people, traffic, and all that. We borrowed the Waterses' car and went for about two and a half hours, into mountains and olive groves. She said it all looked like a Cézanne. We stopped by the side of a road and watched a man with some goats on the hillside. Eloise showed me how goats wiggle their tails. She said she wished she had one to wiggle like that sometimes. Show what you think of people and things. I made a little white goat's tail out of my handkerchief and wiggled it. "That to Rob," I said.

I asked Eloise when she was going to put my ring back on her finger publicly, for good. She turned away from me the way she does when she is going to go against what I want. She said she didn't know. "Are you afraid to tell your sister? She got married, why shouldn't you?" I asked, thinking there might be some kind of a one-way twinly loyalty involved.

She spread a picnic cloth. "I don't know when I'll tell them. Let's not think about it right now."

My feelings were hurt and I said so. Why was she so reluctant about permanent steps? Did she doubt me in some way?

A goat came up almost to us, but when we held out hands to it, it twitched its tail and sprang away. "So much for all of you," Eloise said.

"Even me?"

She nodded. "You, too."

I found that very reassuring, for some reason.

There was some interesting talk about the Gould house again tonight. I won't put most of it down, since lots of it was in front of the Goulds and doesn't count. In the car, coming home, Eloise said she didn't think Rob's plans were as good as other houses he had done. Too commercial. She was really tough on him. Rob was infuriated and started to fight back, but I saw Patricia put a hand on his arm. Afterward I asked Eloise what it was all about.

"It's all about why I didn't marry him," she answered.

She told me that she had worked in Rob's office, and that they simply didn't see eye to eye. "He was lucky, as it turned out. He got someone nearer what he wants and needs. Patricia will be nice to the Fids and the Prissies, and wait for him to outgrow his cheaper ambitions. He knows it, too. I suppose he always knew. But he had some trouble deciding between what was better for him, and what might make him better— do better work, I mean."

"Patricia knows about this, and she doesn't care? You're so much alike and yet that much different," I said in wonder.

"You've seen," she replied. "Those sides of us that touch the other are very smooth and neatly fitting, but the other sides, which face other people, are quite different. Which of the two sides means the more? I don't know. The smooth ones mean more to her and me, me and her; the different ones more to her and Rob or to you and me. But there are two sides. Everything has to have two sides."

"Wonderful," I said. "It's just wonderful."

We had walked into town to buy a bottle of gin, and at this moment turned from the hot, glaring street into the garden of the Villa Chaminade—have I noted that there was a little plaque on the gate saying that "Here, during such and

227

such years, lived Cécile Chaminade, Composer of the Scarf Dance"? "You know, I'm beginning to talk a little like you, Neal," Eloise said, stopping to pick a huge scarlet geranium. "Two months ago I don't believe any of what I just said would have occurred to me. And I certainly wouldn't have said it, even if I'd thought it."

"Our joint side is getting smooth."

"Wonderful," she answered. "It's just wonderful."

I was thinking about San Francisco and twinship today, and I suddenly understood one of Rob's problems. I was watching Patricia sitting alone in the garden. I was supposed to be asleep on a chaise longue and she was reading. The other two were off somewhere together, for they do get along much of the time. Rob talks to Eloise a lot, because even though she hurts his vanity, he knows that her ideas are good. I watched the expressions on Patricia's face as she read, how it would change when there was something funny, settle into passivity when she was less interested, how the corners of her eyes would wrinkle when she had to think. I realized again how much she really did look like Eloise, even though they feel and smell different. And there came an expression on her face and a turn to her head as she looked out to investigate some noise from the direction of the water that suddenly reminded me of the girl in the coffeehouse in San Francisco. It might really have been Patricia. If Patricia had decided to turn Rob down and come to Paris, mightn't I have met and fallen in love with her?

In fact, I think it's a 50-50 chance it was Patricia. She and Eloise are in a 50-50 relationship, so it has to be a 50-50 chance.

I thought: then one part of me will always be in love with Patricia, because of the 50-50. Now doesn't that mean that part of Patricia will always belong to me? And in that case, isn't he right to be jealous? And doesn't that mean that part of Eloise will always belong to Rob? As I thought all this, I got quite jealous of him, walking off somewhere, arguing with Eloise.

All this is so complex that the only thing to do is to hang on to Eloise through it all. Patricia and Rob are geometrical figures in a certain relationship to Eloise and me. They are flat areas, bounded by lines, adjoining other areas. I can't try to understand it all, only relate to them geometrically, according to the laws of mathematics.

It's getting so near the time when the Waterses will move to Florence that Eloise had to tell them we were engaged and were going to be married. She did it three days ago at breakfast, which we have, when we get up at the same time, on a wrought-iron table out in the garden, under some big plants with dark-green leaves. Lots of butterflies and yellow jackets trying to get the jam.

"You can't be serious," Rob said, spilling.

"When, Elly? Good lord, when?" Patricia said.

No congratulations. No cheers.

"Soon," Eloise replied. "I'll drive down to Florence with you as we planned, and Neal will return to Paris for a couple of weeks. Then he can come to Florence, and we'll be married there."

"But . . ." Rob said. He started fresh. "But you don't even know Neal, not really."

"You can't both be unaware that he and I know each other rather well," Eloise said, looking from one to the other.

Rob looked down, and I felt his pain at the fact, now that it was out in the open where he had to deal with it.

"I didn't know I was going to have to go back to Paris," I said.

Eloise nodded. "I just decided that, Neal. Thinking it over by myself. I want you to go back there and think it over yourself."

Patricia and Rob looked at each other. "I should say he might want to," Rob said.

"That's why I'm sending him away."

Everybody looked at everybody else. Typical of the Villa Chaminade.

"I won't back out," I said. "As far as I'm concerned, it's all settled."

We've had a kind of truce the three days since then, as far as group discussions of the engagement go, although I'm sure there have been two- and maybe three-part conversations without me. I guess this from the way Eloise has shown up looking tired and with bad color under her tan. I finally told her yesterday that she wasn't to talk to her family any more, and she promised.

Rob and Patricia have changed toward me. They are more accepting, but also seem almost afraid of me, or afraid of offending me, or something like that. Rob said today when we were alone that he supposed that as Eloise's nearest male relative he ought to know something about me, in case the plan went through. I said it would go through. Was I financially solvent? I told him I wasn't, but that I would deal with the problem, he needn't worry, and maybe I had great expectations.

He took the last remark as pure talk and ignored it. "Eloise is quite rich, you know, Neal," he said.

"It doesn't matter," I replied.

"Yes it does."

"Tell me, Rob. What is wrong with our getting married?" I asked him.

"Never mind. That's not up to me to say. Anyway, your own financial position is no worse than the rest of it. Let's get drunk." And he, at least, did. It was, moreover, intended as a friendly gesture when he asked me to join him. Rob wasn't stupid. He knew, too, that there was some pretty complicated

230

geometry involved, and that he'd better come to terms with it.

I leave for Paris tomorrow, and have already arranged for Eloise to meet me, when I come in on the Paris-Rome Express, at the train station in Florence, the eighteenth of August. Meanwhile, she'll arrange for our wedding.

II.

Have I said how much out of joint my nose had been put by Neal's adventures? Have I hinted at it? It's true. I resented all his luck with Eloise, for instance, not that it wasn't all right if he had a girl, but why did she have to be so God-damned elegant, and so obviously fancy rich, too? When they decided that they would get engaged I couldn't help but draw a comparison between them and Pounce and me, the course of normal love, if you could call it that, with its promise, however phony, of permanence, with what I had. I've already said what I have to say on that subject, I know, but I just don't want it to get forgotten in the midst of all this. Not that I would *really* have chosen marriage for myself. I mean it. But I resented Neal's having a choice which I did not. Then he left to go south, and during the time he was gone, I managed to raise quite a little weed patch of resentment. It was a bad time. In spite of all my ideas for the new films, I had trouble getting into them. I had my studio, and I hired some people who were willing to do rather strange and wonderful things in it (that is a different story), but still, I didn't feel satisfied. There was something I couldn't get around, something I couldn't climb over. I didn't want my friends to fly to some sunny paradise and live in thoughtless happiness there. If Neal had had any consideration, any real gratitude for all I had done for him, he at least wouldn't have planned to leave for so long.

I welcomed him coldly back to Paris, and my feelings were mixed when, two days later, he burst into my room about ten A.M. holding a letter. He shook me in my bed and shouted: "What is leukemia, Ned? Where can I find out what leukemia is?"

I told him what I knew, which wasn't much. I got dressed and we went to a bookstore where we found a medical encyclopedia. I will never forget the general statement about the disease, put with the incomparable detachment of such books. I translate:

"The prognosis is generally unfavorable. There is no known cure, and the disease is invariably fatal, unless some other complication intervenes to terminate the patient's life before the leukemia shall have run its course."

That was what was wrong with Eloise. Those sudden fatigues, that well-bred melancholy. Neal had his beloved, but she, more than most, carried mortality in her very life's blood.

It was shocking, obscene. Even Pounce cried when she heard. I endeavored to purify my own reactions, because it was, after all, more punishment than Neal's transgression deserved.

There were two kinds of the disease, which may or may not be two related diseases: one works like lightning, the other can be prolonged for years. So far Eloise had the latter, and in its earliest stages. She might live for some time—even a decade.

Her letter, part of which I quoted some pages ago, went on to explain all this, to explain that it ought to make a lot of things clear to Neal, and that she should have told him the day they met, that she was marked for death, and that he should forget her.

"But I can't," he said, when he read the letter through to us. "I can't forget her. I still want to marry her."

"You can't marry her," I opined, not without a trace of satisfaction. "Knowing what you do, you would never have a

232

happy moment. She might die any time and it won't be pretty." I mentioned, delicately, one or two symptoms harvested from that encyclopedia.

"So might you or Pounce. So might I. It is possible I will die before she does, and maybe not prettily either," Neal said. I thought about witty Mr. Sick and the little slip of paper he had left on Eloise's drafting board—had he done it the day Neal saw her in San Francisco, if indeed it was she whom he saw? I wonder. Then Neal said: "Now I understand about Patricia and Rob. They are afraid."

"I don't understand."

"Twinship. The hazard of twinship," he said.

"Possibly. It's irrational, though."

Pounce spoke up, having thought slowly and seriously. "Neal, do you think Eloise really wants to marry you? Really? Do you think that she would have married you if it weren't for her sickness?" It was quite bright of Pounce to have put her finger on an essential in the situation, namely that it revolved more around Eloise than around Neal. Slow but sure, my chelonian Pounce.

"How can you discard the fact of her disease, even hypothetically?" I said. "How can any question be asked with any relevance which leaves that out?"

"But do you, Neal?" Pounce persisted.

Neal considered her question. "Yes, I think she would. There is no telling for sure. I don't doubt that it's made a difference. She has needed me or someone more than she ever would have before. I want to believe, yes, that she would have married me, and nobody can disprove that, so it's true, true for me. And I don't care anyway. If she will marry me now, then I will marry her. I think that's what I'm supposed to understand. I know that much from things that were said at Sainte-Maxime. She would forgive me if I backed out, but she will marry me if I don't."

233

"Then marry her." Pounce's decisions, when they finally came, were irrevocable.

"I will," he replied.

And marry her he did, after a fashion. I am not writing a sentimental account of his life, and I'm not going to waste time with any romantic bosh. I don't know what flowers she carried, or if her veil was of tulle. In a way, only disease saved Neal's love from banality. Let us at least thank leukemia for that, and Mr. Sick, too—but I imagine I am writing now in bad taste. I return to events.

Marry her, to repeat, he did. First he telephoned all over North Italy to catch her en route to Florence. He finally got her and told her simply that he was coming on as scheduled, and she should arrange for the wedding. That was all. No arguments.

He came to us from the phone. "It's not really so bad," he said, "when you think about it. Lots of marriages don't last as long as ours may last. My own father and mother weren't married ten years."

"It's the knowing about it," I said.

"True, but . . ."

We were repeating ourselves, yet what else could we do? I thought to myself then how we were reducing the situation to something like normal, talking about it as if it were any other problem, like an unfinished medical education or military service.

Neal asked us to come to Florence for the wedding, but we couldn't go. I didn't have the money, and Pounce wouldn't leave me behind. Neal offered to have me come as his guest, but it didn't seem worth it. Pounce objected, and, after a few second thoughts, I decided it was better not to. There's no point in exposing our worse sides to too great temptation.

Once more we hear the orchestra of love tune up, hear the sweet southern melodies trailing out over the sculptured Tuscan hills on that bright afternoon when Neal and Eloise were married, and illegally married at that. The complications they encountered were prodigious. Involved were the American Foreign Service Regulations, which stipulate that no American official may perform a wedding ceremony abroad, although he may witness one—what happens, may I ask, if the consular official is an ordained minister?—and certain impossible provisions of Italian law. They had to give up the idea of legality and settle for being wed in the eyes of God. That is, Eloise telephoned to Rob's classmate, the one who owned the villa in Florence, up in the mountains where he had gone to escape the heat, and explained their problem. He caught an express train down, married them with the appropriate words from the Book of Common Prayer, cautioned them that what he had done was not binding in any court of law and that they should have it done over once they reached the States and shouldn't mention it around because he would be jailed, and with a twinkle of black sandals he was off for the Cour Majeur again, saying on the train platform that those who could wear linen jackets could stand Florence in August, but those committed to the black had best get out. He didn't stay overnight.

A consular official was there unofficially, pretending not to notice what was going on. After several drinks, postceremonial, he said, with the bureaucratic urbanity of his species, that he wasn't responsible if Neal and Eloise wanted to live in sin, this to that same classmate.

None of this matters. All it meant was that the ceremony wouldn't take in Italy or America, but presumably it was duly noted Elsewhere.

The Waterses, too, were witnesses, and so were a couple of other Americans whom they knew but did not tell all to. There were a few wires sent, and the doctor advised by telephone to San Francisco, Rob on this end. Rob wanted announcements mailed out, since only he and Patricia and now Neal and of course the doctor knew of Eloise's trouble, so nobody else would know how strange a thing it was for her to marry, and would merely think it strange if they didn't send announcements. On the other hand, the irregular nature of the ceremony was a problem. Rob fretted. Was it perhaps better to ignore it and send the announcements when the legal ceremony had been performed back in America? Much thought was used over all this, amidst the general gloom, troubled Waters. It was decided that announcements would be sent at once, because Rob knew his classmate, and he knew that the parson, after getting a couple of Martinis sloshed down behind the pectoral cross sometime, would gossip—about the marriage, not, obviously, about its illegality.

Neal notes in his journal that by this time the presence of the disease seemed to him quite normal. It had been so much talked about, it intruded so little in fact. A mere indefinite certainty, like living over an earthquake fault, or farming on the slope of a volcano. I quite understand what he was trying to say, and have remarked how I noticed it beginning to happen by the time he left Paris. Anyway, after they were a few days on their honeymoon, the problem of the disease had become quite smoothed over, encapsulated in plastic that had neither taste nor texture nor color nor smell, but was just there, quite in the abstract, a laboratory demonstration kept in isolation from real life.

They were, in fact, happy. They saw sights, ate well, drank lots of good wine, even talked about the Black Death (epidemic of 1348) in Siena, he notes, and joked about gentle sister leukemia in Assisi. In Perugia one night they discussed whether or not, had Eloise been in good health, she would have fallen in love with Neal, and whether Neal would have fallen in love with her—that earlier question of Pounce's. They decided it didn't matter. I repeat, they decided it *didn't matter.*

"Eloise says," Neal wrote, "that it is fitting our love should have some sadness in it, too. We both have come to feel that it is more touching, more moving, *means* more that way. Any

236

silly fool could be happy with the view from the terrace behind the cathedral at Orvieto, or wandering through the streets of Cortona. We were happy, too, those places; but our happiness is touched with the sadness of finality. We will never do these things together again; we have done them with so much more feeling, as a result. I suppose it would surprise the average honeymooners that we don't envy them. We really wouldn't exchange with them, for our own has more depth."

Ha! The small problem encapsulated, to become the object, where noticed at all, of a kind of Country Graveyard contemplation. Yes, they finally ended by rejoicing in their very affliction, for it enhanced life. That wasn't the way the Devil intended to leave things.

Shortly before they had to return to Florence to see the Waterses off for Rome and home, they came to Urbino, and remained there overnight. Before dinner, sitting in their hotel room, Neal wrote both his mother and his Uncle David. He sent some snapshots to the former. Eloise, too, wrote her, and after dinner—he doesn't specify the menu—they went out into the town to mail the letters at the main post office. There are several things to see in Urbino, according to an old guide I have consulted (I have never been there)—one of the finest Renaissance palaces, a famous Piero della Francesca "Flagellation." Neal comments on that painting, how he and Eloise stood in front of it in the afternoon and talked about the way the dramatic event has been reduced to planes and lines, all emotions contained within geometrical relationships. He told her about his diagrams, then, of her, himself, her sister, and her brother-in-law. Above all, Urbino is known for its beauty of disposition and for the fine countryside around it. They walked the streets as night fell, looking thoroughly at everything they hadn't seen, looking, looking, looking, hand in hand, happy together. They sat in a square in the lower area of the town and had something to drink at an outdoor café, a simple place, such as a provincial town like Urbino would

237

have, nothing fancy, no awnings, no little orchestra playing gems from Puccini. There were two musicians, who made a few lire in the evenings playing for German tourists who came up from the Adriatic Coast, and they played for Eloise and Neal. An idyl, a veritable idyl.

The next day they got up and drove over the desolate pass that leads from Urbino across the mountains into Tuscany. On the way down the winding road, after the summit, Eloise was driving, to spell Neal; and as they rounded a sharp curve, a driver coming up the slope, made frantic by a slow oil truck he had been trailing for five or six kilometers, passed blind, and there was a head-on collision. It happens all the time in Italy.

The trucker did what he could. He put the other driver in the shade to wait the hours it took for an ambulance to get up the pass; and he mopped up the blood from Neal's cuts. Meanwhile, a guardian devil got out of our friends' car and swaggered off into the dry brush, unseen, wiping a hand on his hairy leg. Since leukemia hadn't sufficed, he had doubled up that eager fist of his and thrown Eloise a real haymaker.

Neal, when he got out the journal of his love affair with Eloise, to give it to me to use for this manuscript, appended a note to it, which will suitably close the episode.

"I could have almost everybody around me who accompanied me or helped me on my rise, my triumphal entry into the City of Manhood and Inheritance, except the person I loved—Eloise. I can't have Eloise. Why? Not because she was an ideal, the thing nobody can ever have. That is not the point at all. She was mine, but I could not keep her. That was a lesson I had to learn. But I keep wondering why. Who is to blame? What is wrong? Is it mortality?"

Don't ask me, Neal. Once I may have known, but I don't any more.

12.

Meanwhile, back in Paris quite a few things had been happening, too. Telling them gives me no pleasure, so let us take them at a canter, looking to right and left as little as possible. I envy the horse his blinders, and rather wish I had one on the eye that sees the past, as well as on the eye that sees the future.

I continued to work on my films, but they continued to give me trouble. The two films, or, if you prefer, the two aspects of one film, began to represent to me the two aspects of life: on the one hand, the permissible, the mentionable, the regular, the O.K., and on the other, the *outré*, the inadmissible, the impossible, the Won't Do. More than that. On the one hand, the endurable, the known, and the charted, and on the other, the strange, the murky, the terrible, which awaits the stray from the common garden of humanity. Strewn though that garden may be with dismembered bodies and horror of every kind, yet it is a garden compared with the pit, and subject to reason, theories, explanations. These contrasts were becoming my constant thought and my obsession. I could no longer laugh much at what was emerging with such painful labor from the womb of my divided mind to take its place on celluloid, for it was taking on meanings all out of proportion to itself. I couldn't regard Number One as merely a clever documentary, original and brilliant, on Love, and Number Two as a naughty movie. Number One was the Garden, where I could walk with Pounce, where I recognized landmarks and familiar attitudes, even tenderness, although it was so often torn up by hate and greed. But I didn't want to stay there. I yearned to jump the fence, leave Pounce and all the rest behind, prowl ultimate jungle on the other side, where the scream in the night took the place of avian twitterings. No admittance,

239

Pounce. That was the sign, and I put it there. There I could sniff blood at will, roll in ordure, consort with witches and imps, and waltz obscenely, rubbing my belly up against the puffed and suppurating thorax of Lady Death. Do I put it too figuratively? Is my language exaggerated? Not, I think, to any of my fellow explorers.

Ahmed had gone permanently to the country with June for all the latter part of August and the first week in September, and he let Pounce and me move back into his apartment during that time. She and I were bickering almost constantly now, a splintering veneer over a dying love, and Ahmed's large apartment was a more suitable arena for us than two small hotel rooms. Sometimes the struggle roared from one end to the other. Sometimes it was desperate; one or both of us might not survive. Pounce had entirely stopped liking me, although she had not quite stopped loving me. One night she said, over and over until I struck her: "Hang on, Ned. Try to hang on."

The nerve of that bitchy, black-haired tomboy.

Bidault and Bliss came back unexpectedly, a few days earlier than he had told us. He was very worried. Business, he said, had made him change his plans. When they appeared that hot evening, I insisted—for I was still in a huff about being moved out for June those many weeks before, and I liked a scene—that Pounce and I leave at once for our hotel. It was awkward, but I put it on the level of consideration and courtesy: they should have their apartment to themselves, etc., etc. But why at once, why that night? Everybody stared at me as if I were crazy, but I insisted. "We owe you too much already, Ahmed," I said, "to risk the slightest additional imposition." He was quite offended by my tone of voice. His great, liquid, stricken animal eyes narrowed. "I want to have a talk with you the next few days," he said, and I knew my subvention was to end—which I had been expecting.

Pounce and I forgot lots of things, leaving in such a hurry, and had to go back the next morning to get them.

The apartment was open and the doors unlocked when we got there, and nobody was at home, nobody at all, neither servants nor masters. I called from the hall, I called into the kitchen, I tried Ahmed's bedroom door—it opened, but it was dark inside, the shutters and curtains all drawn, and nobody was there. I thought it was odd. Ahmed might have neglected to let his servants know he was returning—Pounce and I stayed there without servants, for he had let them go on vacation—but I could hardly imagine his leaving the place open. Well, it was none of our business. We went into what had been our bedroom during our recent stay and collected odds and ends. Pounce had left a movie camera in a closet, and she was fooling around with it, putting it into its case, fixing some gadget, taking her sweet time as she always did, that deliberate Pounce. She was very angry with me for insulting Ahmed the night before, and wasn't saying much. I wandered off.

I went first into the dining room—no clue there. Fresh flowers on the table. The balcony was as usual, and I sat a moment in the sun and wished I could have clapped my hands for service. Then I returned to Pounce, but she was still fiddling, and when I complained she told me to go on without her, so I stayed.

I looked in June's bedroom, which had been redecorated, as Ahmed had said, in a powder blue, with white trim—June's Wedgwood palace, which love had built her. I thought, then, of Pounce and myself, and the days we had spent during that happy, hopeful early time in Paris. Impulsively, I took a heavy fingernail instrument and scratched a large heart deep into the fresh paint above the headboard of the bed. Within it I put my name and Pounce's. It was the last time we would ever be in that apartment, but they would not forget us all that soon.

I passed through the room to a closet, which had another entrance from the room next door, the master bedroom, into which I walked, blinded in the darkness there, for June's room had been fully lighted. I opened a shutter and peeped out, then drew it to once more, but the curtains I left open. As I turned to leave by the main doorway, my roving eye lit upon the bed, which was recessed in an alcove, so that I hadn't seen it when I first looked in.

Believe me when I say that I gasped. I gaped. I gulped. I gagged. But I went nearer. I stopped. Then I went nearer still. Suddenly, in terror, I looked around into the corners of the room, but I was alone.

My artist's instinct did not desert me. When I became articulate, I called to Pounce to come at once and bring her camera. She called back, something I couldn't understand. I ran to the door, almost falling when I had to stop, opened the door, and yelled to her to come and bring her camera. Just this one time she would be allowed over the garden wall, for there was no way to keep her out. I wanted . . . No, let me put it more strongly. I felt—with every nerve, every cell I possessed I felt it—that I had to have pictures of Ahmed and June lying there naked, their severed heads balanced perkily upon the bare breasts of their naked decapitated bodies.

For such is what I saw. That sly old Devil. How he loves an occasional *coup de théâtre*.

Pounce came in, but, irritated by my peremptory order, she hadn't brought her camera. When she beheld my *nature morte*, she backed into a corner. Being Pounce, she neither screamed nor fainted.

"The camera," I whispered, as if I thought someone might overhear, Ahmed or June awaken and pull up the soppy sheet. "Bring the camera. This is something I could never have paid for."

"Ned," she whispered. It was an appeal.

I looked at her. She had turned to face the wall. "This is no time to turn chicken," I snapped. "I don't like looking at them any more than you do, but it's my duty." Cursing, I ran to our old room and got the camera myself, returned, and executed a strophe and antistrophe about that gory bed, trying to find the best angle for photography. Then, happily, I remembered the bad light. "Go open the shutters," I commanded. No reply. "Open the shutters, damn you," I shouted, stamping a foot as hard as I could.

I had left the shutter unlatched, and at that moment—was it the wind, the jar on the floor when I struck it?—one of the shutters swung slowly wide. Light flooded in. I took my footage. Then I did a little rearranging and took the rest of the footage I had left in the camera. I then returned everything the way it had been, and thought about the police.

I turned to Pounce. "What about the police?" I said calmly, feeling better, purged, relieved.

It was too late. She had watched what I had done. To her, I suppose, the double murder was merely an atrocious crime. She could not understand, as I did, all the erotic overtones, the lovely possibilities, understand just why Amor was so inevitably present in that blood-spattered alcove. I will not try to describe how she felt. I do not know what she thought. I do not know, I do not care. All I know or care about is that at that moment, when I finally took time to look around at her, I realized, with a little shiver that traveled from the backs of my knees to my scalp, from the way she turned from me as I went toward her, that she would leave me and I might never see her again. Occasionally such an insight proves to be true.

But I didn't have time just then to mend any fences, for I had the film to worry about. I recalled that the police snoop in a wide circle all around any major crime, and, should they get that spool, it might occur to them to develop it and look at it, and I didn't want it confiscated, nor did I want to get shoved into a French jail for tampering with evidence. So I unloaded the camera and put the film into a light-proof case, then ran out of the building, found a taxi, gave him the package and some money, and told him to deliver it to me in care of our hotel. It was risky. He might have put two and two together after reading the newspapers and gone to the police, or they themselves might have got it when they went through our hotel rooms and questioned the proprietress; but it worked out all right. She hated the cops. She kept it for me until I was able to get it to a locked cabinet in my rented studio. My greatest sequence was saved, for the time being.

Finally I realized just how deadly a game Ahmed had been playing. I never found out exactly what it was, though. He was surely mixed up with the Algerian war in some way. That explained his lack of friends or normal life in Paris, and all his precautions. We were there at a time when the police went around dumping the garbage cans early every morning, to clear them of Algerian corpses before the good bourgeois of Paris should see them on the way to work. Faction was killing faction, and the French participated according to the vagaries of unstable government. I don't know what Ahmed was doing—munitions, espionage?—but whatever it was, some opposing group finally cornered him there with his pale American mistress and delivered them both from the vexations of this earthly existence. What a lark I had always thought his mixed blood. His silly name, half Arab, half French. Too absurd. One so often takes the most serious things about other people lightly.

I called the police, but before they arrived I telephoned the American Embassy. I got some idiot there who thought I was either a crackpot or playing a bad practical joke, but he overheard a little of the conversation with the police authorities when they arrived, enough to make him pay attention. The result was that Pounce and I were protected from possible manhandling—the security forces didn't play around those days, either, any more than the Arabs did. She and I were questioned over and over, separately and together, and held for hours. The detectives didn't believe that we knew nothing of the underground portion of Ahmed's life. Finally they were convinced of Pounce's innocence and let her go. They kept me on for several days. When they finally released me and I returned to that friendly old Carthage et Edimbourg, I was informed that Pounce had left—left Paris, left France, left Europe.

Our proprietress, the one with the crush on Neal, had all the newspapers, and, pretending I was neither suprised nor particularly displeased by Pounce's departure, I sat in her rooms back behind the lobby and read everything she could show me about the crime. The servants, it turned out, were found in a closet. They had merely had their throats cut. It was clear that whoever committed the crime had come in when Ahmed went to open the door for the servants, or even afterward. He was not supposed to be in Paris and was slightly off guard, I suppose, felt a little safer than usual. The crime must have happened only a short time before Pounce and I arrived. I was rather pleased with myself for having insisted that we spend that night, when Ahmed and June returned unexpectedly, in our own hotel. Otherwise . . .

I had a great deal, oh! a very great deal, to think about, as I slowly climbed the dark, musty stairway to my room, the film carton tucked under one arm.

13.

Neal didn't return to Paris until the tenth of October. He had business to attend to in Florence, of course, with both the Italian and the American authorities, all much complicated by the irregularities of that ill-fated wedding ceremony. One of the problems was to straighten out the matter of inheritance, for although the marriage had no legal validity, announcements had been sent out. It was just possible that he stood to inherit Eloise's money, and Rob was outraged by that succession. But she had made no new will, and Neal was glad to renounce any claim he had. He did his legal duty, in any case, but then he vanished for several weeks, leaving the American Express Company, Paris, as his address. I believe he spent them in Switzerland, a perfect place for a truly bereaved person, I have heard, since the Swiss manage to make even the Alps seem inconsequential, a backdrop for dirndls and moo cows—Heidi kayos the Sublime. I got a letter from him telling me what had happened, as curt as a telegram, and that he would see me in a while.

I must now make a confession that is not at all pleasant. I do not much believe in everyday morality, which is at best a shaky sort of foundation on which to set Society, full of anachronisms and justifications for self-interest and the expediencies of larger groups. Nevertheless, I don't care for treachery, and that is what I was contemplating while Neal mourned 'neath the Jungfrau. Look at it from my point of view. Ahmed, my one hope, was dead. Pounce, who at least wouldn't have let me starve, was vanished. I had no friends to turn to, no family which would remit. I had only one reserve card, which might possibly take a trick: I knew where Neal was and David Wallace didn't, at least there was still a chance that he didn't, a chance, that is, so far as I knew, that Neal would not have written him, although, as it turned out, he had. Anyway, that is what I was thinking about, from time to time—while I waited for Neal to show up. I knew Wallace well enough to know that if I took that bribe he had offered me so long ago, I would have to produce the goods.

Neal came in at the Gare de l'Est, and stopped at the Express Company for his mail before coming to the hotel, so he had his letters by the time he reached me. Included were a note from Pounce and a long letter from David Wallace. I was my most friendly when I saw him. I told him to cheer up, that we could still have ourselves a time in Paris, France, and that I had plans, for other films, trips to Germany and Spain, he mustn't give up, the world lay open before us. My voice faltered. He wasn't paying attention.

"Where is Pounce?" he asked mysteriously.

"She's left me," I replied. Then I told him about Ahmed and June, and about Pounce's departure. I was as gay as a canary.

"June. Ahmed," he said slowly, shaking his head, thinking, I am sure, about Eloise. Then he said: "You don't miss her?"

"Oh, not at all," I replied. "That was all over."

"Not at all?"

"Not at all," I said. What did he want me to do—tell him she had taken half of me back to America with her?

"Was there a funeral for Ahmed?"

I didn't know.

"What does this mean?" He handed me the note from Pounce which he had found in his mail. In it she told him to make me tell him about his mother and show him the newspaper notice. He knew, from Wallace's letter, what the reference to his mother must mean.

I muttered something unprintable. "Go to my billfold over there on the table and look in one of those little pockets inside," I said. "You'll find the clipping there."

He did so. Then he put it in his own pocket. "Why hadn't you given me this? Uncle David says she died the end of last year, although your clipping's not dated. You must have had it since then. Why, Ned? Why?"

"I didn't want to spoil your time here."

"What gave you the right to decide that?"

Suddenly I got furious. I rushed over to him, my fists waving, purple in the face, swallowing saliva as fast as I could. "God damn you, you and Pounce both. Why shouldn't I? Who made you what you are? Who created you, Brewster? Why shouldn't I decide what you should read?"

He pushed me firmly backward. He was quite white. Scared, I wondered? "You had no right," he said quietly. He stared strangely over my shoulder, as if seeing something behind me. I looked around. "I will never forgive you for this, Ned. I don't really want to quarrel with you over it; only remember this, that it will always lie between us. I'd even admit that you might have been right, at one time, to have hidden it from me, but not when you did."

I crouched, waiting.

He sighed. "I must go back. Today if I can get space."

Infuriated, I struck out at him. He ducked, twisted to one side, grabbed me, although I am bigger than he is, and while I quite literally kicked and screamed, he tied me up in my belt, a couple of neckties, and the bedclothes. When I was helpless, with Madame Hotelkeeper by now in the room, he said: "God help you, Ned. Get ahold of yourself if you can."

"Get out. Get out, get out, get out," I bellowed. "Get out and don't ever get in my way again, Brewster."

He left, and I heard him talking to Madame in the hall. Eventually she came back in and, when I had calmed down, let me loose.

That was the last time I saw him in Paris. He went home. He left me in the lurch.

I idled for several weeks more, I don't actually remember how many. I did a bit more movie-making, but that wasn't working out at all. Mostly I did some editing, and one of the chief things I did was to take that sequence of Neal and Eloise and splice it in with some of the craziest stuff I had for Film Two, so that they become recognizable actors in a most outrageous part. That gave me some satisfaction—it was really a neat job of editing, implicating them in things they never did. I got a little cranky, I guess, and after a rather unfortunate episode in the lobby of the Carthage et Edimbourg involving an English fairy and his Jug boyfriend, Madame asked me to leave.

That did it. I was really broke, only a few hundred dollars to my name. I sold clothes and cuff links to pay off my room, and looked into freighters, because I figured that I might have a better chance getting my film out that way, and found one sailing from Bordeaux to Baltimore, leaving October 31 —Halloween. I was aboard, but the police got wind of my departure, made a routine search of my luggage, as a last check on the Ahmed affair, found my films. They let me go as scheduled, but I was told, after they saw what they had, that I was henceforth *persona non grata* in France. I imagine they show them now and then at police smokers—*Les Grandes Soirées de la Sûreté*. . . .

Farewell France. Hello America.

Only not quite so fast. Because something happened on the way. I was by myself one afternoon, pacing the deck, such deck as there was on that scow, having offended the other eleven passengers by then so that they gave me lots of room, and came upon the Captain smoking. We stood side by side, looking out at the horizon. A ship appeared there—long, low, flat. I said, in French, that it was an aircraft carrier. He was amused. He mocked me. He disagreed. It was a tanker, he said. A warship, I insisted. A tanker, he said. No, I insisted, more violently: it was an aircraft carrier. But no, he contradicted me, it is a tanker. It was too much. That lousy merchantship captain. I hit him right on the side of the head and almost pushed him overboard.

That is why I spent the rest of the voyage under lock and key, not in my cabin, but in a storage area up in the bow, where they shoved food to me as if I were some kind of wild animal. When we docked I was taken into custody, shipped off to Ohio, and put into an institution. I won't describe it or my experiences there, but it was a state hospital. It was alleged that I was insane.

I sweated it out in that dump for a long time. They let me loose, finally, but I had no place to go. My Cincinnati sister couldn't (and wouldn't) take me in. I had no money and no job. I was desperate. And that is how it happens that I wrote to Neal. I explained my circumstances. I reminded him that I had lost my original job on his account, and was black-listed on his account. I sent the letter in care of his Uncle David, for I was sure they were reconciled. They were sure to be, for I was the only one, in that case, who suffered permanently as a result of their rupture.

I was right. Neal got my letter. He let several weeks go by, more time than was either right or kind, but finally he sent me a letter, which reached me in the little furnished room where I lived my miserable days, my miserable nights—by benefit of a sister's grudging charity.

I was invited to come and stay with him for as long as I wanted. He would make it possible for me to do films again.

He thought of everything. Included in the letter was a check for five hundred dollars to get me there. Ha ha ha! Now where did he think I would find someone to cash that?

I had to airmail it back to him, and have him wire me the money instead.

 PART FOUR

PART FOUR

The railroad station—I have grown afraid to fly; it's unnatural, I now realize—was built of dark-gray stones, heavily
rusticated, and could have been a city hall, a post office, or a
jail, just as well as a station. It had little turrets and slits, so that
Pinkerton Detectives could shoot arrows at striking laborers, I
suppose. But they could also be used by the Authorities to
keep watch on who came and went. I wanted to wait for
my footlocker, which had been checked through, but Neal was
impatient. Such detail was beneath him—I caught that. He
would send a man down for it, he promised; there was no reason for *us* to wait *ourselves*. (My italics.) I wasn't sure it
would be safe. I worried about it, and spoke of it several times.
I couldn't afford to lose it; also, I worry more than I once did.
Neal carried my heavier suitcase and my briefcase, where I
had put lots and lots of papers to be saved. He was already
sun-tanned, was expensively dressed in a spring tweed suit
that never saw a ready-to-wear rack, and had that feeling
about him of people who may have breakfasted on scrambled
eggs with fresh caviar.

It was comforting, though, to be with Neal again—in a way.
After those last painful months, it was comforting. Except
that I could tell, from the casual manner he assumed when
he asked me how I was feeling, that he had been in
communication with my sister and probably with the doctors,
too. "How shall I act with him, Doctor? What should I say to
him, Doctor? Any subjects I should avoid, Doctor? *What if he
gets unmanageable, Doctor?*" And so forth. But I was getting
used to that. People turned out always to know about
me. Those doctors would spill their guts to anybody.

Neal was the only friend I had in the world now. The fact intensified, although it did not necessarily sweeten, our attachment.

I knew nothing of what had happened to him, and was very curious. Oh! but I was curious. Yet I waited. I was watchful. I asked no questions. I let the situation unfold before me. I wasn't going to stick my neck out.

I got my first big clue—that five hundred dollars apart—from the car we drove off in, which caused the people of the town of S——— to take oafish second looks. They might have looked more enviously at a Cadillac, but they looked longer at this stunning British creation in bottle green with its world-famous radiator. We glided soundlessly from the curb, and I reached out to touch the wooden dashboard. Neal noticed.

"Uncle David says I should start out ostentatiously, even vulgarly, since I have to get people used to the idea that I have lots and lots of money," he said.

"I see," I answered grimly. "Vulgar. That's a strange word for you to use. That doesn't sound like you."

"Revisions, Ned. It's time for revisions. Anyway, it's his."

"I see."

"It's like a movie," he went on. "I have to invent ways of showing off. I say to myself, 'Now what would I do if I were a movie director to make all the ordinary people in the movie house know that my hero is rich?' And then I do it."

"That's one kind of movie," I said, offended by the way he spoke of the "vulgar" product as if it were typical of the medium.

"Speaking of which, I've got some plans."

"Really?" I was cool, but a horrible flip of my stomach accompanied the thought that perhaps Neal was going to start experimenting with his own films, that the offer to let me work had been bait, a ruse, that maybe I'd been brought on to be a helper.

He glanced at me in a doubtful way, then came to some kind of decision on how to handle me. I had grown pretty sharp at getting that look, sensing that decision, during those last months. It happened every time.

"I'm staying with Uncle David," he said as we drove along. "He wants you to stay with him in his house, too."

"David Wallace wants me?"

"He's mellowed," Neal said. "Most of the time he wants what I want now. And there's plenty of room, believe me."

The only other talk we exchanged all the way out to Wahnfried, the Wallace estate, was when we passed a large institution, sprawled on both sides of the street as it climbed the biggest hill in town. "This is Wallace College," Neal said, waving a hand. He pointed to a large official-looking building, columns and pediments all over it. "That's the original part of it." Then to a gimcrack gothic building. "That's the School of Music, named after Uncle David's mother." Then we passed a very trim modern building. "That's new," he said unnecessarily. "We're going to have a competition for a new library soon." He stopped for a traffic light and glanced sideways at me. "I'm being made a trustee," he said.

The W.P.A. guide to the near Middle Western state of I——, one of those prepared during the Depression, as some will remember, carried as part of its entry on the town of S—— the following:

"*Wahnfried*, named after the villa of the composer Richard Wagner (1813-1883), is the estate of the Wallace family, the leading financiers and industrialists in the region. It lies to the north of town and commands a fine view of the river. It was built by Benjamin T. Wallace (1851-1911) between 1901 and 1903 in the eclectic style of the period, but differs from the usual mansion of its time in that it was imitative not of English or French prototypes, but of German medieval architecture, heavily influenced by certain romantic imitations built in the 19th century in Germany itself, notably the castles erected for King Ludwig II of Bavaria. Wahnfried contains about 50 rooms, grouped, on irregular levels, in an H-shape around an open courtyard. These include a Great Hall, used

255

for musical evenings and dances, which has frescoes by Gott-
fried Helmshaven (1876-1917), who was brought from
Düsseldorf to execute them. They form a cycle of four murals
based on the story of Wagner's festival drama *Parsifal*. The
house is approached by an imposing gatehouse, also in German gothic style, whose heavy portcullis, which can be raised
or lowered from the house, was especially designed and built
by the Otis Elevator Company. From here a long drive winds
up toward the house, which presents a very picturesque profile from below, since it stands on a bluff and has many turrets and battlements. The house may also be seen from the
road that passes north along the other side of the river: there
is a place to turn out at the best viewpoint, and from this distance Wahnfried is a very convincing imitation of an old castle
on the river Rhine. Electric torches light the courtyard and
great stairs, and there is a small medieval garden with an antique fountain (15th century, Upper Rhenish) within the
enclosure, flanking the main drawing room. The gardens
which lie around this "castle" are informally designed and
contain a gothic ruin, probably the last one ever built, which,
like the house, was planned by the Chicago firm of Radnor
and Feke. There is a small artificial pond, as well as some magnificently planted flower beds, laid out along the edges of
the woods.

"*Not open to the public.* At certain specified times, usually
in the spring, the gardens are opened for one day. A fee is
charged for a designated charity. Visitors must confine themselves to the paths."

What a poor relation I felt myself when I was shown
through all this opulence after lunch—and what a lunch! A
lobster soufflé, a lamb chop curled around its own tender kid-
ney, some tiny fresh green beans, strawberries with cream. It
was May, and the berries must have come from California, but
they were good. We ate in a kind of alcove off Neal's sitting

room, which looked out over the river. From that window, high in a high house on a high bluff, the vast sweep of valley and the country beyond (we were looking away from the city) gave a startling feeling of what that part of America must have been like in the nineteenth century, the time of opening out, the settling of the West. At the same time, I felt the feudal appeal of the whole setup: Lord knows how much of what we could see either belonged to David Wallace or was by him held in fee.

"Nice view," I said.

Neal nodded. "You'll have one, too." I hadn't been to my rooms yet, because we were late getting back from the station and lunch was already on its way.

"Good lunch," I said. I wanted to hit just the right note, appreciative without being gushy. I wasn't sure just how to do it, but I knew it had to be done. Sometimes appreciation is the price of generosity, and I was in no position to refuse payment.

"It's all part of the picture," Neal said.

Then we went on the tour of the house, first of all the library, whose gloomy walls and recesses were covered by rows and rows of books lined up behind glass panels set in elaborately carved oak frames. Certain shelves projected forward, and on these was arranged a part of the late elder Mrs. Wallace's collection of Meissen—much of it was on loan at a distant museum. Her portrait, by Anders Zorn, melted above the fireplace in the dining room; its pendant, of her husband, was above the fireplace in the library. Then we went on through the hallway into the dining room, from there into the great drawing room, which boasted five Sargent water colors on one wall panel, thence to the Great Hall, which was reached by crossing the entrance hall again and climbing a flight of eight stone steps. It was little used, for it had been scaled to life in the nineteenth century, if not a millennium earlier. It was in here that the life-sized murals were painted—

Parsifal amidst the Flower Maidens; Parsifal, Gurnemanz, and Kundry; Parsifal and Amfortas; finally Gurnemanz and the squires, the latter having as its inscription, in elaborate gothic script, *"Durch Mitleid wissend—der reine Thor."* That rang a bell somewhere.

I looked around, at the magnificent floor, the long rows of casement windows along two sides, the vaulted ceiling. "Quite a period piece," I said.

And so on and on and on, including bowling alleys in the basement and the indoor pool, which had now been emptied, since it was getting warm enough for the outdoor one to be filled. I wasn't shown all the second floor, because a lot of it was bedrooms with dressing rooms, but there was a sewing room there which almost smelled of old Mrs. Wallace still—dried rosebuds, woodruff. Above the second floor the house got quite confusing because of its irregular plan, towers and courts, winding corridors and dark stairways leading nowhere. I expressed curiosity, by chance, at one of these which, dark like the others and with slate floors, had a pale-green stair runner and some gilt wall fixtures which seemed out of keeping with the rest of the house.

I craned upward. "Is that where you keep the reserve soap flakes?" I asked. It struck me as silly—I don't know why I said it—and I giggled.

Neal walked on. "That leads up to a big attic," he said.

I held back. I had an idea. "Is it really big? I mean, a really big area? Big enough to use for a studio? I'd like to have a look at it."

"I was planning to have you use a big storage room in the basement," he said.

I resisted. "Underground? No windows? I suppose this attic has windows. I don't know that I could work underground. I'd rather work in this attic."

"It's full of furniture and things, though."

"No, really," I said stubbornly, determined to stand my little inch of ground just then; otherwise I'd have no ground of my own at all. I'd be a possession. "You can always consolidate things that are stored. Or move them to the basement."

Exasperated by my persistence, Neal said abruptly, "I'll have to explain something, Ned. I can't offer you the attic here. Uncle David wouldn't have it. Nobody is allowed to bother it."

"An attic? He cares that much about an attic?"

"Let's say it's a quirk of his."

"What kind of a quirk? I mean, why?"

"I can't tell you."

"You don't know."

"I do. And that's all I can say. But I'm telling you to forget it. If you don't want the basement room, we'll find something else. But forget about this."

That sharpness in his voice, that note of command. The voice of someone learning how to give orders. I knuckled in, rather glad I'd needled him to the point of getting a real reaction, which filled in the way he really felt about me and my being his dependent, staying at Wahnfried, gave it a third dimension. "Maybe the cellar will do," I said. "I didn't understand. Maybe we can contrive some artificial windows down there and light them from behind." I meant that suggestion seriously, but Neal misunderstood and laughed at me. So . . .

We walked then through the gardens, which certainly were beautiful, but which seemed to me rather small for such a big house. I said so, and Neal explained that before the war the formal gardens and lawns had been a lot bigger.

"Someday it will all have to become a public park," he said.

"It's large for one person," I remarked. I was getting surfeited with other people's belongings, filled right to the craw. "I can't say that that would seem a great social injustice to me."

"That's what Uncle David says. He says being adaptable to

change is the minimum history requires of a ruling class. He says it's far better to be a Jew than a dinosaur. Survival—that's what counts."

"I wouldn't have expected him to say that."

"He doesn't always say what you expect him to."

We came to the last of the beds planted with late spring bulbs, from which the land fell away rather steeply. There was a small graveled roadway which led through the woodlands down from the crest of the bluff through a draw which approached some flatter terrain near the river level. There was hammering coming from somewhere, and the sound of a bulldozer working, or a crane.

"What's that I hear?" I asked.

"It's some building going on. My idea," Neal said.

"What kind of building?"

"Why, I guess that's a secret, too," he said.

"Another secret? Wahnfried has two secrets?"

"Why not? It has two occupants. You know my old theory, that everything comes in pairs, has two sides to it."

My temper flared dangerously. "I don't like all these mysteries. I don't feel comfortable with a lot of mysterious hammering and forbidden attics around me. Are you by any chance *planning* something?"

Neal laughed at my anger. "Yes, I am planning something. You've put your finger on it. You'll see eventually. And right now, wouldn't you like to see your rooms?"

I was given two rooms, filled with iris, with the river view I had been promised, but only from one window. The other ones looked in the direction of that winding gravel road I just mentioned, and from that height I could see some evidence of construction work—dust, machinery moving through the trees, the gash of another entrance road. I was uneasy about it, and very very curious, and I was determined, as a matter of pride, a matter of self-assertion, to find out what it was. Yet did I dare to probe that secret, and, incidentally, the other

260

one, the one in the attic? I didn't know by what arcane code this household ran, and there were risks I couldn't take. No more direct questions, no frontal assaults. Rather, stealth, murder by night.

I spent the later part of the afternoon unpacking my footlocker and putting things away, which took me quite a while, because it's important to get each item where it most belongs, and that isn't always easy to decide. Then I lay down to worry until dinner, among other things about meeting David Wallace again. I went to look for Neal about 6:30, but he wasn't in his quarters, so I poked around a little on the second floor, unsure what I was supposed to do. I climbed to a landing between the second and third floors, where there was a view downriver toward the comforting sight of factory smoke and the first bridge, and was standing there when I heard the sound of footsteps from above and voices. I shrank back, but there was nowhere to hide. I was quite certain that it was Neal and Wallace and some woman, and that they were all coming down the stairs from the forbidden attic. A little conference closed to Ned. I really didn't find it at all funny. It wouldn't have surprised me to learn that a room had been prepared up there where I could be put if I got violent—in which case the construction work was for something other than my cage. There was the sound of the elevator door closing, and a moment later Neal appeared, coming down the stairs, dressed for dinner. I pretended surprise and commented on the view. He told me to come along, that his Uncle David would join us soon.

We gathered in the library, amidst all that sumptuous paneling, beneath the expensive-looking portrait of the elder Mr. Wallace, whose son, when he joined us, behaved with his usual cool assurance.

"Now that I am adopting Neal as my legal son," he said, holding out a very skinny, blue-veined hand, "his friends are welcome in my house, which is now his as well. So, Mr. Bates, let

us forget our grudges of the past and grow to like each other."
He smiled thinly.

I shook his hand, a little afraid of his touch. He noticed. Both he and Brewster noticed things, which didn't make it easier. He smiled again. "This is Mr. Bates, Mrs. Gladstone," he said, turning in his wheel chair to the short, stout woman, with round pink cheeks, a golf-ball chin, and spectacles. "Mrs. Gladstone is my nurse, Mr. Bates."

"Are you always in this chair?" I asked. I couldn't help myself; I had to know.

"Indeed we aren't," Ida Gladstone said for him. "Only when we're tired." She shook my hand, keeping her left hand on one of the pushers of the chair. Not death, but only the relaxation accompanying the decay of muscle fibers would ever cause her to let go entirely of Mr. Wallace.

She watched me closely during dinner, which she ate with us that evening, although often she didn't. I knew what she was watching for. I was very subdued, and that reassured her, since she took a coarse view of madness, little knowing how deep still waters can run. But I wasn't pretending. I felt quiet. I was being careful. Should I say how I really was acting? I'll put it in a word. I'll grit my teeth and write that word down.

Humble!

I can't truthfully say that anybody in the house wanted me to be that way. Nothing was ever said. I have never been made to sit a place away from the fire or eat dark meat of chicken. But when life has kicked you a number of times, you get careful. And so I made myself be . . .

Humble!

While Mr. Wallace and Neal chatted about my future—where I should work, whom I should meet—I was doing a little noticing myself. I was noticing what seemed to link them together, how the currents were running, what the resemblances were—I had come to a rather obvious conclusion about their relationship. I was baffled. I was sure I was right, yet

262

there was nothing very definite, nothing that would have justified a person's jumping to his feet. Allowed him, for instance, at a hearing a couple of weeks· later, when Neal and Wallace were seated side by side, Neal arguing for a reorganization of the school system on the basis of some crackpot theory of his (he won, too), allowed him to jump up and point a finger and shout, "Are you going to pay any attention to that bastard?"

After dinner, back in the library with the brandy bottle, Wallace asked me if he could watch my work from time to time, and if I would explain to him what I was doing. "Neal says you have a very great talent," he said.

"Does he?" (Where would I fit that in?) "Yes, Mr. Wallace, I'd be glad to have you. But I don't do ordinary movies."

"I should hope not."

"Movies?" Gladstone said. "You make movies? My, now isn't that interesting." Her eyes, behind those glittering spectacles, were avid. My stock rose in Nursie's bosom. I could be ever so mad, if I made movies.

Wallace asked: "What are you planning to work on first?"

I hesitated—how much ought I to reveal? "I've thought of doing something on the sensation of falling," I said.

He thought this over. "I should have imagined that was concerned largely with nonvisual sensation. But it would be interesting to try." Old fox. He guessed I was withholding.

"We'd better buy cameras by the dozen," Neal said. "I predict a lot of breakage."

"I'll be working in equivalents most of the time," I told him, miffed by such literalness.

"Naturally," David Wallace said. He was tired, and Gladstone was making moving motions. "Well, it will be very interesting to see how it turns out, and I am sure it will be good for you to keep busy." It was the most direct reference which had yet been made to my recent stumble on life's path.

"I need a lot of rest," I said. "I need to spend time by myself."

"Loneliness is not always the same thing as rest," Wallace observed.

Neal put a hand on his shoulder and helped Gladstone get the chair started. "Nobody in this house need ever be lonely," he said.

Again I felt the affection between them, and felt a pang of envy. It should have been perilous, after all that had happened between them, but it just plain wasn't. There was no place to insert a knife, nothing to pry loose. The weld was sound. I was quite depressed when I got back to my room and tried to sleep. I felt left out. Although I had only that day been taken in, I have rarely felt more abandoned than that night.

But I had work to do. And I was comfortable. And they would both be indulgent with me. I sensed that. And then, I had those two mysteries. Who could guess what power might descend to the man who unraveled them?

2.

The attitude of despairing optimism which I have just described did not prove entirely justified. True, life at Wahnfried was comfortable. David Wallace and Neal were considerate and, as I had thought, indulgent with space and promises of money. No barriers which I could ferret out were put in my way; still, something was wrong. My work wouldn't get going. I had my seminal ideas, but I couldn't seem to get them any farther than just that—seeds without sprouts, and, as even the most abotanical person knows, no sprouts no plants, no plants no flowers. I couldn't decide what I would need or where to begin, and spent hours sitting in that basement storeroom, pretending to work, but actually unable even to hit upon so much as the color to have it painted. My notebooks, where once my bright thoughts tumbled like the *drôleries* in the borders of an illuminated manscript, were now chaos, a random collection of jottings which by no exaggeration could have been called a plan. The nearest thing to inspiration I had was to do a film about doing a film—idea, elaboration, shaping up—in the hope that thereby I might be tricked into getting started, but something about it was forbidden. No luck. Nothing would happen. Had Mr. Sick invented a special ticket, just for me?

Neal knew. Mr. Wallace knew. The butler and the maids and the cook knew. All of them were so tactful. Avoid the subject, Bridget, just the right deferential smile. Or, from above, the appropriate clap on the back, the word of encouragement. It wasn't pleasant. Nobody who has not experienced that kind of sterility, that frustration, can imagine what it is like.

Nosey Nursie Gladstone was the first person who really came out and said anything. "How's our movie coming, Mr. Bates?"

"I guess Heaven never intended a madman to make movies, Mrs. Gladstone."

She puckered her pale lips. "Now, Mr. Bates, don't you talk like that. You're no worse than most. Be sure you let me be in it when you get started."

"Give me a subject," I said, holding her at the door. She had caught me on my way out to the swimming pool, carrying half a dozen pencils and several sizes of note tablets.

"Why not do one on nursing? They use a lot of them in the schools now. I'll help."

"Lord God, Mrs. Gladstone, I'm too squeamish."

"I promise you: no blood and nothing you couldn't show to an eight-year-old."

"That *is* an inducement," I called from outside. "I've always made that my rule."

A few afternoons later Neal, too, inquired. He came out to the pool late and saw me surrounded by my equipage—pencils and all. He stretched out beside me on his back to sun his underside, and had to push some material aside.

"How's it coming?"

"You know, don't you?"

"Not exactly, Ned."

"Well, it isn't."

"Any particular reason? Have you tried to think why?"

"What the hell . . ." I flared up. "Of course I have. But there are just times when you can't work."

"I didn't bring it up just to be unpleasant."

"I'm glad to hear that."

"What does it feel like, Ned?"

"Dry earth, waiting for rain."

"There's a psychiatrist here in town. Dr. Legg. I went to him once."

"I'd rather go under without any labels, thanks anyway."

He dropped the subject. I sneaked a couple of looks at him lying there, lanky and very brown, on his blue striped towel. Two sulphur-yellow butterflies danced in the air above his head, and one of them lighted on his arm. I assumed it was a portent, I didn't know of what.

But a day or two later he came back to it. "Have you ever thought of trying to do something—to one side, get going that way?"

"I don't understand."

"Some project other than a movie. Get involved enough in some other project, and maybe the movie will just happen. I was thinking of a book, for instance. Write a book about yourself."

"I hate confessions."

"Then do my biography and put yourself in it."

"What the hell have you ever done to warrant a biography?" I asked angrily, sitting up and flapping my hand at the yellow butterflies, for, uncannily, they had returned to Neal that day, too.

"I seem to be getting what I want, and nobody the wiser. That's a good reason right there. But I was thinking more of a double project. Twin lives, both starting at the university, both ending here at Wahnfried. It might be interesting."

The clarity of the contrast smarted in my eyes, as if I had opened them to the sun.

"What has happened—that's always the question, isn't it? It would be a way of knowing that. See what turns we took, why we are what we are," he added.

"For you the answer is simple—money."

"Partly. Anybody needs money. Money is a means."

"Money is an end. Money is an absolute. With money anything is possible."

"Except, apparently, to make a movie," he said.

There was never any point in trying to argue logically with Neal. I flopped back down and flipped over on my stomach. "You're getting delusions of grandeur."

"Naturally. I have grand plans."

"Like what?"

"Maybe I'll be President."

"I'll write the book when that happens."

"Suit yourself. It's not a bad idea, though."

I thought about it. The sun burned down in the beneficent way it has in June, and a pleasant dry breeze blew over us. Now and then the odor of cut grass scented the air. From far away I heard the honking of a car, from down below, that hammering.

"Could it be my book? Could I say anything I wanted? I mean, in spite of the fact that I'm living here, your guest?"

"Of course. I'd let you use any papers I have, too. Just one stipulation, that you make two copies, one for each of us."

"What about the attic? What about the work going on down below? I'd have to know about them."

"Not for a while. You'll begin at the beginning. They're here, now, at the end."

The idea had some appeal, not the idea of doing Neal's biography—such colossal ego, really—but the idea of going into the past. The appeal any scheme has that seems to nullify the mutilating erosions of time. Backward, backward to Paris, and beyond, backward, to Pounce, to the vacation in the woods, backward to Mrs. Peters's third floor. The reversals, changes in latitude and longitude, all the drift, taken back, canceled, turned to play and make-believe, the object of my imagination, subject of my pen. The menacing teeter-totter, on which I seemed to find myself so hopelessly held, high and helpless, while Neal thumped his chest in triumph on the ground, upended, its cycle closed.

"I'll start with the telegram about your mother," I said.

"That might be a good place. Yes."

"You were at your worst then."

"Just as you want."

A little later in the afternoon he had to go into the house, and when he returned, he brought with him those "Thoughts on an Autobiography" which I transcribed so long ago. "Here," he said. "Maybe you can use these." He glanced through them. "They date from quite a while back."

I, too, had a look. "What a lot of bull," I said to him. "Such pride. Such conceit."

He smiled. He didn't mind. "They're part of the case," he said.

His imperviousness exasperated me, as if he had so many important things on his mind he just couldn't be bothered to let me get under his skin. "Metamorphosis. Metamorphosis, indeed. Just remember this: that for every worm that gets turned into a butterfly, there's a prince changed to a toad. It all depends on who's waving the magic wand."

And so, *j'ai reculé pour mieux sauter*, unknown reader. I began this manuscript, which has been my hobby, my sport, my relaxation during the last few months, and I found that as I delved backward through the medium of memory, I myself became like the person I was reconstructing, a parallel Ned Bates existing on a different stratum of time, a revived Ned, a regenerated Bates. Mysterious powers have governed—intensified, diminished, modified—this phenomenon, and I have permitted them to do so, have relaxed and let them have their way. But, on the dark side, I also discovered that turning back the hands of one clock is not the same thing as turning back the hands of all clocks, for it had no effect on Neal, who continued to swing in his new orbit, impervious to the baneful influence of sunny Ned, e'en though I was burning bright once more.

And my projects . . . They began to jell just a little bit. I got some equipment—two cameras, lights, tape recorder, props, about twenty-five books on physics; for my mind began to leaf out from that original idea of "falling" and to play with the possibility of a presentation of related examples of kinetics—inertia, deflection, trajectories—it was filled with rolling balls, falling objects, palpable vectors. All this was paid for by the House, needless to say, and became quite a little investment in Bates & Co. I wasn't ready to begin photographing anything, but those essential preliminaries, at least, were getting done. For the first time since Paris, things were looking up; and I therefore had energy to spend on peripheral problems, too, such as the mysterious attic.

3.

The best channel I had to the solution of the mystery was Gladstone. She was the weakest of the major members of the household—because of her proximal position with regard to David Wallace, I counted Ida as a major figure; her comings and goings revealed his own.

I talked to her when I could find her by herself, and used the movies as bait to draw her out into the open. I asked her if she would like to try out for me, and she was "tickled pink" with the idea; so I told her I thought a good way of doing it would be to have her read a little Shakespeare—the Nurse from *Romeo and Juliet*, for example. I gave her a copy of the play to read, which she did in one night, and the next morning, agog with titillation, took me aside while David Wallace had a second cup of coffee with Nepot Neal, and accused me of being vile-minded and making fun of her. She had understood more than I had thought she would. How those spectacles glittered, how those round cheeks plumped up with outrage. Gladstone really was an actress. "To the pure, all things are pure, Mrs. Gladstone," I said. "What do you mean?" "It's all right. It can't touch you," I replied. "Just give it a try. You read the Nurse's lines, and I'll read all others."

Act II, scene 4. Gladstone: " 'I pray you, sir, what saucy merchant was this, that was so full of his ropery?' " Oh, my lovely. My lovely sag-arsed Gladstone, that starched white uniform truly concealing an honest biddyful of false virtue. " 'Scurvy knave! I am none of his flirt-gills, I am none of his skainsmates. And thou must stand by too, and suffer every knave to use me at his pleasure.' "

Ned as Peter: " 'I saw no man use you at his pleasure. If I had, my weapon should quickly have been out, I warrant you. . . .' "

Then, "What hours are best for you to practice, Mrs. Gladstone?"

"He naps from two to four. I can do it then."

"So do I, often. What about later?"

"After dinner, maybe, Mr. Bates."

"No, that's too late. You must be tired by then. Before dinner or in the mornings?"

"He's very active in the mornings. When he's out I could. But I can't before dinner."

"Doesn't he ever read before dinner? Couldn't you get away?"

"No, I couldn't."

"Why not? It's too bad. I think it would be the best time."

"I just can't, that's all."

There was my clue. Gladstone was busy, secretly busy, every afternoon, just before we gathered together for dinner. I kept a log of everyone's activities, and I checked times against each other. Mr. Wallace never appeared at those hours, either, nor could he be reached by telephone—I made several tries from outside. Neal, too, was generally unavailable at that time. I took to the upper halls and landings in my stocking feet, carrying sandals I could slip on in case I met a maid. It was soon settled, and amounted to this. All three of them spent those hours up in the forbidden attic, nearly every day. Why, why, why? It fairly made my teeth chatter with curiosity. I set my alarm clock one night and arose at 4:00 A.M., when the palest dawn first faded the eastern skies. I crept up that green-carpeted staircase, prepared for anything, even a ghost. Nothing doing! The door was locked. I noted the type of lock, though, a great pseudo-medieval affair, which would take a fancy key, and I remembered that one such was attached to the ring that Gladstone carried. I plotted accordingly. Gladstone's key would be my key.

I told her one evening that I wanted her to be sure to study her scenes that night if she could, for I wanted to run some tests with the cameras the next day. David Wallace overheard and asked what we were up to. It was a dangerous moment, for he might have been offended by the absurdity of my project—Gladstone was, after all, his essential helper. But when he heard, he was amused.

"I think she'd be very good as the Nurse," he said. We were all sitting in the library, I with a postprandial whisky in my hand. He stretched out a crustacean pincer toward one of the bookshelves. "Neal, would you get me the *Romeo and Juliet* from that set?" he asked. But before Neal could do it, nimble Ned had jumped to his feet and handed the old man the volume with a deferential smirk. He gave me a sharp look, then smiled, amused by my eagerness. "I will reread it," he said.

I told Gladstone I thought we would work on the speech that begins "Then hie you hence to Friar Laurence' cell . . ." and told her to memorize and practice it, for there would be lights in her eyes and she wouldn't be allowed to have the text before her. "I'll prompt if necessary," I said, and she was thrilled by the professional sound of the offer. We separated, David Wallace to nod a few moments over Act I, I to work for a bit on this manuscript (I had Neal home to see his sick mother at about that time), Neal to study a manual of parliamentary procedure, and Gladstone? Gladstone to stay up half the night, soaking in her new role.

The next afternoon I met her down in the basement in my studio, where I had set up the floodlights, a director's chair, one or two pieces of furniture, and an old dressmaker's dummy that wobbled on a springy metal frame, which I had found and draped with a sheet—a lissome Juliet. Gladstone came down from putting David Wallace to bed for his nap, and when she came in blinked like some bespectacled old fowl, for I snapped on the floodlights in her face. I myself wore heavy dark glasses.

"Have you learned your lines, O honey Nurse?" I asked. "Art sure won't stumble, good sweet Nurse?"

"My lands, I stayed up half the night. I have that little speech by heart, Mr. Bates, for certain," she said. Fond Gladstone.

"Then try it," I said sternly, stepping backward into shadow.

She faced me, those hot lights beating at her. She set her shortish legs astraddle and started in. " 'Then hie you hence to Friar Laurence' cell,/ There stays a husband to make you a wife./ Now comes the wanton blood up in your cheeks . . .' "

I stopped her. "Please, Mrs. Gladstone. *Please*. This is poetry. This is drama. It is not arterial blood; it is not venous blood: it is *wanton* blood. You know what wanton means?"

"I looked it up, Mr. Bates."

"Make it sound that way, Mrs. Gladstone, or you'll never be *my* sweet, sweet Nurse."

She started over, and I let her finish. "Again," I said. She did it again. "Again, and take it slower this time," I commanded. She did it. I picked up the megaphone I had beside my chair and shouted at her so that she jumped. "Slower, slower." She tried it yet slower. "Get across the idea that it's hard to 'climb a bird's nest,'" I said. She tried. "Once more," I commanded, not even listening to her any more. She was showing fatigue.

"Now go through it with gestures. Put life into it," I said. A moment later I interrupted. "Haven't you understood those lines? Are we to see your career collapse before it has even begun? When you say 'I am the drudge, and toil in your delight,/ But you shall bear the burthen soon at night' I want you to smack your lips."

"I can hardly bring myself to say those lines," Ida said.

"It's only a play. You're only acting," I told her. "Besides, it's Shakespeare. And they're the heart of the thing. They're the kernel of the nut which you must crack if you really want to see yourself in a movie."

Gladstone tried again, and this time I listened, and I must admit that she wasn't bad. She must have been too worn out to be self-conscious. Many an artist has reached new heights because of having been out too late the night before.

"Now for the costume," I said. "And then the tape recorder and perhaps even the camera."

"Costume?"

"Of course. I can't have you looking like Florence Nightingale instead of Juliet's sly nanny. I have prepared a costume." I handed her some lumpy stuff which would make a great hot cloak. "Take it behind that curtain and change," I said. "We must hurry if we're going to get through this afternoon."

Trusting Gladstone did just that. And as I had hoped, her own clothes were left hanging in the curtained area, for it was much too hot in the basement by this time to throw my woolens over her uniform. It was a simple matter to keep her occupied while I sneaked behind the curtain with a flashlight and found her key ring. I crept back to the camera without her noticing I had gone at all. Then, while she recited, I fingered those keys on top of some cotton batting I had brought down to quiet the noise. The ring opened on a simple principle, and in just a moment I had the very gothick key itself, and was pressing it between two plastic blocks, to get a mold.

"I'm getting pretty hot and tired, Mr. Bates. I don't know how much more of this I can stand."

"Acting in the movies is hard work," I said. I fooled with the camera and got it to make noises. "Now go on." I was nearly finished, just about ready to replace the key on the ring, the ring in the uniform.

" 'I am the drudge, and boil on your delight . . .' Oh, Mr. Bates, I made a mistake. I just can't do any more this afternoon. Say, what time is it getting to be?"

"The bawdy hand of the dial is now upon the prick of noon," I said.

"What's that you say?"

"Never mind. It's nearly four. Still time for another try."

"Didn't I hear a car? Maybe Mr. Neal is back."

"Go to, good gentlewoman. Pray proceed."

"I'm just too tired. I can't. Maybe tomorrow, Mr. Bates. Mr. Bates?"

I had just then vanished behind the curtains to replace the keys, and she might have caught me out; but I called that I was listening to her from that side, and thought the acoustics were better, and I would put a microphone there for the final shooting. I skipped back to my place. "You want to give up, do you? All right. We'll have another go at it in a day or two."

Gladstone hurried in to change. "What time is it now?" she called.

"After four," I replied.

"Really? I've got to fly."

"Now you know what those poor things in Hollywood go through," I called to her, as she thumped up the stairs to the main floor.

And then, as soon as she was safely out of the way, I took my plastic blocks, hurried up the stairs myself, got the keys to one of the cars from Mr. Wallace's driver, and sped to the best locksmith in town.

4.

Delicately, using a pillow to muffle any sound, I thrust the key into the lock. Would it turn? Would it let me in?

It was midnight. What other time would have done?

The locksmith had told me it was a crude job, since my mold was hardly professional, and he was unused to that kind of work. But he thought it might do, for the lock itself was normal, even simple; only the stem and handle of the key were complicated with medieval ivy. He had examined it with interest. "I never saw anything quite like this," he had said, "except some of the keys for the Wallace place." I had laughed hollowly, as it is sometimes put—I should have known to go to the second-best locksmith—and told him I was from Cincinnati. "Why didn't you bring in the original key?" he asked. "An eccentric old relative," I replied. He was curious, but he did the work.

I turned the thing to the left, which is what one would have expected to work. Nothing happened. It wouldn't budge. I diddled it, pushed, jiggled, moved it out and in, did every trick I knew to do to a lock, my actions casting horrible shadows there at the top of the stairs, for the only light was from a flashlight which was standing on its end in a corner, throwing a round spot of light on the ceiling above the door, converting everything else into ghostland. I swore every oath I knew and stopped to think.

It occurred to me next to turn the key to the right. Maybe this silly lock worked in reverse. I tried, and there was a click. Hissing with triumph, I turned the handle of the door and pushed inward. Nothing happened. I shoved harder, but, though I could scarcely believe it, it was still locked. I reversed the key and then threw the lock again, thinking that perhaps the bolt hadn't quite cleared. It wouldn't open. I worked at it for ten minutes or so, meanwhile discarding caution and my pillow, and finally, cursing my luck, the locksmith, Gladstone, Wahnfried, David Wallace, and, of course, Neal, I had to give up. Above all I cursed trick double locks, for that is what I felt must be involved here. There was nothing to do but to put the lock back in its original position and try to think of another way to get in. I did so, and then, with that compulsive gesture people make who have been baffled by locks and can't quite believe it possible, I pushed the door one last time.

It opened. Had the last person to leave forgotten to lock it, or was there some other explanation? For the first time, I hesitated, almost afraid to carry my project through, aware, for the first time, that terror might await me on the other side of the door.

But I *had* to go on. I picked up my flashlight and crept forward, playing it into the vast space of the attic.

Exposed to my eager eyes was something very like the set to a drawing room, separated from the rest of the area by partitions, painted a pale green. My dancing beam picked out little marble-topped tables, spindly French chairs, a large couch, large enough to stretch out on, Sèvres bric-a-brac. Everything was in precious veneers, gilt-bronze, satins and brocades. Clearly it was a woman's apartment—but whose?

To one side, a false hallway was constructed out of board

276

which, like all the partitions, ran only to about eight feet, leaving a large gap between its uppermost level and the ceiling of the attic, which was at least twenty feet high. I found another doorway and went through it into a bedroom, furnished in Empire style, with a large bed mounted with ormolu sphinxes. A dressing table aglitter with perfume bottles. Chests, closets. I looked in the latter and found lots and lots and lots of clothes, including some very fancy items.

I had by then penetrated the secret of the place. It was Mrs. Brewster's apartment, reconstructed, in part, in the attics of Wahnfried. "All right. So far so good," I said aloud to myself. "But what in the devil do they *do* here?" I looked all around the bedroom again, and stopped to examine those gilt sphinxes more closely with my light. "Can you tell me?" I asked; but they, accustomed to posing riddles, refused to answer one. I shrugged. "You must have seen a hell of a lot in your time," I remarked, then turned to go through the drawers of the main dressing table. "Christ, what a lot of stuff! Now what's this?" My fingers had plunged into a great mass of some soft stuff that felt like hair. When I pulled it out, hair it appeared to be. Buns and wads of it, hanks of the stuff, all the Brewster chestnut color. Mrs. Brewster must have used it when she was going out somewhere very much as the grand lady. I dropped it like something unclean. It was too creepy. I made a face, and shivered.

But then I grinned. Suddenly I was delighted. All this was more than I had ever hoped to find. A loving monument to a dead mistress, a most doting piece of necrophilia.

"Wouldn't *this* cause some embarrassment if it got known outside," I said.

I explored enough more to make sure that no other rooms from the Brewster apartment were reconstructed—no kitchen, no dining room, no other bedrooms. Only Mrs. Brewster was to be worshiped in this place.

"I ought to file a petition to have her grave opened," I said,

277

"to make sure she's really in it." Involuntarily, as I uttered these dangerous words, I looked behind me. Anything could have been watching me from the shadows, and I rather thought that something was. Nevertheless, I forced myself to do one more thing before I hurried away. I went to feel under the couch and found that beneath the richly pleated skirts was an interval between floor and underpinnings quite large enough for a person to get in. I tried it, and while it wasn't spacious, it was certainly no more confining than a coffin. I was even able to adjust myself so that I could take notes. My next move was decided.

David Wallace was reciting a poem:

> *"If God there be,*
> *And not just whim,*
> *What's good for me,*
> *Is good for Him.*

"That's what my father used to say, Neal, whenever the subject of religion came up—if it came up in private. He was an old-fashioned freethinker."

From my position, quite literally directly beneath the old man, I mouthed a silent "Ho hum," and made a note with a hard pencil of the childish little quatrain. The endless lectures by Mr. Wallace, which I had been listening to, seemed to me to have all the pertinence to contemporary life of a series of sermons on the causes and consequences of the Deluge.

A quick laugh came from above the other pair of ankles I could see, the ones that were placed by the legs of an armchair to one side. These tedious disquisitions seemed to interest and amuse Neal. He listened to them, as far as I could tell, rather ritualistically, like some relaxing lord listening to a well-known saga, repetitive and worn.

"An admirable man. A formidable man. Stern, though you

278

would hardly guess that from his irreverent attitude toward the Almighty." I blinked when a shift of position above caused a mote to fall into my left eye. How sick I was of hearing about Benjamin T. Wallace, builder of Wahnfried, cannot be imagined. Uncle David had only a very few subjects that he wanted to talk about, and I had been listening for days and days. "He married my mother ten years or so after the Civil War. She was of German stock. Did you know that? Revolution of 1848. Her maiden name was Ackermann. Needless to say, nobody in Father's family had ever married anything but an Anglo-Saxon before, and it came as quite a shock when Father did so. Steps were taken to prevent it, I believe, but he insisted, and my grandparents had good sense enough not to permit it to cause any permanent rift in the family. They were always kind to her, although she doubtless knew how they felt."

"Poor thing," Neal murmured.

I grimaced, and wished that instead he had told his "uncle" that he had conveyed precisely this information not four evenings before.

"I think that this unsuitable marriage was the reason my grandfather decided to send Father out west, and to expand his interests here, feeling it was better, under the circumstances, for both of them to be somewhat nearer to the frontier, and farther from Wilmington." He was quiet for a long time, but a foot tapping perilously near my nose was proof that he had not gone to sleep, which did happen once in a while. "Well, the arrangement certainly turned out brilliantly from a financial point of view," he added.

The whole matter of Madame Brewster's reconstituted salon had turned out to be innocent enough, an old man's nostalgic whim. He had loved the woman, David Wallace had, and when it became necessary to clear her apartment, he had had her furniture moved into storage space in his own house, and then later had had the idea of setting it up in its familiar or-

279

der, later still of going there to sit and dream. Once I had
found out that nothing more occult or scandalous was involved, I would have stopped my daily visits and been
spared that ludicrous position under the couch, except for
one thing. Mixed in with his reminiscences of dusty ancestral
tradition were occasional real indiscretions, particularly when
he touched on business matters, which he did now and then—
after all, he was really doing all this to instruct Neal. And
those I wanted to hear.

"They were in Europe a great deal," he was continuing.
"Mother liked it very much, partly because she so loved music. She was one of the first Americans to grow to know Wagner, to become his partisan, one might say. As a result, incidentally, she met Bernard Shaw and had several letters from
him which are now in the library of Wallace College. She
used to go to Bayreuth nearly every summer, and she knew
Wagner's family there and visited them. Out of that grew
this house and its name. Hence also the decorations in the
Great Hall, those rather dated things from *Parsifal*. How she
loved that opera. I think she loved to imagine me as the Knight
of the Grail—but I hardly qualified as the pure fool illuminated through pity—*Der reine Thor*. . . . Not with my father there."

"Why not?" Neal sounded more sharply interested than
usual.

"Because he wouldn't have had a fool for a son in the first
place. My mother was not unlike your own in looks—very
elegant and stately. A wonderful woman, but exceedingly,
perhaps excessively, emotional. Very near tears and laughter,
very sentimental, not at all stoical. My father indulged her
and was always patient and understanding, and frequently
amused and delighted by her tenderness and humor, but of
course he wasn't like her at all. I have taken after him, quite
deliberately. I have thought that it was quite right for women
to do what they pleased, if their circumstances allowed it, and

that it was to be expected that they would cry and laugh more than men. Men should present tougher, more composed figures to the world. They are absolutely responsible for themselves, women only partially so. This is what I want you to learn today, Neal. It is part of the duty of being a man to maintain an evenness and a consistency and a determination. Men need self-control and a sense of duty, along with a clear sense of what their duty is. Nor will I permit it to be said that I am old-fashioned and out of date."

Won't you, dear David Wallace? Well, that is precisely what was being said, even as you talked, from under the couch.

He came back to the subject a day or two later. "Principles such as those I mentioned simply do not go out of date, although they may go out of fashion. Regrettably. That has been the basis of my life. I learned it from my father, he from his, I imagine." He raised his voice, usually rather feeble in those afternoon sessions, until it rang from that high attic ceiling. "I hope you will learn it from me. I believe a man should be dignified, restrained, reserved, reasonable, energetic, and that above all he should have will and determination; and he must have power in order to carry out what he wants. Then he has a right to be as exacting of others as he is of himself. By God, what this country needs is more Romans. Compare Dwight Eisenhower with a Cato and you will know what is wrong with us."

"You ask a lot, Uncle David," Neal said.

"And what I don't like? Self-indulgence, weakness, vacillation, inattention, irresponsibility, stupidity, and sympathy that is not really kind or understanding, but only hazy and fuzzy."

The next day, Wallace combined two of his favorite themes, his principles and his mother. "My mother agreed with what my father believed, although she didn't try to live up to it, and was herself so different." As soon as I heard this introduction, I more or less turned off my mind; once I came near snoring, for I was on my back, let me repeat. "Like your own mother. When I first went away to school she addressed me in her letters as *Mein kleiner Held*. And that was what she wanted me to be—a young hero. I must admit that I think your mother was sometimes a little too easy with you, Neal. But it's all turned out all right."

As the last sentence or two was said, I made a little prediction to myself, and turned to see if I was correct. I was. Neal began to wiggle his feet. It was his usual accompaniment to references to himself and his mother.

"The point is not to be cold. Far from it. We all have emotions, but we should limit their display."

"I think the point is to have them, Uncle David."

"But assuming you do, then they must be kept under control."

No sooner were those words out of his mouth than I began to itch right under the left knee. While Wallace went on about Neal's mother, what a splendid woman she was, if difficult, that itch grew, magnified, spread, and pulsed down the leg, up the leg, around the leg like a horrible great crawling insect exploring my tortured flesh with hundreds of scrabbling little feet. I put a hand to my mouth, ready to gag myself if necessary. I gnawed my knuckles. "It was her choice that we should never marry," he said, just as I drew in breath for a yell of torment, but that statement surprised it out of me. What had I been missing? Then, to reprieve me, Gladstone came in from the "bedroom," where she passed her time knitting while the men talked out in the parlor—knitting and eavesdropping. Naughty Gladstone.

"Almost six o'clock," she said. "Time for our dinner."

"Yes, yes, thank you. Remember, Neal, that she was a woman well worth our love," was Wallace's last statement.

"I've been thinking about her a lot, Uncle David, and I believe you're right. I'm understanding that more and more.

Only it's a little easier to do it now than it sometimes was then."

Wallace replied that there were doubtless good psychological reasons for that, and may even have mentioned one or two; but I didn't care, for my itch was returning and I went wet with sweat for fear I would have to reveal myself—it was July and by no means cool in that attic, although there were great exhaust fans off in one end. I trembled while deliberate Gladstone helped Wallace to his feet and out of the room. To top it off, Neal chose that particular afternoon to putter around, examine things, finally get out the photograph album and leaf through it. (I had a look later—it was full of Mrs. Brewster, all dressed up.) But I managed to lie still. When I was caught, it was not because of any itch.

It was, I think, because I grew careless as I grew wise. As I heard more and more about the Wallace empire, secrets of his far-flung business organization, tips on stocks, thumbnail sketches of partners and state officials, the most intimate secrets of family life, I began to assume that I had a kind of omnipotence to go with my burgeoning omniscience, that I, in my worm's position under the couch, was as secure as Neal, for example, sitting up where the grownups sit. Wahnfried, the various businesses, the boards of trustees kept in a pocket, all the rest, began to seem as if promised to me because I knew so much about them. I licked my chops over all those figures, all that gossip. Not that I was foolish enough to think it would all happen without effort on my part, but I was getting the necessary arms for a showdown. A real scandal, if possible, something frankly usable for blackmail, would have helped—I already knew quite enough to embarrass David Wallace, but I knew from of old that he was a formidable enemy. I needed something that could be sent to a safe-deposit box, to be opened by an opposition congressman in case of violence. Then I might yet taste my revenge for the way I had been treated so many many months before.

283

Yet that doesn't explain why I became careless. After all, the great carnivore isn't careless. What happened was that I began to think them already beneath my paws, I believe. What, after all, is the distinction, in such a situation, between thought and actuality—if there ever is one? Without the idea of power, the fact cannot be. Ultimately all power rests on faith, the faith of the Master, the faith of the Servant—faith, in both cases, in the existence of the power. In this case I came to believe in my power, but they didn't even know of it. That I didn't count on. The trouble was that they were uneducated.

Ida Gladstone caught me because, thinking myself strong, I left traces.

I don't know what all of them were—a slip of paper with a note on it was one of them. Perhaps a cigarette stub, which I left in an ash tray without thinking. Or was it that I ceased to be properly attentive to her—let the acting project drop, snubbed her once or twice—and so turned her to counter-espionage. She was a born watchdog, capable of the most intense loyalty and of the greatest ingenuity and subtlety in protecting her own. Ida Gladstone, Guardian of the Masters. And so one afternoon I heard the door locked from the inside after all three were up there. Oh the irony—for it was I who had taught her to take the dramatic outlook on life.

"Why did you do that?" David Wallace asked.

"Mr. Wallace, I think someone has been coming up here. I wouldn't be surprised but that someone was here right now. I want your permission to look around."

"Someone up here? Who could be coming up here?"

"We'll just see if I'm not right."

I could see her white feet, broad and stubby. The toes pointed immediately toward the couch. I was caught.

She went down on her knees and lifted the skirt of the slip cover. I was revealed, flattened ignominiously, a great, pale larva, unable to run anywhere, an easy prey, helpless, wiggling. And so I remained, unwilling to move in the humiliating manner necessary to extricate myself before the eyes of my captors, throughout the brief scene that followed, only my head fully visible, thrust out from under, face turned upward, displayed by Gladstone, who continued to hold the curtain for what was, in fact, her greatest scene.

The old Wallace got off to one side to reduce the angle at which he must stoop to see. He was more dumfounded than anything else. "What's *he* doing here?" he asked Neal.

Neal bent over from his chair and stared at me quite a while before he answered. I had never seen his face from that angle before—it greatly emphasized the cleft in his chin and the high cheekbones, and I couldn't see the chestnut hair, so it hardly looked like Neal. It was the face of some dream image which recalls a person one knows in peripheral ways without being that person, an enchanted impersonator, what comes out when you uncork the wrong bottle, I don't know what all.

Something terrifying happened to the face. It flew into its component parts, twisted, writhed. I felt nauseated. It was too much, coming on top of my being discovered. Then I understood. It was a smile. Neal was amused.

"He's doing research," he said.

"Research!" Wallace said. "Research on what? Confound it, this is intolerable."

"Research on himself, I should think," Neal answered.

"On himself? Under your mother's couch? Here in your mother's living room?"

"Who else? Isn't all research research on oneself?"

"Neal, you know how I dislike the obscurities you sometimes play with." The old man came closer and looked straight down at me, resting a hand on stout Gladstone's shoulder. "I find this inexcusable, Ned. Infantile prying . . ."

I interjected a reply before Neal could say anything. I

wanted to register my defense. "I was told I couldn't use this attic as a studio. I wasn't told that I couldn't try to find out why."

"Common decency, man. Respect for other people's privacy."

"He means he wasn't forbidden access to the room. He has broken rules of courtesy, Uncle David, but he hasn't violated any magical prohibitions. We don't have to have his head chopped off and put on a pedestal."

"That's it," I said, glad someone understood.

"This is all too much for me," David Wallace said. "I am going back downstairs. You will have to settle it; but I won't have things like this going on in my house as long as I am alive."

The real moment of danger was over, so I was free to maneuver a bit myself. The worm could turn psychologically, if not, under the circumstances, physically.

"I've heard quite a lot since I've been coming here," I said. "More than any stranger ought to have heard, I should think."

Wallace stopped. "How long have you been assuming that grotesque position?"

"Several weeks." I mentioned a couple of the business facts I had overheard, one or two evaluations of influential men. "I can't be ignored, everything considered. It goes beyond harmless eavesdropping, doesn't it?"

I should have waited. I should have been more subtle. A real frontal assault like that was something which, even in his enfeebled condition, Mr. Wallace could deal with. He returned to stand above me, and his voice, when he spoke, was like stilettos and icicles and hypodermic needles.

"Consider one thing, Mr. Bates. Who is going to take your word against anybody's, much less mine, or pay any attention to an addled confidence man like you whatsoever, when they learn of the record? One might begin with your being discharged from the university library for unseemly conduct, continue with your arrest by the Paris police and the subsequent confiscation of your films when you left the country"—so he had found that out!—"and terminate with the period you spent in a state insane asylum."

"Now, now, Uncle David," Neal said soothingly. "Let's let the matter drop for the moment. I know Ned, and he doesn't really mean any harm. If he did, he'd do more. You go downstairs, and we'll talk about it when we've had a chance to think." He waited until the old man had disappeared, leaning on Gladstone. Then he said to me, "I do hold one thing against you, Ned: you let yourself get caught."

Gladstone had forgotten her knitting, and hurried back in to get it. She took a last look at me. "Huh," she said contemptuously. "I'll come back after dinner and straighten up," she told Neal, as if somehow my being there had created a distasteful disorder.

They both left, leaving me under the couch to think about what had happened.

I remembered, then, that while I had wanted to stay where I was, once I was discovered, it had not occurred to anybody to invite me to come out. How devastatingly can one have one's true status brought home?

5.

I didn't go to dinner that night. I hid in my room with the lights out, and when Neal had something sent up to me, I sniffed it like a wise old rat accustomed to amateur attempts at rodenticide, but eventually I ate it. All I got was the hiccups.

Where did I stand? What were they deciding downstairs? I suspected—with good evidence—that David Wallace would want me sent away, Neal would vote that I stay. Neal would win, but did I want to go through a period of probation, like a delinquent child? I couldn't stand that, not after all I'd been through. I was in a real frenzy of worry and anxiety. I needn't have bothered, for I was rescued from my predicament by the sudden surge of events, an unexpected readjustment of forces at Wahnfried, triggered by me.

But let me go back a moment. The other thing on my mind, aside from the question of what they were going to do to me, was: how would I get my revenge on Gladstone? My feelings toward her had changed entirely from what they had been earlier in my stay, when I had toyed with her over the movies, teased her about her profession, even talked to her about her family. In fact, I thought, as I sat like a criminal awaiting judgment in my darkening room, of going back to that earlier passage in this manuscript, in which I spoke of Gladstone and her prurient mind with such understanding and affection, and marking it out, changing it to conform to my hatred for her, now that she had betrayed me to her masters. But I decided not to; for I am interested in the true palimpsests of Time, not in forgeries. So I let the earlier Gladstone remain, although in my mind she was replaced by a nasty, snooping old bitch, bent on seeing that no influence other than her own should work in the household.

These worries, these thoughts of vengeance, warred for space in the convoluted corridors of my consciousness, until my mind was nearly addled by it all. Was it a dream, what happened next? I am not quite sure. I have wondered. Did I in fact do it, or did I not? Was it as I remember, or was it not? Have I been indulging in ex post facto explanations of real events to increase the significance of myself? In pure fantasy? I do not think so. The one piece of evidence, with which I could prove what happened, was removed when Mrs. Brewster's furniture was taken away. I refer to the slip of paper that I pasted underneath the couch that evening.

I took a piece of paper from my smallest note pad (3″ x 5″) and on it I wrote a little spell which, if I remember correctly, read: "Curse the Master and the Dog." Then I took it and a spool of plastic tape and my great gothic key—they hadn't thought to confiscate it, the idiots!—and crept upstairs while the others were still down talking about me. I entered, for the last time, that strange vast place, devoted to the worship of the dead, snapped on a light, and looked around. Emotions spurted through me like poisoned blood, burning everywhere it touched, as I thought of my ruined hopes, dashed by that one cruel sentence of Wallace's, his summary of my career, and by Gladstone's snooping. Truly I owed them a debt, and long, long ago Neal had pointed a safe way to pay one off, with his own little scribblings. I went, for the last time, to the couch, and with a shiver wriggled under it, and there, using the tape, I attached my curse, and wriggled out again.

Then I cast my red-rimmed eyes around, looking for something that might give me an idea how to supplement my message, another prank that might prick a little. As if directed there, they fell upon the photograph album, a book dedicated to the glorification of one American woman, filled with pictures of Mrs. Brewster *en grande, moyenne,* and *petite tenue,* and I seized it, hugged it close to me, and rushed for the bedroom. Once in there, I turned the stiff and crackling pages, stopping from time to time to go to the closets and check what was hanging there. Near the end I found what I wanted —husky, handsome Harriet Brewster, in a floor-length gown shot through with metallic threads, and with a great puffy collar. She smiled from the glossy print, snapped at some kind of party, smiled out at me, and I smiled back. I recognized that costume. It was recent. It still hung in its place. I turned to it. I would add my jot and my tittle to the endless Wallace-Brewster hierology I had heard expounded in this accursed attic.

As I did so, I realized that I was not alone.

I am serious. I do not believe it was a trick of the mirrors or of the dim light and heavy shadows. It was not my excitement, or the great strain of the preceding events. No. I believe that I had been joined by a revenant, come back to those rooms prepared for her dwelling place with all the care spent on an Egyptian burial chamber to make her feel at home. Mrs. Brewster, dressed in flowing orchidaceous robes, had come to watch the fun. I bowed my head.

"Good evening," I said into the obscurity that palpitated with her gorgeous ectoplasm.

"I'm going to give Gladstone a scare," I said. "I'll need to borrow a few things."

She allowed me to pass through her, and I went to the chest of drawers where her spare hair was kept. I opened it and took out several hanks of the stuff, along with a heavy net I found beside it in the same drawer. I put them on as best I could, fiddled and adjusted them, unwound one, bunched another up, and then held them in place with the net. I went to look at myself in the mirror, and what a strange effect it was; like some monstrous dummy fitted with human hair I grinned at the mirror-image Ned, and he grinned back. More work, more work. Hurry, hurry, hurry. Off to the closet.

There I took that green dress, hastily put it on, which disarranged my coiffure, so that I had to adjust it again. Then I went to the dressing table, smeared eye shadow all around my eyes, and added a horrible crimson mouth, then found a veil and used it to obscure all other details of my face. There was one thing left—how to move, how to progress.

I practiced before the mirror, and found that if I bent my knees until the bottom of the gown rustled across the carpeting, then moved forward in a kind of bandy-legged duck walk, my greater height was concealed, and at the same time I seemed to float along without skeletal movement—Gladstone would not have X-ray vision, after all. There remained my arms, but I found that if I thrust my hands a little way into some white gloves, hunched my elbows into my body in order to utilize a sort of cape-like sleeve on the dress, then held a candlestick between my flopping fingers, nobody was likely to notice that there was something wrong. And so I was ready, except that I had to be sure there would be no sudden glare of electric lights to reveal my impersonation.

Just in time I hurried into the living room and disconnected all the plugs. Before Gladstone had a chance to get down and reconnect any of them, she would have her attention distracted by an unexpected visitor. Look out, insidious Ida!

The sound of slow steps on the stairway outside sent me quickly back into the bedroom, where I turned out those lights, and prepared a match for my candle. Then I tiptoed forward, feeling my way with a free hand, until I was at the entrance into the living room. I waited, listening to the sounds of the door, the snapping of the light switch. A board creaked. Someone was moving forward to find another light and try it. I visualized Gladstone's plump hand outstretched, her fingers eager. I struck my match, lighted my candle, and holding it so that most of the light was cut off except just a little, which flickered over my veil and revealed the horrid dark pools of my eyes, my cannibal red mouth, I flowed forward into the crepuscule of the living room, moaning.

I heard a wheeze as someone stood up, someone who had been stooped down working at a lamp cord.

Onward we came, for Mrs. Brewster was behind me, I sensed that. How could it be otherwise? And then someone said, "My God!" and there was a horrible gasp, and the sound of a body falling to the floor. I stood paralyzed, but pricklings in the back of my neck told me that Mrs. Brewster was withdrawing, leaving me alone.

For the voice had been that of David Wallace. Of all the nights to break his routine! David Wallace had come up for a second time. And when I bent over him, I discovered something else, too, although I took a feather from under the couch

—I knew where to find them—and tried it on his lips, just to make sure. He was dead, all right. No wonder Mrs. Brewster had come back that night. She was probably lonely.

But it does leave the question, which one of us was it who caused the old man's heart to stop?

6.

There has been a great conspiracy. It has all been hushed up. He died peacefully in his bed, they say. A man like David Wallace could never die anywhere else—that is the implication.

My part, whatever it was, in the "sudden, though not unexpected" death of David Wallace (newspaper account) has never been discovered by those who do know the truth of *where* he died. Isn't it strange that it never occurred to anybody to wonder if he might have died of foul play? It would always be the first thing to occur to me; but then, I'm not everybody.

I have wondered now and then in the weeks which have passed since that great scene—will it be the last one?— whether I should confess what I did to Neal. Only, what exactly would I confess? That I know the truth? That I was there? That I had passed a curse? That I impersonated his mother? That I was with his mother? After all, would he believe me? Wouldn't he think I was taking credit for an event planned and executed by Mr. Sick?

Nobody believes me much any more anyway; nobody thinks I'm worth bothering about. They haven't even mentioned my getting caught under that couch. I'm the half-wit child here at Wahnfried, allowed to remain on because one can't, after all, be cruel to a thing which isn't responsible for what it does.

Well, facts should be recorded, including the facts, the true facts about the death of Mr. Wallace. I do feel that. After all, I was once something not unrelated to an archivist, and still have respect for documentation. But I guess it is not so important where or how they are recorded, and it is not expedient for me to confess to Neal, to tell the truth. I don't know how he would react, and however intolerable his tolerance may be, nevertheless he does still house and feed me—his own house, now, his own grocery bills. Recorded the facts have been, in any case, in this manuscript.

This manuscript . . . It has turned into my chief consolation, my singular companion. I have spent these weeks bringing it up to date, until it and life have become temporarily identical, the mood of retrospection supplanted by one more urgent. I threw myself into the task with something of my former energy, as if I hoped through my efforts to come upon something unexpected, worked in gold, casting light on a whole civilization. Without it I could not have survived the black despair of these past weeks, for truly I have been to one side of all things important. They have been such boring weeks, filled with business for Neal, but with nothing for me. Fifty times I have been introduced to the mighty only to see the poor-relation expression come over their face when they met me, only to see them turn away, too important to bother with me. And my other work? What stupidity, to have hoped I could ever do it. My shy muse has refused to join me in a house where I have murdered. Once I knew her, but she knows me no longer. Neither does anybody else. I am alone.

The will has been read, and was no surprise. Neal is now as rich as Croesus, and maybe richer. He is called "my beloved son" in the will—but then that wasn't too indiscreet, since he was legally adopted by David Wallace. I am sure the old man had dreams of imperial Roman precedent, such were his delusions of grandeur. Anyway, discreet or not, there is nothing for the locals to do but accept it, and they will, for such is the power of power. If poor Ned were a ditch-born child, the contempt he would meet would be even greater than it is now, but a golden mirror reflects only smiles. The details of the will—cash, real estate, foundations, etc., are too long and too vast and too uninteresting. Let us say it is a fairy story, of great unearned success, magic, and let it go at that.

I went to the funeral, which was held in the fashionable Episcopal church, although David Wallace hadn't been in it in years; but Mother Ecclesia will always forgive her erring children in the end, particularly when they have left a juicy estate. The bishop imported for the razzle-dazzle made a reference to Wallace's lack of faith, if I heard correctly, although just then I was counting the number of bouquets banked around the coffin. He said something, I believe, about how Wallace had not been a religious man in the common sense of the word, but that by their fruits, etc., and all the town was filled with the results of his benefactions and those of his family, the finest spirit of public service. We then had a catalogue, from Wallace College to the Charlotte Ackermann Wallace Home for Foundling Children. And, that episcopal voice rolled on, great as the benefactions of the living Wallace had been, the surviving family had assured him those of the dead Wallace were greater still. Several heads turned toward Neal, sitting all by himself, except for a distant female cousin from Wilmington, who had come on to represent all that was left of the eastern branch of the family. How she must have detested Neal; for they had lost their money, and but for him would have been entitled to more than buttery crumbs.

Neal didn't raise his head. He mourned David Wallace then, and he still does. He is glad to have his inheritance, I think, but I believe he counts, or pretends to count, the cost too high. Else I would probably confess my part in events, after all, and claim some reward; I'll do it the day I catch him with the latest stock-market reports and an adding machine, just wait and see if I don't.

He wept at the grave. It was a blistering hot day, and everybody was panting; but two present added the salt of tears to their salt sweat: Neal and Gladstone. After the prescribed handful of earth had been thrown in, Neal went to the edge, looked a moment, then raised his hand in a kind of salute, or a wave, as if his Uncle David had been down in the bottom, watching for him to say farewell, waiting for the heavy weight of the rest of the earth to shut him down there forever. As Neal walked away he passed by his mother's grave, for she had been buried beside the Wallace plot and nowhere near his father, who was buried out of town where he had originally come from. Neal stopped to read her tombstone, and the first thing he did, upon returning to Wahnfried, was to give orders for that attic to be cleared and all her furniture sent away.

Everything about that day seemed pointless to me. I looked on without real understanding, except for the flowers. They made some sense.

One major decision remains to be made. I have grown fond of this book, not because I claim any particular distinction for it as books go, nor do I think it proves anything. Nobody will emerge from a reading of it knowing that the earth is flat and the sun travels round it. Yet I am coming to believe that it alone must stand for all the possible children of my mind, those unborn children, sealed somewhere behind a damp wall, strayed from the doorway that leads to birth. It will be my greatest achievement, paltry though it be in comparison with what I had hoped for. For what else will I ever do now?

The remaining decision is this: where should I end? My search into time past, to borrow a phrase, is now complete. The *then* has become the *now*. Tortoise Time has overtaken me. I am faced not by enigma, an incompletion, but by an oppressive present, and an ominous future which scratches at the door, snuffles at the bottom crack—I can smell its foul breath. All those Neds of yesterday, the Ned who loved Pounce, the Ned who saved Neal, the Ned who might have renewed art, are face to face with the Ned typing this very page. The past offers many pleasant avenues, one for each Ned, but the present Ned can face in only one direction at once, and there he sees only darkness and oblivion. I went in search of my various selves, and they have found me out; and now we must all march abreast, a shuddering phalanx which lumbers forward to its doom.

I have tried to turn hither and yon, left and right, to climb up, to jump down, but I am not able. Powers and Principalities move faster than I in order to block me. I don't even know how they do it, I don't even know why. I don't ask. I only know that nothing else will ever happen.

Only one thread is left to be examined, then clipped and tucked in. The second mystery of Wahnfried.

Actually, I have a good idea of what it is. I could have found out all along if I had bothered to read the newspapers. Neal has told me as much. He was quite surprised when I mentioned it to him the other day, laughed in a condescending way and said he thought I would have found out about it long ago. He was joking, or mostly joking, when he had told me it was a mystery. It is to be a children's play park, which he has had built on a corner of the Wallace property, and which has now been left by his "uncle" to the city, along with a large slice of woodlands down by the river, several hundred acres. The children's part is to be opened in a couple of weeks.

It is going to be done as a memorial to David Wallace. But one more benefaction, the first of those posthumous hundreds which Father Protestant Episcopus promised us all.

7.

I shouldn't have gone to the opening of the park. I knew it, but I went anyway. Why should I not have done so? Simply because I knew something would happen if I went. Something final and terrible, a terminal statement about my life. I would be ground under a merry-go-round or fall off a swing; or someone there would identify me wrongly, and I would be mobbed, arrested, taken away. I didn't know what. I only knew something would happen and that I ought not to go. But certain danger has its certain appeal, so one man scales cliffs, another keeps a mistress, and the third stares insolently at strangers.

I did delay until long after the opening ceremonies, at which the governor and mayor spoke. Does that show that I am trying to hang on? A sickly self-preservation? Or was I merely playing?

I walked down the hill from Wahnfried, following that small road I had noticed months before, moving quickly through the bright gathering leaves, my pace set by the brisk day and by my body's instinct rather than by my shrinking and reluctant will. The descent was symbolic; everything was. I was approaching the entrance to some desperate place oozy with febrific miasmas. It turned out to be simple enough, well ventilated and lighted, nothing but an enormous gate with iron grilles and a high stone entablature which bore a carved inscription:

THE DAVID WALLACE MEMORIAL CHILDREN'S PARK

But what a world of meaning may be concealed behind such prosaic appearances!

A happy attendant stopped me. His uniform, of red, yellow, and blue, clotted with braid, and with gaudy feathers on the helmet, was a child's conception, or a savage's. He wanted to know what I was doing without a child along, and I told him I was a house guest up at Wahnfried, hoping, at the same time, that he would abide by his instructions and I therefore might yet be turned back. He was skeptical, so I had to try to argue—that was a part of the game. I pointed out that I

297

had come down from above—"From *above,* you understand?"—and could easily go back there for authorization of
some kind, or I could go off into the trees and get over the
fence or dig my way under. He listened to me, grinning. He
had been chosen for his good temper, and he let me by, a too-
accommodating Cerberus.

Smiling my weak thanks, I forced myself to go on in.

Children everywhere. The whole compound literally was
alive with children, crawling with children. Every child from
five to ten years old in the town and county must have been
there, every nursery emptied out, every orphanage voided for
the day, the schools abandoned, the playgrounds silent as
death. Little imps ran madly in every direction, screaming,
laughing, dancing, and cavorting through the pens and
groves and structures of this delectable underworld which
had been laid out for their witless pleasure. There were thickets of children, flocks of children, herds of children, clusters
of children, galaxies of children, agglomerations of children,
braids of children, concatenations of children, sequences of
children, knots and tangles of children, cords reams and drifts
of children, a detestable and hateful sight. Here and there an
adult stood out above the flailing sea around him, and each
time one did, I looked to see if it was Neal. I wanted to see
just how he was taking it all, all this orgy of innocence, whose
impresario he was, but I couldn't find him anywhere in sight.
He was off somewhere inhaling the fumes of gratitude which
bubbled up out of every fissure and hole, and smiling to himself at the dangers, the traps and pitfalls and madness and
folly of his garden. Yes, his benefactions, Mr. Bishop, may
be myriad, but they will always have a catch to them, opening up danger just where they seem to give away the most.
I know.

It was important that I find Neal. I had to find Neal, but
where was he?

There was nothing to do but to investigate the sideshows

and diversions, of which there were dozens, some permanent, some just set up for opening day. I began with a maze of metal bars joined into rectangles, with flopping squares of colored plastic falling to make curtains between cubes. This was for the child-as-ape, the monkey babies, who clambered atavistically over and under and hid and peeped out, chattered and scratched. A good place to break a back or bruise a cerebellum. I stuck my head into a space a few feet above ground and nearly had my nose bitten by a tiny red-haired tot whose mother must have adored him, he was so sprightly. I backed away hastily, and got my backside pinched by another. It didn't do to lose too much altitude in that mad garden. I stood up and looked through the structure—would Neal be perched somewhere at the top?—and my balance reeled with the complicated dimensions of it, until I had to turn away and hold my hand over my eyes. Then I started to run, but tripped and staggered to my knees, leaving behind me a screaming hazard rubbing a barked shin. I dashed for the nearest cover, two little houses built side by side, with a party wall; but when I got there a strong arm blocked the doorway.

"Say, mister, you can't go in here without a twin."

"Why not?" I asked, trying to push by. "Let me in."

"Don't shove. Can't you read, at your age? This is for twins only."

I looked at the sign over the entrance. Sure enough, there it was, clearly stated: FOR TWINS ONLY.

"What's in there?" I asked. "Is Mr. Brewster there?"

"Who's he?"

"All this belongs to him."

"Is he a twin? Nobody's in there but twins."

"I don't know," I said. "Please let me in."

"Go away, mister," he said. "I can only see one of you, so you may as well just go away."

"Blind, blind, blind," I howled, and dashed off until I almost fell over the counter of one of the several stands set up to give away candy and ice cream and popcorn. Over it, in blinking blue neon, was a suitably anthropophagical aphorism: "That which is not good to eat is not good for anything."

"You're never too old for this," a female attendant said, thrusting a box of popcorn into my trembling hands. I thanked her automatically and took a handful into my mouth, on which I nearly choked when I noticed that dangling from her five-foot-high chef's hat were furry spiders, which bobbed up and down on the ends of lengths of elastic. She noticed my look of horror. "Don't mind them, they're just hungry," she said with a giggle.

I backed away from her, holding the corn in front of me, spilling from it, then turned and ran again, right into the arms of Gladstone, who was supervising the feeding in a half-professional sort of way.

"My lands, slow down or you'll hurt yourself." She noticed the half-empty box which I held between us for protection. "Don't you wish you were a little boy, Mr. Bates, so that you could enjoy all this more?" She stared into my face and puckered her lips—how I detest her mouth, and those lips that smack as if she had hyperviscosity of the saliva. "We don't look too well. Too much excitement?"

"That's it, Ida," I yelled, and once again I ran off, until I came to another building, labeled "Dentist's Office." That seemed a possible haven, something cold and scientific, and I went inside; but as my eyes grew accustomed to the scant light I saw that even here the terrible solicitude of the De-signer had prepared a nightmare. The entire end of the room was filled with an enormous face at least fifteen feet high, its great jaws open, the lower one falling beneath the floor, bristling with teeth. Perched upon a stool, straining to get at a molar, was a robot dentist, holding a four-foot-long drill with which he was attempting to dig a hole. But while I watched, he gradually worked farther and farther into the mouth; and then, while all around me the Innocents screamed with joy, the great green eyes in the face lighted up and rolled about, there was a bellow of pain, and the dentist responded with a yet more ecstatic lunge for the nerve. Then gradually—the dentist too engaged to notice—the massive lower jaw began to close, until the dentist was caught, and as I ran from the room, there was a crunch, and he was being chewed up and swallowed.

I was back in the undertow, caught in the currents of wriggling infancy, drawn along. I looked about me with horror, envying Herod. A little boy grabbed my hand and took me with him. I looked down, hoping I might find him kin, hoping at least he was frightened. No. He was being friendly. It turned out that he was taking me to the auditorium, which was the largest building as yet finished in the park. Most of the children were now moving in that direction, I noticed, and then I remembered that Neal had mentioned that there was going to be a show in the later afternoon. That explained everything, of course. Neal would be in there, overseeing preparations.

A show. I tugged on that small hand and stopped. Now what kind of a show would it be? Ought I to go? My hackles rose, and I knew that whatever it was that was so dangerous for me had something to do with the show. No, I hadn't better go in. Yes, I had. "Yes," I cried aloud. "Yes, I must see the show. Take me in with you, little boy."

But he couldn't. This time I needed a ticket, so he abandoned me by the door—and what a door it was. It was only three feet high, and it, too, like Dante's, had its exhortation: "Break or you'll have to bend," it said.

And this time the attendant was firm. No ticket, no entrance, no matter how low I was willing to bend, no matter in how many pieces to break.

"You need a ticket. You aren't qualified," he kept saying, which was such an odd way to put it that I thought it must mean something, perhaps that he had been told about me in advance.

"Well, we'll just see," I said angrily.

Then I climbed as fast as I could back along the road up to Wahnfried, sure that the butler would have extra tickets, for he had just about everything. I couldn't find him, though —I expect he had gone down to see the show—and the only servant there, a maid whom I caught watching television in the library, didn't know anything about tickets. What to do? I paced; I bit my nails. Then I fled from the house and ran back downhill, determined to try again. By this time there was almost no one left roving in the park. Everybody was in the auditorium. I had to get in. I simply had to get in. Perhaps a back entrance . . .

The man who was supposed to be posted there must have sneaked in for the show too, because the stage door was open and unguarded. I pushed it and found myself in a hallway, lighted by a small red lamp. From somewhere ahead came sounds of screams and laughter, and I felt my way toward them, testing the floor ahead of me with a toe, for who knew what preposterous devices might not have been installed within that building to catch trespassers. But I tripped no alarms, set off no firecrackers, and soon I found myself behind stage. There were people there, and I ducked back. I turned and took another passage, this one leading down some stairs. I hoped it might go into the pit under the stage, even into the orchestra pit, and I turned out to be right about that. There, under the stage, I found myself in almost total blackness, for only the tiniest lights were burning. Up front I could hear the band, but before I got to it I bumped into a stairway which seemed to lead up to the stage itself. Then I knew where I was—the prompter's box. I could get into that and see without being seen, and that was what I wanted. I found a trap door and the latch. I lifted my head cautiously, like a little animal scouting from its secure hole in the ground.

302

The loud-speakers were roaring something about a daredevil feat, something about danger, but they were drowned out by applause, and I saw the feet of three clowns twinkle by in front of me, a curtain call. Then there was a thumping fanfare. Everybody grew quiet and the lights went out. I raised my head a bit more. I heard scraping and rattling, something metal being moved forward, then strange sounds, scrambling, a muffled thump, and heavy breathing. Blinding lights went on again, and I found myself looking into a great cage a couple of feet away from my face, and leaping into it came a trio of lions, all females, their tails snapping, measuring its dimensions with their great velvety strides.

"Direct from the jungles of Africa," I heard the barker cry. "Hungry man-eaters, thirsty for blood." At the back of the cage I saw three stout, lion-sized chairs, each of them with the name of its occupant-to-be: Pearl! Opal! Ruby! Then the voice cried, "And now the man who is going to test his courage against theirs, risk his life. Presenting the Lion Tamer. Here he comes. . . . Presenting . . ." And the name was drowned out by yells from the audience, but I saw him. I saw the Lion Tamer, although my eyes were dazzled by floodlights. I saw him open a little door at the back of the cage and slip in. I saw him raise his whip to bring them to order and command them to go to their places. He was tall and slender, all made up, and he had long curling mustaches and a false beard.

That was all I saw, for just then one of the beasts, passing by the front of the cage, saw my head, and with a snarl leapt against the bars, her great paws open. Instinctively I threw up an arm to protect myself, which caught the attention of her sisters, and they all darted forward. That was the last thing I saw, those three fierce muzzles snapping at me through the slim bars of the cage. I passed out cold and fell from the prompter's box.

*

Apparently I spent several minutes lying there, I have no idea how long. When I came to, I could hear the sound of furry feet on the boards above me, and hear the audience shrieking. I crawled to the doorway and collapsed there, feeling my bones for breakage. What a strange destiny governs our accidental looks over our shoulders—for Gladstone, passing by on an errand, happened to look behind her, thinking she heard a sound, and saw me there. She called an attendant, and together they rushed me to an emergency first-aid station, where a doctor, also on call, visited me. By then I was quite conscious, and told them it must have been something I ate, which sent Gladstone into a fit for fear all those hundreds of children had eaten the same thing and would all vomit at once. I was handed some spirits of ammonia, told to take it easy for a while, and she and the doctor rushed back into the auditorium to direct operations should the mass nausea take place.

Eventually I got to my feet, straightened my tie, and returned to Wahnfried. I didn't want to have to think about anything just then, so I took a generous pinch of sedatives and blacked out again, after leaving a message that I was still unwell and wouldn't be down for dinner.

8.

The past week has been spent on my recovery, and has been climaxed by a visit from Pounce.

I did not rise from my barbituric slumbers refreshed and renewed. I was really quite sick, almost delirious, running a high fever. They had to have a doctor look at me again, but he could diagnose nothing, and merely prescribed palliatives. There were no cures for what was wrong, I knew that.

I have been staying in my room most of the time, and the day before yesterday Neal, serious, worried, came to see me early in the morning, and said that someone was coming to visit us. I asked who.

I was aware that he had taken a chair facing mine and was looking at me. I don't look at him any more if I can help it, but I can sense what he is doing some of the time.

"Pounce is stopping by on her way out to the Coast," he said.

I didn't even jump. "So? Will she be here for the night or just for dinner?"

"For the day," he said. "She's taking the night plane out."

"Does she know I'm here? Isn't that too much of a surprise?"

"She knows, Ned."

"I wish she weren't coming," I said.

"Why?"

"Oh, she'll just complicate things," I replied.

"How?"

"I would rather forget." I thought about my manuscript, this manuscript, where the old Pounce lives. "Her file is already closed," I said. "There's no room for more about her."

"Ned, Ned," Neal said, "I wish you would let us help you."

I was rupturing the yolk of my second egg, and even when he said that, I didn't look at him.

When we took her down to see the Children's Park, she remarked—trust Pounce to manage such a crude therapeutic move—what a wonderful place it would be to make a movie. She looked so much the same—dark-browed, a little thinner, the same square-cut style, ready for California.

"Make one, then," I said.

"Why don't you make one, Ned?" she replied.

"It's a dead art. I sincerely believe it is a dead art," I replied. "Only throwbacks or fossils make movies these days."

The only part of our visit down below that interested me was when we went into the small zoo, which is unfinished, and has only ponies, a camel, and those lions as yet within it. Workmen were all around, and a guard. The cats were in makeshift cages, not very stout, separated one from another by sliding doors which operated from above. They were noisy and restless, and Neal explained that they had to be kept separated, and the day workmen kept away, because they were litter-mates and were all three coming into heat simultaneously and were unmanageable. They had nearly had to cancel their act at the opening, he said, and couldn't possibly have put on the show now.

I found the courage to pop the question that has been festering in my brain. I seized him by the elbow and bent my face to his ear.

"Was it *you?*" I whispered.

He frowned at me and disengaged his arm. "Was who me?" he asked. "What are you saying, Ned?"

Betrayed, evaded once more, I turned aside. "Nothing," I replied.

A moment later I added, "All that preposterous business about Opal, Pearl, and Ruby you wrote in your letters. All of it was lies, of course. I never believed it." But he didn't hear me, for I found that I had walked away from them, and they were behind me, speaking to each other. They stopped, of course, when I came back.

Right after dinner I excused myself and went to my room, saying I was tired. They let me go then, but before her plane left Pounce came up to see me.

"Will you talk to me, Ned?" she asked.

"Tell me how to and I'll do it," I said.

"How do you feel?"

"That's pretty obvious, isn't it?"

"When Neal felt that way he went on a trip," she said.

"You didn't hear me. I already said I think that was lies."

She was holding each elbow in the opposite hand, and she shrugged the whole rectangle of arms and shoulders. "In any case, he did go away somewhere. On a trip. Far away," she said.

"What is it you want to tell me?"

"Nothing. Nothing, really. I'm sorry things aren't going better, that's all. I wanted to say that to you before I left."

"I'll be all right," I said.

Neal insisted that I go with them to the airport. The last I saw of Pounce, she was striding out toward the waiting plane, carrying a small bag, her tailored coat flapping in the cold wind. At the gate she had kissed Neal good-by, but I held our farewells to a hearty handshake.

9.

I have just read this manuscript all at once, from beginning to end—the first time I have dared to do it. I wonder what has happened to Neal. I began with a Neal I could define, three Neals, in fact, but now there seems to be a fourth, a Neal who has vanished almost, a Neal no longer accessible to me, whom I cannot reach, cannot comprehend, have not captured in my prose prison. A question therefore vexes me as I sit here working for the last time—for the book is surely finished now. Is there any longer such a person as the Neal within these pages? There was, but is there now? Is there a secret continuity which eludes me, or is there no hope? Such a Neal as does exist, what is his connection to the Neal of this book? I am breaking my poor brain over the question.

I might have found my answer. If I knew the truth about the person in the cage the other afternoon, that might illuminate all mysteries at once. But I won't ever ask again.

A journey. That's it. Pounce was right. Pounce always had her insights about me, her rough way of cutting cleanly into my complexities, the way a dumb animal senses the advent of a bad mood long before its owner is even aware of it. I will take a long, long trip somewhere. I have no idea where it will end, and I don't care—I'm no metaphysician—but I do know, now, ever since we visited below yesterday afternoon, where it will begin. I was looking closely all the time. There are locks and latches I couldn't work, but those three are simple enough for me, given the will.

Neal! You, there, Neal! The Neal I can't touch. You, it seems, will be the only reader these pages will ever have. I notice I have addressed you from time to time as I went along. Yes, this book is for you. I will leave it for you. You have disappeared from it now, yet here and there I sense your presence in it, even yesterday. On a different level from me, in a different dimension, a new course, an orbit which my own eccentric one intersects but rarely—and the last time tomorrow, when you open your bedroom door and find this (both copies) in the hall outside.

Perhaps, if I had the ingenuity and the energy, I could go back and pick up your trail, stalk you once more. I don't. Neither the ingenuity nor the energy. I am worn out.

Well, read my book carefully. Everything is here that I know how to put in, everything that ought to be, the good and the bad. I cannot logically ask that the good be used to augment my memory if I do not let the bad remain to diminish it. Here, such as I was and am, is Ned Bates. Here, such as I could catch you, is Neal Brewster.

Now I walk below for a last visit to the three who are waiting there, restless, irritable, itchy. If I open my window and listen, I can hear them coughing in the dark.

ECCE! DUO INTER LEONES IERUNT, ETIAM IN LUSTRA LEONUM: UNUS SOLUS EGRESSUS EST.

I wonder if anyone will think to cancel their regular feeding.